T0161732

TEARS OF HONOR

James A. Ardaiz

Pace Press
Fresno, California

Published by Pace Press
An imprint of Linden Publishing
2006 South Mary Street, Fresno, California 93721
(559) 233-6633 / (800) 345-4447
PacePress.com

Pace Press and Colophon are trademarks of
Linden Publishing, Inc.

Cover design by Tanja Prokop, www.bookcoverworld.com
Book design by Andrea Reider

ISBN 978-1-61035-900-9

135798642

Printed in the United States of America
on acid-free paper.

Library of Congress Cataloging-in-Publication Data

Names: Ardaiz, James A., author.
Title: Tears of honor / James A. Ardaiz.
Identifiers: LCCN 2020049164 | ISBN 9781610359009 (paperback)
Subjects: LCSH: World War, 1939-1945--Participation, Japanese
    American--Fiction. | Japanese Americans--Evacuation and relocation,
    1942-1945--Fiction. | GSAFD: Historical fiction.
Classification: LCC PS3601.R415 T43 2021 | DDC 813/.6--dc23
LC record available at https://lccn.loc.gov/2020049164

TO THE READER

A number of years ago I was asked to give a speech about the American judiciary, of which I have been privileged to be a part. My focus was on the failures of the American judiciary, when the values of our laws have been severely tested by unpopular issues. One case I discussed was *Korematsu v. United States*, 323 U.S. 214 (1944), the United States Supreme Court decision permitting the detention of Japanese Americans during World War II, and particularly the dissent of Associate Justice Robert Jackson expressing his rejection of the Court's actions as unconstitutional. If anyone has an interest in what it means to be a judge, that dissent expresses it. It was the Court's conservatives who expressed outrage at what I consider to be one of the American judicial system's great failures to stand up to a monumental wrong. When confronted with that obligation, it failed.

After giving the speech, I began to read about the Korematsu case's background and the history of Executive Order 9066, by which President Franklin D. Roosevelt ordered the forced relocations. What caught my attention consistently were the references to the young Japanese men who left the relocation camps to fight in Europe, leaving behind parents and loved ones in concentration camps. Why would they do that?

I set out to find the answer to that question. This book is the result. In addition to several years reading numerous sourcebooks, it took me five years to write this novel. While I consulted many books and documents, my primary sources for the war were interviews with men who participated in the specific events described, such as Colonel Young Oak Kim, Captain Martin Higgins, and Private First Class Al Tortolano. I was privileged to speak to many people who had been inside the relocation camps, as well as people who had seen it happen from the outside. As would be expected, most were quite elderly, but their memories were clear. Listening to them, I knew this was an American story that had never been told from the different perspectives of the many individuals whose actions so deeply affected each other.

I decided to tell this story from three of those perspectives: the people relocated to guarded camps, far from their homes; the government that ordered that relocation; and the men who fought in the 100/442nd Regimental Combat Team—the most decorated, the most wounded, and the fiercest fighting unit of World War II.

It was very difficult to weave the stories together. There is so much history and there are so many individual stories. I tried to create representative characters, and those characters are composites. The Miyaki, Shiraga, and Machado families are fictional. But I didn't create fictitious incidents. I placed my characters within the events of history.

In addition to sticking to the facts, I tried to capture the personality of a time I did not live through. So much changes and yet, so much stays the same. But how people talked and described their experience in those days is very different from today.

As for the actual men and women who helped orchestrate these events, I used their names. Because I chose to do this, I was very careful with their words. It was startling to find out that much of what was said by government officials with respect to the relocation was recorded and transcribed. I had access to those transcriptions through the efforts of historians who spent what, I know, were countless hours cataloging historical moments.

I found it unnecessary to embellish the actual words to provide context and a sense of history. The words came from the men and women to whom they are attributed, including Earl Warren, later Governor of the State of California and, finally, Chief Justice of the United States.

The words attributed to President Roosevelt and to the functionaries, aides, and generals surrounding him are, with minor nonsubstantive exceptions for context, their words. In order to assure the reader that these are actual quotes, the quotes are preceded by an asterisk (*). To me, this device was the least disruptive method to signal actual quotes. It's my belief that the actual words allow readers to make their own judgments.

To the extent statements are attributed to actual historical characters, but not preceded by an asterisk, the statements are consistent with the context and historical documentation of what occurred. I did edit the asterisked quotes to make them read more smoothly, but I made every effort to ensure that nothing was taken out of context, or presented in a misleading light.

I make no judgments about the members of our government who orchestrated the relocations. Their words are portrayed accurately, as are their actions. Some were well-meaning, and some were not. What surprised me was who some of the people were who demanded and supported the relocations, and how cynical their motivations were.

Many people given the responsibility of governance did wrong even though they believed it was right, and many people did right and were treated as if they did wrong. It's easy to say what you might have done when you can look back at history. I don't think it's quite so easy when you are confronted with history-making events.

All government documents referred to or quoted are actual documents. They were gleaned from the National Archives, academic compilations, and resources at the University of California, Berkeley, and Stanford University. While there are numerous selected references to documents and transcribed statements related to the relocations, the most comprehensive is the nine-volume work of Roger Daniels, *American Concentration Camps*. This compilation of documents includes many transcribed statements from historical figures involved in the relocation, and was a primary source to ensure accurate quotations. Mr. Daniels' meticulous attention to the relocation's history is invaluable, as are his other detailed academic works about the relocation. There are also many other documents obtained by historians and utilized in subsequent research material. I have included the many primary reference materials in the Source Materials list at the end of this book.

I was also allowed access to the archives of the Go for Broke Foundation, which graciously permitted me to review documentation and recorded interviews with members of the 100/442nd Regimental Combat Team preserving their experiences, although almost all of them have passed on. Those interviews included people who were detained in the camps created for the relocations, and I was privileged to speak to many of them, although for the sake of their privacy I refrain from listing their names here.

It seems common that men and women who have lived through the ravages of war as soldiers do not like to talk about it. I had the privilege of being allowed inside that circle of warriors who fought and bled for this country, while their parents worried and grieved behind walls of wire. I also had the privilege of individual detainees providing me with private recollections, which I wove into this book as part of the composite story.

Many of the events described in *Tears of Honor* seem unreal. They actually happened. The combat descriptions were taken from National Archives battle reports, interviews, and other well-documented resources. The bayonet *banzai* charge described in this book actually occurred. It was, to the best understanding of historians, the only *banzai* charge ever made by Americans.

The description of the Lost Texas Battalion's experiences was gathered through personal interviews with the surviving commanding officer, Marty Higgins, and with Al Tortolano, a surviving member of the Alamo Regiment, and from confirmation by independent source documents. The location of the honors ceremony was altered to provide literary continuity.

Last, but not least, a major character in this book, Colonel Young Oak Kim, was a real person. His account was gathered during six months of interviews. The events in which he is portrayed as a participant were described by him and confirmed by independent source documents, including daily battle reports.

The author has been privileged to know many brave men. Young Oak Kim's exploits are the stuff of legend. They really happened. He was the bravest of them all. The author was honored to attend his funeral. I watched officers from three countries stand and salute, and I watched the long line of men from the 100/442nd give him one last measure of respect. Floral wreaths were sent by France, Korea, and the United States. It was a privilege to interview men who once stood proud as soldiers and now, for those left, stand bowed with age but unbowed as men. Kim is buried with his men, as he requested, in the National Memorial Cemetery of the Pacific (Punchbowl) in Honolulu.

Kim and Higgins are gone now, but it was an honor to know them. They were real American heroes, as were the men who stood with them. Listening to them and Al Tortolano was profoundly moving, as were my discussions with so many men who spoke with humility, even though what they did was profoundly brave.

This book isn't a documentary. It's a story. I've done my best to accurately relate what happened. If there are mistakes, they are mine. Hopefully, those who remember because they were there will feel that I honored their story. Hopefully, those who were not there will now know the story.

I tried to tell this story as best I could. I cannot say that I did it as well as it could possibly be done, but I can say that I tried my utmost to honor the men who fought and died for this country, and to tell the story of their parents who submitted to the unjust demands of their country. And I tried to tell the story of the government that decided to incarcerate so many loyal Americans simply because of the color of their skin and the set of their eyes.

When I finished this book, it reminded me of why I am proud to be an American. I hope that when you, the reader, finish this book, you'll feel the same way. I can say that to a man, the participants said the same thing: They were Americans.

—James A. Ardaiz

**"Honor has not to be won;
it must only not be lost."**

Arthur Schopenhauer (1788–1860)

DEDICATION

This book is dedicated to the many men and women who fought for our freedom during World War II, including my mother, First Lieutenant Ruby Morris (South Pacific), and my father, Captain Harry Ardaiz (Aleutians). Whether the battlefield was in the Pacific islands or the bloody fields of Europe, young men and women sacrificed their lives because they believed in something greater than themselves.

No one made a greater sacrifice then the young Japanese Americans of the 100th/442nd Regimental Combat Team and the MIS (Military Intelligence Service). In order to serve their country, many left concentration camps created by their own country. They left mothers and fathers, sisters and brothers behind wire fences with armed guards who wore the same uniform they proudly put on. I dedicate this book to them. They are American heroes.

I also dedicate this book to the memory of Colonel Young Oak Kim, a man who never failed on the field of battle.

Last, but never least, I dedicate this book to my wife, Pamella, who tolerated and supported the countless hours I spent trying to tell this story.

PROLOGUE

April, 1998
Manzanar, California

It wasn't a memory that came often. Like all things trapped in the recesses of an aging mind, small things—smells, the air, the place—pulled fragmented images to the present and left them there to bring back emotions of the past. For the old man this day, it was the time of year and the blast of cold air blowing in his face. He shivered briefly as his mind's eye held the image before him.

The air hung heavy with the damp of ending winter. Moving quickly down the muddy road the soldiers, his soldiers, tugged their fatigue jackets close as the air rushing past their transport vehicles chilled them even more. He was their sergeant. He pulled his collar up against his face. It was cold but nothing like it had been in the mountains of France. He had never been as cold as that French winter. The new men, the replacements, complained about weather he would once have been grateful for.

The new men knew nothing of war. The veterans like him wanted nothing more of war. His mind drifted to thoughts of his family. Soon, maybe, he might rejoin them. He had given that thought up as the war with Germany pulled him through days and months and years. Maybe it would be over soon. Everyone said it, but he knew that was mostly because everyone wanted to believe it.

He held up his arm to halt the column. The air smelled different. At first the men looked at one another, catching only the acrid hint of diesel exhaust from the trucks, the oily miasma penetrating their nostrils. There was something different—a tincture of decay settling over them.

Through the trees he saw a drifting smudge of smoke slowly spreading, like the last breath of a fire. Certainly, he had seen enough of the detritus of war, the sounds of battle and the consequences of destruction, but there had been no shelling for days. The German army was in full retreat. There were so many enemy soldiers surrendering that he had started taking their weapons and pointing them down the road to the main column. The war was already becoming something that he could see an end to, an end that he had made it to. There was a time when he had given up hoping to make it and had lived each new day with resignation at what he would face and acceptance of what he had faced.

His driver, a young Japanese American with eyes shaped just like his, waited for him to speak. Nobody questioned his leadership or his orders. He had been transferred into the unit, the 522nd Field Artillery Battalion, from the 442nd Regimental Combat Team, the all-Japanese unit that had fought its way through Italy and France. From a combat infantry unit to an artillery unit, the faces were all the same—Japanese Americans with a sprinkling of Caucasian officers. That is what they had been at the beginning and that was what they were now, but nobody questioned their ability or their loyalty anymore. The 442nd had proved that in Italy at Salerno and Anzio, in France at Biffontaine, and at so many other nameless killing fields. He had nothing to prove. He didn't talk about what he had seen. His face told it all. He told his driver to move slowly down the road toward the smoke.

He had learned that in battle, you always move to the sound of the guns. If there was smoke, then maybe there was battle, but probably there was just the wreckage of battle. He sent scout teams ahead with orders to report back. They would move slowly until they knew what was in front of them. He could hear the murmur from the new men. He knew he would hear nothing from the veterans, who would just wait, having already learned that most of war is waiting and terror would come soon enough.

As he approached the direction of his scouts he saw a wire enclosure with the gate open. One of the men had used his carbine to shoot off the chain that held it closed. What he saw were ghosts wandering aimlessly through what was left of a military camp. The smell was stronger, almost stifling. He had smelled it before. Death had settled here. What he saw were survivors, if they could be called survivors. It was hard to tell the difference between them and the bodies scattering ground smudged with patches of dirty snow. He looked at the people moving toward them, recoiling reflexively at the sight. They looked like skeletons with skin stretched over bones, clothes hanging on them like rags drying in the sun.

He turned to the scout who walked up to the jeep and said, "They say this is a prison camp. They say they're Jews. They want to know why Japanese have come."

He had heard of these places, death camps for Germany's reviled and unwanted. He got out of the jeep and walked forward through the gate, moving away from clawlike hands that reached for him, the voices a garble of words he didn't need to recognize. He knew the sound.

He turned to his driver. "Get the Captain. Tell him we need doctors. We need food. Tell him—tell him to come." He didn't know what else to say. He looked at the wire fence and the guard towers. He had seen those before, too. "And tell them we're American soldiers."

His mind slowly drifted back from the memory. Isamu Miyaki could feel the weight of each of his seventy-four years. Every year pressing down more heavily than the one before. He settled back into the softness of the leather car seat, savoring the moment and the luxury of the air conditioning blowing cold air on him, even as it stirred memories of the past.

Today he rode here in a Cadillac. The first time was on an old school bus, when President Roosevelt ordered all Japanese on the West Coast into detention centers. As he looked back on it now he was amazed at how peacefully they had gone, obedience to authority ingrained in them, convinced that their government would do what was right, until they saw the guard towers, and the guns of their guards closing them inside of the wire walls of Manzanar.

He braced himself for what lay ahead. He knew the memories would come back again. That was part of why he came and part of why he wished he'd stayed home. He breathed in the filtered air of the luxury sedan one more time and reached for the door.

The dragon's breath of Manzanar touched his face. The old man drew back from the sudden change in temperature. *It's not the same, and then again, it is.* Still, the heat of the high desert felt different to him now—age, perhaps.

As a boy he didn't mind the spring heat. He looked forward to its relief from the cold winters of California's San Joaquin Valley. Those times when the fog bathed the farm in gray mist and the workers were merely shadows with voices. The farm had been his home. It still was. But this place had been home, too.

Each year, on the last Saturday of April, they gathered in remembrance at Manzanar. Men and women bowed with age. Middle-aged children guiding elderly parents to the gathering place. Small children riddled with impatience—no rides, nothing to see except an empty place. Nothing to listen to but the voices of the old, or the whispers in the wind of the dead.

"The young need to see," he had told his grandson. "The young need to carry our memories. Someday, you'll understand."

The old man accepted his grandson's impatience. It didn't seem so long ago that he had been just as impatient with the murmuring of old men.

Manzanar. The fences were long gone to rust, but to Isamu Miyaki it was still a place with walls of wire. Walls you could see through but could not walk past, except with permission. Barbed wire binding the alkaline dirt where he and others like him were free to stay, but not free to leave. Immigrant parents and American citizen children herded together and driven from their homes with nothing except what they could carry inside the wire walls.

He walked out along the few fence posts still standing, the last sentinels of his days here, dried out in the sun, the sap long since turned to dust. *Just like old men.* He remembered the dust. It still filled the air. It tasted the same. He wondered if it was the same soil he had shaken off almost sixty years ago. He remembered the words from walks to the cemetery, ashes to ashes, dust to dust. Always the dust and always the wind—hot in the summer, cold in the winter. *The seasons of Manzanar change, the dust of Manzanar endures.*

There was little left now, just a few buildings, not even the tower. Manzanar—"apple orchard" in Spanish—just down the road from Independence, California. The irony of that name still touched him. For Isamu, Manzanar would always remain the place where he arrived as a boy and left to become a man, him and so many others. Some now like him, old men, and others long returned to dust.

Still, Freddy always said it was better than Arkansas. His friends were sent to the Jerome War Relocation Center in Arkansas, while his family was sent here. It made it worse to be torn from old friends. His mind drew back for a moment to days long past. *There it was, the sentry house. It looked smaller now and less forbidding. There, where the guard tower once stood.* Gone were the machine guns and sentries—nothing now but shadows that could no longer shake him in the night.

Isamu walked slowly through empty dirt streets now marked only by the stone foundations of buildings long lost to the wind and the sun. He looked across the ground that no longer held a sign or landmark. *Once we built a park right over there.* The earth still held the outlines of the ponds so carefully tended, their beauty once a respite from the parching sun and wind, now only dry depressions in the ground gathering puddles of muddy water from infrequent rain. He paused silently. *And there, there were the stones lying quietly in the earth marking the passing of those who would never leave this place.*

Isamu turned his gaze back to the edges of Manzanar. Gone was the barbed wire. Gone too was the flapping tar paper that covered the walls of his house, Barracks Ten, room three. One room to share with his parents and his brother.

He tasted the dust in his throat. He felt it rise up. He swallowed hard and looked down at his feet. Still the same dust. Still the same taste.

Isamu turned to his son Fred, named after his childhood friend, and pointed. "There—there is where I played ball. Me, Akiro, Tom, all of us. There is the place."

Fred led his father slowly across the road to the empty lot. To a player it was still a ball field. Isamu imagined his son only saw dust, rocks, and weeds. There were no baselines drawn, no bases, no mound. Very little grew where his feet had once pounded to each base, sliding to safety and rising to sweep the dust from his pants. They had pressed the ground rock hard with their base running, and the earth seemed to retain its memory of those days. Maybe he and his friends had beaten the ground into submission.

To him it was still a ball field, waiting for another game. *Well, my friends who have made life's final journey before me, do you still play?* The image startled him. *Perhaps they were playing here now,* he thought, as he stepped off what once had been a baseline. Someday soon he would know. Certainly in the next life he would return to the days of summer and not the hills of Italy, or the forests of France, or the ravaged land of a vanquished enemy.

Fred's son, Matthew, called out, "Grandpa, catch the ball. Catch the ball." He looked around but saw nothing through his eyes except blurred motion. His eyes were watering. *It must be the wind. And the dust.* He could hear his grandson calling to him even as his mind began to drift back to the voices of his youth. Standing perfectly still, he could hear them even now.

PART
I

CHAPTER 1

June, 1941

Calwa, California

"Isamu, catch the ball. Come on, we don't have much time. My dad'll kill me if I'm late to the store again."

The impatient tone of Freddy's voice grated on Isamu as he responded. "Call me Sammy! You know I like that better than Isamu." Both Freddy and Mickey laughed.

Freddy grinned. "Better not let your father hear you say that."

"Yeah, at least your father named you Fred."

"That's true, but your middle name isn't Clarence." Sammy laughed. It was true. Some names sounded better in Japanese.

Mickey stood off to the side, waiting for the other two to finish their exchange. "Hey, you two going to play ball or gripe about your names?"

"Take it easy, Mik-i-o." Sammy drew out Mickey's full name and smiled at his friend. Mickey was the oldest and had just graduated. The other two were still in high school. All three would have looked alike to the casual observer. Dark from the summer sun, baseball caps pulled low over eyes slitted by heritage and the force of the sun. If not for their eyes, they would have looked no different from other boys in the central San Joaquin Valley of California, discarding their shirts at the first opportunity to play ball in the amber light of the late afternoon. All three were of Japanese descent and American by nativity. Ordinary boys playing the American pastime at every opportunity, stealing as many moments as possible away from their chores.

The three young men threw the ball back and forth in the perpetual game of catch they had been playing since they were little. Neither of the younger two was very tall for their seventeen years, but neither came from very tall parents. It was a matter of concern to both of them. Sammy was slim and bronzed from work outdoors. His black hair was short because of the summer heat, easier to care for with his baseball cap constantly on his head. Freddy was a little taller and just as dark. Mickey was the tallest at about five foot six. He was also the most muscular, having worked on his father's farm and its row crops. Mickey was not an athlete. He played for love of the game and the love of his friends. For him, that was enough.

Baseball was their first love. It held everything: excitement, physical activity, and challenge. There were few times when one of them didn't have a baseball or a glove nearby. Sammy loved the feel of the ball in his glove. Left hand curling around the ball and pulling it into the soft, worn leather, reaching with his right hand and throwing in one fluid motion. He knew he was good, but it wasn't enough. He wanted to be great.

Freddy was always a half-step off of his friend's pace. For him, baseball was a passion but not a destination. Sammy wanted to play ball for a major league team, but Freddy and Mickey just wanted to play. It had been that way since they could remember. Mickey was still trying to figure out what was going to happen in his life. Since graduation he had been more quiet than usual.

Sammy turned to his two friends, "Freddy, have you decided on next year? Where you're going to go after we graduate?"

"I guess I'll go to Fresno Junior College. Dad thinks I should keep on in school and maybe be a doctor or a lawyer. And I have a better chance of making the ball team there than at Fresno State."

Sammy snorted. "You? A doctor? You get sick cleaning fish."

Freddy's face reddened a bit. "Well, at least I can catch fish. What are you going to do?"

"Same thing, go to Fresno JC and play ball. Then I'll decide. Coach says I can make the team. All I know is I'm not going to be a farmer."

The mention of making the Junior College team took Freddy by surprise. "Coach didn't say anything to me about making the team." His face showed the realization that Coach's silence spoke volumes.

"Don't worry," Sammy said, catching the uncertainty on his friend's face, "if I make it, you'll make it."

Mickey watched silently. Sammy and Freddy had been talking about the same thing all summer. Their senior year hadn't even started yet, and it seemed strange to them to make decisions about what they were going to do beyond that.

Freddy changed the subject. "You think DiMaggio is going to be able to keep up his hitting streak?" Joe DiMaggio had hit in over thirty straight games for the New York Yankees, and his streak was an object of national obsession.

Sammy shrugged. "I think the Clipper will hit fifty or sixty games, you watch."

Freddy snickered. "Yeah, sure. Nobody can get a hit every game."

Sammy just laughed. "You watch. He can do it. We have a few more minutes. Let's work on grounders. You need a lot more practice if you're going to make the team."

Sammy looked over at Mickey. His friend had been fairly quiet, even for him. "What are you going to do now that you've graduated? You planning to go to JC?" Even though Mickey was a year older than the other two, the three had been inseparable.

Mickey held the ball in his glove and toed the soft dirt. His face lost its boyish lines for just a moment, reminding Sammy of his father. Mickey looked down at the ground and then turned his face away before answering. His voice was quiet but firm. "I'm going to volunteer for the draft." He looked back at his two friends, waiting. This was not something he had discussed with them.

Neither boy said anything for a moment. Keeping secrets was not something they had often done. Sammy waited for Mickey to say something more, but Mickey kept staring at them, his face expressionless. The silence filled the empty space of the makeshift baseball field. Sammy finally broke the awkward quiet.

"You're kidding, right?"

The draft had been put into effect in the last two years, but it wasn't something Sammy or Freddy thought about much. They were still in school. Sammy twisted his glove with his right hand. He overheard some of the teachers at school talking about war. His father talked about war in hushed tones with his mother. But he didn't think about war. He was going to be a senior.

Mickey shook his head in that way that his two friends recognized from years of being together. The decision was made. "I got reclassified 1-A. I've been thinking about what I want to do. I know Dad wants me to help with the farm. I just don't want to spend my time hoeing and digging up onions and pulling off tomato worms. I talked to the guy at selective service and asked if I could just go now and they said okay. Besides, it's only for a year. It'll be something different." He turned his face away from his friends and looked off at the brown hills of the coastal range, cut sharp against the sun. "Different than here, anyway."

Mickey looked at his friends and suddenly said, "I'll see you guys later." He turned and started walking in the direction of his family's truck farm.

Sammy and Freddy tossed the ball back and forth, each waiting for the other to say something. Nobody talked and they fell into the silent rhythm of catch. But the thought of Mickey's decision affected both of them. They had always been together. They had always been here. It never occurred to either of them that someday their lives would be different. Both boys couldn't help feeling a tinge of resentment. Mickey was changing their lives. Unconsciously each of them began to throw the ball harder, the thudding of the ball into their gloves filling the uncharacteristic silence between them.

The long light of the summer hid the time. Neither boy paid any attention to the hills of the coastal range to the west, their color shading from brown to purple in the late afternoon. To the east the foothills stepped up to the Sierra Nevada range where, even in the summer, some caps of snow could still be seen. The heat of the great Central Valley of California did not begin to wane until after dusk and even then, the warmth rose up from the valley floor like an oven cooling.

Calwa wasn't a big town. Sammy knew it wasn't really a town, more of a place. But it was next to Fresno, the city, so at least they could go to the movies. Sammy's father, Shig, didn't like movies very much. Sammy guessed it was because it took him time to form his words in English and he was slow to speak, ensuring his words were correct. Words spoken quickly were difficult for him to follow. Shig was Issei, first generation. Sammy was Nisei, second generation. Born and raised here in Calwa. An American. An American who played baseball.

Someday I'll be like "Joltin Joe" DiMaggio. They'll call out my name—and I'll be Sammy Miyaki—feared by pitchers everywhere. He just hoped he would outgrow his father's five foot three stature. His father always said, "More rice." But somehow Sammy didn't think that was going to do it.

Freddy's impatient voice disrupted his daydream. "Sammy, the ball! Come on." Sammy whipped the ball, skipping it across the rough ground. It popped up at the last moment and caught Freddy square in the lip.

"Sorry, Freddy." Next time Freddy would remember to move to the ball. "Iron Man" Gehrig always moved to the ball.

"Let's go home. Maybe tonight we can catch frogs by the ditch."

Freddy just grunted, his lip already starting to swell.

"My mom's going to kill me. We're having our picture taken tomorrow."

"It'll go with your fat head."

Freddy just grunted again. "Maybe we need to look like twins." The threat was empty. Sammy knew Freddy wouldn't stay mad. He never did. Anyway, the lowering sun made it difficult to see the ball. Sammy picked up his shirt, the signal that it was time to start for home. The grape picking would start early in the morning and Sammy's father would expect him to work. "There is honor in work," his father said. His father looked at everything in terms of honor—even baseball. Somehow Sammy couldn't see the connection between picking grapes and baseball, but he wasn't going to spend time thinking about it. Picking grapes was work. Baseball, well, that was something else.

~

Sammy walked down the dirt road that separated the main house of the ranch owner, Mr. Bagdasarian, from the home of the ranch manager, his father. The rows of grapevines pushed up against the soft edges of the dirt path. Dark green leaves hung over the wire trellis strung between wooden stakes, next to gnarled grape stumps that lined the dusty roadway. The smell of the heavy fruit held the air, closing out everything else. Sammy brushed at the gnats that swirled around his head. He kept thinking about Mickey leaving. He didn't want things to be different. He wanted to do something else, too. He inhaled the heavy sweet odor. He was sure of one thing. He didn't want to be a farmer. He didn't know what he wanted, but at least he knew that.

Sammy got home just as his mother, Setsuko, was looking through the kitchen window. He could see his father watering her roses in the yard. His father never seemed to stop working, moving from task to task.

Sammy could feel the pride his father gained from a hard day's work and harbored a deep respect for his father's commitment to the farm. He stood for a moment at the edge of the dirt roadway that led to their yard and watched his father tend to the roses.

Sammy had often thought that his father put as much care into keeping up the beauty of the roses as he did to the crops in the field. To his father, all growing things brought something to the quality of life. Sammy felt a mixture of emotions as he watched. It wasn't sadness. Perhaps regret that he couldn't feel what his father and brother felt for the land. To him it was little more than dirt, but he dared not share that thought. Somehow, he suspected his father knew. Certainly, his mother did.

"Isamu, are you ready for dinner?" His mother's soft voice came through the kitchen window screen. She was never loud or abrupt, always soft in voice and manner. Sammy's father had the gruffness of a farmer. The calluses on his hands and crusted skin were those of a man long accustomed to working in the weather and sun. Yet Setsuko had the softness of a flower. To Sammy, his parents had always seemed like a gnarled vine with a rose growing next to it: His father strong to the soil, pulling seasons into the twists of his character, his mother with scents and petals.

Setsuko had been a "picture bride." His father had written home to find a wife, and his family arranged to send Setsuko after an exchange of photographs. Setsuko came to America to meet her husband for the first time a few days before she married him. To Sammy, it was a mystery how a man could marry a woman he had only seen in a picture.

"Isamu, have you washed for dinner?" His father's voice was disapproving. He knew Sammy had been out playing ball. It was difficult for him to reconcile his son's ball-playing with his own commitment to work. Shig took some pride in Sammy's talent on the ball field, but he had difficulty with anything that did not resemble work.

"I'll be ready in a minute, Pop." His father took a swipe at him which Sammy easily avoided. His father did not like to be called "Pop." He preferred *otosan*, or Papa, but Sammy liked to tease him.

"You have been playing ball with Freddy and Mikio?"

"We were just doing a little practicing. Freddy needed to work on his grounders so he'll be ready when we start school."

Shig took off his hat and wiped his forehead, the line of the brim marking the sunburned skin from the rest of his face. He sucked air through his teeth. It was a sound he made when he heard something he questioned. "So you were doing it for Freddy and not for Isamu?"

"Maybe a little of both, Papa." He changed the subject. "Did you know that Mickey is joining the Army?"

Sammy's father turned and looked at his son, his face suddenly very serious. "I think there will be lots of boys going in the Army. I'm sure his father will talk to him."

"No, I mean he's going in the Army now. I think he wants to get away from the farm. But I can't believe he's going so soon."

Shig sighed deeply. "Maybe Mikio decided that he has to make a choice." Shig paused, his eyes showing that he understood what his son might be thinking. "You don't have such a choice. You stay in school. That is what you need to do to help the family. Wash for dinner now, there will be much to do tomorrow and you must go to bed early."

"I want to listen to *The Shadow* on the radio. Will that be all right?"

"*Hai.*" Sammy smiled, a small victory. Maybe he could get his father to let him listen to *Amos and Andy*.

Sammy removed his shoes before entering the house. Even in America, the family retained the custom of removing their shoes and placing slippers on their feet. Sammy walked into the kitchen to greet his grandmother, who waited at the kitchen table.

"*Obasan*, grandmother, are you well?" It was a ritual they practiced. His grandmother always responded the same way. Her words tumbled out in the jumble of what, for her, passed for English. "As well to do at my age." He bowed to her in respect and waited for her smile.

Obasan reached out for his face and rubbed his cheek. Her skin had become thin, filled with blue veins. Her hand felt like tissue touching his face. She spoke very little. Her days were spent by the furnace or in the sun, depending on the season. In a Japanese household, even though it was his mother's home, the mother-in-law was given the respect as the head of the home. Setsuko always treated *Obasan* with great deference. She was a quiet, gentle soul, much loved by his mother and the rest of the family.

Setsuko moved around the kitchen, murmuring to no one in particular. As always, his father sat at the head of the table. The first portion of food was given to his grandmother. Steam continued to rise from the bowl of rice as each member of the family took their share. While

Sammy appreciated the traditional foods prepared by his mother, he also appreciated more American dishes. Tonight, his mother laid the platter of golden fried chicken on the table with a flourish. As always, grandmother took the leg.

~

It was still dark outside as Sammy chewed on a cold ball of rice, walking with his brother out to the field, beginning the ritual of turning grapes into raisins. His older brother, Toshio, walked next to him, smiling. Toshi looked forward to this day. He was a farmer. That was what he wanted to be. The early morning still held some of the coolness of night, but not much. Even in the dark, the earth had not lost its heat. Soon the sun would take the last measure of comfort from the air, just as the heat would slowly take the last measure of energy from the field workers. To Sammy, it was hard and dirty work. The only satisfaction he discovered came at the end of the day, when it was over.

The wooden trays were stacked near the heavy posts at the end of each row of vines, ready for their load of grapes. The pickers would lay the bunches on the tray to start the drying process. Row after row of grapes lying on trays, sitting on the smoothed ground.

The flashing curved knives of the pickers moved down the rows. They crouched beneath the vines, where the humidity was trapped under the canopy of grape leaves. Heavy clusters of grapes were quickly cut from curled wood cane stems, winding along the wire trellis. It was hot, hard work and the workers had to move quickly. They piled the bunches into pans and then arranged them on the trays, their fingers moving rapidly. It was not a neat process, as they were paid by the tray

His father was the foreman for Aram Bagdasarian, who owned the ranch. While Mr. Bagdasarian treated Shig like family, it grated at Sammy that his father couldn't own his own land. Mr. Bagdasarian said that many other Armenians could not buy a house in some parts of Fresno, just as Sammy's father could not own land. It was the law. *Someday I'll buy my father land*, Sammy thought, *but I won't carry trays, I'll carry a bat.* He swung the trays in an arc and heard his brother's laughter as they scattered.

Sammy hurried to pick up the trays and moved down the row. He could smell the bleeding stems as the pickers sliced the grape clusters from the vine. "Look for the brown in the stem," his father would say, pointing to green bunches picked by anxious and careless pickers. The brown meant sugar and sugar meant good raisins.

Sammy watched the workers, mostly Mexicans with some sun-reddened white laborers—all with their children working alongside them. Sammy remembered the sting of his father's hand when he referred to the sunburned pickers as Okies. "Do not dishonor working men. Do you like it when they call us Japs?" The lesson remained after the sting was gone.

The workers stopped at noon. Numerous clusters of friends or families quickly gathered into groups. They built small fires, using old grape stumps and pruned canes. Soon, Sammy smelled the tortillas and the cooking meat. Sammy could hear the lilt of Spanish and the drawl of the women from Oklahoma. It reminded him of the holidays when his aunts would work in the kitchen with his mother, Setsuko, Japanese mixing with English, a sound that meant something good to eat was on its way.

José Duran called out to Sammy to join him for lunch. José was lean and tall, with a slender build that belied his strength. His body was hard from working in the fields. José was popular with just about everybody at school. The handsome young man didn't have to work at it very hard. His quick smile, easy going manner, and exceptional physical ability made him a natural leader. Or least as much of a leader as he could be. The son of a farm worker, even if he was the best pitcher on the baseball team, was still a farm worker.

The Durans worked as field laborers, helping with the watering, discing, and picking. They lived in a worker's shed on the ranch. It was built onto the equipment shed, unpainted boards and a rusting metal roof, one room, only fifteen by fifteen feet. Sammy always felt a special warmth when he was welcomed inside his friend's home. The room had a scent. He could smell the chilies hanging from the nails in the walls, spices that were different than those his mother used, but still made him hungry.

The smell of chilies and frying meat filled the air around the Duran family. Sammy moved into the group and José's mother handed him a tortilla, just as she did to her son. José ate quickly. If they hurried, he and Sammy could play a little catch before they had to go back to work. José was a pitcher with a fastball that could crack your hand. He loved to throw hard.

José turned to his friend. "I think we're going to leave for Texas this winter. I have an uncle there who has some land. My dad wants to plow his own fields. Maybe I can finish a school year." He said it in a matter of fact way, even though it would uproot him from his life.

Sammy was startled. "You're leaving?" First Mickey and now José. "What about school?"

José looked at Sammy. "If I can go to school, I will. My family needs me."

José saw the confusion in Sammy's face. "I don't have a choice." He said it with a conviction that left no room for more questions. José accepted the responsibility of his family, and he put that before anything else. Sammy waited quietly while José reached into a bag and pulled out his glove. José grinned. "Let's play."

As Sammy and José walked away from the resting workers, they both watched Carmen, José's sister, amble over to a shade tree by the side of the ditch carrying water to the ranch. A young man stood waiting for her. Sack Pritch had been working on getting Carmen to go out with him for quite a while. José's father did not approve of Carmen seeing a white boy, even an Okie, so they were trying to be discrete.

Sammy and José watched Sack try to talk to Carmen. It was like watching a slow dance where nobody touched. Sack kept shuffling his feet and moving around. Carmen stood and slowly swayed. Her honey-colored skin and black hair contrasted with the ruddy sunburn and auburn hair of the young man near her. Every time Sack reached for her hand she pulled it away, knowing her father was watching. José laughed and whispered to Sammy, "My father will chase her with a switch if she lets Sack touch her. But I've seen them at night by the ditch."

Sammy remembered Sack's oft-told story of how he got his name. "Well, my real name's Billy, but when I was born they put me in a flour sack to keep me warm. Every time they moved me they grabbed hold of the sack. Pretty soon I just became Sack." The Pritches—Frank, Mae, and Sack—followed the crops and moved up and down the Central Valley, and sometimes up to Oregon and Washington when the apples were ready for picking. But they always came back to Bagdasarian's farm to lay the grapes on the trays.

Sack said he was going to do something different, maybe join the Navy. "No more grape pickin' for me, no sir. I'm going to be a sailor and go everywhere." Sack wasn't the only one Sammy heard talk of dreams and different places, but most of the time they came back the next year, looking older and harder.

Sammy walked down the rows, sweat dripping down his face, caking into muddy rivulets on his cheeks. Soon the sun would bake him browner. Just like the grapes.

~

Freddy rubbed his lip. It was still sore from the day before and he hadn't received any sympathy from his parents. His mother was upset about the family picture. His father said that he shamed the family by his lack of consideration. It was only a picture, but that wasn't a suitable answer to any of them. Mas and Satomi Shiraga were people who lived on a schedule.

Their store, M and S Grocery, was in the center of Calwa. There were a few other businesses in the area—a garage that had been there so long the words on its sign were baked off by the sun, a pharmacy operated by the only Chinese family in Calwa, and a hardware store. It was all the people in the area needed.

Freddy picked up the broom from behind the counter. He couldn't understand why the old building had to be swept twice a day, inside and out. His father said that keeping the store clean was an honorable thing. Freddy shook his head. *What did honor have to do with something nobody would see?*

He carried the dustpan outside and down the creaking wooden steps. The whole store sagged just a bit, showing its age. Wood cleaned by the wash of rain and dried by countless summer suns. Boards stretched tight, pulling against nails that left dark stains where the iron bled into the grain. It was an old building warming itself and everyone inside with the summer heat.

Freddy walked over to the counters, bending under the weight of summer fruit: grapes and watermelons, peaches and plums. Each day the Machado family brought in fruit from the local farms. This was the way of things. People brought in food for Mas to sell and he either paid them cash or traded with them for food and other supplies. Mas said it was a good way to live. Each person working to help the other while at the same time helping themselves.

13

Freddy watched his father clean the counter as his mother walked in from the back of the store. Satomi always seemed to float across the floor, never far from her husband or her children. They were her life, all that she wanted. She and Mas met when he first came to Calwa. She was just fifteen and he was twenty. Mas had come to Satomi's father's farm to buy fruit. Mas often said he saw her and spoke to her father that very day. Mas didn't order Satomi to do anything, never even asked. She just knew. Freddy's parents simply were part of each other in everything they did.

Satomi worked in the area behind the counter. She carefully cleaned the glass of the display case and orbited her family while they worked together. There was a harmony to her movements. While Freddy did not really think of his mother as beautiful, he could sense that there was something about her that was beautiful, the center of the family around which their life revolved.

Freddy's sister Betty was filling the candy jars on the counter. Under their father's watchful eye it was hard to sneak a piece, but Betty always seemed to get something. Fifteen and just beginning to get looks from the boys at church, she would walk slowly by the boys at school as if they didn't exist, but her eyes were always turned to the side to see if they watched. And she always made sure she was around when Sammy came by. Freddy knew Sammy had been watching her, just like he had been watching Rose Hayashi, Mickey's sister.

Freddy walked out back to clean the truck. The 1923 Ford flatbed was his father's pride and joy. Already fifteen years old when his father bought it, the sides of the truck bed were boards worn smooth from the loads of many years. He ran his hand over the fender. The black paint was almost blue in the sun, in some places so thin that it barely tinted the metal beneath. But it was clean, and sometimes his father let him drive it around the neighborhood

As Freddy swept the bed of the truck, Mr. Machado drove up with a load of boxes, pulled up to the side of the store, and got out of his truck. Short and powerfully built, he looked like a bull pushing at the boxes. He waved Freddy over to help. The smell of fruit mixed with the dusty smell of the tomatoes. "Right out of field, Freddy." His Portuguese accent still thickly covered his English. When his father and Mr. Machado would get together at the end of the day and have a few beers or some sake, it was hard to understand either of them.

His father came out of the store to greet his friend. "*Hola*, Luis." Freddy grimaced at his father's effort at Portuguese with a Japanese accent. He waited for what he knew was coming.

"*Konnichi wa*, my friend, I bring peaches. Fresh picked." Mr. Macha-do's Portuguese accented Japanese was just as bad. It didn't really matter since they both knew what the other was trying to say. Besides, Mas said the effort meant more than the result. They were both trying to respect the other's heritage.

Satomi came out of the store to greet Mr. Machado and cast her own critical eye on his fruits and vegetables. She was the one who would be stacking the fruit in displays and she wanted the fruit to be perfect. She made a point of picking out a peach with some bruising on the skin, then put it back with a show of deliberation rather than saying anything.

"Hello, Mr. Machado. How is Maria?"

"Hello, missus—my Maria is fine. She will be by later today."

Satomi went back into the store. She would not criticize the fruit or vegetables in front of either man. Her husband would lose face if his wife asserted herself in front of his friend, especially while they were doing business. She only wanted to make a point and be sure her husband was reminded of it.

Mas eyed the tomatoes and squeezed a few on top. "Peaches are good sellers, but the tomatoes look a little green."

"Mas, Mas, I pick the best for you."

Freddy's father laughed. This was part of the trading and he looked forward to it. Luis was a good friend and they always made a fair agreement. Why would they not? After all, tomorrow they would trade again.

Both men lifted boxes off Luis' truck, talking about the heat and engaging in whatever gossip they had heard during the day from their customers. Mas had heard about the Hayashi boy from Freddy. He knew Luis stopped at Jin's, Mikio's father, to get tomatoes and onions.

"Mikio is going into the Army, I hear. Did Jin say anything?" Luis pushed a box towards Mas and stopped. Mas caught his change in expression. Suddenly Mas could see the concern in Luis' eyes. His friend pulled a box of tomatoes off the truck and sat it heavily on the ground. Luis spoke slowly. "Everybody say that war is coming. Everybody say that Japan wants war with America. Germans already at war. People dying young and old. I don't want no war. I don't want our boys to be soldiers."

Mas looked down at the tomatoes. What Luis said worried him, too. He left Hiroshima as a young man to make a new way in life. At home he would be working as a peasant. In America he had respect. But there was so much talk now, and when he came around people lowered their voices. He could hear them talking about "the Japs" and "the Krauts." Even Mr. Schmidt talked about the Krauts like he wasn't German. The talk was bad. And it was getting worse.

The two men stood silently with their thoughts for a moment. Then both of them pulled fiercely at the boxes and said no more. War could not come. It was too painful to consider.

CHAPTER 2

August, 1941

Fort Ord

Monterey, California

The Pacific Ocean slapped the beach dunes at Fort Ord, snug against the coast of Monterey, California. The fort looked more like a resort than a military installation until the view filled in with soldiers running along the dunes in double time, rifles against their chests. It had only been active for a few months when Pvt. Young Oak Kim arrived from his induction center at Fort MacArthur, near San Pedro and the Los Angeles harbor. In fact, his group of recruits were the first to sweep out the new barracks.

Basic training hadn't been so bad. Kim enjoyed the challenge. It was much different than what he had experienced growing up in the Bunker Hill section of Los Angeles, better known as Little Italy. At first he felt the excitement of a new adventure, being an American soldier. Now he chafed against boredom. He had won promotion from private to corporal, but Kim still felt a restless dissatisfaction. There was a certain sameness to it now: fog in the early morning, sun in the early afternoon, and chill in the evening. Still, he couldn't argue with the scenery. Even though he had grown up within several miles of the ocean, he couldn't see it every day. Kim never tired of the ocean. He only tired of the boredom.

Compact, slender, and of Korean descent, Kim sat in the back of the motor pool area reading the latest letter from Ida, his high school sweetheart. She was studying at the University of Southern California to be a nurse. As soon as his time in the Army was over he planned to marry her, but for now he was finishing his year in the service. He idly batted away a fly as he contemplated the dismantled truck in front of him. He didn't want to be a mechanic and he didn't want to be in the motor pool, but it was better than where he started. It was hard to forget that they first wanted to make him a cook.

Kim had worked for a while in his father's store in Los Angeles and then for a Chinese meat dealer, where he helped butcher cattle. All things considered, he figured taking apart a truck wasn't much different. He couldn't help but consider the irony of being drafted. When he had tried to volunteer back in 1939, he had been turned away because he was Asian.

Kim remembered going in to enlist and the recruiting sergeant who looked him over and laughed. "Boy, the army don't need no Koreans or China boys. Now if you was Filipino, that'd be different. Them generals and admirals always need good mess stewards. Don't need no Koreans. You go on home now and work in the store." But now with the draft they were taking everybody, including him. The incident left a bad taste in his mouth. He felt more sadness than anger at his treatment. He didn't like feeling different. He was an American, but not a good enough American to be a soldier until they started taking everybody.

Kim received his draft notice in January. He was happy just to be in the Army and out of the butcher shop. The first day he put on his uniform he felt like everybody else. He looked like everybody else. But right after basic training he ran into Sgt. "Bull" Durham. As far as Sergeant Durham was concerned, the Army didn't have a place for Kim as a real soldier. He remembered what Durham told him: "You aren't like the rest of us. You can be a cook, a clerk, or a mechanic." It had taken him a moment to realize what "the rest of us" meant.

But Kim wanted to be a soldier. He received the best score on the rifle range and was the top of his recruit class. It wasn't in his nature to give up easily, especially when he thought he was right.

"I already told you," Durham repeated, "you're going to be a mechanic. We already got enough cooks and clerks anyway."

Kim knew Durham didn't think Asians could fight. All he wanted was a chance. But right now, all he was going to fight was a carburetor. He carefully folded his letter from Ida. He would read it again later.

Durham walked into the motor pool area. Kim saw him out of the corner of his eye and stood up. "You busy?" It wasn't really a question and Kim knew it. He looked up at the taller man. At only five foot seven, Kim looked up to many people.

"What do you need, Sergeant?"

Durham smiled, "We got a new load of recruits coming in on the bus around 2:00 p.m. I want you to take a truck and go pick 'em up. Let 'em know what a real soldier looks like. Bring them boys back to the training compound. I'll be there waiting for 'em."

Kim bit his lip rather than say anything. One of these days he and Durham were going to have to talk, but he knew it wasn't going to be today. He went to get a truck ready. It was going to take a lot more than Durham to get to him. A memory of his mother came to him, causing him to smile.

When Kim was twelve, he had done something that made his mother angry. He couldn't remember now what it was, though he remembered that he deserved to be punished. His mother cut several switches off the tree in the yard and told him to stand on a stool. He rolled his pant legs up before she switched him. He could still remember jumping up and down on the stool, but he wouldn't cry. After she had broken all the switches, his mother fell to her knees and hugged his red legs. "You are either going to grow up to be a very famous man or you are going to end up in prison," she said. It was the last spanking he got.

He went over to the truck to make sure it was fueled up. As he walked away Durham called out to him. "Kim, when you get back I want you to come by my office, okay?"

"Yes, Sergeant." *What did that asshole want now?* He'd find out soon enough. He climbed into the seat of the truck and nursed the starter until the engine fired. It started pretty slow. He made a mental note to check it when he got back.

~

Mickey sat quietly on the bus looking at the empty countryside. He'd never been further from home than Fresno, which was now hours behind him. He'd never been on a train, either, but the excitement of that wore off quickly. There were no other Japanese on the bus and he was not used to feeling so alone. He had heard most of the young men talking about being in the Army but when he tried to strike up a conversation, he didn't get much of a response. Finally, he gave up and decided to just look out the window. The earlier train ride from Fresno to Stockton had not been unpleasant, but the farther he got from home, the lonelier he began to feel. It would help if he saw a friendly face, one that looked like his.

The countryside looked flat, just like home. The grass was dry and yellowed by the sun, except for some patches of green fields. Finally, the bus rose over some hills and dropped down into another flat area, where suddenly everything looked different. There was more green than he was used to. When they stopped the air was different, colder.

Already the excitement of going in the Army was beginning to wear thin. He started to wonder what Sammy and Freddy were doing right now—playing ball probably. Same as he would be doing. Yesterday he had walked over to Sammy's home. He was pulling trays from the stack near the end posts. Workers were busy moving down the rows, checking the drying grapes to see whether they were ready to be turned. The once green fruit was slowly withering in the summer heat, turning a brownish rose color. Mickey had seen the same thing every summer of his life.

He tried to remember each detail, and was surprised that it seemed so hard. It was only yesterday. The heat had rippled the air in the distance. The mountains surrounding the great Central Valley had begun their shimmery dance on the horizon. The air was clear and dry except under the vine foliage, humidity still trapped under the heavy canopy of leaves. The streaming sweat of the men showed on their backs as they bent over the wooden trays bunched with drying fruit, turning the browning grape clusters so they dried evenly. Sammy was just as sweat-stained as the others, just as brown.

He had yelled at his friend as he approached, scuffing the powdery dust of the roadway through the field. Sammy stopped pulling trays, eager for a respite from the tedium. "Mickey, what's going on?" Sammy knew he seldom came over to the field unless there was news.

"I'm leaving tomorrow. I wanted to let you know. I have to catch a bus in the morning and go to Monterey."

"What's in Monterey?"

"Some place called Fort Ord. That's where I start training. At least it isn't too far away. Look, I'll write as soon as I can and let you know what it's like. It's right next to the ocean, so at least it won't be as hot. I got to get back home. Everybody's waiting. I just wanted to say goodbye."

Sammy remained strangely silent for him.

His friend walked him part way back down the ranch road, puffs of dust rising from their heels. Sammy wiped his palms on his pants and stuck his hand out. "Good luck."

And that was it. Now he was on his own for the first time in his life. He couldn't help but wonder if he would make a good soldier. Anyway, it would all be over in a year.

Mickey began to idly munch on the pickled vegetables his mother packed for him as he watched the bus pull up to a gate. The soldier at the gate looked over the bus and waved it through. The bus stopped at a wooden building that appeared newly painted, tan in color with a green tar paper roof. The driver turned.

"Okay, everybody off. This here's Fort Ord and you boys is in the Army."

The boys shuffled off the bus and stepped down on the gravel in front of the building. Mickey could see a tall, lanky man watching them and a shorter Asian man standing by a truck. His first thought was one of relief. At least there would be some people here like him. All of a sudden his attention was drawn to the taller man who, when he spoke, sounded like a barking dog. "You men form a line. You're in the Army now and you better get used to it. I ain't got all day." Mickey and the rest of the boys jostled to get into a semblance of a line. All the while the tall soldier kept eyeing them and yelling for them to hurry up. He took out a clipboard.

"When I call your name, answer up." He yelled out, "ADAMS!" A short, heavyset blond boy said, "That's me, sir."

"Boy, when I call your name you answer 'here!' You understand? And when you talk to me you say Sergeant! Understand?" Adams stammered as the sergeant barked at him. "UNDERSTAND?" He waited until Adams answered and then got right in his face. "I can't hear you, Adams. You got a problem we need to know about, boy?"

Finally, Adams got out an answer that seemed to mollify the sergeant. Mickey concluded that it wouldn't really make a difference what Adams said. Whoever was first was going to be made an example. Name after name was called out while Mickey watched, concentrating on what seemed to be the wrong answers and what didn't provoke any more attention than necessary.

"Hashi!" The sergeant looked around and yelled again, "Hashi–Mik-e-o Hashi." The sergeant looked directly at Mickey. "You Hashi?"

Mickey answered, "I'm Mikio Hayashi, Sergeant."

The sergeant squinted his eyes and moved directly in front of Mickey. "What you say your name was, boy?"

"Hayashi, Sergeant."

The sergeant rocked back and looked over Mickey's slight frame. "Your name is what I say it is, Hashi. And when I call it you better answer. Understand?" Mickey decided that the only acceptable answer was "Yes," even though he couldn't believe he was answering to the name of "Chopstick."

"Yes, Sergeant, I understand." The sergeant looked at Mickey for a moment and then made a check on his clip board.

"Johnson!"

"Here, Sergeant." The sergeant kept on going until he identified everybody in the line.

The sergeant pointed in the direction of a truck. An Asian man in uniform was leaning against the door. "This here's Corporal Kim. The first thing for you to know is he's got two stripes on his sleeve and you ain't got none. He'll drive you to the reception area and tell you what to do. Get in the truck."

The sergeant spat on the ground, evidencing his obvious disgust with the new recruits, and walked away. Mickey looked over at Corporal Kim and walked with the others to the truck as Kim dropped the tailgate.

Kim smiled as the young men stumbled over each other, trying to get in the truck as quickly as possible. By the time Mickey got there, both bench seats were full and nobody was moving over to make room. Kim turned to him and said, "Get in the front with me." Then he turned and got in the driver's seat. Mickey climbed onto the passenger seat, grateful to not get yelled at.

Mickey almost hit his head as the truck lurched into gear. Kim watched him out of the corner of his eye. "What's your name?"

"Hayashi, Mickey Hayashi."

Kim laughed. "Well you better get used to being called Hashi, because that's what everybody is going to call you from now on."

Mickey grimaced.

"I'm Corporal Young Oak Kim, by the way. I'd like to tell you the worst is over, but it's not."

Mickey looked over at what seemed like a friendly face. "You Chinese?"

Kim's hooded eyelids narrowed even more as he answered. "Korean."

Mickey smiled. "Well, it's nice to see a friendly face."

Kim relaxed visibly and smiled back. "Yeah, I know how you feel."

Kim pulled the truck up near the recruit training compound but didn't get out. He had been here before. He didn't like it then and he didn't like it now. All those drill sergeants yelling at boys who didn't know where to go and couldn't understand what the drill instructors were saying anyway. Eventually some of them would realize that if they just kept their mouth shut it would all be over with soon enough. He turned to Mikio.

"Look, Hayashi, just do what you're told. No matter what you do they aren't going to let you think you got it right the first time. They need you and they can't do much of anything to you. Just don't talk back. I'll see you around." Kim stuck out his hand.

Mickey nodded his head. "I understand. Thanks." He turned and climbed out of the truck. The first thing he did was stumble and fall on top of a drill instructor. Kim shook his head and drove off. He could hear a sergeant yelling "Hashi! What the hell kind of name is Hashi? You some kind of potato?"

By the time Kim got back to the motor pool it was close to 5:00 p.m. He still had to check on the starter and go see Durham. He yawned. The starter could wait until tomorrow. There wasn't that much to do anyway, so it would give him something to work on. Besides, seeing Durham would most likely put him in a foul mood. He fueled the truck and parked it inside the motor pool area.

He walked over to the headquarters. When he walked in the company clerk looked up, smiled, and nodded his head towards Durham's office. Obviously the clerk knew Kim was expected. His eyes showed a question, but the clerk just shrugged and told him to go on in.

Kim knocked on the door and waited for Durham's raspy voice.

"Door's open." He walked through the door and saw Durham sitting behind his desk with a stack of paperwork. "Evening, Kim."

"Evening, Sergeant. You wanted to see me?"

"Lock the door and take a seat." Kim was unnerved at the sight of Durham smiling. The man didn't smile much. Kim took a chair in front of the desk and waited for Durham to speak.

"Look, Kim, maybe you and I haven't gotten off on the right foot. It's never been personal with me, you know. I just been around a long time and I know how the Army works. But maybe you and I can do things a little differently from now on—if you can you keep your mouth shut?"

Kim turned his head slightly to the side and narrowed his eyes.

"Yes, Sergeant, I can keep my mouth shut."

Durham pointed to the piles of paper in his box. "See this? I get piles of this every day. I got ten months to go until I got my twenty in and then I can retire. But I got a little problem. My eyes are going bad on me. Can't see the paperwork anymore and I can't do the reports I need to do. I need you to do the reports for me and I'll sign 'em. If the Army finds out I can't see well enough to do my job they'll put me out to pasture, and I'll lose my retirement. Whatta you say?"

Kim didn't give anything away by his expression, but he had to admit he was stunned. This was not what he expected. "Why me, Sergeant? You got a clerk out there."

Durham's face momentarily flickered with discomfort. "If the clerk finds out then he's gonna talk. I need somebody who's gonna keep his mouth shut. I need somebody who I can depend on. I done most of my duty in Hawaii and there's a couple things I learned over there. Asian people, well, when they give their word they keep it. It's an honor thing with them, right? Well, I figure if you give me your word you'll keep it."

Kim sat silently for a moment. Durham was asking for a favor. It was tempting to tell him to go to hell, but it also was an opportunity to gain the upper hand. He stared straight at Durham, dragging out the moment. "Okay, Sergeant, I'll do it. When do we start?"

He could see a look of gratitude on Durham's face. "Kim, I appreciate this, I really do. I'll figure out some way to repay you. I'll show you how the reports need to be done and then I'll sign 'em. You just come by at the end of the day after the clerk's gone."

"All right, Sergeant."

"Thanks, Kim—and it was never personal, you know. It's just the way things are in the Army." Durham stuck out his hand and waited. Kim stood there for a moment. It may not have been personal for Durham, but it was personal for him. He stuck his hand out. Holding a grudge wasn't going to get him anywhere. Better to be friendly with Durham than continue as enemies.

"I'll take care of it, Sergeant."

Kim walked out of the HQ and pulled his fatigue cap over his close-cropped hair. That was part of the trouble with being near the ocean. It was great to look at, but the nights were cold. He walked back toward the barracks, listening to the crunch of gravel beneath his boots. He knew what Durham thought of him. But the Durhams of this little world were in charge, and he had to live with it. That didn't mean he had to let them get inside his head. He was a good soldier. He was a better soldier than most of the men around him. He knew it and, he suspected, so did they. *Maybe someday I'll get my chance.*

CHAPTER 3

September, 1941
Calwa, California

Sammy walked down the dirt path from his home toward the main road and the bus stop a half-mile away, the sound of his new jeans chaffing against the inside of his legs. The long rows of vines had not yet begun to turn yellow. There had been no frost. The drying grapes were still on the trays, gathering in the last of the summer heat. It would be a late harvest. Soon they would be dry enough to pick up and place in the sweatboxes. The bunches that had been left hanging because they were too green to lay down for raisins had turned yellow, the grapes at the bottom beginning to turn dark and split. The dried raisins on the trays gave off a heavy sweet odor. The smell of the decaying fruit and the more subtle aroma of the browning raisins hung heavy over the rutted access road.

Sammy brushed away the gnats that spun in the sunlight of the dirt road. The smell of the decaying fruit matched his mood. It was the first day of his senior year and he couldn't seem to lift his spirits. For the first time in his life, the certainty of what each day would bring was gone.

For as long as he could remember, there had been three of them. Sammy kicked at the dirt. Mickey's decision had not just changed his own life. Some days he didn't know whether to envy Mickey or resent him. He kicked another dirt clod. Everything was changing.

More and more his parents spoke in whispers. More and more the men gathered reading the newspapers, talking about the Germans sweeping through Europe and the Japanese Empire marching through Burma and Singapore. Even in his own home Sammy could sense unease.

His father listened to the radio reports from London and talked about their relatives in Japan. When Shig looked at his sons, it was clear he was worried.

Sammy walked from the ranch and turned down the worn pavement of the main road that reached through every path in Calwa. *The main street*, he said to himself, *the only real street. Everything else was just dirt roads going to where somebody had built something.* The road had been roughened by the seasons more than the passage of vehicles. He looked at the pitted asphalt. The street seemed tired.

Sammy looked up when he heard the noise of students. The bus stop was just a corner, near the pharmacy. Sammy was thinking about all the times spent waiting at the bus stop with Mickey when José caught up to him.

"You still going to run for student president? I'll help you put up signs and stuff."

The question distracted him from his effort to stay depressed. "Yeah, I've decided to do it. I guess Ferdie Diamico is going to run too. I haven't heard of anybody else."

José grinned. "You're going to win. Everybody likes you and Diamico is kind of a jerk."

"Ferdie isn't so bad, he just doesn't think before he talks."

"Well, I think he's a jerk so I'll get some of the other guys and we'll put up signs and stuff, okay?"

"Yeah, okay. I gotta make a speech at assembly at the end of the week, so let me know if you hear anything."

Sammy walked over to Freddy, who was already at the bus stop. "Can you believe we have to go back to school already?" It seemed like summer had only lasted a few short weeks and now it was over. Seeing Freddy started to change his mood.

"Yeah, but this year we're seniors. I can't wait to work over the freshmen."

Both boys had spent a considerable portion of the summer thinking of things to do to the new kids. After all, it had been done to them and now it was their turn. Dutch Schmidt walked up as the boys were talking. Dutch was the biggest guy in the senior class and the center on the football team. But, as Freddy frequently pointed out, the guy had played too much without his helmet.

Dutch moved close by. "How ya doing? I haven't seen you guys since school let out. I spent the summer workin' in the old man's butcher shop. Cuttin' meat is a good workout. I'm in great shape for football." Dutch didn't say anything to José, just kind of nodded in his direction. José nodded back.

Dutch towered over Sammy and he reached out and grabbed the smaller boy and rubbed his head with his knuckles while Sammy protested. "Hey, Dutch, come on, lemme go."

The bigger boy laughed. "Seniors got to stick together, right? You find me some freshmen and I'll make them squeal like pigs. They got to get used to it."

Freddy caught Dutch's attention. "Hey, Dutch, Sammy's going to run for student body president. What do you think?"

"I think you should be taller than a freshman to be president. But I guess I can vote for him. Just as well vote for him as for that stupid wop, Diamico." Freddy laughed uneasily. He wasn't comfortable with names for groups of people.

Sammy hesitated. "I don't think we should use words like wop, Dutch. I think we got problems enough without that."

"Wop, Jap, spic, what difference? So I'm a kraut and you're a Jap. You are what you are and that's the way it is." Dutch looked at Sammy through narrowed eyes. There was a challenge there but Sammy wasn't ready for it.

Dutch nodded. "Don't worry, little man. I pick smart guys to side with. 'Sides, you're going to help do my homework, right?"

"If you'll help with the election, I'll help with the homework." Sammy could feel tension easing, but none of this conversation sat right with him.

The first week of school was an adjustment, even for a senior. At least he knew where everything was. Sammy spent the week preparing for his speech.

Students running for office spoke to the rest of the school at the first assembly of the year. Sammy sat nervously, waiting for his turn to speak. He twisted his speech around in his sweating hands until the paper no longer crinkled. Diamico was going to speak first because he had won the coin toss. Sammy shuffled his feet around while Freddy poked him.

"Hey, don't worry, Diamico will screw up, you watch. What's he going to say, anyway? He'll promise better food in the cafeteria and a bunch of other things he can't deliver." Freddie started laughing. "Look at his hair. He's got so much Vaseline in it you could grease a car."

Ferdie Diamico fumbled with his tie and pulled out his speech. Freddy was right. Diamico's hair looked like it was painted on. He was leaning against the podium, trying to look taller. As usual, it took a minute for everyone to quiet down.

"My fellow students, my name is Ferdie Diamico and I'm running for student body president. I ask that you vote for me because our country is going to war and at the end of this year some of us will be going off to the Army. We need to take sides now. We all know who we're going to fight. I ask you to vote for me because we need to elect somebody who is on our side. I am one hundred percent American and my parents have been here a long time. Everybody needs to think about this because things are going to change this year. We need to elect people who think like us and who look like us. It's the American thing to do."

Ferdie smiled and looked over at Sammy as he walked off the stage. There was a lot of hollering and clapping. Sammy walked slowly up to the podium and took out his speech. He unfolded the paper and looked at the words, but he couldn't speak. A cold lump stuck in his throat, and he could feel the heat rising up his face. He looked out at the students, waiting for the words to come.

"My name is Isamu Miyaki. Everybody calls me Sammy. I'm running for student body president and I wrote out my speech but now I guess I have something else to say. I heard what Ferdie said and at first I was ashamed that he was talking about me. Then I was mad because he was talking about me as if I wasn't here. But I am here. Look around this room. There are a lot of us here that look different from one another. Our families all came here for the same reason. To make a better life. Even Ferdie's family. I guess he forgot that. I don't know if there's going to be a war and I don't know if it is going to be with Japan. So, if it bothers you that I look different, then don't vote for me. If it isn't important to you that all of us look a little different, then please vote for me. I don't have anything else to say."

Sammy could feel the blood rushing to his ears as he walked back to his seat. He couldn't hear anything. He wanted to throw up.

That afternoon Sammy sat through his English and history classes with his head down. He could feel everybody looking at him and he didn't like it.

Finally, his last class was over. As he got up to leave, Mr. Williams, his teacher, asked him to stay a moment.

"Sammy, I was at the assembly today. If it means anything to you, what Ferdie said was wrong. What you did took great courage. You acted like a leader today." Mr. Williams stuck out his hand. Sammy took it and looked at the kind face of his teacher.

"I don't think I'm going to win."

Mr. Williams' eyes narrowed slightly. "It isn't important if you win. It is important to stand up when the wrong things are said or done. You remember that."

Sammy saw Freddy waiting for him at the bus stop. "I heard some of the kids talking and they're going to vote for you. You did all right. Never mind what Ferdie said."

José was standing nearby. "I told you he was a jerk, didn't I?"

"Yeah, but that doesn't make it any easier." He heard the soft voice of Freddy's sister Betty behind him and he turned when she touched his shoulder. It was like a small jolt of electricity.

"I heard your speech today." Her gentle voice made Sammy strain to hear it. It matched her face, soft and warm. All he could see were her eyes, like the crystal glasses his mother brought out for special occasions, sparkling clear. She turned her head and let the blue-black hair fall toward one shoulder. He couldn't even remember what she had said.

She smiled at his discomfort. "I heard your speech today. You were wonderful."

All he could think to do was mumble his thanks.

"I'll vote for you tomorrow. What that boy said hurt all of us."

Sammy was still trying to think of something to say as everybody shuffled on the bus. He looked for an opportunity to sit next to her, but Freddy moved in front of his sister and sat.

"You okay?"

"I guess. I just wish it hadn't happened." Dutch walked by and punched Sammy in the arm. "Don't let it get to ya." The large young man looked down at Sammy. "My dad came on a boat, too." Sammy looked up with gratitude and then quickly looked down when Dutch said in a louder voice, "But he didn't swim cross no river to get here."

He could see the muscles tense on José's neck, but José never turned around. Sammy felt tired. It didn't make any sense for people to distinguish between themselves based on name or skin color. He leaned back in his seat. He stared at the burnt umber color of the back of José's neck before looking down at his own brown hands.

His father noticed his face at dinner and asked about his speech. Sammy didn't have the heart to tell him what happened. He just said that he had been very nervous. But Sammy's friends had let everyone know, and Toshi spoke up before he had a chance to stop him and told their father everything.

Sammy gave his older brother a quick look and waited for his father's reaction. His mother passed food quietly. The meal continued in silence while Shig slowly chewed his food and stared at his son. Then Shig stood and placed his hand on his son's shoulder. "Let's take a walk."

Sammy followed his father outside and down the dirt road that led from their house towards the vines. They walked silently for a few minutes, long shadows falling across the road as the sun set. The soft dust of the roadway remained silent under their feet. The only sound was the slight rustle of the vines as the heat of the ground rose up through the leaves, Sammy waited. He knew that when his father was ready to speak, he would.

He looked up at the sky and the slowly emerging moon. The crescent shape had lost its sharpness. He could feel his eyes watering. He turned his face away from his father, rubbing his eyes with his sleeve. If his father saw it he kept silent, walking slowly until they came to the ditch running through the ranch. The water was low. Irrigation water wasn't in much demand now that the crop was in. The water looked like a moving mirror of the sky. Sammy stared at it, listening to the frogs hiding in the grass of the ditch.

Finally, his father stopped. As always he spoke slowly, each word weighed and measured.

"Isamu, there are days when you must face the hatred of other men. Sometimes it simply comes from ignorance and sometimes from envy, but mostly it comes from fear. If you remember that such words often hide the fear of the other man, then you will not be afraid of such a man. If you look at him and never step back, you will conquer him in the end. If you did not let him see your shame or fear, then you have done what a man must do. I am proud of you. What happens tomorrow will not be remembered by many. What you said today will be remembered by all."

Shig placed his hand on Sammy's shoulder. "Let's go back and finish eating. Your mother has prepared a good meal." The two men, one older and bending with fatigue, one younger and straightening with pride, walked back to the house.

When Sammy got to school the next day he could see that some of his signs had been defaced. The word "Jap" had been painted on a few of them. Freddy walked ahead of him and started to pull them down. Sammy called after him, "No, leave it up. If somebody is going to pay attention to that, then tearing the sign down won't make any difference." He walked into his homeroom and got ready to vote.

The vote wasn't as close as Sammy thought it would be. Sammy won by 223 votes. He was the first Asian to become student body president. Still, there was something vaguely unsettling about the victory. He couldn't stop wondering how many people voted against him because he was Japanese.

José was jubilant. "I knew you could win. I knew you'd beat that asshole."

Sammy just smiled.

"Maybe you were sure but I wasn't so sure, especially after yesterday."

José looked directly at his friend, pulling him closer. "Look, Sammy, I've never said anything to you about this, but a lot of us voted for you because you're not white like them." José hesitated for a moment, thinking about what he wanted to say. "We wanted you to win, especially after what happened yesterday. I know there are things I'm never going to get a chance to do and nobody will ever say why. That's the worst part, always wondering if you didn't get a chance because of what you are. Now you got a chance for all of us."

Sammy's eyes widened at the vehemence in his friend's voice. He had never heard José speak that way. He never even knew he felt that way. José's deep-seated anger disturbed him. Sammy couldn't help but wonder if that same anger would one day come to him.

CHAPTER 4

September, 1941
Fresno, California

The Japanese community in the area surrounding Fresno was not large but it was significant, and it loved baseball, or *besuboru* as they called it. Almost every Japanese church or Buddhist temple in the area had a team, and the rivalries were fierce. Every Sunday they gathered to worship and then meet on the baseball diamond to fight. Scores were kept and arguments over umpire calls simmered all week until the next game.

Sammy and Freddy attended a Congregational church like any other, except the congregation was entirely Japanese. The Lord's Prayer sounded distinctly different recited in their native language. Carved wood in the front and bright paint distinguished their church from others in the area. The corners of the roof flared upward, and shoes were neatly lined up at the entrance. Sammy's father said how a church looked was not the point. What it taught your heart was the point.

Families came in from the city and surrounding farming towns to gather, worship with their families, and watch whatever games were scheduled between rival churches or the all-star teams. People from Fowler, Selma, and even as far as Reedley, forty minutes away, made the trip. Stands were set up with people selling sweet rice cakes, savory skewers of meat, quilts, and crafts made by the ladies of the different women's guilds. There would be a baseball game later in the day with the Fresno Athletic Club and the Florin Athletic Club from up north. The great

Moon Kurima was going to pitch for Florin. And, almost more important to Sammy, Betty would be there as well.

Sammy was surprised to find such a somber gathering at the church. When the Miyakis arrived, there were crowds of men talking quietly and the women were all together in the shade. Sammy joined Freddy and they moved near where a circle of men had gathered. The men all seemed very agitated and it was clear something was wrong.

Sammy and Freddy heard their fathers and the other men talking about Japan. The word *senso* was repeated over and over again. They had all been reading the paper and the stories about the possibility of war with Japan. Europe was already at war with Germany. Every night they listened to the BBC broadcasts from London that talked of the plight of the English people. That war felt very far away and still the boys heard their fathers at night engaged in quiet conversations with their mothers and the whispered word *senso*—war.

Everyone was passing around a week-old article from the *San Francisco Examiner* that somebody brought to the church. The headline read, *"SECRET PLANS OF JAPANESE GENERAL STAFF PREPARING FOR WAR WITH A WESTERN POWER."* The *Examiner* claimed it had obtained a secret document prepared for the Japanese Minister of War last October. Dr. Akagi, the Miyaki family doctor, was reading the article out loud, detailing Japan's intention to use a place called Manchuria to obtain war materials and invade Korea. But the worst part was what Dr. Akagi read next. Japan was preparing for war.

Sammy heard his father and other men repeating the line in disbelief. A Japanese economic conquest of Manchuria, Korea, and even Mongolia. An invincible position in the Far East. Foundation for the military conquest of the Philippines. All the men sucked in their breath when Dr. Akagi read, "in contemplation of war with the United States."

Sammy stepped back from the circle of murmuring men. He wasn't sure if what he heard was right. War was something he studied in school. The Civil War—men standing in lines shooting at one another. He had watched parades on Armistice Day, old men in uniforms that were too tight, carrying rifles and talking about the Great War. Even the war in Europe was just a thing to talk about in class. His thoughts were a jumble. *We're going to war with Japan? Japan is a small country. America is big, much bigger—much stronger. This can't happen. It makes no sense.*

He felt his father's hand brush his shoulder as Mas and Shig moved back from the gathering of men The boys followed, looking at one another, not sure what this meant.

"Japan will be sorry if they do this," said Mas with resignation. "Masaji says he will go back to Japan if there is a fight."

Shig looked down. The same thoughts weighed on his mind. Both of them were born in Japan. They still had family there, and now they had adopted a country that would be against the home of their birth. They did not think as leaders of countries. They did not think of war between nations. They thought of war between families. Japan was not a stranger to them, as it might be to some Americans who called for war. America was not a stranger to them, as it was to swaggering Japanese military men chafing for *bushido*. For them war meant blood spilled between families. For them, to choose sides meant raising their hands against those they loved, no matter which side they chose.

Sammy and Freddy followed behind the heavy steps of their fathers. Finally Shig said, "We are now Americans. Our children are Americans. We must act like Americans. This is our home now. Let us pray this does not happen."

Mas's face reflected his anguish. He spoke slowly, so the words would not tumble out. "It is more than I can bear to think of my brother's children fighting against America. Our sons will be soldiers against our families."

Shig touched his friend on the shoulder, "We will do what honorable men do. This country is our home now and we must be her children. So must our sons." The two friends walked back to the church slowly.

Church seemed to take forever. Sammy tried to get his mind around his father's words. Finally, he decided it was more than he was prepared to contemplate. There were things outside he would rather do. The smell of incense filled the church. They were used to it, but today they wanted the smell of the grass and the dirt of the game. But first, they wanted to eat.

The smell of sizzling meat and shrimp filled the air outside the church. Freddy and Sammy moved through the food lines, picking up savory rice and chicken in sweet sauces. Freddy's sister Betty edged into their line. Sammy watched out of the corner of his eye while talking to her brother, whose mind was on whether Moon Kurima could throw as hard as people said. "Do you think Zenimura can hold up against Moon?"

Freddy was a big fan of Moon Kurima, even though he played for a rival team.

"Zenimura will show those strawberry farmers how baseball is played," snorted Sammy. The Florin team came from a strawberry farming area, and it had been difficult for them to make this game because it took time away from the constant attention a strawberry field needed. Still, the attraction of playing Fresno was too strong. Besides, Kenichi Zenimura was a legend. He had played against Babe Ruth. Moon hadn't done that. Freddy would see.

"Let me help Betty with her plate." Sammy held her plate while she reached for a napkin.

"She doesn't need any help, Sammy. Let's go find some shade."

"Just a minute, we should wait for Betty." Sammy could feel the heat rise in his face when Betty smiled at him.

"She's going to follow us now, I hope you know that." Freddy's exasperation was beginning to show.

"So what. She's your sister, you should be taking care of her."

Freddy sniffed at his food. "You seem to be doing that okay. She's not going to get lost. Just sit down."

Betty sat down closer to Sammy than to her brother. Sammy couldn't help but notice how gently she laid her napkin in her lap. Her hands were soft and delicate.

Freddy snapped him out of his reverie. "Hurry up and eat. Maybe we can get to the park a little early and see Moon warm up." He was already on his feet, wiping his hands on his pants and heading for the field.

The players were already there when the fans arrived. Sammy could see Zenimura working the players. He was the coach and a player. To play for Zenimura was a great honor. He had already won a Japanese American state championship and taken an elite team to Japan.

Sammy could see two of Zenimura's best players talking about their own glory days. Johnny Nakagawa was sitting next to Charley Hendsch. Nakagawa was a legendary player and everyone called him the Nisei Babe Ruth because of the number of home runs he hit. Hendsch had played for Fresno State and ended up playing semi-pro ball. He was a big hitter and a popular player. Both men were laughing about the old days when they could play in the sun all day. Age had slowed them down, but that didn't mean they didn't want to be out there on the field. Sammy could hear them laughing as Zenimura yelled at his players.

Over the laughter and excitement, the voice of old Mr. Honda could be heard talking about the day Babe Ruth and Lou Gehrig came to Fresno in 1927 and played an exhibition game. Mr. Honda couldn't hear very well and he had no idea how loud he was speaking. Sammy had heard the story at least a thousand times, but old Mr. Honda told it well. Sammy couldn't imagine what it must have been like to go up against Babe Ruth and win. If you did only one great thing as a baseball player, that would have to be it.

Sammy looked around the stands and saw José sitting on the edge of a bench seat on the first base line. He walked over to say hello.

"What are you doing here?"

"I hitched a ride with Sack. I wanted to see Moon Kurima pitch."

"Sack's here, too?" There was surprise in Sammy's voice.

"I don't know why you're surprised, my sister's here."

Sammy looked around and saw Carmen over by the gate talking to Sack. He walked over to say hello and give Sack a hard time. But as soon as Sammy saw them up close, he decided that it wasn't the right time for teasing. Sack looked very serious. He rested his hand on Carmen's shoulder. She was leaning in, her head not quite touching his chest. Sammy had never seen them so close. Carmen's shiny black hair fell alongside her face, hiding her eyes. Sack was talking, but his lips were barely moving.

"Why the long face, Sack?"

Sack turned at the sound of Sammy's question. Carmen kept her face turned away. His voice was hoarse, almost guttural. "I'm leavin' tomorrow, Sammy. I tole' you I was gonna join the Navy and I did. They got me shippin' out tomorrow for San Diego. I'm gonna try to be a gunner's mate on one a' them big ships." Sammy stepped back and thought about what everyone had been reading earlier in the day. He could see the wetness on Carmen's face as she looked down at the ground.

Sammy backed off. He wasn't sure what to say, but he knew he had interrupted something private. "Be careful out there. The ocean's a lot deeper than the ditch behind the house."

Sack moved his head almost imperceptibly, as if giving serious thought to Sammy's observation. "Guess I'll hafta learn how to swim.

I could always stand up in the ditch." Sack looked at him and then at Carmen. "I'll be back, Sammy. Me and Carmen got plans."

"Does José know?" Sammy asked.

"Yeah, but he won't say nothin' to Carmen's dad. We're gonna wait 'til I get back from my first year. Then I can take care of her."

Sammy decided it was time to leave. He turned to find Freddy. There was a lot to talk about.

The boys walked over to watch Moon warm up. "Freddy, who's the guy in uniform sitting with Stewie?" Stewart "Stewie" Tamura was sitting next to a young man in an Army uniform. People were talking to him, but he seemed to be concentrating on what was going on in the field.

"His name's Otani. He's home on leave. Look at everybody around him. That uniform really does it for the girls."

The players took the field to wild cheering and catcalls from the fans. The Japanese were normally reserved in behavior, but baseball was an excuse to let go. Sammy could hear the betting start. Good-natured goading over how many runs Fresno was going to win by were responded to by snorts of derision. Shouts of "We'll see" and "Just wait" were heard all over the field. Sammy found a seat and noticed that Betty sat down next to him.

"Sammy, you watching the game or not?" Freddy asked.

"Of course I'm watching."

The game quickly stretched out, with neither side scoring until the bottom of the fourth. Moon was pitching. A pitcher's job is to control the plate. He faces a batter much like a gunfighter. Kurima certainly knew his role and Zenimura was at bat. He knew his role too.

A pitch is the culmination of the massing of muscle propelling the arm forward and delicately twisting the wrist to the elbow to place spin on a ball the size of an orange. So beautiful when done skillfully, forcing the ball to a speed of ninety miles an hour at a glove sixty feet away, and over in less than two seconds. To hit a ball well-thrown is the hardest thing to do. Everyone knew Moon was a good pitcher. Zenimura had seen Moon before. It was timing and reflex, timing and reflex.

Sammy watched in fascination as Kurima pushed dirt around the rubber bar in the mound. Somehow, he looked like a coiled snake as he pushed his leg high in the air and snapped his arm forward. They could hear the grunt as the ball left his hand. To Sammy it happened in slow motion. He could see the ball as it struck the bat. A hard skimmer between the short stop and second. Zenimura was around first and edging towards second before the center fielder pushed him back with a hard throw.

The shouts of fans were all over the field. Zenimura was almost forty but he could still play. "Hash" Hashimoto was up. Freddy and Sammy leaned forward. Hash was a good hitter but he didn't like to hit an inside fastball.

"Ball one." The umpire shouted. It looked high, but Moon was throwing for the inside.

"Strike one." The booing and heckling drowned out the umpire, but it looked like the inside corner of the plate to Sammy.

"Strike two." You could hear the cheering when the crowd heard the crack of the bat, then hear the groans as they watched the ball curl up and over the backstop. Foul ball.

José was sitting behind the boys. "Watch this. He's going to throw a curve."

"Naw, he's going to throw another fastball, you watch."

Moon shook his head at the catcher's sign. He wiped his forehead on his arm.

José laughed. "Watch his hand, he's rubbing the ball. He's going to throw a spitter."

"He isn't going to throw a spitter. You watch. It's going to be a fastball, low and inside."

They could hear the crack of the bat all over the field. Hashimoto caught the ball on an upswing. Everyone was on their feet, willing the ball over the fence. Willing the ball to drop before the fence.

It landed over the fence. A home run. The cheering mixed with the groaning. Zenimura trotted the last few feet to home and stood to slap Hash on the back as he crossed the plate. Two runs for Fresno, nothing for Florin.

This was looking good, but Sammy's interest in the game was beginning to wane. He looked over and saw Otani, the soldier in uniform. For some reason he couldn't get Sack and Carmen out of his mind. He looked over at the spot at the end of the bleachers where he had left them, but they were gone. With José's family leaving for Texas, Carmen would be going with them. Sack wouldn't have a reason to come back.

Freddy's exuberance jarred him back from his thoughts. "Could you believe Kurima? A home run in the ninth? What a smack he put on the ball."

Sammy just laughed. He hadn't even been aware of what was happening. "Yeah, he did it to us all right. He's a good player."

Freddy couldn't restrain himself. "He's the best. He's the best." He looked at Sammy for a response, then shook his head. Both young men watched the game quietly, each caught up in his own thoughts.

CHAPTER 5

September, 1941
Honolulu, Territory of Hawaii

The two young men dressed as soldiers walked along the shore of Oahu, kicking at rocks in the dirt above the beach. It was another day of pointless drills. One minute they had been in the 289th Hawaiian National Guard on Oahu, and the next minute the unit had been federalized and they were in the Army for real. The spurts of rain blowing onto the shore did little to relieve the heat and humidity. It was just part of life in the islands. The sun shined while rain fell from passing clouds. The pie pan helmets on their heads didn't help, either.

The two men were trying to stay in the little shade along the road above the beach. This was definitely not part of their plan. The National Guard hadn't been a bad deal when it was only weekend duty, but after the National Guard 298th and 299th Hawaiian units were federalized, the men became more aware of how close they were to being real soldiers. They both complained but also knew they had little else to do. They would complete their military service and get paid. At least they got to go home most nights and could usually get a weekend off if they needed it.

There were reasons to have a local military presence added to the significant military presence on the island. Theoretically, the men in the National Guard were part of the first line of defense for the islands. Of course, none of them took that seriously. This was Hawaii, not Los Angeles.

Right now, their minds were not on defending their homes. Tug, the smaller of the two men, seemed to move forward as slowly and relentlessly as the work boat he was named after. The other man, Yuki, moved ahead swiftly then looked back, as if his look could drag the smaller man forward. A fast cruiser and a work boat chasing her.

"Tug, move a little faster will you? I want to get back so we can find some shade."

The smaller man just grinned with a smile that matched his size. Five feet four inches tall and just as wide. That's why all the boys called him Tug Taniguchi instead of George. He didn't mind. He liked being called Tug. It seemed to fit. Together they made a strange pair. Yukio Watanabe was five feet ten inches, tall for a Japanese and even taller when next to Tug.

"Taniguchi, you should have been a sumo wrestler."

"Be careful, Watanabe, or I'll push you all the way back."

"First you'd have to move."

"Hey *brah*, I move but see no reason to move in this heat."

"Stop with the beach boy routine. You sound like some surfer boy down at Waikiki working on the tourists."

Tug grinned, his white teeth showing.

The clothes of both men were stained dark with sweat. It ran down their backs and down their legs. Salt rings seeped through their shirts, under their arms, and on their backs. Even though they had both grown up on the island and were used to the heat and the humidity, they weren't used to being dressed in such clothes. The heavy uniforms just didn't make sense in the humidity of August. Tug kept complaining, wondering why he couldn't wear an Aloha shirt and shorts.

Finally, Tug's mind moved off his discomfort. "Yuki, you're pitching tomorrow against the Wanderers?" The Wanderers were a team of *haoles*, white boys, who played in the Hawaiian Baseball League. "You should be able to beat hell out of those *haoles*." Tug grinned at the thought of teasing his white friends, who would be rooting for the Wanderers.

"Maybe, but for white boys they're pretty good. This is going to be a tough game. We'll see."

Tug grunted. "You always say, we'll see. Why don't you just say you're going to beat them? It's bad luck to have doubts."

"Maybe so, but it's just stupid to be overconfident. We'll see."

Tug snorted. "You wouldn't be playing for Asahi if you couldn't beat those boys."

"Yeah, and they wouldn't be playing for the Wanderers if they couldn't beat us. We'll see."

But both young men knew that Asahi was the best. The team to beat. It was one of the oldest teams in Hawaii and the premier Japanese team. Yuki knew that tomorrow was going to be a tough day if he didn't pitch his best. His height normally helped him to bear down on a hitter, but the boys who played for the Wanderers weren't like the Chinese boys who played for the Tigers or the all-Filipino team. Many of them were just as tall as him and a lot beefier.

"Yuki, I've decided I'm not cut out to be a soldier. We been doing this since October when they activated us. How much longer you think we're going to have to stay in? I don't think I need money this bad to walk around in the sun dressed this way. You like this stuff. I know I don't plan to spend any more time in a uniform than I have to. Our rifles don't even have bullets in them."

Yuki made a face. "They don't have firing pins either. Why do you need bullets? You going to be attacked by a seagull? Stop whining. We're in 'til they say we're not. All I know is I'm going back to school when I get out."

"What do we do if the Japs come?"

"The Japs aren't coming, Tug, you know that. We're too big a country. They couldn't be that stupid. Besides, they aren't going to take on the whole Pacific fleet." Both boys gave no thought to the fact that they were of Japanese descent. To them, Hawaii was home and they were Americans. Their guard unit was made up of Hawaiians, Chinese, Portuguese, and just about everything else, including local boys of Japanese descent. Japs were Japs. It wasn't the same thing.

"Stop worrying. Besides, if they do come they're just going to think you're a big rock because you move at about the same speed."

Tug and Yuki eventually made their way into the Guard post office. It wasn't that much cooler in the office, but at least it had shade and a fan.

"What took you two so long?" snapped Lt. Coehlo. Usually Coehlo was fairly soft-spoken. Yuki figured it must be the heat and decided to be agreeable. Tug, however, couldn't resist baiting Coehlo.

"We were watching the water to see if the enemy was coming. We almost got attacked by a coconut." Coehlo didn't laugh, but then Coehlo never laughed. He took everything seriously, including walking along an empty beach guarding against seagulls.

Coehlo's face showed his disgust with Tug's lack of military bearing. He couldn't keep the sarcasm out of his voice. "You never know, but if they do come you two won't see them until they walk on the beach."

Coehlo's bad humor didn't faze Tug. "Well, Lieutenant, if I see them coming I'll just fire a warning shot from my rifle so you can get ready for them."

"Taniguchi, there's a reason why we don't give you any bullets. It starts with your mouth. Less talking and more watching and maybe I wouldn't worry so much. Anyway, I need you two to go over to Schofield and get these supplies. Bring them back tomorrow."

Yuki's face fell. "Coehlo, you know I'm supposed to pitch tomorrow."

Coehlo looked at both men. "That's Lieutenant Coehlo to you, Corporal Watanabe. You don't think guarding the island is more important than baseball?"

He waited for Tug and Yuki to think of something else to say but both men stood quietly, their minds already on how to get back in time for the game.

"Anyway, I didn't say what time you had to bring back the supplies, did I?" Coehlo's face had just a hint of a smile. "Make sure I have a good seat at the game."

~

By noon the next day the sun was steaming everybody in Honolulu Stadium. It was the best diamond in Honolulu. Sometimes called the Termite Palace, rumor had it that the University of Hawaii was conducting a study of the effects of termites on wood and was using Honolulu Stadium as their testing area. People said that it was only the termites holding hands that kept the whole place intact. The fans didn't care. The place hadn't fallen down yet.

The Asahi team had been around since before the Hawaiian Baseball League was formed in 1927. There was always an intense but friendly rivalry with the *haole* boys. Many of the younger men on the two teams had played together in high school, so the heckling was going to be fierce on both sides. That was part of the entertainment. Everyone was polishing up their insults. The competition would be heated and no quarter would be given. It promised to be a great day for baseball.

"Doc" Komatani stood near the dugout, watching his players warm up. Doc was a dentist whose passion was baseball, and he was part owner of Asahi. Yuki could hear him shouting instructions to the players as they went through their warm-ups. He had a face that reminded Yuki of a bulldog, and sized to match. When he laughed, everybody laughed, mostly because of the way his whole body shook.

Doc turned when he saw Yuki walking towards the bullpen. "You ready to throw today, Yuki?"

"I'm ready, Doc. I got the heat."

"Uh-huh, uh-huh, just throw the heat and we'll be fine." Yuki laughed and kept walking.

Tug followed Yuki into the bullpen to help him warm up. Tug caught for Yuki on the high school team, but he wasn't good enough to play for Asahi. In this heat it wasn't going to take long to warm up. Yuki stretched out his lanky frame and pulled his right arm behind his head, then his left arm the other way. Back and forth until he felt the muscles begin to loosen. Tug tossed him a scuffed ball from the bag and waited for Yuki to throw.

"Come on, Yuki, just toss a few to make sure your elbow is loose."

Yuki had a bit of a side arm pitch. It was tough on his elbow, but it made him throw a natural slider that was tough to hit if it was thrown with velocity. And Yuki had velocity.

Yuki loved the feeling of standing by himself on the mound. He felt like the Lone Ranger on the radio. Just him against the bad guys.

The first pitch slid through the damp air, gathering moisture from the humidity. When they played, the ball reacted to the dampness and got a little heavier. Today was going to see many heavy balls.

Joe Takata stood, watching Yuki warm up. Joe was the star outfielder, playing centerfield. He was also in the Guard.

"Hey, Yuki, you come to play?"

"Takata, I always come to play. You just do your part and hit, okay? Hope you didn't stay out too late with Florence last night."

"Yeah, *brah*, don't you worry about old Joe. I'll hit the ball. You just make sure those *haole* boys don't hit the ball." Joe walked over to the dugout to sit and think about the game.

Yuki took his hat off and rubbed the sweat from his forehead. He wondered how many more chances he would get to pitch before the Army decided he could make better use of his arm holding an empty rifle and guarding the other side of the island. What were they all so afraid of? Didn't they read the paper? Just the other day the *Honolulu Star Bulletin* said, *"A Japanese attack in Hawaii is regarded as the most unlikely thing in the world, with one chance in a million of being successful. Besides having more defenses than any other post, it is protected by distance."*

Yuki toed out the dirt in front of the pitcher's rubber on the mound and laughed to himself. *I wonder what the Japs would think if they knew we didn't even have bullets in our rifles?* He squared off and took one more practice throw from the mound.

CHAPTER 6

October, 1941
Calwa, California

Sammy walked over to the Duran family's room next to the equipment shed. He was hoping maybe he and José could get in a little catch before his father reminded him again of his chores. He saw that the Durans were packing their few belongs into cloth bags and two open suitcases. Carmen was tying a string around a box of her mother's prized cooking utensils. The nails where the chilies and other spices had hung were empty.

"José, what's going on?" Sammy knew the answer but didn't want to hear it.

"We're going to Texas, Sammy. My father wants to leave on the bus early in the morning." José's voice betrayed the emotion his face was trying to hide. "I guess I won't be playing ball with you this year."

Sammy hung his head. First Mickey and now José. He wasn't sure what to say.

"How will I get letters to you? Sack is going to keep sending letters to Carmen and he sends them to me first."

"I got an address from my mom. Here." José handed over a rumpled folded piece of paper. "Send the letters to me and I'll make sure Carmen gets them."

Sammy walked out of the small house and turned. "I'll be right back." He hurried to his room and rummaged through his drawers until he found what he was looking for. He raced back to his friend.

Sammy handed José a bag. "Here, take this with you. Maybe you can use it." Silently, José reached out and took the bag. He didn't need to look inside. He knew it was Sammy's best baseball.

"I'll write you and let you know where I end up. We'll see each other again, don't worry."

"Yeah, we'll see each other again." Both boys stood awkwardly waiting for the other to make the first move. José stuck out his hand and Sammy reached for it. "Take it easy."

"Yeah, you too." Sammy walked away. He kicked the dirt as he made his way back to the house. His father would be waiting. There was work to do.

CHAPTER 7

October, 1941
San Diego, California

Sack was alone when he left Fresno. Carmen wasn't at the bus station, nor did he expect her to be. His parents had already pushed on to the crops in the north. Sack had been doing odd jobs around the ranch and sleeping in the shed where the raisin trays were stored. He was able to catch a ride from Mr. Bagdasarian, who dropped him off and wished him well. The rancher also handed him a few extra dollars. "For the trip," he said. "Keep yourself safe, boy." He stood at the curb as Mr. Bagdasarian drove off, watching the rancher's truck pull away. Then he turned and walked into the bus station alone.

Sack held onto the ticket he received from the Navy recruiter as others at the bus station said goodbye to their families. It only made leaving harder. He and Carmen said their goodbyes by the canal where they had met secretly for months. Both searched for the right words but were left with only long moments of silence between them.

Sack spent the first hours on the bus staring at the small valley towns that hugged the highway. Every stop seemed just the same, a dusty farm town with new passengers climbing on the bus who looked the same as the ones who stepped off. He only spent a few moments watching the new arrivals before he lost interest. Most of his thoughts were about Carmen and whether she would be there for him when he came back.

He stared out the streaked window of the bus at the flat, open land. When he had followed the crops with his parents, they stayed on the back highways and farming roads. The view was always the same, brown earth and green crops. The view from the bus wasn't any different than it had been from his parents' truck.

The bus crawled over the twisting mountain pass called the Grapevine that bridged the Central Valley with the Southern California basin. Cars sat beside the road on the steep mountain grade, their radiators steaming from the strain of the climb. He had never been this far south, but he sympathized with the families standing beside their cars crowded with their few possessions. He had also stood beside his father's overheated truck many times. He knew how it felt to watch others pass you by.

Now, as the bus left the mountain road and came down into Los Angeles, all he saw through the window were palm trees and blue skies. As the bus followed the coastal highway he saw the ocean, stretching blue and frothing as far as he could see. He couldn't take his eyes off the endless expanse of water. It was the first time he'd seen the ocean.

When he arrived in San Diego, he looked out over a harbor sheltering massive ships that he had only seen before in the posters outside the recruiter's office. With a few other enlistees, he found his way to the ferry and crossed San Diego Bay. He stood on the blunt-nosed bow of the ferry, feeling the spray of water and looking at the blue-gray ships hugging the harbor edge. A massive battleship rode at anchor, her guns cocked at the sky like the prickly spikes of a porcupine. He looked down at the harbor's green water and then up at the guns of the huge ship. *One day I'll fire those guns.*

When he arrived at the San Diego Naval Training Station, Sack walked through the wooden gate and stopped to read the sign over the entrance:

WELCOME ABOARD
You Are Now Men Of The United States Navy
The Traditions of the Service Demand Your Utmost Effort
Give It Cheerfully And Willingly

He felt the rush of anticipation. He was in the Navy. He *was* going to see the world. Already everything was different. The air was balmy, a sharp contrast to the heat of the Central Valley. He let the warm breeze flow over him. It was one of the few times he could remember welcoming the sun on his face instead of feeling it burn into his back.

Over the excited voices of the other young men standing near the entrance, he heard a bellowing voice that sounded like a fog horn. A grizzled older man approached them. He had stripes on his sleeve that ran from top to bottom.

"Welcome to the Navy, boys. Now get your asses in line."

It was time to begin.

~

Two months passed quickly after Sack had walked through the gate, and he still had a month of basic training to go. He sat down heavily on his locker and picked up the boot he had just removed. So far, all he had seen of San Diego was the way it looked across the sparkling water of the bay. The first day hadn't been so bad, except for the haircut. He never realized how big his ears were until he saw himself in the mirror after the barber shaved his head. The auburn fuzz made him look like a peach. Then he walked into a supply warehouse, still rubbing his head, and was handed a sea bag and piles of clothing. Nobody asked him his size, except for his shoes, and even then he didn't think they paid any attention. After a little trading between the new recruits, almost everybody found something that fit.

He pushed the polish rag into the creases of the boot. He kept one boot on in case his trainer came in. Sack learned quickly that whatever the Navy wanted done, they wanted it done *now*. One boot off at a time meant only one boot to be tied in a hurry. He fell into the habit of taking any opportunity to shine his shoes, because he never knew when another would come. The Navy didn't seem to care if he slept as long as he kept his boots polished and his bunk made. As much as he hated to admit it, Navy life wasn't much better than working in the fields. He still got up at 5:30 in the morning, and there was still always someone with a big gut yelling at him to work faster.

Sack worked the polish into the boot, carefully scraping away flecks of paint from a ship-painting drill. He learned to make a bunk with square corners. He learned to march around in circles and squares, and he learned to stand in line for everything that he might enjoy. He learned how to row a whale boat. He could throw a line off a ship to the dock. As far as Sack was concerned, none of it meant anything because he still hadn't been on a real ship. His only advantage came when firing a rifle. He had fired a rifle many times to get a stray rabbit for dinner. Most of the boys in the barracks had never seen a gun, except during the Saturday matinee.

He kept pushing the polish around, ignoring the sound of the other men in the barracks. He missed his family as much as he missed Carmen. Every day he answered mail call, but the letters were few and far between. He knew better than to expect anything from his mother and father. They weren't much for writing. He didn't even know where his parents were. His family followed the crops. It took him some time to realize that he had never been away from home before, though home was no specific place. Sack looked around the barracks. This room was the closest thing to a real place to live he ever had. But it wasn't home. Home was wherever his parents were. Wherever the crops were. *And now*, he thought, *home was Carmen.*

He started another letter to her, but it was always a struggle. He knew how he felt about her, but somehow it never came out right on paper. For Sack, writing was almost a painful experience.

A few of the other men in the barracks were also writing letters. There wasn't much to do with the little free time they had, except to write letters and tell lies about the girls back home. He didn't talk too much about Carmen. Mostly he kept to himself and Buford, the recruit who had the bunk directly next to him.

He wondered what the future held for him and Carmen. He wanted to tell her that he was going to try to be a machinist when he got out, so he could support her. He didn't want to spend his life picking grapes and apples. Sack wiped the polish from his hands and unlaced his other boot, carefully removing the leggings that kept his pants bloused. He reached for the unfinished letter. Maybe he would tell Carmen about the rumor they were all going to the Pacific Fleet.

Buford lifted his head from his bunk and rolled over on his side, facing Sack. "Pritch, ain't you through writin' that gal of yours? We gotta get our gear stowed for inspection. I don't want no potato detail again."

"Stop yammering, Bufe. I'm done writin'. We got some time. 'Sides, the only thing you like to eat is potatoes. Don't you never get enough?"

"I never get enough of anything when it comes to food." Bufe Douglas laughed, his ruddy complexion almost hiding his freckles. He was a big old Oklahoma boy, at least six feet one and well over two hundred pounds, at least when they started basic training. He had slimmed down some from the daily running, but he did his best to add the weight back at every meal. Bufe was born poor and stayed poor until he joined the Navy. As far as he was concerned, any place that kept his belly full was all right with him.

"Sack, the poop is we're gettin' our orders pretty quick. Where you want to go?"

Sack usually kept his ambitions to himself, but he didn't mind sharing them with Bufe. "I'm hopin' for a battlewagon. Those big guns are the thing for me. I'm hopin' for Hawaii. I sure would like to see them islands. And the women."

Bufe laid his head back on his pillow and laughed. "What do you care about the women? The only woman you ever talk about is Carmen."

~

It was well into November, and there was only one more week to go before training was finished. They had their orders. Bufe walked into the barracks and threw two letters on Sack's bunk. Sack looked at the envelopes and the tiny writing, already several weeks old. He held the letters, savoring the moment as long as he could, then he looked up to see Bufe staring at him. Bufe's hands were empty.

"You get any letters?"

Bufe shook his head. "Nah, folks ain't much for writin' but my sister tries. Nothin' today 'cept for you. Sack nodded and turned back to the two thin envelopes. He carefully opened the one with the earlier postmark and unfolded the paper.

Carmen told him that she was sorry she hadn't been able to write. Her father watched her closely. She received all of his letters. The family was leaving soon for Texas. He stared at the penciled marks on the paper. *She's probably already gone to Texas. She doesn't want me to work with guns. She wants me to be a cook. She thinks being a cook is safer.*

He looked up when he realized Bufe was still standing over him. "What'd she say? She still likin' you, or you gettin' one of them Dear Johns?"

He carefully folded the letter and put it in his pocket. "Yeah, she still likes me." He patted his shirt pocket. The best part of the letter told him that she had talked to her mother about him. That was a start.

Sack saved Carmen's second letter until Bufe took a shower so he could read it without interruption. He carefully opened the second envelope, written a week after the first, and unfolded the paper with its pages of neat script.

She missed him every day. Her mother said that she would talk to her father. They were moving to Texas. She would write as soon as they had settled. She still wanted him to be a cook. His eyes lingered over her signature: *with love, Carmen*. Carmen's last two letters were enough to get him through the last week of Basic.

Sack sat on his bunk, trying to think of what to write back. He had hoped to get back to Calwa before Carmen left for Texas, but there hadn't been enough time. He finished the last line of his letter without putting anything down about his orders, except to say that he was going someplace else. He had been ordered not to write anything about them until he got to his new duty station.

Bufe straightened his bunk. "Quit writin'. We gotta get moving if we're gonna catch the bus into town."

Sack sealed the letter. Hopefully, Carmen would write soon. The Navy said that mail would be sent on to wherever he was in the Pacific Fleet. He was both disappointed and excited. There would be no leave time to see Carmen. But he was going to a battleship, just like the one he had seen riding at anchor when he crossed the bay on the ferry.

Bufe could not control his excitement or his impatience.

"Buddy, can you believe it? We're going to Hawaii."

CHAPTER 8

November, 1941
Calwa, California

Mas walked into the store from the back rooms of the family area. The rest of the family was beginning to stir in the early morning but he liked to be up first, to feel the air and the silence that came before the day began. The dusty smell of the potatoes left in the bin mixed with the sharp odor of the first pomegranates of the season. Mas caught the heavy odor of peaches. He held the remnants of the summer harvest in storage as long as possible. He looked at the last pale yellow fruit in the wooden box. Most were showing some bruising. He could tell by the smell that he would have to sell them today, or have Satomi use them to make preserves.

Mas walked out onto the front porch and looked at the entrance. This winter he would replace the boards that covered the area between the steps and the front door. Shuffling feet had worn the wood planks down. He liked the old wood with its ripples and stains.

There was a chill to the morning air and the days were growing shorter. He looked at the tall elm tree out front that shaded the dirt area, the store's parking lot. The leaves were turning. Winter was closing in. Mas stepped down to the dirt and began to walk around the store, his morning ritual of gratitude, reminding himself of the long journey that had brought him here.

He stopped on the side of his grocery, quietly looking at the paint running in drips down the wall of his store. The thickly brushed words were still wet in the early morning damp. His first reaction was anger at the vandalism, before the words began to sear his mind. He could feel his throat tightening up. It was only paint, but he felt shame that others would see it and worse, that someone put such ugliness on his home.

Mas hung his head, his lips set in a straight line. He knew that the words on the wall were the same words people walking by whispered. *People think that whispers conceal their words*, he thought. But he knew the air carried hateful sounds much farther than ordinary ones.

The sound of gravel underfoot came from the back of the store. The long shadow of a man carrying something large drew itself into the bright morning sun as the footsteps approached the back corner. Mas turned, waiting to see if the vandal was coming back to look at his work.

"Hello, Mas." It was Luis, carrying a bucket and a brush. He was startled to see Mas staring at the wall. "I'm sorry, my friend. I hoped to wash it off before you saw it."

Mas could feel his chin start to tremble and his eyes fill. With such a friend, he would not bend or break to this.

"My boy Tony's coming to help, too. This wall needs paint anyway. See, you wait too long to paint and someone does it for you."

Luis was trying to joke, but it was hard for Mas to laugh.

"Why would someone do this, Luis? We've lived here a long time. Everybody comes to my store. I give credit if people need help."

Luis shook his head. He had asked himself the same question. His face reflected Mas's anguish. "War makes people afraid, Mas. People who live in fear try to gain control of their lives by hating someone else." He nodded reassurance to Mas. "We start now and clean the wall, eh? Before the family sees."

It was too late. Freddy heard the men talking and had walked out to see what was happening. He stopped just as he came around the side of the store. His eyes caught the bright color bleeding from the sun-bleached walls and darted across the red slash of painted words. He felt the anger move over his body and the shame burn down his face.

Freddy turned his back to the wall, his words coming out in a hiss. "Who did this?"

Mas turned to face his son. There was resignation in his voice. "I don't know."

Freddy's response cut his father off. "We need to find out who did this. We need to stop them." Freddy looked back at the wall. "They won't do it again."

Mas considered his words before answering his son's threat. Luis was right. You did not gain control over your own life by hating someone else. "No, you will do nothing except clean the wall. We must not give more reason for hate."

Freddy clinched his fists. "You're wrong, Dad. We have to fight back. I'm not afraid to fight." Freddy immediately regretted speaking out to his father. He did not talk back to his father and had never challenged him. But it was too late. The words were already out.

Mas looked at his son with sadness. "We will clean the wall." He said nothing else.

Luis sensed the tension between father and son. "Tony's coming to help." He gave a reassuring look to Freddy. "Maybe you can get another bucket?"

Freddy nodded his head, grateful that Mr. Machado had given him an opportunity to walk away. He felt ashamed. His father was no coward, but he didn't understand. If you didn't fight back when somebody did something wrong to you, they would just do it again. Do it worse.

Freddy walked to the back shed behind the store. He saw Tony Machado coming up behind him. Tony's black curly hair framed a handsome square-cut face, and his dark brown eyes took in the words on the wall. He shook his head. His father had come into his room, awakening him, asking him to come to the Shiraga store. He hadn't told him why.

"Who did this?" Tony's voice was edged with anger.

Freddy shook his head. "My dad doesn't want to know."

"Doesn't want to know? What the hell? Why not?" The words came out in an angry rush, the muscles in his neck tensed like cords of rope. Tony was built just like his father, only bigger. He was a year older than Freddy. Nobody messed with him but then he never messed with anybody else, either. He carried himself with the easy grace of a young man who had confidence in himself and didn't need to prove it.

Freddy shook his head. "I said some bad things to my dad about not fighting back. I shouldn't have said anything."

Tony looked at the younger boy, his quick anger diminishing as he realized that his own father would hurt more over what his son said to him than what others had done. He formed his words carefully. "Sometimes we say things we don't mean. I think your dad knows that. Cleaning this off will help."

Freddy looked at the paint cans his father placed near the wall. "Dad, Tony and I will handle this. Maybe you and Mr. Machado can go inside and get the store set up." His father looked at him and nodded.

"Luis, we will have coffee, maybe?"

"Coffee would be good, Mas. Coffee would be good. Let the young men work, eh?"

Freddy scrubbed fiercely at the still-dripping paint, his thoughts a chaotic tangle of anger, resentment, and confusion. He struggled with his father's reaction. *He has to be wrong. You can't just let people hurt you. You have to fight back.* It didn't make any sense to him. His father was no coward. *But doing nothing? Wasn't that what you did when you were afraid?* He remembered the look on his father's face as he stared at the wall. *That wasn't fear. What was it then?* He felt shame for questioning his father. He stabbed the bristles of the brush into the grain of the wood, smearing paint over the letters, taking back his home.

Tony painted silently, reaching his brush into the bucket and slowly covering the words on the wall. It occurred to him that they were merely covering them up. The epithet would always lie beneath the surface of the paint, hidden but not gone. *It's no different than leaving hate unsaid*, he thought. *It's still there, even if you can't see it.* He could sense Freddy's anger as he watched him out of the corner of his eye, pushing the paint into the wood, attacking the letters. Tony drew his brush over the words carefully. Freddy was his friend. Mas was his father's friend. It was as simple as that. All the other differences didn't mean a thing.

Tony thought about telling Freddy what he had done, but decided against it. He hadn't told his own father yet. He would ask his father's permission out of respect, but it was done. He had to make his own choices and this was his decision. He hid the copy of his enlistment papers in his closet. He had joined the Marines. So he understood how Freddy felt. Sometimes you had to fight.

～

Mas drove his truck past Fresno's Courthouse Park, the white dome rising above the thinning leaves of the trees. Freddy and Sammy were riding in back. Mas maneuvered the truck next to the curb in front of the old brick Basque Hotel, across the street from the Fresno train station. Nobody stayed there, except sheep herders when they weren't out with the flocks. The smell of roasting meat from the hotel caught the air as the boys jumped down from the truck. It reminded them that they were hungry.

The word FRESNO was carved in the front wall of the station for visitors and engineers to see as they approached. Even though it was almost Thanksgiving, the ivory-colored walls and red clay roof tiles of the station still showed the heavy dust of summer. Winter rains had not yet come to wash the building clean, and the dust dulled the normally bright roof. November sun gave thin heat to autumn air.

The boys followed Freddy's parents across the street to the train platform. Mas and Satomi had come to stand with Luis and Maria as they said goodbye to their only son. They weren't the only ones gathering. Clusters of mothers and fathers, sisters, brothers, and girlfriends circled other boys who stood with suitcases or sacks holding a few items of clothing. Everyone had a bag of food for the trip. Their boys, like Tony, were leaving. It wasn't hard to pick out the mothers and fathers. Their faces were already worn from lack of sleep. The talk of war was in every conversation. Mothers and fathers held close to their boys, touching them as they strained to listen for the approaching train's whistle.

A Marine stood at the edge of the track, also watching for the train. He held the day's list in his hands. The sergeant could feel a twinge of regret. He had signed these boys up and soon, he knew, they would be going off to a war that was surely coming. He had seen war. He knew some of these young men weren't going to come back. He knew that those who did would be far different from when they had left. The Marines would train them, give them every chance. In some ways the sergeant envied their sense of new adventure, for soon enough they would learn the hard lessons ahead of them. He remembered when he had stood at the bus station as a young soldier, saying goodbye to his mother. He blinked at the memory of her standing in front of him, twisting the folds of her Sunday dress as she whispered in his ear to come home safely. He came home three years later, but only to put flowers on her grave. She hadn't lived to see him again and he hadn't been back since. The sergeant watched the huddled families. He would give them as much time as he could. Until the train came.

Sammy looked around at the other families. Some of the young men carrying bags weren't any older than he was. Some of the people on the passenger platform stared in their direction. It wasn't hard to tell what they were saying, and it wasn't long before they were saying it loud enough to hear. Sammy noticed that some of the young men looked down in embarrassment at the comments of their parents. He had heard the words before, but that didn't make it any easier. He grabbed Freddy's arm as he headed toward the loudest of the men.

"Don't do it, Freddy. It isn't worth it. We're not here for them anyway."

"Let me go!" Freddy said, as he moved his arm away. Just then Freddy felt another hand on his shoulder, pulling him back. There was no mistaking Tony's grip.

"I'll take care of it." Tony walked over to the loudmouth. Nobody could hear what he said. The family turned away and Tony walked back to Sammy. "He said he was sorry. Now let's forget it, okay?"

Tony went over and touched Mas on the arm. Mas nodded quietly. The whispered words, the painted words, it made no difference. Mas had seen what happened. He knew, but there was no point in saying anything. This wasn't a time for angry words.

Maria looked up at her son, so proud and so straight he stood, so handsome—a man now. But the memory was there of the small boy crawling up on her lap and crying over some small hurt. Fear gripped her, a cold lump in her stomach. She couldn't help herself and brought her shawl up over her eyes. It didn't seem so long ago that she was drying his tears. Now he reached over and brushed them from her face.

"Mama, please don't cry. I'm going to be fine. I promise."

"Write to me, Tony, please. I need to hear from you."

"I'll write to you, Mama, don't worry." His father stood quietly, trying to carve a picture of his only child into his mind. Luis reached for his son's arm and pulled him close. He could not bring himself to tell Tony how much he loved him; those weren't the words of one man to another. But he had to hold him one more time. One more time to feel his arms around his son before he left. The sound of the whistle was growing in the distance.

"You listen good, Tony. You do what they tell you. Keep yourself safe."

"I will."

The whistle got louder. The hiss of steam from the braking engine blew warm humid air onto the platform. The deep voice of the sergeant startled everybody and drew their attention toward the slowly moving train pulling the passenger cars in front of the platform.

"You Marines form up on me. I got papers for you."

Sammy and Freddy stood near Luis and Maria, waiting for a chance to say goodbye to Tony. Luis and Maria stepped in front of them as Tony turned and hugged his mother and father one more time. The little cluster of family and friends watched as he walked over to the sergeant, firmly gave his name, then got on the train. Tony looked back as he climbed the steps. One last look, one last wave, and then goodbye.

Each young man started to pull away from his parents and friends. Arms reaching out for one last touch, one last hug, one last endearment.

And all with the same last whispered words: *You come home to us.*

And all with the same response: *Don't worry. I'll come home.*

CHAPTER 9

November, 1941
San Francisco, California

The Presidio overlooked San Francisco Bay. The panorama of the military installation gave it a postcard view of the harbor. Broad expanses of green lawn curled around the high-ranking officers' large Spanish-style homes, and stuccoed buildings dotted the hills like a private college. City traffic rolled off Lombard Street and snaked around the edge of the open fort as it headed to the Golden Gate Bridge. The fort's wide lawns and rolling hills belied its status as the headquarters for the Western Defense Command of the United States Army.

Mickey looked out his barracks window at the tree-shrouded hill, with the hints of the bay in the distance. The only good thing was the ocean, but it was only a distant temptation. Here he could walk down to the water in his free time and look at the bridge, without anybody yelling at him to keep running. He looked at the bay's whitecaps, trying to pull his eyes away from the window and concentrate on his studies, but he was tired. The slashes and lines were all beginning to look the same. He rubbed his face. He had no time to be tired. There was too much to do.

Basic Training at Fort Ord hadn't been so bad, he thought. He turned his head away from the window, back at the book in front of him. The text was in Japanese.

About half way through Basic, he was called into the Captain's office. The Captain wanted to know if he was Japanese. Mickey smirked now at the thought. *The Army just discovered I was Japanese?* He told him he was an American, but then the Captain asked if he was of Japanese descent. He guessed the officer couldn't tell by his name. After Mickey confirmed he was Japanese, the Captain wanted to know if he could speak the language. He told him that he grew up speaking Japanese at home.

The next thing he knew, he was packing some of his gear and being driven to the Presidio. When he walked inside, rows of soldiers were sitting in chairs with papers in their hands. All of them were Japanese, too. Nobody said anything. They were all too afraid. They sat around staring at one another until a secretary started calling them in, one by one.

When called, Mickey walked through a door and sat down in front of three men perched behind a large table. Two were Japanese and one was white. All of them spoke to him in Japanese. He hadn't heard a white man speak Japanese before. It startled him, but he responded. He was asked to write something in Japanese. They looked at what he had written and told him to go back outside and wait.

The next thing he knew he was sent over to a barracks, told to stow his gear and wait for further instructions. The other men in the barracks didn't have any idea what was happening. Some were afraid that the Army was looking for spies. Mickey began to wonder if maybe he should have kept his mouth shut. So far, it hadn't been a good thing to be a Japanese man in the Army.

It turned out the Army needed men who could speak and write Japanese. No more Basic Training. No more running. They were going to attend school. Between the sand hills of Fort Ord and the grassy hills of the Presidio, it hadn't seemed like a difficult decision at the time. So he volunteered.

Mickey wondered if he was going to regret that decision as soon as he was assigned to an abandoned airplane hangar that was part of Crissey Field, the Presidio's airport.

Just after being accepted to the unit, he quickly wrote a letter to Sammy about what he was doing. At the time, he hadn't thought it was a big deal. Now he knew that it was. He'd been selected in the first class of the MISLS, the Military Intelligence Service Language School. It was made very clear to him that their work was top secret. He was to improve his Japanese language skills. He was to help translate military documents and other communications as necessary. He needed to talk to Sammy, to tell him and Freddy not to say anything about his letter.

The school itself didn't seem like much. Nothing in it was new; everything came from someplace else. Lieutenant Colonel John Weckerling served as commander and a former Army private named John Aiso, a War Department civilian, was the academic director. Another PFC named Kaneko and two civilian Japanese Americans made up the faculty. The textbooks and curriculum were created by the instructors. It seemed to Mickey like nothing had been prepared in advance—the Army had decided to let the instructors figure it out. But it was clear that the men selected to the MISLS were a special group. There were only sixty of them and all were Japanese, except for two white boys.

The work was hard. Most of the documents he read concerned military Japanese called *heigo*. It was like learning there was a separate hidden language inside of the language he spoke as a child. All the men were struggling. His *sosho*, military cursive writing, was still poor but it was better than most. Mickey stayed up late at night going over his lessons. After lights out, he used a flashlight under his blankets. Sometimes he went into the latrine to study. He thought often about the fact that he had traded school for the Army, and here he was in school while in the Army. Life, he was learning, had a funny way about it.

～

"Destroy the letter." Shig handed Mickey's letter back to his son, turned away, and stared out from the porch.

Sammy took Mickey's letter out to the refuse pile. He read it once more and then burned it with the rest of the trash. His father read the letter when Sammy asked him why the Army would send Mickey to school to learn Japanese. As his father read the onionskin pages of Army stationery, his face darkened, the anxiety evident. Sammy watched the edges of the letter curl in the fire. His father's answer kept going through his mind. *The Army expects war with Japan.* Sammy stirred the ashes of the letter, watching the last words darken and crumble.

CHAPTER 10

December 5, 1941
Honolulu, Territory of Hawaii

The smell of flowers filled the air around the Matson Terminal in Honolulu Harbor. The S.S. *Lurline* readied herself for the voyage back to the mainland. It was Boat Day. Friends old and new gathered under the gaze of the stately stone Aloha Tower that dominated the berth where Matson passenger ships carried excited passengers to the gentle islands and carried them back with memories of paradise. The clock tower jutted into an azure blue sky, the flag at the top of her spire moving rhythmically in the island breeze as the crowd came to wish the passengers bon voyage. Every passenger paused one more time to hang a lei around their neck and take in the music of the islands. The scent of mountain maile and plumeria filled the gangway for the voyage home. Paper streamers fluttered down as passengers lined the ship's railing.

Yuki and Tug walked along the pier as part of the military presence guarding against sabotage. As far as they were concerned, it was another stupid assignment, another part of the building war hysteria.

"Yuki, everybody looks like they're in a good mood. What are we doing this for?"

"Somebody's got to justify what we do. Besides, it's better than guarding the beach."

Tug pulled at his uniform, the heavy material sticking to his body in sweat-darkened patches. "How long we gotta do this?"

"I guess until the ship leaves."

Tug stepped back to let a man and his wife pass. They could feel the eyes of the two *haole* passengers and couldn't help overhearing their conversation.

The man looked back over his shoulder at Yuki and Tug and then leaned into his wife. "Can you believe that they got Japs guarding the docks? We're one step away from war with those little yellow bastards and they got them guarding the docks."

"Be quiet. They'll hear you."

"I don't care if they hear us. I can't believe they got Japs guarding the pier. Son of a bitch. They're everywhere."

Yuki could see the muscles swell under Tug's shirt as he muttered. "Who they calling yellow bastards? Stupid son of a bitch. We're here to protect these people."

Yuki just stood quietly. "Just ignore it. Everybody's scared. When people are scared they say stupid things."

Yuki stared out at the *Lurline*. Her white upper deck glistened in the sun, set off by her gray hull. "Everybody's leaving. What I wouldn't give to take a trip on one of those. Anyway, forget it, Tug. We know what we have to do." Yuki heard the band playing "Aloha Oe," and just then the *Lurline* blew her whistle. Seamen began moving the passenger ramp away from the ship as the rumble of her engines began to rise.

Tug watched with envy as the big ship started moving away from the pier. Leis and confetti filled the air. All his life he had lived on the same island, and the farthest he had been away from home was fishing with his uncle. He wondered if he would ever get a chance to go on a big ship.

Yuki followed the *Lurline* as tugs moved her out of the harbor. In the distance he could see massive ships floating light blue against the dark of the sea.

"Tug, look at that!" Even in the distance they could tell that the two massive ships moving in a line were battleships, the queens of the Navy's fleet. The smaller destroyers looked like fishing boats framed against the mass of the battleships surging through the sea toward Pearl Harbor. At night when the Navy fired those fourteen-inch guns, the distant sound could be heard rumbling like thunder rolling across the sea.

Tug looked over at his friend, whose mind was obviously somewhere out with the ships on the horizon. "Yuki? Which ones are they? Is that the *Oklahoma* or the *Nevada*?"

"I don't know. One of them I guess." He kept his eyes on the last ship in the line, the *Arizona*'s flags providing small dots of color against the crystal-blue sky.

~

Sack and Bufe arrived in Oahu in early November by Navy freighter. Both young men stood on the dock at Pearl Harbor, taking in everything around them. The air had a different feel to it, a softness that made them feel like they were walking through something, even though nothing was there. It was as though they were breathing flowers, the smell so heavy with plumeria. Oleanders crowded the water near the dock were they stood waiting to go out to their ship. They looked at each other and grinned.

The sunlight reflected off the blue harbor water, dancing points of light that sparkled in the morning sun. Sack took it all in, the water, the smell of salt and flowers, the warmth of the breeze. All his life he had sheltered small dreams within him. Now he stood before those dreams.

Bufe turned to Sack. "Well, Seaman Pritch, pretty soon we're going out there." A line of battleships lay moored in a row, like massive steel buildings climbing out of the gently lapping water of the harbor, small craft darting around their hulls like birds picking at some huge beast. And there toward the front was the mighty *Arizona*. Even from shore, she was huge. Over six hundred feet long and bristling with guns like tree trunks. Sack could only wonder what it would be like to work on those guns. But he and Bufe knew that it was going to be a long time before they got to do anything important on board. They were Seaman 2nds, as far down the pecking order on a ship as you could be. But it didn't matter. They were in Hawaii and they were going to be on a battleship.

A rough voice pulled their attention away from the ships. "You boys standing here for a reason, or are you planning to get out to your ship?" The boatswain's mate staring at them looked like he had been at sea since before they were born, and the dark bands of color on his faded shirt sleeve showed that he had already lost more stripes than either Sack or Bufe had earned.

Bufe blurted out, "We're going to the *Arizona*."

"That right, huh." It didn't sound like he was impressed.

"Let me see your orders." Sack and Bufe immediately dropped their sea bags and fished out their paperwork.

"Well, you boys are in luck cuz that's where I'm going today and you'll be seeing a lot of me. You two sorry clowns will be working for me. Name's Smitty, but you can call me Bosun Smith for now. Let's go."

Sack and Bufe followed Smitty down to the dock and into the boat bobbing by the gangplank. Three other men were already sitting there. They looked up but remained silent. They were too busy looking around, and, like Sack and Bufe, were afraid to say anything until they knew they wouldn't get into trouble.

Smitty looked over in Sack's direction. "You, what's your name again?"

"Pritch, but everybody calls me Sack."

"I don't care what everybody calls you, Pritch. I ain't calling you shit and that's too good for you as far as I'm concerned. Now grab hold of that line and toss it when I tell you to."

Smitty gunned the motor and waited until the boat started to pull away before telling Sack to let go. Smitty laughed when Sack almost went over the side.

"Let go, stupid. Can't you see we're pulling away?"

It wasn't a good start, but Sack's attention soon focused on the hull looming over them. The *Arizona* had steel sides like canyon walls, and that didn't count the thirty feet her hull drew below the water. Her bow pulled up in a graceful flair like she was rising out of the sea, the turreted barrels of her fourteen-inch guns poking defiantly at the sky. As far as he was concerned the *Arizona* was the queen of the fleet. To him she was the most beautiful thing he had ever seen. Except for Carmen, of course.

Pritch heard Smitty's voice rasping through his reverence for the great ship. "Well, Seaman Pritch, does she meet your fancy?

"She's beautiful."

"Yeah, well she wasn't so beautiful just a few weeks ago. We just got her out of dry dock. She got hit by the *Oklahoma* while we was out on maneuvers. We was doin' war games and zigzagging to practice for subs, you know. I heard the engines go full astern cuz the *Oklahoma* started headin' straight for us. She hit us right in the side and peeled us like a tomato can. But she got fixed and now she's back in business. It takes a lot to put down the *Arizona*."

"Where were you when the ship got hit?"

"I was below decks workin'. But you boys is special. You get to work on deck to start."

They quickly found out that working on deck wasn't what they expected. Their first weeks were spent scrubbing the teakwood deck with holystones. They took turns pushing the stones back and forth across the deck with a broom handle stuck in a hole that penetrated the stone, while the other threw sand and water on the deck. When they finished the whole process, the deck would dry to a gleaming white. If they weren't doing that, they were chipping paint and polishing brass. Smitty's harsh laugh stuck in Sack's mind the whole time he and Bufe scrubbed the deck and polished brass. Life on board any ship of the line was the same for a lowly seaman.

~

Sack and Bufe sat on stools peeling potatoes in the *Arizona*'s galley. It took a while, but they had moved to mess duty—below decks, but better than scrubbing brass. Bufe gave Sack a sly look as a peel curled off the spud in his hand.

"I thought you told Carmen you didn't join the Navy to be a cook?"

Sack laughed and reached for another potato in what looked like a bottomless pile.

"I'm not a cook and I ain't going to be one. I didn't join the Navy to make biscuits."

All they did was set up tables, clean tables, and scrape dishes. Then they started all over, getting ready for the next meal. There were advantages, however, which both young men quickly recognized. First, they got tips, so there was a little extra money. Second, they got extra food. As far as Bufe was concerned, this wasn't a bad deal. Some of the guys said Smitty was actually doing them a favor.

Bufe wiped the starch from the potato skins on his pants. "Hey, the food's pretty good and I like that cornbread they make. It could be worse, we could be up on deck scrubbing."

"You think anytime you get extra food that everything's okay. I think you dream about extra potatoes."

"And you dream about that gal of yours. Both of us got to dream about something."

"Better to dream about a girl than a warm biscuit."

"Yeah, maybe, but right now that gal ain't giving you no warm biscuits so I figure I'll stick to dreaming about a full belly."

Sack picked up another potato. So far, he hadn't done anything except drill, scrub decks, polish brass, and peel potatoes. Other than adjusting to the slight rock of the ship in the calm waters around the islands, he didn't feel like much of a sailor.

~

For the last few days the *Arizona* had been cruising around the islands and laying off of the island of Maui at the Lahaina anchorage. They practiced maneuvers for two weeks and there had been one real drill, when the pocket ships picked up possible Japanese submarines. Everybody was pulled up to battle stations, even the mess cooks. Sack and Bufe were assigned to fire duty and went to the stern to man the hoses. Men moved up and down ladders at the same time. The yelling and cursing as men looked for their helmets and tried to make it to their assigned station only increased the sense of panic that something might be out there waiting for them. All of a sudden, the war seemed very real.

The *Arizona* moved out to sea for gunnery practice. It was the most exciting thing Sack had ever experienced. The noise from the guns was so great that those on deck would burst an eardrum without proper safety equipment. All Sack and Bufe had were potato peelers and dish towels. They stayed below decks, but could feel the 33,000-ton *Arizona* lurch to the side when she fired a broadside. Sack couldn't wait until he was on the big guns.

They headed in for refueling on a Friday afternoon. Sack had a few minutes of free time to go on deck as the fleet passed by Honolulu Harbor and Diamond Head. The dark green and gray-brown crag looked like a silhouette against a crystal-blue background. The warm island air blew against him as the *Arizona* surged through the dark blue water. Soon they would be at the mouth of the Pearl Harbor naval anchorage.

He and Bufe had Saturday night leave. Rumor had it that they were going home for the holidays. He decided he would write a quick letter to Carmen and tell her he was on the *Arizona* and might be home for Christmas.

~

The *Arizona* was going to spend Saturday filling her fuel bunkers for what everybody expected to be a trip home. The repair ship *Vestal* was alongside. The *Arizona* faced the shore of Oahu and would be turned around over the course of the day so she could move out to sea. Most of the men had drawn some sort of work detail but somehow Sack and Bufe got lucky, finally getting part of a day off. They were both in their whites and they swaggered a little as they stepped on the pier. Sack looked for a taxi to take them to Honolulu. It was a beautiful Saturday afternoon and Sack wanted to make the most of their time. They had to be back on board ship by midnight.

"Okay, Seaman Pritch, what's the plan?" Bufe was more excited than Sack at the opportunity to go ashore in Honolulu.

"Well, I figure we can catch a cab downtown and grab something to eat and a beer, then figure out what there is to do. And I'd like to get back here in time to go over and see the battle of the bands. They say the *Arizona*'s boys got a real good chance to win. I'd like to hear some good music."

"Sounds good to me. I know a couple of the band boys, so I'm okay with going to listen."

The cabdriver looked at both men and asked where they wanted to go.

"Downtown."

"Where downtown, sailor boy?"

"Any place you think we'll have the most fun."

The driver looked over his shoulder at the two young sailors. "You boys looking for a good time because I can fix it up."

Bufe grinned and reacted first. "Hey, that sounds good to me. How about you, Sack?"

"I guess, but what exactly you got in mind?"

The cabdriver looked at him as if he was stupid. "I got in mind you getting your bell rung. That's what you want, don'tcha? You boys want your bell rung, right?"

Bufe looked over at Sack and then at the driver. "What do you mean, get our bell rung?"

The cabdriver looked disgusted. "A screw, stupid. What else. Where you boys from, anyway?"

Sack felt his face redden. "I got a girlfriend back home."

"Well, she ain't here, sailor boy, so what's it going to be?"

"Just take us downtown, thanks."

The cabdriver laughed. "Okay, guys. I'll take you to Hotel Street. You'll see a lot of sailor boys there." The cabdriver eyed the two young men. "But be careful. There are a lot of people who will take advantage of boys like you, if you know what I mean."

Sack looked over ruefully. Five minutes into his first leave and already spotted as a rube.

~

Hours later, Sack felt like he was still on ship but his sea legs were failing him. Somehow, one more beer seemed like a good idea. All that Chinese food made both him and Bufe thirsty. The two men staggered as they reached the door of Rosie's Bar. Everybody was laughing and making noise, so they started laughing too.

"What time is it, Sack? I can't see my watch." Sack looked at his wrist and raised his eyebrows to keep his eyes open.

"It's 11:30. We already missed the bands. We got to get back to the ship or we're gonna be late. We gotta find a cab."

Out on the street, Yuki and Tug carefully avoided the groups of drunken sailors that came into town for Saturday night beer. Fights between sailors and soldiers were common and the slightest shoulder bump on the side-walk could lead to a brawl. Neither of them were in the mood for much drinking. They had to be on duty in the morning. Both of them moved out of the way of the two sailors staggering out of Rosie's Bar.

Sack and Bufe moved unsteadily out the door. The cabbies weren't too excited about taking drunks back to the dock. Two of their shipmates yelled out of a cab that they had room. Bufe fell off the curb trying to get to the cab. Two soldiers standing near them grabbed him before he fell, laughing as they handed him back to Sack. He grinned and then caught sight of the Japanese faces smiling back at him. Sack nodded his thanks and pulled Bufe across the street to pile into the cab.

The cab pulled up to the dock. Sack could see that they were late. All four men raced as fast as they could, given their condition, to the end of the dock for the launch. Smitty was standing there.

"You two are late. What kind of fools you make of yourselves?"

Smitty was laughing as he looked at the four swaying sailors. "You boys ain't gonna feel so good in the morning. Get in the launch. You puke in my boat and you'll be lickin' it up tomorrow, so keep it inside your stomach or make sure you feed the fish. Got it?"

All four climbed into the launch, grateful they wouldn't be late. When they got to the *Arizona*, one of the other sailors assigned to the launch grabbed Bufe and helped him up the gangway. Smitty laughed again and yelled, "Hope you boys got laid, cuz it's gonna be a long time before you get off again."

~

The next morning, Sack stumbled from the crew's quarters to the showers. He had to be in his mess area by 6:00 a.m. to prepare for Sunday breakfast. It wasn't too much of a rush because on Sunday the men could eat later, and many slept in. He woke Bufe on his way out. He could feel the throbbing of his head with every step. He wasn't used to drinking. It was going to be a long morning.

He rubbed his face and tried to will his eyes open. The sting of cold water woke him up, but it didn't take away his headache. Sack hurriedly shaved and got dressed, anxious to get something in his stomach. When he got to the mess area, the coffee was already brewing. The cook, a huge man with a belly that hung below the edge of his T-shirt, looked up and laughed. "You don't look too good, boy. You get in trouble last night?"

Sack grinned and felt his jaw ache from the effort. "Me and Bufe had a little too much fun last night, Cookie. I could sure use some coffee." The cook just grunted and scratched his belly. He wasn't too concerned about a lowly seaman with a hangover.

"You get that coffee in a pot as soon as it's ready and take it topside. We got to get it to men in Turret Four, then set up for the church service."

Sack was more than happy to take coffee back to the stern area, near Turret Four. He was anxious to get to know any of the gun crews, so he could get assigned there when his days in the mess area were over. Sack started gathering up a few rolls that still looked pretty good. *No point in going empty handed,* he thought.

He started slowly setting up the silver and the plates. Most people were going to wander in a little late because of the band competition and last night's movie. Sack had wanted to see the new movie, *Dr. Jekyll and Mr. Hyde*, but going to town was more of an attraction. Besides, they'd show it again.

Sack carried the heavy coffee urn up to the top deck. The ship was unusually quiet. The fantail was being set up for church services, and it was only a few minutes before the raising of the colors. He reached the deck and stepped onto the stone-polished teak. It was almost eight o'clock. The cool morning air had that soft feel to it that he remembered from his first day on the dock. Sack sat the coffee urn down and looked out across the harbor. The crystal blue of the morning sky erased the faint reddish tint of dawn. The air carried the scent of flowers. He inhaled deeply. *No wonder they call this paradise.*

Sack looked up at the sound of the aircraft engines. He didn't spend that much time on deck so while he had heard them before, they hadn't sounded so loud. He looked over toward the shore and saw a cloud of planes streaming toward the anchorage. The sailors on deck were looking, too. One petty officer said that they must be the Army practicing their gunnery runs again. *Didn't they know it was Sunday morning and guys were trying to rest?*

The strains of the "Star-Spangled Banner" drifted across the water from the *Nevada*. Strange snapping noises fractured the skirling crescendo. The cracking sound caused Sack to startle as small plumes of water danced toward the *Arizona*. Then he saw the wing of the first plane as it pulled up over the ship. A blood-red ball was glinting from under the wing.

CHAPTER 11

December 7, 1941
Pearl Harbor, Territory of Hawaii

A hot fist of air hit the fantail just as a tremendous roar sounded around him. Sack looked back across the anchored row of battleships at the *West Virginia*. The battleship *Oklahoma* folded inward like crinkling paper, her steel-plated hull buckling as explosion after explosion hit her side. Dense smoke poured from the gaping holes, flames flashing through the blackness and joining the smoke roiling from the *West Virginia*.

Sack heard screams of confusion and the piercing sound of alarm claxons drowning out the voices of the few officers on deck. It seemed like the sky was raining metal. He ran forward and pulled into a corner near a door, crowding next to another sailor. Both men tried to squeeze themselves into the small, confining space. Then Sack felt his companion slide to the deck. He looked down into a pulpy red mass, shards of white bone jutting through the gore, a faceless body lying at his feet.

Sack heard shrapnel hitting the deck and smelled the sour odor of burning metal and fuel. Smoke hung over the harbor like a funeral pall. Men were running on the deck half-dressed, trying to get to their duty stations. Some held only their shoes, their naked bodies still wet from interrupted showers. Sack kept thinking that he couldn't stay here. He had to do something or go somewhere but there was no order, only chaos.

The alarm for general quarters sounded off. Over and over the boatswain screamed into the loudspeaker, "THIS IS NO DRILL! THIS IS

NO DRILL! GENERAL QUARTERS! ALL HANDS! GENERAL QUARTERS! WE ARE UNDER ATTACK!"

Sack ran toward the stern of the ship, hoping that he could find somebody in charge. The deck moved upward as he ran toward the fantail. He recoiled in horror as he realized that bullets were tearing the teakwood planking apart like teeth ripping into flesh. The man in front of him turned into a red cloud and slowly sank to the deck. Holes opened in the sailor's back like crimson blossoms. Sack slipped in the blood as he kept charging toward the stern. Bullets hit the metal superstructure repeatedly. Everywhere he saw men lying on the deck looking up blankly, their last vision a red ball emblazoned on a wing spewing fire. He began to panic as he realized there was no safe place to run. There was no pattern to the ripping fusillade. He could hear the *Arizona* shrieking as bullets tore into her skin. Screaming men shared her agony.

A strong concussion of air pushed against Sack as he tried to keep moving toward the fantail. He turned to see the battleship *California* move sideways with the force of an explosion in her side, a swirl of white water rimming her hull, just as there would have been if she had fired her guns in broadside. But her guns were silent as burbling flame cascaded from her ruptured fuel bunkers and she began to list. The strength of the blast caused him to reach for his ears in pain. The *Vestal* was still alongside his ship, tethered by hawsers as thick as a man's wrist. Sack saw a man race by with an ax and start hitting the lines with great thwacking blows, severing the lines one by one, allowing the *Vestal* to break free.

Everything moved slowly, so slowly that no detail escaped him. The smell of blood and burning flesh mixed with the bitter odor of used gunpowder. The cacophony of screams, orders, and cries for help melded into the staccato gunfire of panicked efforts to strike back at the silver planes swirling over the harbor. Everywhere he looked the harbor ships were on fire, metal tearing loose from riveted hulls as one by one the great ships of the line gave up their bellies against the attacker.

Sack ran against the tide of men trying to find direction. The stone-rubbed teak decks were stained with blood and scattered pieces no longer identifiable as men. A sailor staggered toward him, reaching out with burning hands. Sack saw his mouth moving but there was no sound, no face, only an open lipless mouth and eyes red and wild. He tried to grab the man to wrestle him down, to smother the flames all over his body, but he jerked to the side and toppled into the water. Men tumbled over bodies and fell on the deck now slick with water and blood. He had no place to go except toward the stern, so Sack started running. He had to get to the stern.

Sack heard the plane before he saw it bank down the flank of the *Arizona*. The chatter of its guns ripped through the decking and caught a man as large holes opened in his chest. Sack shook as he realized it was one of the mess boys that he worked with. He spotted Smitty by the stern, pushing men over the side as they froze in panic. Sack could see the dark smears on Smitty's white T-shirt, red and black, as he stood feet apart, squaring himself against the flailing arms of frightened sailors.

~

Commander Mitsuo Fuchida circled above the green-rimmed harbor. He allowed himself to embrace the moment. Clouds clung to the mountains of Oahu, the verdant peaks sharply defining the canvas against which the lines of battle were drawn. So beautiful, so peaceful against the startling blue of the sky. The sunlight flashed off the silver of his wings. For one brief instant there was no sound, and the silence of his mind embraced the beauty of it all. It was almost too perfect. The pale blue ships with their mighty guns fixed and silent. All of them strung out in a row, like trinkets on a bracelet. So beautiful in their moment of death.

Fuchida could see men on the ship decks walking as he skimmed the surface of the azure-blue waters and unleashed his guns, the mist streaming off his wingtips as the chilled metal sliced through the warm island air. For a moment he felt pity for the men on the decks as they began to point and then run, when the string of deadly projectiles tore into them. Even as commander of the attack wave it was a moment he could not deny himself, winging across the sparkling water and rising through the twin towers of a mighty American floating steel fortress, a moment of defiance as he rose up to circle—to watch from on high as the din of battle fell softly against his ears.

Lieutenant Shojiro Kondo watched from his cockpit as Commander Fuchida led an assault on the ship he had been trained to know as the Arizona. He watched Fuchida's streaking plane throw a stream of fire across the great ship and then pull up to circle the field of battle. He gripped the lever, freeing the eighteen hundred-pound, armor-piercing bomb, feeling his plane lurch upward in its moment of release. The seconds drew out. There was a pause that seemed interminable. Have I failed? With a roar, the Arizona spewed orange and black flame. Smoke reached up toward him, opening its fiery maw in a futile attempt to grasp him.

Fuchida rode the air above the battle as he felt his plane shudder from the concussion of the blast. The Arizona rose out of the harbor, heaving upwards and rupturing in half as she bled flame from her wound. He gave himself the luxury of a moment's contemplation on the colors of violence: the green of the mountains, the dark blue of the water, the heated orange and yellow of flame, the blackness of smoke, and the crystal blue of the sky. He cleared his mind to focus on the planes slicing across the harbor, as oil and fire mixed with steaming sea water and dying men. His pilots were firing into the thrashing masses in the water. He did not think of them as men. Slowly Fuchida turned his plane as the second wave maintained the assault. His mind was already on the return to battle.

~

For one brief moment Sack saw Smitty's eyes settle on him. Then he felt the deck rise up beneath him. A mighty roar took hold of the ship, the lurching deck pushing up as his knees hit the teak. All he could hear was the twisting scream of metal ripping away from the steel bones of the ship. All he could see was a great billow of orange and black flame towering over him as the *Arizona* convulsed in her death throe.

The water in the harbor was thick with oil from the battleships' ruptured fuel bunkers. Many had their bunkers filled in anticipation of a return to the West Coast for Christmas. Fuel oil cascaded from gaping ruptures in the once-mighty Pacific Fleet, now sunk in the harbor's mud, fire taking the last of its dignity. The oil erupted in patches of flames, streaming across the water. Men struggled to swim ahead of it, but their churning arms only took them through more oil. It was like swimming through molasses. Pieces of bodies floated in the water. Some men clung to the floating corpses of their comrades, desperately trying to save themselves from the same fate. Bullets tore through the water, making a ripping sound as they hit the oil, and then a sickening thump as they hit a body, dead or alive. Sailors stuck on flaming decks themselves became fiery torches, leaping into the oil-soaked water, hissing as they extinguished themselves in the dirty sea. The roar of the flames on the water and on the ships mixed with the screams of the dying and terrified, drowning out any effort to communicate. There was little need to communicate. Everyone had the same thought.

Heavy fingers of thick fuel oil lay over the swirling water, feeding flames that gave the shallow harbor water a crackling, hissing sound. The thick tendrils slipped around and squeezed the broken *Arizona* with their fiery tentacles. Men were jumping into any open water, trying to find a way to Ford Island a hundred yards from Fox Eight, the quay where the *Arizona* was moored. Enemy planes continued attacking the hordes of men struggling frantically for any place to escape the burning sea.

Smitty was in Turret Four when the attack began. He didn't know what had happened, but finally he and the others decided to get out. He climbed out into a conflagration fueled by confusion and burning oil and moved towards the stern. Men were standing by the rail look-ing at the burning fuel, their faces a distorted mask of panic and fear as they searched for an open area of water. He hesitated over jumping into the flames and open water and taking control. Smitty turned and began pushing men over the side. There was no haven on the ship.

Smitty felt one brief moment of confusion as the deck pushed up against him, throwing him into the air. The *Arizona* rose up out of the water, the deck angling up with an explosive roar as the huge battleship tore herself in half. The concussion threw him back over the fantail, his ears filled with the loudest noise he had ever heard.

The next thing he knew he was immersed in a pocket of clear water ringed by flames, a mixture of oil and salt burning his eyes and choking him as he tried to breathe. He looked up, only four feet below the deck. The *Arizona* was settling into the muck of the harbor, her top deck just above the water. Frantically he began to swim as men called out for help. He had no help to give. His eyes burned and his mouth bled as he strug-gled against the viscous flotsam of oil, paper, and wood swaying on the surface.

Smitty passed a screaming seaman struggling to stay afloat. He could see the terror in the boy's eyes as he kept sinking below the surface and grabbing fistfuls of seawater in a futile attempt to pull himself up. Smitty grabbed at the boy's shirt and felt himself pulled down. He tried to calm the boy, but nothing registered with the terrified seaman. Smitty made his choice and let go. He began pulling toward the island, an oily mist of smoke floating a few feet above his head. He closed his mind to the screams from the boy until he couldn't pick them out from all the others.

He was heaving by the time he reached shore, covered in oil. He dragged himself up the short beach to the grass and lay panting, staring at the sky and a banyan tree. The branches swayed slightly, weighted down by unrecognizable debris caught in the leaves and limbs. It was only when he wiped oil from his eyes that he could make out the body parts hanging there. He kept vomiting until there was nothing left inside of him.

Smitty stood up and looked over the once-pristine harbor. Ships were on fire everywhere. The *Arizona* was broken in two, the bow section a twisted mass of metal, with part of her superstructure sticking out of the water in impotent defiance. Men floated on the shore, their battle over. Others struggled out of the water with their clothes hanging in blackened strings. Smitty turned away when he realized it was not clothing but shreds of skin. Finally, he walked to the water's edge and started pulling men out of the water. Some were only floating, but others were moving enough to show they were alive. Smitty reached for the ones that moved as the survivors pulled man after man to the grassy area of Ford Island.

One man rolled in the water, his mouth moving soundlessly as he reached for what was left of his arm. Smitty pulled at him, tugging anywhere he could grab hold, ignoring the fact that he was pulling on skin and hair. The man looked up at him, his voice a raspy whisper, "Smitty, is that you?"

Smitty looked without recognition at the blackened face and body. He reached underneath the young man and as gently as he could pulled him from the black water and dragged him up to the grass, next to a growing line of bodies. Men and women rushed back and forth, looking at the bodies lying in tangled rows. Smitty took one more quick look at the young man. His arm resembled a charred stick of wood. His face and hair were covered with black oil, blood running in thin watery streaks from his nose. The only part of him that showed white were his eyes, rimmed with red, staring upward.

He put his hand on the boy's face. "Don't you worry, son, you're gonna make it." Then he walked back into the oil-slicked water.

The burned boy looked up at the sky. There was no sound. Only the sky, a patch of clear blue, untouched. The sky had been blue the last time he saw Carmen. He could feel the grass cool against his back, but nothing else. He could only feel the grass and he could only see the blue window in the sky. He wanted to show her that perfect blue. He closed his eyes to pull her into his mind. She was almost there. He could feel her. And then he could feel her slipping away into darkness.

PART
II

CHAPTER 12

December 7, 1941
The White House, Washington, D.C.

Icy night wind swirled through the trees around the Capitol, pulling at the last few dry leaves still clinging to gray branches. The normally busy streets of Washington, D.C., were almost empty as the city prepared itself for the uncertainty of war. The sparse traffic was mostly government cars moving rapidly to and from the War or State departments.

Across from Lafayette Park, the White House stood starkly pale against the night, its own lights glowing through drawn drapes. There were no darkened offices within its rooms tonight. Outside the Oval Office of the President of the United States, papers were being carried between desks, and the usual ring of telephones had become a constant din as staffers tried to respond to calls with questions that couldn't be answered. The man sitting inside the Oval Office had closed out the sound hours before. He looked at the photograph of his cousin, Theodore, who had occupied this same chair. The robust face stared back at him through round spectacles, the face of a man of action. There was no question in his mind. *Teddy would act decisively.*

The President of the United States looked down at the document on his desk. Today Franklin Delano Roosevelt didn't feel like one of the most powerful men in the world. His Pacific Fleet lay a smoking ruin in the waters of Pearl Harbor. The attack they all feared had occurred. He thought it would be the Philippines. No one had thought it would be at Pearl. He read reports on a daily basis that traced the progress of the war in Europe, and now America was drawn into it with the devastating destruction of its Navy.

The President closed his eyes with the fatigue of stress. The reports were coming in hourly and each one was worse—more men dead, more ships lost. Nothing to hang his famous optimism on except the confidence that America would in the end prevail.

He read the document in front of him one more time. It was prepared in anticipation of this day. When he was much younger, he himself had written that the Yellow Peril was overestimated. *It was one thing for them to march through primitive countries like Manchuria and China, but this? How could such a backward nation have accomplished such a devastating attack?* The President shook his head. *Today their diplomats stood in the State Department, making overtures of peace while their forces attacked. These people cannot be trusted.* Even the ones that lived in the United States, he felt, were aligned with the emperor of Japan. The Germans were not much better. They would have to be dealt with too, as would the Italians.

The President inhaled deeply on his cigarette. The Italians could be handled later. Hitler was a different story. But neither the Germans nor the Italians had dared to attack American territory. It was only a matter of time before America would be at war with all of them. But today, America was at war with Japan. He was not going to let these people hide in the United States as insurgents and spies.

Franklin Roosevelt reached for his pen. This would at least be a start. He read the most important part of the text one more time.

*"NOW THEREFORE, I, FRANKLIN D. ROOSEVELT, as President of the United States and as Commander in Chief of the Army and Navy of the United States, do hereby make public proclamation to all whom it may concern that an invasion has been perpetrated upon the territory of the United States by the Empire of Japan.

"And, acting under and by virtue of the authority vested in me by the Constitution of the United States and the said sections of the United States Code, I do hereby further proclaim and direct that the conduct to be observed on the part of the United States toward all natives, citizens, denizens, or subjects of the Empire of Japan being of the age of fourteen years and upwards who shall be within the United States or within any territories in any way subject to the jurisdiction of the United States and not actually naturalized, who for the purpose of this Proclamation and under such sections of the United States Code are termed alien enemies, shall be as follows ..."*

President Roosevelt scanned the list of regulations. They seemed sufficiently comprehensive. If more were needed, he would add them later. Even if they had lived most of their lives in the United States, those born in Japan could not by law be citizens. They were still citizens of Japan. They had no loyalty. *They're like a growth inside us waiting to explode.* It was important that immediate authority be issued: the power to arrest and detain; to confiscate their firearms, shortwave radios, and cameras; to restrict their travel. As for all the rest who might or might not be citizens, the FBI already held lists of the dangerous ones. They'd know what to do.

The President looked up at his secretary waiting for his signature. He laid the proclamation down, covering the speech he had been laboring over. Where it said, "By the President," he signed in a firm hand. He lifted the document up for a moment to let the ink dry. "Transmit this to Secretary of State Cordell Hull and a copy to Attorney General Biddle."

He eased back in his wheelchair and stretched his back as best he could. He had to prepare his speech to Congress and the nation tomorrow. The President could only hope that these words would begin the long struggle ahead. He had to inspire. He had to lead. He looked down at the draft of the speech on his desk, his mind wandering over the first line. *Yesterday, December 7, 1941—a day which will live in infamy...*

CHAPTER 13

December 7, 1941
Schofield Barracks
Honolulu, Territory of Hawaii

It was almost 9:00 p.m. Tug kept complaining about being hungry. They received field rations, which they ate in the dark. Yuki's squad crouched in its trench, trying to see anything in the pitch blackness of the parade ground. Smoke from fires still burning in the harbor drifted through the night air. The men had been ordered to keep quiet. Even Tug was quiet, with the exception of his rumbling stomach.

It had been a long day. They'd been in a cab on their way to the barracks when they heard a series of muffled explosions. They both looked in the direction of Pearl Harbor and saw the black smoke billowing into the air. Planes were circling and diving, but they couldn't see what they were attacking or why. Silver planes zoomed over them and pulled into sharp turns, racing back toward the harbor.

The cab driver was screaming and driving all over the road, trying to get out of the way. He hit the curb and ended up on a lawn as a plane roared over them. Yuki jumped out of the cab. He heard the explosions and the roar of antiaircraft fire coming from the harbor. The smoke roiled up in massive black clouds, planes swarming over the harbor. Tug looked over. "Who's attacking us?" The answer became immediately clear as a silver plane with a red ball on it came streaking toward Schofield, in the direction of Wheeler Army Airfield.

By the time Yuki and Tug got to their company quarters, everything was a mass of confusion. Orders were being shouted by so many officers and sergeants that nobody paid any attention to anyone but the ranking officer closest to them. The supply sergeant was handing out rifles and bayonets. Another sergeant was helping men put firing pins into their rifles. Ammunition clips were sitting in piles. Yuki grabbed a rifle and inserted a firing pin while Tug grabbed a couple of ammunition clips. They hadn't used live ammunition since Basic. Men were shoving their clips into the big Springfield rifles when a round went off and ricocheted off a cement walkway.

They gathered their gear and marched to the parade ground. The bullet-pocked walls of the buildings and cratered concrete walkways were fresh reminders of what had happened only a short time before. The carefully manicured lawn was reduced to a series of crude trenches forming a defensive perimeter. Night fell quickly amidst the smell of dirt and the burning harbor. The men huddled together in the freshly dug trenches, waiting for the enemy to come through the dark.

Finally, Lieutenant Coehlo moved down the trench and found Yuki, who could barely make out the lieutenant's face as he whispered instructions. There was another man with him, but all he could see was an outline in the dark.

"Listen up. I want you to take three men and meet me at the parade ground office over there." Yuki strained to see where Coehlo was pointing. It was almost impossible to make out anything, but he could catch the outline of the roof in the silhouette created against the night sky. "I want you to go with Lieutenant Halder here and he'll move you across. Understand?"

"Yes, sir." Yuki stared at the shadowed face of the man behind Coehlo. Coehlo moved off down the trench and left the shape of the lieutenant behind.

Yuki heard his voice but still couldn't see his face.

"Are you Corporal Watanabe?" This guy didn't sound like he was through puberty yet.

"Yes, Lieutenant. Everybody calls me Yuki."

"Well, Yuki, pick three men and follow me." The lieutenant jumped out of the trench and offered his hand. Yuki turned and told Tug, Kazo

Suzuki, and Johnny Kitahara to follow him. He grabbed the lieutenant's hand, and then Tug's, so that they would all stay together. They followed Halder over to a building while moving in a crouched position. All of a sudden, they froze at the sound of the bolt action of a Springfield jacking a round into the chamber.

A voice hissed out of the darkness. "Who is it?"

Halder looked in the direction of the voice. What came out of him sounded completely different from the way he sounded in the trench, his voice deeper and more authoritative. "You're supposed to say, 'Halt. Who goes there?', soldier. Not, 'Who is it?' Anyway, it's Lieutenant Halder, so you better not be pointing that weapon at me." They all heard the weapon being shouldered.

"Sorry, sir."

Halder didn't seem to notice the contrition. "And get that round out of that chamber before you shoot yourself in the ass. Everybody here is on your side. If the enemy comes, they aren't going to be walking across the parade ground."

"Yes, sir." Yuki was relieved to hear the clip being ejected and the sound of the bolt action pushing the bullet out of the chamber.

They moved inside one of the buildings, where there was a low light hidden by shades taped to the windows to keep in the light. Lieutenant Coehlo and a captain Yuki didn't know were looking over a map and whispering. Coehlo glanced up as they came in.

"Yuki, I want you to take your men out and set up a machine gun emplacement down by the perimeter of the fort. Lieutenant Halder will show you where we want it."

Yuki coughed nervously and looked at Coehlo. "Er, Lieutenant, could I speak to you for a minute, sir?"

Coehlo walked over. "What is it?"

"Sir, I don't know how to use a machine gun."

Coehlo stepped back. "Halder does, he'll teach you tonight. Besides, I don't have anybody else who knows how either. Now move out."

Halder motioned for Yuki and his men to follow him and they went out to a waiting truck, its engine idling. Yuki and the rest jumped in the back with four other men that they couldn't see well enough to identify. Sitting in the middle of the truck bed were two .30-caliber machine guns laying across folded tripods. The water-filled cooling casing around the barrels looked like large metal pipes. Yuki couldn't take his eyes off them as the truck lurched forward and started moving away from the parade ground area with its lights off.

They didn't go very far. The lieutenant got out of the truck and ordered the men to grab the machine guns. It took two men to wrestle each of the heavy weapons off the truck. They waited for instructions.

"Watanabe, you and your men take a machine gun over near that little hill over there."

"Yes, sir." Yuki looked over at a little rise that covered one of the entrances to the fort. "I'll be over in a minute." Yuki and Tug carried the one hundred-pound weapon over to the hill and sat it down while Suzuki and Kitahara lugged ammunition. They looked around the area they were covering. Evidently the two crews were expected to be a first line of defense. Halder walked over and showed them how to properly set the tripod to support the machine gun.

Yuki looked over at the lieutenant. "Sir, I don't know anything about machine guns."

Halder nodded. "Well, you're gonna learn real quick. This is the trigger, this is the feed and this is the belt. Got it? You open the top here, put the belt in and close the top. Pull back here on the bolt and you're ready to go." He pulled Yuki down next to the gun. "Put your finger on the trigger here." He grabbed Yuki's hand and wrapped his finger around the trigger. "Don't pull the trigger unless you want to shoot." Yuki settled in next to the gun.

"If you see an enemy plane, try to shoot it down. This gun has tracer bullets so you can see where you're firing. Just remember to fire in front of the plane so it flies into the bullets. Have this man help feed you the belt." He pointed at Tug. "We'll send men out to relieve you in a couple of hours, okay?"

"Yes, sir."

The lieutenant walked off to help the other machine gun crew, positioned approximately one hundred fifty yards away.

Yuki looked over at the others. "What the hell are we supposed to do if a Japanese plane comes?"

Tug looked back and grinned, his teeth showing florescent white against the dark of his face. "I guess we shoot it down, *brah*, what you think?" Suzuki and Kitihara laughed nervously and tried to find themselves comfortable spots. All they could do now was wait.

It was almost 1:00 a.m. before anyone came up the hill to relieve their crew. Everybody was stiff from staying in position. Yuki turned the gun over to a sergeant he had never seen before and asked where the truck was. The sergeant told him they had to walk back. The men lined up and started walking through the darkness back in the direction of the parade ground, hoping nobody was going to shoot them.

All of a sudden they heard the rustling of leaves and branches. A soldier came out of the bushes, wearing an armband that said "MP." They couldn't see his face, shadowed by the pie pan helmet strapped to his head, but they weren't really looking at his face. He was pointing his rifle at them.

Another MP came out of the bushes and looked closely at Yuki and his men. "Hey, Carl, these are Japs!" Immediately the first MP worked the bolt action on his rifle, while the other one pointed his .45 at the four men.

Yuki stared at the two guards. "We're not Japs, we're American soldiers with the 298th. We've been manning a machine gun at the perimeter of the fort, so let us go through. And by the way, I'm a corporal and in case you haven't looked at the stripes on your sleeve, you're a private first class." The man with the .45 kept poking Tug in the ribs.

Yuki looked over with disgust. "Well, Private, either take us prisoner or let us get going because I need some sleep. I don't have time for your bullshit."

Both MPs looked at each other, trying to figure out what to do. Finally, the first man said, "Hey, Corporal, no hard feelings, okay? We gotta be careful."

Yuki grabbed Tug by the arm and pulled him along. He turned and led the men back along the road toward the parade ground. Suddenly, they heard a burst of machine gun fire. They heard the plane and saw the tracers from the area of their machine gun arcing up toward it. The new machine gun crew obviously didn't know any more than Yuki and his men. The plane veered off from the direction of Wheeler, pulling the tracer fire with it until it was out of range.

Yuki and his men approached the parade ground area very carefully. Even though their eyes were used to the inky blackness and pinpoint starlight, they could barely make out the outlines of the trenches and the trees. After what happened before, they didn't want to get shot.

It was pretty obvious that there were a lot of nervous people with loaded guns around. Company First Sergeant Joe Ka'ne was sitting near the parade ground office when they walked up. The huge Hawaiian moved his massive bulk slowly as he looked up with half-closed eyes. "Hey, Yuki, was that you firing that machine gun?"

"No, Sergeant, that was the replacement crew. I don't know who they are but I'm glad it wasn't us."

"You right about that, Yuki. The captain was out here swearing about whoever started firing. I wouldn't want to be them. Anyway, what they expect? Everybody nervous and scared. You tell them to shoot if they see something and they shoot cuz they always see something. Best to stay in back of guns, I think." He laughed with a deep rolling chuckle. It was hard not to like Ka'ne.

"You take your boys and find a place to stretch out by those trees. Just be careful about walking around in the dark. You take a pee around here and you likely get your dick shot off. And that's if you're lucky."

"Thanks Sergeant. We could use some sleep. Listen, you got any idea what happened down in the harbor? We still don't know for sure."

Ka'ne looked down and spoke in a low voice. His usual lilting Hawaiian accent seemed lost in sadness. "They say whole Pacific Fleet is sunk in harbor. I heard that thousands of men got killed and wounded. Captain say he heard they still got men in those ships and they're trying to cut them out. Men still floating in the water. Too many to pull out. My brother work in harbor in dry dock. I don't know what happen to him, yet. Maybe he make it, maybe not. I don't know."

Yuki took his men around the edge of the parade ground until he came to a group sleeping in a scattered cluster. It wasn't long before Yuki was asleep, even with Tug's snoring.

Sergeant Ka'ne found Yuki and Tug a few hours later. The sky was beginning to lighten as the sun broke over the horizon. Ka'ne could see black smoke in the distance over the harbor. The air was still heavy with the smell of burning oil and carried whispers of expended gunpowder from the frantic efforts to fend off the attack.

"Yuki, wake up." Ka'ne shook the young platoon corporal until Yuki sat up, rubbing his eyes. "I need you to get a couple men together. The lieutenant needs some men for a detail. I want you and some of the other boys to go with me."

Yuki wasn't quite awake yet, and it took a minute for everything to register. "Yeah, yeah, who do you want?"

"Get Tug and a few of the other boys we can count on. Bring them over to the command post and I'll explain everything."

Ka'ne walked back toward the command post area, leaving Yuki to get himself completely awake. He didn't have much of a beard but he could feel the stubble on his face and the oil on his skin.

He pushed Tug in the shoulder. "Tug, come on, we got duty. Get up." Tug just turned over and kept snoring. "Come on, we got duty." He shook him awake.

Tug finally opened his eyes, "Okay, I hear you. What we got to do?"

"I don't know. All I know is that Ka'ne is taking charge of it himself, so it must be something important. Grab a few of the guys and let's go."

Within minutes Yuki led a small group of his fellow soldiers into the command post. Coehlo didn't look much better than they did. The lieutenant waved them over to a few chairs. Ka'ne was standing near Coehlo's desk. Several other soldiers straggled in until they had about fifteen men waiting for instructions.

Coehlo got right to the point. "Look, we have orders to send a detail over to Pearl to help with clearing vital areas. This isn't going to be pleasant. Just remember that the Navy guys over there have it a lot worse than we do. Those are their boys you'll be picking up." He looked at the Japanese men in the group. "You boys are probably going to have a harder time. I wish I didn't have to send you. First Sergeant Ka'ne here will lead the detail. Just do what they ask and Ka'ne will take care of you. I'm sorry I have to ask anybody to do this." The lieutenant's voice trailed off.

When Coehlo fell silent it was clear that the meeting was over. Ka'ne called the men outside and they walked over to a canvas-covered truck. Ka'ne told everyone to climb in the back while he got in the front with the driver.

It didn't take long in the early morning hours to get down to the gate leading to the base. There wasn't much traffic, except for military vehicles and military personnel in private cars. Bullet-riddled cars were up on sidewalks, where drivers had turned in desperate attempts to get away. The closer they got to the harbor, the more they could smell the oily smoke coming off the burning fires. When they reached the gate, the guard walked to the back of the truck and looked in.

The first person he saw was Tug. He stepped back immediately and put his hand on his holstered .45. "Hey, you got Japs in here!"

Ka'ne got out of the truck and walked back to the guard staring into the truck. Ka'ne towered over him. "I got no Japs in here. Only American soldiers in this truck. You got something you want to say?"

"No, First Sergeant, but, well you know, there's a lot of hard feelings here. The Japs shot a lot of men in the water."

Ka'ne leaned down. Yuki couldn't hear what he said, but they could all see the guard's face redden. The guard walked back to his post and raised the gate arm. Their truck rumbled on, past the officer's club to the dock at Merry's Point. Everybody got out and climbed into an open boat. The sailor manning the helm kept giving hard looks at Yuki and the other Japanese boys, but he didn't say anything as he pointed the craft toward Ford Island.

It was an image of stark contrasts. The morning sun was sparkling across water strewn with floating debris and ribboned with thick tendrils of oil. The blue Hawaiian sky framed the destruction of the fleet. The familiar scent of flowers had given way to the acrid smell of burning wood and metal. Warm tropical breezes fanned oily fires from ships that once graced the harbor with their majesty. There was nothing majestic about them now, their blackened hulls no longer riding high in the blue-green water.

The men moved up the channel, with the dry docks to their left. Yuki and the others couldn't keep their eyes off the water. Its rainbow hues were broken up by pieces of paper and floating clothing, as well as wood and other wreckage. Men in small boats were using long poles to pull objects close. It was readily apparent that they were looking for the bodies of men rising to the surface of the once sapphire-clear water.

Flotsam hit the boat as they moved out into the main channel, with Ford Island ahead. The men went silent as they passed down the once-proud battleship anchorage. Small tenders moved around the various ships where men could be seen on the decks with acetylene torches and sledge hammers, pounding at frozen hatches.

They crossed to the stern of a ship turned on its side, its screws thrusting out into the air. Her propellers would never again take a bite of the sea. Men were walking crab-like across her upturned hull as they hauled cutting equipment. The letters showing out of the water on the stern revealed her to be the *Oklahoma*.

Smoke was still boiling up from a ship that was sunk in the mud, with parts of her deck awash. It looked like a giant had broken it in half and dropped it back in the water. "That was the *Arizona*," the helmsman said. "Japs hit her while men were sleeping. They still don't know how many of our boys are inside." The way the helmsman said "Japs" wasn't lost on the men in the boat. He spit the word through his lips while looking at them.

Oil was still bubbling out of ruptured bunkers, and the helmsman made little effort to avoid it. He plowed right through until he came to a dock where another seaman caught a rope and tied them off. The small boat only waited long enough for them to disembark before heading back into the harbor.

Yuki stood on the dock, looking out over the channel. He and the other men had not said very much. But now their eyes were focused on the far end of the dock, where trucks were unloading. The cargo was unmistakable even if the shapes weren't recognizable. Bodies were being laid out on a grassy area. Yuki watched in silence as men carefully moved their comrades over and laid them next to others. Men and women moved along the rows, examining the bodies and then directing their movement to others who carried them down to open boats by the dock.

Ka'ne finished talking to an older man in a filthy uniform. He walked back to his waiting men. "They want us to move down the beach here and help with the men still in the water." He pointed down the shoreline, where the row of battleships had been moored. "Let's just do what we need to do." Ka'ne started walking down the dock past the truck unloading bodies. Tug and Yuki looked over at the men being carefully moved off the truck. Most were badly burned, and a few looked like they were asleep. They couldn't keep their eyes off them, even though it somehow felt disrespectful.

Ka'ne found a crew working and came back with directions. "Look, we need to get in some of those trees over there. Just be careful when you do it. If you see anything that looks like identification, make sure that you don't separate it."

Yuki and Tug looked at one another. They walked closer, staring at objects in a banyan tree. Tug turned his face. "I can't do this."

Yuki locked eyes with his friend and climbed up the tree, as he had done so many times with so many banyan trees. It would never again bring the same memories of childhood. He reached for what was left of an arm. There was a glint of gold from a ring still on the hand. The profile of an Indian warrior was inset, encircled with writing. A high school class ring. He barely kept from choking, but forced himself to take hold of the dismembered arm. It was cool to the touch, the skin flaccid, splotched gray and red, blackened where it had once joined a shoulder.

Tug and the others were on the ground looking up. "Just drop it down, we'll catch it. What else we gonna do?"

Yuki dropped the arm down to the men below and moved through the tree, doing the same to other objects. There were only a few human remains caught in the branches. It was mostly clothing and pieces of metal that had blown clear of the attack. His stomach was heaving by the time he finished.

Yuki moved over to a grassy area and sat down. His hands were covered with oil and other residue that he didn't want to think about. He put his head down against his knees and began to cry softly. The others moved quietly around him.

Ka'ne stood at the water's edge, watching men in small boats maneuvering around the wreckage between the battleships and the shore. They were trying desperately to find everything they could. The oily smell of smoke still lingered, but now a different odor drifted faintly over the water as the harbor water gave up the dead.

After a few minutes Ka'ne waded into the water. He looked around for a minute and then gently lifted what looked like an oil-soaked bundle of rags from the greasy water and carried it back up to the beach. They all watched as he laid what was left of a sailor on the grass. Then they waded in to do the same. They each knew that for the rest of their lives it would be difficult for them to walk back into the waters, along their island beaches, without thinking of this day.

CHAPTER 14

December 7, 1941
San Francisco, California

The news reports from Pearl Harbor were coming in constantly and rumors were all over the place. *Japs had parachuted into Honolulu. Ships were burning at Pearl Harbor and men were still trapped inside. Thousands were dead. The Pacific Fleet was on the bottom of the ocean.* Cpl. Young Oak Kim didn't know what to believe. He had taken the last bus out of San Francisco in order to get back to Fort Ord.

When the bus pulled into the front gate, the driver made a point to wish him and the other soldiers luck. "You boys go give 'em hell." Others on the bus echoed the sentiment. *Yeah,* Kim thought, *I'll give 'em hell from the motor pool. Maybe I'll throw a carburetor at them.* He hurried to his barracks.

When Kim walked into the company compound, all the lights were on. Blankets and field equipment were lying in piles outside Supply. Men were bumping into one another as they ran back and forth across the center of the compound. Everybody was moving, but nobody seemed to know why. He threaded his way through the compound toward the lights of his quarters.

Inside his barracks, everyone was pulling gear from foot lockers. The normally neatly made beds were rumpled and covered with clothes and folded fatigues. His bunkmates had already started packing up his equipment and were clearly relieved to see him. Tommy Johanson spoke up.

"Hey, Kim, where you been? We're moving out. The buses are on their way. They're going to be here in less than forty minutes. We got some of your gear ready, but we didn't know what you wanted to do with your personal stuff."

Kim thanked him and then went to work finishing his field pack. Most of his personal things he put in his footlocker. He would come back for it later. Sergeant Durham yelled for the men to roll out and form up. He barely had time to finish before he and the others were outside.

"You men get on the buses and shut up right now. There'll be plenty of time for talking later."

One man shouted out, "We gonna protect against an invasion, Sarge? We don't got no rifles or nothin'."

Durham's eyes focused on the soldier who asked a question he couldn't answer. "I told you, there will be plenty of time to talk when you get on the bus. You ain't gonna need no rifles where you're going. Now move it."

The buses followed one another into the hills above Fort Ord. There was very little talking. Most of the men spent their time looking out the bus windows and wondering what was coming next. As the buses climbed away from the beach, the cypress trees gave way to gnarled oaks and then to low lying brush. In the dark, it was difficult to see much. Kim began to wonder, *If we're up here to protect against an invasion, then why are we so far from the beach?*

When they got deep into the hills, the buses stopped and everybody got out. Kim looked around. There weren't any buildings or tents, just bare ground with a few scrub trees.

The soldiers milled about, waiting for some type of instruction. As usual, nobody told them anything until well after the rumors had started. Kim sat down and watched the confusion. He overheard men saying that Japanese subs were spotted off the Monterey coast and that they were up here to form a perimeter line of defense against the invasion. *That doesn't make sense. If we're the perimeter line, then we should be setting up near the beach.*

Johanson turned to Kim. "You think the Japs are going to invade?" The tremor in his voice gave his fear away. He didn't sound any different than a lot of the men. There was a lot of fear. Mostly because nobody knew what was happening.

Kim looked at Johanson, his heavy eyelids squeezing into slits. "I don't think the Japanese are going to invade Monterey. They'd have to come inside the harbor and take the whole coast. Besides, I can't believe they made it all the way to Pearl Harbor. Go to sleep. Nobody's going to bother us up here. At least, not tonight."

He found himself a spot and unrolled one of his blankets from his field pack. *How were they going to stop an invasion? They didn't even have any weapons and hadn't been near a rifle since Basic.* Just the thought of giving a private a live bullet scared the hell out of the NCOs. They locked up and accounted for every round. Nobody actually fired ammunition because of the paperwork involved.

Finally, Sergeant Durham called his men together and told them that they were going to spend the night where they were. It didn't take long before somebody asked why. The obvious answer was because that's what they were ordered to do, and it didn't take long for Durham to give it. Eventually he looked around and said, "I figure they moved us up here cuz they don't want us to get killed if there's an invasion. They're going to need every man, so better to keep us away from everything until they can figure out what to do."

Some of the men started muttering about fighting the Japs and that the Army needed to stand its ground. Kim looked around at the milling men and officers. *So the Army has decided that if the Japs come, we aren't in a position to defend the beach? That meant the Army wasn't prepared for this.*

He concluded the best thing he could do was to get a good night's sleep. He pulled his blankets around him and turned over on his side, quickly falling asleep. That was another thing he learned in the Army— sleep when he could. He didn't know when he was going to get another chance.

Kim pulled his blankets closer around him. No matter how tightly he wrapped himself, the nighttime damp seeped in. The hills above Ord were colder than down near the beach. A low mist formed over the area. It was barely light, but he could make out men setting up field stoves. He opened his eyes a little wider. At least there was the possibility of warm food and maybe a cup of coffee. He figured he would wait as long as he could before getting up. No sense moving around any sooner than he had to.

The sun began to break through the morning mist when Kim saw Durham moving. He didn't look any better than the rest of them.

"Kim, not much need to get up right now. Nobody's told us what to do. I haven't seen an officer since we left last night on the buses. I don't think they know what to do."

Kim nodded. "What're we going to do, Sergeant? Nobody has given us weapons or anything. We just going to sit up here and watch the war?"

"If there's a war, Kim, we won't be watching it. Somebody will come along shortly and tell us what to do. I may as well get some coffee. You too, before everybody else. Listen, there's gonna be a lot of paperwork when we get back. I'm gonna need some help. Okay?"

"Sure, I'll come by as soon as we get back." Kim walked over to the makeshift mess area and pulled out his canteen cup. Cooks were pouring coffee into large canisters, steam still rising from the pots. The air was filled with its strong scent. He poured a cup and walked back over to his blankets and sat down. He wondered how much longer they would be stuck here.

Around 10:00 a.m., buses rumbled back into the makeshift encampment. It wasn't long before sergeants were yelling, "Everybody up, we're moving out!"

Kim stuck close to the men of his barracks as they piled onto the bus. "Where to now, Sarge?"

All the men asked the same question and everybody got the same answer. "We'll know when they tell us." He settled back against his seat and watched the countryside. It quickly became obvious that they weren't going back to Fort Ord. Especially after they pulled through the gate onto the coastal highway. He watched quietly while the countryside began to move by in a constant stream of green.

The bus moved up the highway, hugging the rugged coastline until they reached San Francisco. They didn't stop. The line of Army buses crossed the Golden Gate Bridge. The coastal area gave way to rolling farmland. Kim kept quiet and waited several hours until the bus pulled into the town of Santa Rosa. The driver kept going until he came up to a gate that said "Fairgrounds." Men started looking at one another. They pulled up near the race track and stopped at the stables. They all piled out again and made a ragged formation near the bus.

Sergeant Durham walked over to where Kim and the rest of the men of his barracks stood. He didn't look particularly happy. "You men go inside and pick out a stall. Make sure you look on the floor before you put your bedroll down. Otherwise you're going to be sleeping in horse shit."

One of the men looked around and said, "At least they moved the horses."

Kim settled himself in the cleanest stall he could find and looked over his new quarters. The cold air pushed through the gaps in the boards. The hard-packed dirt floor held the winter dampness and whatever else had soaked into it over the years. He wondered how long it would take to get used to the odor. Two days after they had been attacked, he was sitting in a horse stall. He didn't feel like much of a soldier. He didn't feel like much of anything.

CHAPTER 15

U. S. Naval Hospital
Hospital Point
Pearl Harbor, Territory of Hawaii

The young man opened his eyes and looked around. The white room held groaning men all around him. He could see beds everywhere, men shoved into the room until it wouldn't hold any more. He saw the glass bottle with the tube running down to his right arm. He closed his eyes and turned his head toward his left. When he opened his eyes, he already knew what he was going to see. The bandages extended to just below his shoulder. After that, there was nothing. For some reason he could feel pain as if the rest of his arm was still there. He lay there for hours staring at the empty spot.

Nurses and doctors moved around, looking like they hadn't slept in days. People moved past him without stopping, their faces drawn with fatigue. The white uniforms of the nurses and the white coats of the doctors were a patchwork of stains. The smell of old urine hung heavy in the air. Constant moans from others in the room lingered. Everybody was covered in bandages on some part of their person. Many had their faces wrapped.

The young man shuddered to himself. At least he could see. He wasn't sure if that made it any easier, because what there was to see left him somewhere between despair and anger. He felt a slight shudder moving up his body as his mouth tightened, trying to control himself, to keep the tears in.

He didn't remember how he got into this room. He remembered being in the water and Smitty pulling him out. He barely remembered that. But he did remember what happened right before he felt the deck buckling, as the pain once again crept into his body. He felt a twinge of guilt about saying anything. So many men around him were so much worse off. He was tired, more tired than he had ever been in his life. He closed his eyes and tried to think of Carmen. She didn't even know where he was. Tears began to gather at the corners of his eyes. He couldn't control them. Right now he couldn't control anything. He remembered lying on the cool grass and staring at the blue sky framed by dark black smoke. It was the bluest sky he had ever seen.

~

He felt a hand gently touch his face. A woman dressed in white looked at him. There was a softness to her face, and the pale flush of her cheeks brought out the blue of her eyes. He struggled with the fogginess in his brain, trying to focus on what she was saying.

"So you're finally awake? Can you talk? We have your chart, but you didn't have any identification when they brought you in. All we could tell is that you were a sailor. What ship were you on?"

He looked at her, trying to form words. He wasn't quite clear why he was here, but it came to him slowly. When he spoke, his voice was raspy and rough. "My name is Billy Pritch. They call me Sack. I'm on the *Arizona*. Do you know what happened to her? I have friends on her."

She looked at him and set her mouth in a firm line while she began writing on a chart. "Billy, how do you spell Pritch? What is your rank? I need to get information down." She kept looking down at the chart and then back up at Billy. He could see there was concern in her eyes, even though she spoke in a businesslike manner.

"P-R-I-T-C-H. I'm a seaman second on the *Arizona*. Ma'am, can I ask where I am? Do you know what happened to my ship?" He hesitated. "Ma'am, do you know what happened to my arm?"

Her face showed fatigue as her mouth closed tightly, the blue eyes softening as she stared at the young man. All her tears were gone, used up on the dead. The only thing she could give by way of comfort was the truth.

"I'm Lieutenant Morris. Billy you've been here for two days. This is the U. S. Naval Hospital, Hospital Point, and men are in here from all over. When they brought you in, some of the men found you with others that had been given up for dead. They thought you were dead, too. Do you remember the attack?"

"I remember that planes hit the fleet. People said they were Japs. Everybody was running around and then I remember being in the water. What happened to my ship?"

She looked at him for a moment and then answered carefully. "Billy, you need to keep control of yourself. The *Arizona* blew up. She split in two. I hate to tell you this, but not many men made it off. They're still trying to get men out of different ships in the harbor. I haven't been out of here for almost three days, so all I know is what I've heard." She put her hand on his face. Her touch was cool and dry against his skin.

"Your arm's gone, Billy. It was burned too badly. I'm sorry. You were lucky they were able to save you. I know you're having a tough time right now, and I wish I could talk to you some more, but I have to keep going to help the others in here. You hang on. Somebody will be around to give you something for the pain."

She patted his good arm and moved slowly to the next bed. Billy could see blood seeping into bandages around the knees of the unconscious man whose chart she picked up. There was nothing below the wet bandages. It was hard for Sack to think of himself as lucky, but at least he would be able to walk. At least he could see. He put his head back on his pillow and closed his eyes against the pain.

He spent most of his waking hours staring at the empty space where his left arm used to be. There wasn't much to do, and he didn't have any news about his ship. The hardest thing was waking up and seeing empty beds. Nobody talked about the empty beds.

"Hey, Pritch. You still layin' in bed, boy? How long you gonna goldbrick?" Billy's head turned to the sound but there was no mistaking that gravel pit of a voice. He struggled to control his emotions, his mouth trembling. He searched for words. He didn't know what to say, what to ask. He never thought he would be glad to see Smitty.

Finally he got something out, his throat still a raspy whisper. "Smitty, how ya doin'?"

Smitty didn't answer. His face was stubbled with a beard showing gray and black, dark smears of oil and dirt on his blue work shirt. The black circles under his red-rimmed eyes showed how little he had slept. He stayed at the foot of the bed. The older man looked down at the empty air next to Sack's shoulder. It wasn't hard to follow his eyes, it was the first place everybody looked.

"Yeah, they had to take it off. The nurse here said that it was burnt like a piece of wood. I guess it wouldn't have done no good to keep it."

Smitty nodded. He didn't say anything for a moment, as if waiting for what he knew the next question was going to be.

"Do you know what happened to Bufe? What happened to the ship?"

Smitty licked his lips and sighed. He had looked through the wards trying to find his boys. There were so few left. The magnitude of the loss weighed him down more heavily than the frantic efforts of the last few days. The ones he found all had the same question. He hated the answer.

"Look, Sack, a lotta guys didn't get out. I been back to the ship, or at least what's left of her. The Japs dropped a bomb right through the deck and it hit the powder magazine. The old *Arizona*, she just blew herself right in half. If you hadda been on the bow section you wouldn't have made it. The only guys that made it for sure were on the stern, like you and me. And that's only cuz most of us got blown clear. I jumped after I came out of the turret, but we was like peas in a can when she blew. My ears is still ringin'. I heard Captain Van Valkenburgh and Admiral Kidd was on the bridge and they just disappeared. There was little piles of ashes all over the ship cuz she burnt so hot them men just got cooked. It was hard to stomach, I'll tell ya. Hard to stomach."

Smitty walked to the side of the bed. He reached out toward Sack's arm and hesitated. Then he squeezed it. He turned away and moved to the end of the bed, uncomfortable with the gesture. "I'm sorry about Bufe. He seemed like a good enough boy. I'll be back soon's I get some time." Smitty stood quietly. It seemed like he had used up all his conversation. Finally, he stepped back.

"You take it easy, boy."

Sack watched Smitty turn to leave. He blurted out, "Smitty, thanks for what you did, you know, pulling me out and everything." Sack reached out with his right arm, his hand extended.

Smitty stood there for a few seconds looking at Sack's hand, then moved around to the side and took it. Smitty gave him a slight smile and nodded. His weathered face blazed redder for just a moment. His eyes were watering. He rubbed his face with his sleeve.

"Old Smitty didn't save you for nothin'. There's gotta be some reason I saw you in that water. You try and figure out what it is. God knows a lotta good men died the other day. There ain't many of us boys left from the *Arizona*." He paused, his voice breaking slightly. "Ain't many of us left." He turned and walked out of the ward without looking at the empty beds on either side of the aisle.

~

Lieutenant Morris came by late in the afternoon on Thursday. Sack was still thinking about what Smitty had said. He kept thinking about how he made it and they didn't. No matter how much he tried, he couldn't think of a good enough reason why.

"Billy, how are you doing? I saw a petty officer talking to you the other day. Was he one of the men on your ship?"

"Ma'am, he was the one pulled me outta the water. He saved my life."

She looked at him like she knew exactly what was going through his mind. "And you're wondering why you made it and other boys didn't. Is that it?"

"Something like that, yeah."

She walked closer to the edge of his bed. "Listen, Billy, a lot of boys didn't make it on Sunday and a lot of boys did. You have to leave the why of it to God. What you have to think about is what you're going to do with your time now. What about your family? Do you have a girl back home?"

"Yes, ma'am, I have a girl. Her name's Carmen and we was plannin' to get married when I got back. Guess that's not gonna happen now. I can't do what I was plannin' to do to support a family and her pop didn't like me none too much when I had two good arms."

She smiled. "Well, I'm guessing that Carmen will make that decision for herself. Maybe you should write her a letter? You think about it and I'll come by later and see if I can give you some help. Okay?"

"Yes, ma'am, thank you, ma'am." She reached over and put her hand on his forehead. The feeling of another human being touching his skin was warm, her soft hand barely resting on his face as she left it there. He saw her eyes looking down at him. There was sadness there. She lifted her hand and smiled at him, but there was no happiness in it. For a brief moment he understood. It wasn't just him she was looking at. It was all of the men she had touched that day.

~

Lieutenant Morris came by Sack's bed around 7:30 in the evening. The ward was dark. Most of the light came from the hallway. Her rubber-soled shoes made small chirping noises on the linoleum floor. She brought a young blond woman with her, also wearing a white uniform. The lieutenant put her hand on the side of Sack's face and turned toward the other woman, her voice low.

"Donna, this is Seaman Billy Pritch. I think he would like to write a letter home to his girl. Will that be all right? I have to make some more rounds and if I stop moving I think I'll just fall asleep." Her eyes were almost half-closed, and the dark circles under them were evident.

Sack looked at her and realized she was trying to do her best. "Ma'am, I appreciate you takin' the time with me. I'd be happy to talk to Donna here, if that's okay with her?"

Lieutenant Morris nodded and gave a weak smile. "Donna is helping us out here. She's studying to be a nurse, but she thinks she can be more help here. Right now, we can't argue with her."

Donna turned to Lieutenant Morris and told her goodnight. "Billy? The lieutenant says you want to write a letter home, is that right?"

"Yes, ma'am, I want to write to my girl but it's pretty hard to write with just this one arm all tied up the way it is." He pulled at the IV tube to make his point.

She smiled and stopped his hand from pulling at the tube. "You don't have to call me ma'am. I'm not an officer. Just call me Donna, okay? Tell me what you want to say and I'll write it down." Sack nodded in gratitude. He didn't write that well when he had two good arms, so he knew she would be an improvement.

"Donna, most folks call me Sack." She gave him a puzzled expression. "It's what I'm used to. It's what I always been called. The letter has to go to a friend of mine cuz he knows where my girl has moved to."

"What's his name?"

"Sammy Miyaki. He lives in Calwa, California, at P.O. Box 455."

Donna's face blanched at the sound of the name. "You're sending a letter to a Jap? After Sunday, you still trust a Jap?"

Sack looked startled. "Well, I guess Sammy's a Jap all right, but I known him a long time and he's been a friend to me. I guess I don't think of him that way." He could see hesitation in her eyes, but right now Sammy was the only way he had to get hold of Carmen.

"Well, tell me what you would like to say."

"Start it with something nice, please."

"You mean like 'dear'?" He nodded.

"What's her name?"

"Carmen Duran. We were plannin' on gettin' married. I don't know if she'll feel the same way about me when she sees I got only one arm."

Donna smiled and her face showed her sympathy. He looked at her and realized she wasn't much older than him. "Please say that I'm okay. Don't tell her about my arm. Just say that I got hurt and I'm in the hospital but I'll be fine."

Donna looked up at Sack. "Don't you think you should tell her the truth? If you were my boyfriend, I'd want to know the truth."

"No, Donna. I'm not ready to say that yet. Tell her I got hurt and that's all. Tell her I think I'll be comin' home but I don't know when. Say my ship was sunk in the attack. I sent her a letter right before the attack and told her I was on the *Arizona*, so if it got mailed then I guess she would be worried. I want her to know I understand if she doesn't still feel the same way about me, and for her to send me a letter and let me know. I don't know where my mail will go. Could you find that out and put it in the letter?"

Donna shook her head. "Look, Sack, why don't I write the letter and you let me know if it's okay. I'll bring it to you tomorrow and you can decide. Why don't you get some sleep?"

Sack knew he wasn't going to sleep. He was already thinking that maybe he shouldn't put Carmen through this. Maybe he should just go home and try to make a new life without her. He needed to think about this. His life would never be the same again. He would never be the same again. How could he give her what they had both dreamed about?

He nodded. "I'll look at it tomorrow." He turned his head so she wouldn't see the gathering tears.

Donna went to the small nursing office and looked at her notes. She started writing.

Miss Carmen Duran
c/o Mr. Sammy Miyaki
P.O. Box 455
Calwa, California
Dec. 11, 1941

Dear Carmen,
By the time you get this letter you already know that there was an attack at Pearl Harbor. I don't know if you got my letter saying I was on the *Arizona*. When we were attacked I ended up in the water. I got hurt and I am in the hospital but I will be okay. I will be coming home in the next few weeks but I don't know where yet. I know a lot can change when two people are apart. I want you to know that I understand if you have changed your mind about me. Please write me and let me know so I know what I am coming home to.

This letter is being written for me by Donna Hardy, who is helping here at the hospital.

Love, Sack

Donna set the letter aside and began writing a second letter.

Dear Miss Duran,
My name is Donna Hardy and I am helping here at U. S. Naval Hospital in Honolulu. I wrote the letter for Seaman Billy Pritch that is enclosed. I decided to write another letter and not tell Billy. I am doing this because I think you would want to know the truth. I can tell that Billy loves you but he is very worried about what you are going to think when you see him. You need to know that he lost his left arm when his ship, the *Arizona*, exploded.

There are a lot of young men here at the hospital that feel the same way Billy does. They don't want their girlfriends to feel obligated to them just because promises were made when they left home. I have a sense that Billy wants to do the right thing and that speaks well for his character. He seems like a very nice young man and I hope that you will let him know that he is still the man you love. Maybe some people think that I shouldn't say anything. But I think you need to know so that when you see him you will know what you want to do.

I have written letters for a lot of the boys here at the hospital and I think, as hard as it is for everybody, that they want to know where they stand. I do understand how you might feel and I wanted you to have all the facts. After knowing everything that I have said, if you have not changed your mind, then when you see Billy you will do it with an open heart. I know if and when he sees you he will have all of his emotions exposed and he will need all of the support he can get. Whatever you do, don't let pity influence your decision. He deserves to know the truth. No matter how hard it is, the truth is better than him living with a lie. Eventually he will find out and you will both suffer for it.

Donna Hardy

Donna wrote the address on an envelope and placed the first letter in it. The second letter she carefully folded and placed in her uniform pocket. She pulled her writing pad close and began to write another letter. There were a lot of men on the ward who needed help.

~

The next morning, Donna walked down the aisle of the ward, stopping briefly to say hello to boys still in recovery. When she got to Sack's bed he looked up and smiled weakly. It always amazed her how most of these boys managed to smile. Arms gone, legs gone, eyes gone, but they didn't let go their hope.

"Good morning, Sack. How're you doing this morning?"

He shrugged. "Guess I'm doin' okay. I woke up this mornin'. That's better'n some of the boys here."

She looked around at the empty beds scattered around the ward. Not everybody was going home. She tried to smile, but it was difficult to deal with so many slipping away. "I have your letter. Would you like to read it?"

He took it, struggling with the folded paper, and then handed it back for her to unfold. "Sorry, Donna, I haven't figured that part out yet."

She took the letter back and carefully unfolded it. "No, I'm sorry, I wasn't thinking."

Sack read the letter carefully and handed it back. "Yes, please send it. The doc says they're sendin' me back on a hospital ship and then if I want, even though I'm Navy, they can get me to the hospital at Fort Sam Houston in Texas. That's right near San Antonio, where Carmen is."

Donna looked at the eagerness in his eyes. "Well, Sack, maybe you want to go to a hospital in San Diego until you hear from Carmen. What do you think?"

He didn't say anything for quite a while. Then he spoke in a hoarse whisper. "You think she won't want me cuz of my arm? She's not like that." It was obvious she had struck a chord of insecurity, because he repeated it.

Donna forced herself to smile. "No, I'm sure she's not, but I just thought you would want to make sure you were in as good a condition as possible before you saw her, that's all." Donna softened her voice. "Look, do you want me to mail the letter the way it is?"

He nodded

"I'll make sure it gets mailed. Take care of yourself, Sack. Have a good life, okay?"

She walked back down the aisle and pulled the second letter out of her pocket, waiting until she was through the ward doors before putting both letters in the envelope. Maybe it was wrong, but she felt it was something that she needed to do. She straightened her skirt. She looked back over her shoulder through the glass doors to the ward. Sack had his head turned toward the window above the bed next to him. Sunlight was streaming in on a now-empty bed.

CHAPTER 16

December 18, 1942
Calwa, California

Luis pulled his coat around him against the winter chill. The December air had settled into a gray dampness that held onto everything it touched. Soon the valley fog would set in and blanket everything until the end of January. It was the same every year. The New Year brought fog so thick it made buildings across the street invisible. There was no break in the gray skies for weeks, day after day without sun, while they waited for news. Maybe today there would be a letter. He took the few steps that led into the small post office and went to his box.

Luis held the brittle envelope in his hand as gently as he would a piece of ripening fruit. It was from Tony. He felt a twinge of guilt. He should wait and share it with Maria, but it had been so long. He slid his thumb under the lightly glued flap and pushed it open carefully. The familiar printing spread across the thin stationery used by the military to keep the mail as light as possible.

His eyes traveled slowly over the single page of penciled writing. He lingered over every word. The training was difficult. Pearl Harbor had changed everything. *Tony might be home for Christmas.*

Luis stared at the single page, nodding his head. Tony was right. Pearl Harbor had changed everything. More and more boys from Calwa were joining the service, leaving the small community. People's faces carried concern about the future. When he delivered fruit or vegetables, the talk now was always about war and sons gone off to fight. He hated what was happening to good people, the anger, the suspicion. Mas's store had been painted again. People spoke openly about the Japanese in the community, people who had been neighbors only weeks before.

Tony would have to fight in war. Luis understood war. He had seen it as a boy. There was nothing good about it. He wanted his son to come home. He wanted all the boys to come home. He carefully folded the single page and put it back in the envelope.

"A letter from Tony?" Luis looked up at the sound of Shig's voice.

Luis smiled at his friend. "Tony maybe will be home for Christmas."

Shig hesitated. He didn't want to ask more questions. He turned away and opened his box. Inside there was a letter from Sack for Isamu.

Shig looked at the letter as he walked up to the house. In some respects, he was upset with his son for accepting the responsibility of furthering the relationship between the Pritch boy and Carmen Duran. It was not what her father wanted, and Shig felt very strongly that a father's wishes should be honored. He had difficulty accepting the attitude of the next generation that they should be allowed to decide what was best for them. They knew nothing of the world or its harshness. Not yet.

Shig carried the letter carefully. For some reason it burned in his hand. He could only hope that the Pritch boy had not been hurt. The shame of what Japan had done was already too great.

It would become more unbearable if people he knew personally suffered as well.

~

José traveled into San Antonio and picked up the mail, as he did once a week. There was a letter. The days since December 7 passed with painful slowness. Carmen had received a letter from Sack before the attack. Since then, they heard nothing. All they knew was that Sack was on the *Arizona*. They read every scrap of news. They saw the pictures. His sister cried every day. José tried to tell her that a lot of men made it off the ships. He'd gone into town to see the Navy recruiter for any news, but very little was available.

Carmen went to church every day to light a candle for Sack. In her heart she knew he was alive, but she also had a deep sense of dread. Something had happened to him, she could feel it. Her mother tried to comfort her. Her father paced the floor, angry because of his daughter's pain. He told her to end it with the Pritch boy and was now convinced no good could come of this. But still, he could not stand his daughter's grief. He didn't know what to say. It was not in his nature to find soft words.

The December cold was penetrating. The Texas wind drove itself right through his coat. José hurried to the house and opened the door. The warm air of the heavy cast iron stove heated their small house and made his skin tingle as it drained the chill from his face. He could smell the *masa* as his mother prepared to make tamales. The dough was spread out next to the corn husks. The meat for the filling was staying warm on the stove. He resisted the urge to grab a piece of the dough, as he had done so many times as a child. The letter was all that was on his mind.

He went to see his mother. She needed to be there for this. Her hands were covered with the cornmeal dough. Esperanza turned to him and looked down at the letter. All she said was, "Get your sister."

José walked to the back of the house and knocked on the door to the small bedroom. "Carmen, there's a letter."

Carmen came out of her room and looked at his empty hands, her eyes questioning. "Mama has it." Carmen walked quickly into the kitchen, her hands shaking. She grabbed the letter from her mother and wordlessly pulled it open, looking at the unfamiliar handwriting on the front. It had been sent on December 11. From Hawaii.

Her mind immediately considered the worst. So many boys died at Pearl Harbor. She pulled out the sheets of paper and forced herself to look at the first page. Sack hadn't written it, though it was written as if it came from him. She read it quickly. It took only a few seconds for the tears to form. She had trouble speaking.

"He says he was hurt but he's okay. His ship, the *Arizona*, was attacked but he isn't badly hurt. He had someone write the letter for him." She continued looking at the other sheets of paper. It was only a moment before tears began to fall. José grabbed her as she threw herself against his chest. He had never seen his sister like this.

"He lost his arm. He lost his arm. Why did he say he was all right?"

Carmen held tightly to her brother. He could feel her tears through his shirt, her head against his chest. He took the pages from her hand as his mother turned his sister around and began to speak to her softly in Spanish. The letter had been written by someone named Donna. José searched for any words that would help.

"I guess he just wanted you not to worry. Look, he's alive, right? You got to thank God that he's alive. Lighting those candles did good, right?" José felt helpless, his words awkward.

Pedro came in from the shed. He looked at his daughter and his wife, the letter in his son's hands. He knew it was news about that boy.

Esperanza held her daughter while she cried. "Mama, he lost his arm. He's going to die, I know it." It caused Esperanza great pain to watch her daughter like this. Love carried with it so much pain. She knew this but her daughter had not yet learned the lessons of life. She was so young.

"*Mija*, he will not die. You must be grateful that he is alive. You must write to him. You must tell him how you feel. That woman who wrote the letter to you is right. You must think what life with him will be now. You must tell him the truth."

"What's best, Mama? I can't let him go. He needs me. I want to tell him that we'll be okay. Help me with this, Mama, please."

Esperanza pulled her daughter close to her. "I will help you, *mija*. But it is time now to talk to papa. He must know what you know. What is right is a hard thing."

Pedro Duran listened quietly while Esperanza told him the contents of the letter. He was glaring at his son for deceiving him, and shifting between anger and anguish over his daughter's relationship with this white boy.

Before he could say anything, Esperanza placed her hand on his arm and leaned in toward his face, whispering quietly in Spanish, "You must consider what is in her heart. You were young once, too, and so was I. Remember?"

Carmen looked at him through eyes clouded with tears. *My beautiful little girl.* There was no greater pain that a parent could feel. His words came slowly, carefully.

"There will be many young men coming home with wounds we see and wounds we will not see. They will learn to make their way. If this is the boy you want, then I will treat him as my son. Your mother and me, we will help." He gathered his daughter up in his thick brown arms and covered her inside his embrace.

"*Mija*, you have chosen a hard road." He shook his head. He knew what a difficult life the two of them would have. "But you are not alone."

Pedro was out in the field, working on a ditch to get ready for spring planting. His few acres weren't large by any standard, but they were well tended and it was a start for his dream of owning his own farm. He heard his son walking up. Pedro took pride in the fact that his son could be in school while his father worked. Now, maybe his son would not have to follow the same path of pulling things from the ground. He looked up and took off his hat, wiping his forehead. It wasn't warm outside, but the work was hard and he still worked up a sweat. He waited for José to speak. His son had papers in his hands, and it was obvious he had something to say.

"Papa, I decided to join the Texas Army National Guard unit in San Antonio. They said I could join now and still finish school."

Pedro dropped his shovel and looked at the ground. Dust rose around their feet. "I thought I made it clear, no Army until you finish school. I want no more talk of it."

"Papa, I already did it. This way I can finish school like you and Mama want, and I'll get promoted faster as soon as I start training."

"You already sign papers? You do this without asking my permission?"

"I'm eighteen, papa. They let me sign on my own. It's what I want to do. I'm not going anywhere until school is finished. Some of the other guys at school are doing the same thing. I want to be a part of this."

Pedro stared at his son. So many things were different now. All anybody talked about was the war. Every day was filled with women crying in his home. Now his son would make more tears. Pedro looked down at the shovel. Hard work was all he had ever known. It was all he could do to show his family that he cared. He stared down at his rough, calloused hands, turning them over back to front as if there was some wisdom there. He had taught his son to work hard. That showed the character of a man. It was what his father had given him. Pedro reached down and picked up the shovel he'd dropped. He handed it to his only son.

~

There were very few lights showing in Calwa, even though it was Christmas Eve. People kept their curtains drawn in fear of an air raid. Tony Machado didn't need much light to find his way. He had walked these streets since he was a child. His parents' home was a welcome sight in the moonlight. The porch, with its wooden steps, still held his mother's flower pots, empty until spring. Tony stood for a moment at the end of the walkway. He could see slivers of light through the curtains. He knocked at the door and stood outside grinning when Luis opened it. "I forgot my key."

Maria didn't care about anything else. Her son was home. She could not help looking at him with pride. He looked thinner in some ways, mostly in his face. His thick black curly hair was gone, and she didn't like the short haircut. All that mattered was that her boy was home. Luis kept touching his son. It was hard for him to keep from crying. He had been so worried he tried not to think of it now. There was so little time. Tony told them that he only had a few days before he had to be back at the camp.

Maria did not like that he had hitchhiked from San Diego. "Look, Mama, it was the fastest way. People were really nice. What with the war and everything, people are picking up guys in uniform and trying to help. I never had to wait very long for a ride."

It didn't matter to Maria. "I would rather you take the bus. Rides from strange people are dangerous."

Tony laughed. "You mean strangers, Mama. Anyway, I met some really nice people and the last guy was a truck driver who was coming into Fresno. He even drove me out here before he went to drop off his load. Said it was important for me to see my family because it's Christmas Eve."

Luis could see a new confidence in his son's eyes. "What kind of training you get down there? What kind of Marine are you going to be?"

Tony looked at his father, his expression growing serious. "Look, Pop, I'm training in a new kind of unit. They call them Raiders. We're training to fight in special kinds of missions. You only get in if you're at the top of your group."

Luis looked at his son and turned his head away for a moment before he spoke. "Just be safe. Do what needs to be done. I raised you to do that." It was as far as he was willing to go. He felt pride but fear as well. In war, he knew that young men died while old men beat their chests and talked of glory. So he would talk of it no further. Now was a time to celebrate. His boy was home.

~

Shig and his small family went to church for Christmas Eve service. Most of the congregation was there. Sammy saw Freddy and his family two pews in front of them, and his heart beat more quickly when he saw Betty turn her head and smile. He felt his mother pat his hand when his face reddened.

There wasn't much of a sermon. Rev. Ishii looked out on the congregation, lifting them in prayer before he spoke.

"We are facing a terrible time in our world, but we must be strong. Jesus said that you must turn the other cheek when your enemy strikes you. There is much hatred in the community, so we must turn the other cheek. We have friends who are calling for calm, and we must not do anything that will arouse suspicion or cause more hatred. Tonight must be a celebration of our faith. We must pray for our families and ask God's blessing on them and on our future."

Freddy stopped listening, not seeing the point. He was tired of doing nothing. He and Sammy had been talking about all of this. What Japan did hurt him too. Now people openly referred to Japs while looking at him with suspicion. He burned inside with the desire to do something. To show them they were wrong.

Sammy sat quietly. His thoughts weren't on the sermon. Since the attack, things had not been going well at school. Almost everybody had a brother or a cousin who enlisted. The only enemy ever mentioned was Japan. Nobody thought about the fact that they were now fighting Germany and Italy too.

The war news was not good. The Philippines were going to be lost, and the paper was full of reports about General MacArthur. Now there were pictures that made the Japanese look like cartoon characters, with buck teeth and round glasses. Nobody was careful about using the word "Japs" around him or in the papers. He looked like the enemy and couldn't help it.

The words from the pulpit became a dull murmur in his ears. Sammy made up his mind. He was going into the Army as soon as he graduated. Freddy agreed. They would go in together.

CHAPTER 17

January 3, 1942
Sacramento, California

The sky was a crisp January blue against the dark metal dome of the state capitol, the golden cupola flashing in the sun. With the exception of the evergreens, the trees outside in Capitol Park had lost their leaves. California Governor Culbert Olson sat in his private office and stared out the window, lost in thought. He couldn't help thinking that he spent a lot of time lately lost in thought. There was too much to think about: the war, the public outcry over the Japanese issue, the frenzy being whipped up by people wanting to run against him. Tall, gray-haired, and dignified, Olson looked like a governor even if there were increasing comments from the Republican Attorney General, Earl Warren, that he wasn't much of one.

Warren was traveling the state, talking about the governor's failure to do something about the "Japanese threat." Olson sighed. Warren had plenty of company in the press. Damon Runyon, columnist for the Hearst newspapers, wrote columns *claiming that it was foolish to doubt the existence of enemy agents among the Japanese population.* Daily broadcasts were coming out of Los Angeles from a commentator telling the people that ninety percent of American-born Japanese were primarily loyal to Japan.

Olson glanced at the newspaper editorials urging the government to*"Herd 'em up, pack 'em off and give 'em the inside room in the badlands. . . . Have no patience with the enemy or anyone whose veins carry his blood."* And the Scripps newspapers joined in the clamor, writing that *"The Japanese in California should be under guard to the last man and woman right now and to hell with *habeas corpus* until the danger is over."* Even Leo Carillo, the cowboy movie actor, was making public statements that the Japanese should be moved off the West Coast.

The governor shook his head. He'd been in political life long enough to know that reality was based on perception, not facts, and it was the people's perception that politicians had to respond to if they wanted to stay in office. Olson looked outside at the traffic moving along J Street. *What exactly am I supposed to do?*, he thought.

Olson's secretary knocked on the door to his private office. "Governor, we have another letter from General DeWitt."

Olson looked away from the window. DeWitt was the Army West Coast commander, and he was worse than the newspapers. "Do you have his last letter?"

"Yes, sir." The secretary, a legal advisor as opposed to a clerical assistant, placed a folder on the governor's desk and stepped back. Olson opened the manila folder and took out the letter dated December 19th. He passed over the usual salutation and reread the lines that he knew were aimed at putting him squarely in the cross hairs of public opinion.

DeWitt had been publicly claiming there was proof of fifth column activity and sabotage and that it was *"vital to the safety and well-being of all our people, as well as to the accomplishment of the mission of the military forces engaged in protecting them and their activities," that Governor Olson through every means at his command "bring the actual and potential sources of such activities under the closest possible surveillance."*

Olson shook his head. DeWitt wanted him to designate some responsible and competent state official to coordinate, supervise and direct the activities of all regular peace and other law enforcement officers and coordinate all measures for state and civilian defense, in cooperation with the military. But DeWitt couldn't give him any troops to help.

If Olson had this letter then so did Attorney General Earl Warren, who desperately wanted to be governor. Warren would use it against him.

Olson dropped the letter on his desk and shook his head in disgust. Politics. *What am I supposed to do, raise my own army?* DeWitt was dropping the responsibility for the safety of the entire state against sabotage on *his* shoulders. It was only a matter of time before Warren started talking about his failure to protect the people against the alien menace and citing the Army's concern. *How am I supposed to deal with Germans, Italians, and Japanese? Hell, doesn't DeWitt know that half the people in San Francisco are Italian?* He wasn't going to touch this. But the Japanese were a separate issue.

He looked at the figures again. Perhaps there was a way to move the Japanese away from the important military installations? He rubbed his chin. *That might be it. Move the Japanese somewhere else.* But DeWitt had to understand that this kind of thing created enormous political problems. He leaned back, lost in thought, and considered what these actions might be.

~

January 29, 1942

San Francisco, California

The view from the office of the Commanding General of the Fourth Army and the Western Defense Command was compelling. The winter sunlight filtered through the leafless branches of the trees dotting the Presidio. Lieutenant General John DeWitt turned his chair to contemplate the dark blue bay, whitecaps flicking the water. He sat quietly polishing his steel-rimmed spectacles, leather chair creaking as he leaned back. Short and stocky, with close-cropped silver hair, he considered his current situation. Three silver stars ran to the point of his collar. It had been a long climb from second lieutenant to commander of the Western Sea Frontier. But now it was his responsibility, all that was before him: the bay, the hills of San Francisco, the entire Western United States.

He told them all a long time ago this was going to happen. As a staff officer at the Pentagon, a colonel, he told them all that when war with the Japs came, and he knew it would, something would have to be done with these people. He told them that martial law would have to be declared in Hawaii. *Register them all, intern the ones who were a security risk.* He warned them all. Now it had happened.

DeWitt mused to himself. Some of the newspapers were telling people not to panic, to be tolerant of the Japs. *How could you be tolerant of the enemy?* You couldn't tell whether they lived here or whether they just crawled ashore from some enemy submarine. They couldn't be trusted. Pearl Harbor proved that.

The Japanese problem was growing increasingly burdensome. He paused for a moment, examining his spectacles for minute traces of dust. His career had been primarily in the Quartermaster Corps—keeping the Army well-stocked and calculating supply logistics. He was a meticulous man and he believed that attention to detail was a hallmark of a good leader. Now he was a general because of this attention to detail.

DeWitt replaced his spectacles and pocketed his handkerchief. He could not clear his mind of the concern that Washington bureaucrats were meddling in matters of military security. *The Japanese problem was one of national security. Couldn't they see that?* It wasn't enough to just restrict the movement of Japs, even though the Attorney General had been signing his proposed restrictions. They even had Japs in American uniforms walking around his own command at the Presidio, studying the Jap language in special classes.

Just a few days ago, the Army deputy provost marshal told him that *"the representatives of the Department of Justice were very apologetic in reference to their handling of alien enemies on the Pacific Coast and promised to do better."* DeWitt could feel the throbbing in the back of his skull. He didn't need apologies and he didn't need excuses. He needed authority. He was rubbing the short gray hair on his temples when a knock at the door pulled him from his brooding.

"Sir, I have Major Bendetsen on the line from Washington. Should I put him through?"

DeWitt looked up, the dull ache in the back of his neck reminding him of Washington. "Yes, put him through." Hopefully Bendetsen had some good news out of that swamp. Karl Bendetsen, a lawyer, had been sent out by the provost marshal to help him with legal matters. Bendetsen had already given him a memo that supported his beliefs: The Army could restrain aliens whose freedom of action was inimical to the national interest. The President laid out the basic authority right after Pearl Harbor. But what he needed now was specific authority. He had to be able to round up the dangerous ones.

DeWitt felt Bendetsen was the right man for the job—he knew how to say it all in the right words, get the job done. *The President is going to do another Executive Order that will give me all the authority over the Japs I need, if the damned Congress will just get the guts up to do what needs to be done.* So far Bendetsen had navigated his requests successfully through the Washington marble wonderland.

DeWitt hit the switch allowing him to listen to Bendetsen's call and continue with the endless paperwork of command.

"Hello, General DeWitt, how are you, sir? I just came from Capitol Hill where I attended a meeting of the California delegation of Congress. I stated that the position of the War Department was this: that we did not seek control of the program, that we preferred it to be handled by the civil agencies. However, the War Department would be entirely willing, upon consideration, to accept the responsibility, provided they accorded the War Department, and the Secretary of War, and the military commander under him, full authority to require the services of any other federal agency, and provided that federal agency was required to respond. That was the sum and substance of the meeting, General."

DeWitt leaned back in his chair. Finally, some reaction from those bureaucrats. He sighed with no small satisfaction. *"It's crystallizing very rapidly out here. As I remember, there is some division, something you read that would indicate something about dual citizens, people with American citizenship and also Japanese, German, or Italian citizenship. If you're going to predicate anything on dual citizenship with Japanese, you're never going to be able to prove it, because, under the Japanese law, if a child is born out here he's registered fourteen days after birth with the local consular agent to become a Japanese citizen. But all the records were destroyed when war was declared."*

Bendetsen responded, *"Of course it would be impossible to prove. As I see it, I believe the thinking on these prohibited areas, in order to reach what they term 'dual citizens,' has got to come to this."* He let the words hang in the air before continuing. *"That out of military necessity some of these areas would be prohibited to everybody concerned, whether they are citizens, white or Jap or black or brown, it doesn't matter, everybody is barred and can only enter on a pass or permit without any arbitrary classification."*

DeWitt's confidence in Major Bendetsen was beginning to grow by the moment. *They would get these people out whether they wanted to go or not. Military necessity—that's the key.*

He considered his words carefully. *"The question of patriotic compliance doesn't hold water. I think there's a little politics in that maybe. They ought to cut that thing out. There are going to be a lot of Japs who are going to say, 'Oh, yes, we want to go, we're good Americans and we want to do everything you say,' but those are the fellows I suspect the most."*

"Yes, sir, General, definitely. The ones who are giving you only lip service are the ones always to be suspected." Bendetsen waited before saying anything further.

"That's the idea. I'm going to read that thing over carefully and talk to you again tomorrow about it." There was a momentary pause. "Oh, and good work, Bendetsen. By the way, what kind of name is Bendetsen?"

Bendetsen didn't answer immediately. "Uh, Danish, sir."

"Yes, yes, Danish. Good people, the Danes."

"Yes, sir." DeWitt hung up the phone abruptly, already moving on to the next task at hand.

Bendetsen sat for a moment with the receiver in his hand. He made the decision long ago that his Jewish heritage would not be an advantage to an ambitious man. That was part of the past. The only issue now was the future.

~

January 30, 1942

Washington, D.C.

Major Karl Bendetsen walked quickly from the meeting with congressmen from the Western United States. Tall, black-haired, and wearing a crisply tailored uniform, his pants razor-creased, he paused on the Capitol steps and looked down across the National Mall. Educated at Stanford Law School, he was cautiously ambitious. It was clear that the war was going to make and break careers. Yesterday, he spoke to representatives over at the Justice Department and then to General DeWitt out in California. The problem was that they couldn't just move out some of the Japanese—they had to move them all, including the ones who were citizens.

Lieutenant General DeWitt had also been quite clear in his instructions that he was to get the regional congressmen's stamp of approval on an evacuation plan. DeWitt was sick and tired of "the bureaucrats" interfering in something they didn't understand.

Bendetsen agreed with his commander. These were politicians trying to resolve issues best left to experts. He ran his thumb across the dry, heavy-bond paper envelope in his hand. He had a copy of the letter that would be going to the Secretary of War, Henry Stimson. It was all that DeWitt could want, at least at the moment. He walked briskly to his office at the War Department. He couldn't restrain himself from taking one more look at the embossed letterhead and the authority it carried, a recommendation by Congress to the President. Authority that *he* had secured.

Bendetsen stood for a moment, feeling the subtle weight of the paper that carried so much power. The War Department would have complete control over all enemy aliens, as well as those with dual citizenship. They now had the authority to intern the Japs, evacuate, and resettle them according to their discretion. All that remained was the endorsement of the President and that executive order was already being prepared. He knew because it bore his hand.

This letter was the passkey to resolution of the Japanese problem. Bendetsen folded it carefully and placed it back in its envelope. He would be the one to give it to General DeWitt. He could already feel the gold leaves on his shoulder turning to silver.

~

February 1, 1942

Washington, D.C.

Provost Marshal General of the Army Allen W. Gullion did not relish the thought of a conversation with General DeWitt. He wasn't going to be happy, and right now there wasn't much Gullion could do about it. *Justice just is not going to roll over and let DeWitt move American citizens into camps or anywhere else against their will, and neither is State.* Gullion frowned. Attorney General Francis Biddle had not liked this idea from

the beginning and the FBI's J. Edgar Hoover argued that it was unnecessary and unrealistic. The combination of the Attorney General of the
United States and the head of the FBI was almost unstoppable. It was
going to take more than just the argument that DeWitt had problems on
the West Coast. He buzzed his secretary.

"Get me General DeWitt on the line, please."

"It will take a few minutes or more, General."

"Just get him. I'll wait." Time always passed slowly when he waited
for a telephone call to go through. At least now the military received
priority over everyone else, so it wasn't as bad as before the war.

"I have General DeWitt on the line."

*"Thank you. Hello, General. Bendetsen is here in the office with me.
General, I've just returned from a conference in the Attorney General's
Office. Present were J. Edgar Hoover, our Assistant Secretary of War, Mr.
McCloy, Major Bendetsen and I, and Mr. Biddle and a few of his people.*
I have a press release."

Gullion read very slowly and carefully. He did not want DeWitt to miss
the clear rejection of his proposal regarding Japanese American citizens.

*"The government is fully aware of the problem presented by dual
nationalities, particularly among the Japanese. Appropriate governmen-
tal agencies are now dealing with the problem. The Department of War
and the Department of Justice are in agreement that the present military
situation does not at this time require the removal of American citizens
of the Japanese race."*

DeWitt felt his neck muscles tighten as he clenched his teeth. *"I
wouldn't agree to that. I'll read it over carefully and then give you my
comment."* He was struggling to maintain his self-control. *Mindless
bureaucrats. Even Hoover is against me on this. They just don't understand.
This is war!* He tried to make his point more emphatically that unless
the Japanese were moved, he couldn't change the negative impact of not
removing the Japanese. *"It can only be made positive by removing people
who are aliens and who are Japs of American citizenship away from the
area. Until they are moved, we have no positive assurance that sabotage
will not occur because they are still present to accomplish it."*

Bendetsen had been listening carefully to the conversation between
the two generals and it was clear that General DeWitt had a definite
direction, one that he too would follow. He stepped near the intercom.

"Yes, sir, General DeWitt. There are a few things that arose that might be well to have recorded for your consideration. As far as any action is concerned, looking toward evacuation of persons involving citizens of the United States of Japanese extraction, they will have nothing apparently whatever to do with it. They say that if that comes to pass, if we recommend and it is determined that there should be a movement or evacuation of citizens, they say hands off, that it is the Army's job; that is point one that came up. Point two, they agree with us that it is possible from their standpoint, from a legal standpoint, that we can designate certain areas which are absolutely prohibited to all except those whom we permit to come in; in other words, the licensing theory that because of military necessity we say this is a prohibited area to all persons, irrespective of nationality and citizenship, and only those who we license can come in or remain in. They agree with us that this could be done as the legal basis for exclusion, however . . ."—he paused to emphasize the next point—*"we insist that we could also say that while all whites could remain, Japs can't, if we think there is military necessity for that. They apparently want us to join with them so that if anything happens they would be able to say 'this was the military's recommendation.'*

"They know here that there's a very heavy sentiment on the West Coast for a Japanese evacuation but that is the immediate occasion for it—Attorney General Biddle wants to, as you say, have the people mollified on it by being able to put forth the statement that in view of the military situation there is no occasion for it. Well that of course is to protect themselves."

DeWitt reacted,*"I tell you, Bendetsen, I haven't gone into the details of it, but hell, it would be no job as far as the evacuation was concerned to move 100,000 people."*

Bendetsen considered the general's position, but he felt the need to make it clear. * "Put them on trains and move them to specified points."*

DeWitt responded immediately. *"That's right. We could do it in job lots, you see. We could take 4000 or 5000 a day, or something like that."*

"Yes, sir, I see. We would have to put them in shelters that we could find inland—3 C camps inland, or National Guard areas under tentage inland, etc."

General DeWitt reflected on the finer points of his proposal before responding. *"Yes, you see we would move the men first, then move the women and children after."*

Bendetsen could not help thinking to himself of the logistical nightmare ahead. *"Of course, there is a large administrative problem involved in keeping the record straight."*

"Oh yes, we could work this up, but I don't mean to say that it is an impossible task, or an extremely difficult task. I don't think so."

So, DeWitt's position is clear. Bendetsen now had direction.

"No, sir, I agree. All right, sir, we will keep you advised. Goodbye."

As usual, he heard the call being terminated just as he said "goodbye." Bendetsen turned to General Gullion. *"Well, I think General DeWitt's position is clear, sir. We will just have to wait until Tuesday or Wednesday but I think he will know how it should be done."*

Gullion waited a moment before responding. *"State and Justice aren't going to dirty their hands with this thing, Bendetsen. If General DeWitt wants this to happen then we are going to have to make it clear that it's a matter of military necessity. They aren't going to get in the way of military necessity. Not in a time of war."*

Bendetsen looked down at his notes of the conversation. *Move them all by train, four or five thousand a day, move them straight to concentration camps*. He closed his notebook. *Yes, that could be done.*

CHAPTER 18

February 3, 1942
Washington, D.C.

Even though it was midafternoon, the sun had not poked through the winter overcast of the nation's capital. The grounds outside the War Department were already beginning to darken in rapidly descending twilight. The graying light outside matched his mood. Slightly overweight and already bald, Assistant Secretary of War John McCloy sometimes wondered why he had left a Wall Street law practice for this job. Besides the war already raging across the globe, he had another battle closer to home: the fight between civilian and military forces over the Japanese threat.

He was not happy about the situation. He wasn't happy with the intransigence of the Army and he certainly wasn't happy with the lack of cooperation from Justice, particularly Attorney General Biddle. Justice didn't seem to understand that there had to be some flexibility in times of war. As far as Biddle was concerned, the Constitution wouldn't allow any flexibility on what to do with the Japs, even though they had bombed Pearl Harbor. And evidently the Army was not getting the point and General DeWitt on the West Coast was failing to recognize that civilians were in charge of the population, even though the country was at war. To make matters worse, he was just handed the transcript of a conversation between the Army Chief of Staff, General George Marshall, and General DeWitt.

DeWitt told Marshall that he had already met with the Governor of California and several representatives from the U.S. Department of Justice and Department of Agriculture, with a view to removing the

Japanese from their homes to other portions of the state. According to the transcript, DeWitt agreed that they could solve the problem by getting them out of the areas delimited as the combat zone. That would take them about 100 to 150 miles from the coast. DeWitt had said that he thought this was an excellent plan, and he was only concerned with getting them away from around aircraft factories and other places.

McCloy told his secretary to get DeWitt on the line immediately.

He waited for the call to go through. *DeWitt needs to be reminded that nobody in the Army, including him, should be taking positions with politicians regarding withdrawal of Japanese from the coast.* This was an incredible political problem. It was obvious something had to be done, but he had a sense of unease about it all. DeWitt formulated a plan that would move both Japanese American citizens, as well as Japanese who did not have citizenship, away from the coastal areas. He also intended to move Italian and German noncitizens.

McCloy took a deep breath. Half the Army were descendants of Germans and Italians. Many of the Japanese living in this country were citizens. He looked at the outlines of DeWitt's plan, laid out on his desk. It went too far. DeWitt was like a bull in a china shop, and he had his own junkyard dog in Major Bendetsen. Everybody knew Bendetsen was drawing up the plans.

McCloy turned his chair toward the wall, looking at the pictures of him with the President and Secretary of War Stimson. He made his money advising corporate clients. He was a realist because business was reality. Still, the Constitution was something he hadn't spent a lot of time thinking about since law school.

People aren't going to ask about the Constitution if Japs start marching through Los Angeles. Damn DeWitt. If the word ever gets out that the Army is really taking a position on mass withdrawal of not just Japs but Italians and Germans it will cause political outcry, maybe even panic. No, I have to pull DeWitt back in. Show him who's in charge.

After a few minutes his secretary buzzed his intercom. "General DeWitt is on the line."

He decided to deal firmly with DeWitt, let him know that he was clearly subordinate to the War Department.

DeWitt was taken aback by the tone of McCloy's comments. Not only did the War Department already know that he had talked to

Governor Olson, but they were placing limitations on him. *"Mr. Secretary, I haven't taken any position."*

DeWitt decided he needed to make his point about the problem. The difficulty with people like McCloy was that they weren't soldiers. *"Sir,"* he began patiently, *"the registration of alien enemies of the Japanese race and the furnishing of each such alien an identification card, and the requirement that they carry such identification card on their person at all times, would not solve the problem or insure [sic] the denial of entrance to such restricted areas. By these steps alone, Japanese American citizens could not and would not be distinguished from alien enemy Japanese. To protect the Japanese of American birth from suspicion and arrest, they should also have to carry identification cards to prove that they are not enemy aliens, as the enemy alien by not carrying identification card on his person could claim to be an American Japanese. In other words, all Japanese look alike and those charged with the enforcement of the regulation of excluding alien enemies from restricted areas will not be able to distinguish between them. The same applies in practically the same way to alien Germans and alien Italians, but due to the large number of Japanese in the State of California, approximately 93,000, larger than any other State in the Union, and the very definite war consciousness of the people of California, the question of the alien Japanese and all Japanese presents a problem in control, separate and distinct from that of the Germans or Italians."*

DeWitt let his point hang in the air before continuing. *"Due to those facts, the removal of all male adult Japanese, over 18 years of age, whether native or American born, from that area of California defined as a combat zone is appropriate."* DeWitt paused for emphasis. *"The problem of the alien Germans and the alien Italians, while a difficult one, has not the same features as the Japanese problem and can be handled without consideration of their removal from the state or scattered areas within the state."*

DeWitt hoped his emphasis on the German and Italian situation that rejected compelled evacuation would show the bureaucrats in Washington that he was trying to deal with the Japanese problem in a realistic way. He could feel relief setting in. *Perhaps the War Department is not on a different page.*

He decided to press forward as if the plan was accepted. *"The Governor is looking at the map and going over the various agricultural areas, some of which are close to and are really superimposed on the restricted areas. There are other areas adjacent to them and not far from them, about 100 to 150 miles from the coast, that these people could be moved to, and it wouldn't involve very many Japanese, that is to say, he thought the total amount in the whole state would be around 20,000."*

McCloy considered the figure. *"The total amount that would have to be moved?"* *That doesn't sound like much.*

"Yes. There are 30,000 but that's men, women, and children. When you take the male over 14, it'll cut that down quite materially, how much it's going to be we don't know yet; that's what they're figuring out now. His idea is that you don't have to worry about the alien enemy group. The other group, the American Jap, the civilians, the citizens, to move voluntarily under the leadership of these . . ."

McCloy still had concerns. *"I have no doubt that if the thing were properly organized there could be a big voluntary mass movement, but there would be bound to be cases, I should think, where some of them would not move, and in that case we would be up against the question as to whether we could move the American citizen of Japanese race. We have felt here that there are so many complications involved in a compulsory movement of any great size that would involve Japanese Americans, that the best way to solve it, at least for the time being, would be to establish limited restricted zones around the airplane plants, the forts and the other important military installations, but do that merely on a military basis, and when you've done it on that basis, establish a system of licensing whereby you permit to come back into that area all non-suspected citizens. You may, by that process, eliminate all of the Japs. Now that has sound legal basis for it."*

DeWitt considered what McCloy was actually saying. *You have to read between the lines with these bureaucrats, and it's always difficult because they try so hard not to say anything committing them to a fixed position. They are willing to move all the Japs, but they want to do it in a way that they can justify politically. As long as I get them all moved, that is the objective. I leave the politics of it to the politicians.* It was obvious that the Germans and the Italians were much more of a political problem for Washington. He decided to feel out McCloy on the issue of the Germans and the Italians to see if that was where the real reservation was.

"Particularly about the Germans and the Italians because you don't have to worry about them as a group. You have to worry about them purely as certain individuals. Out here, Mr. Secretary, a Jap is a Jap to these people now."

McCloy took a second to respond. *"Yes, I can understand that."*

DeWitt sat back in his chair. *"The Governor said yesterday that if something isn't done and done very promptly, why in certain sections of the state they're going to take it into their own hands."*

There was a long silence on the phone before McCloy responded. *"Yes, that's what we fear."*

DeWitt could sense McCloy was starting to come over. *If the Germans and the Italians were the problem, well, I'll deal with that later.*

McCloy sat back, thinking. He made a note and then came back to the conversation. *"Yes. Now let me get one more thought clear. If these fellows do not proceed apace with this new suggestion of theirs, I wonder whether it wouldn't be practicable to put into effect a withdrawal from these limited restricted zones, a withdrawal which would include not only Japanese aliens but also Japanese citizens on the basis of excluding from a military reservation any one that you wanted to."*

DeWitt waited as if he were letting the realization just occur to him. *"Oh, I see."* *So I'm right.* McCloy saw the wisdom in his proposal, he was just looking for a legal way to do it or what would, at least, be arguably legal.

McCloy took the thought further. *"You see, then we cover ourselves with the legal situation taken care of in that way because in spite of the Constitution you can eliminate from any military reservation, or any place that is declared to be in substance a military reservation, anyone— any American citizen—and we could exclude everyone."*

DeWitt smiled with satisfaction. *Lawyers, you have to admire the way they justify whatever position they decide to take.* Clearly, McCloy had come around. Now it was just a matter of finding the legal justification, the right words. *Bendetsen was right. All they needed was the justification.*

"Thank you, General. I think we understand one another." McCloy slowly placed the receiver back on its cradle. He made a final note. *Military necessity. Military necessity would do it, and the lawyers would make it constitutional.*

~

February 4, 1942
Washington, D.C.

Attorney General of the United States Francis Biddle sat behind his desk at the Department of Justice. A Harvard Law School graduate and former law clerk for Supreme Court Justice Oliver Wendell Holmes, he had risen to his position almost by accident. He served as a judge on the federal Third Circuit Court of Appeals, which he left to become Solicitor General before the President made him Attorney General.

Thin, bespectacled, and balding, he was shaking his head as he reviewed the latest proposed restriction of Japanese as well as German and Italian aliens on the West Coast. *What was it that these Army people don't understand? These are American citizens. We can't just be moving American citizens around.*

He looked up at his assistant, James Rowe. "If DeWitt has his way we will be moving all the Japanese, Italians, and Germans off the West Coast. Just exactly where does DeWitt think we can put these people? Even J. Edgar Hoover thinks this is ridiculous." He looked down at the latest proposed restriction. "I have already sent out three of these and they still want more. I can't believe it has gotten this far."

Rowe looked at his boss and nodded his head. *"It's hard to believe but it has taken on a life of its own. This is what the Army wants and it is what the War Department wants."*

Biddle snorted. *"Then let the Army do it. If they think there's some military necessity then let them make their case to the President. As far as I'm concerned, they haven't made it to me. All right, get this memo out. We need to let the War Department and DeWitt know that we are getting really tired of this. It's my name on these proclamations."* He looked down at the press release, declaring the entire California coast line a restricted area regarding movement of foreign-born individuals of Japanese, Italian, or German descent.

Biddle looked up at Rowe after reading the press release.

"This is a dirty business, Jim."

Rowe nodded quietly. "Well, McCloy over at the War Department seems to be leaning in the direction of a determination of 'military necessity.' If that determination is made, then it will change the constitutional question as far as the movement of noncitizens, but it's the citizens I'm concerned about. Besides, let's be realistic. It's one thing to talk about the Japanese; it is quite another to talk about Germans and Italians. I read the other day that Joe DiMaggio's father isn't a citizen. Are they going to detain Joe DiMaggio's father? I don't think those people have thought this through. It's my recommendation that we distance ourselves from this and place the responsibility directly with the War Department."

Biddle nodded. "Yes, I agree. I want you to start working on a letter to Secretary Stimson over at War. Let him do this if he has the stomach."

"I'll get to work on it, Mr. Attorney General."

The Attorney General stood up and walked over to the window, flanked by an American flag. *I need to talk to the President before this goes any further.* The other day he'd been told that *"it was a question of the safety of the country and the Constitution—why the Constitution was just a scrap of paper."* *How can I argue that American citizens who haven't done anything except be born represent a threat? The sins of the father? What sins? There hasn't been a single reported case of sabotage by these people.*

He stood silently, looking out at the people walking. The Washington Monument was beginning to glow as night fell. He started his career as a law clerk for Justice Oliver Wendell Holmes, the greatest man he had ever known. Now he was the chief law enforcement officer of the United States. *Justice Holmes wouldn't have hesitated. The Constitution of the United States is not a scrap of paper.*

He turned and walked back to his desk, lifting a pen from the holder at the edge of his desk.

He began to write on the lined pad, "Mr. President . . ."

CHAPTER 19

Brooks Army Hospital
San Antonio, Texas

S ack was glad to finally be off the train from California. The ride was long and difficult. All his thoughts revolved around Carmen and what was going to happen when she saw him. By day he stared at the rushing landscape of brown to green to brown. At night he stared at his reflection in the window, framed in the blackness of the American landscape. It just didn't matter where he was if his life was going to be lived alone.

He had begun to move around. He needed to do something to take his mind off his destination. There were a lot of men on board who were badly injured, and he offered his time and help to break up the monotony.

One of the nurses directed him to a young man who sat by himself staring out the window. "Maybe you can talk to him? He's having a rough time dealing with his injury. I think he was on the battleship *California*, so maybe another Navy boy can help him out."

Sack had looked at the young man, sitting with his face turned away. He walked slowly down the aisle and sat down.

"Mind if I join you? Us Navy boys got to stick together. Nurse over there said you were on the *California*? I was on the *Arizona*." He waited for a response. None came, so he persisted. "Going to Texas so I can be near my girl. Or at least I hope she's still my girl. Name's Billy Pritch but folks just call me Sack on account . . ."

The young man kept his face turned to the window, his profile etched sharply against the blackness outside. Finally he spoke quietly, the words hissed through clinched teeth.

"Look, I don't care why they call you Sack. Just leave me alone." He kept his head against the window. His voice softened, and he opened his mouth slightly as he spoke. "Nothing personal, just go away."

Sack remained silent for a moment, then tried again. "Hey look, I didn't mean no harm or nothin'. They just said maybe you might like to talk to somebody and I figured two sailors might find something more to talk about than one of them Army boys."

The young man slowly turned his face to Sack and waited for a reaction. Sack couldn't help it. It was like looking at melted wax. The dark hair came down to a line of skin drawn so tight that it shone. Most of the right side was rippled and scarred, cracks in the skin showing where movement broke the burn-hardened tissue. The ear was gone and the skin was an angry purplish red.

"I don't want to talk. Do you understand?" He looked at Sack with an intensity that made his dark eyes glint like obsidian.

Sack tried to regain his composure, but his face still registered shock. "Hey look, I'm sorry, didn't mean to stare. I just wasn't expecting it. I mean, I got burned too. Lost my arm." He held his empty sleeve. "Maybe I'll just leave you alone." He started to get up.

The sailor kept his gaze level, only slightly turning away as he spoke.

"Name's Tim. I was on the *California*. Got blown against one of the bulkheads that was red hot from the fire. Guess I left the side of my face there. Don't know. Buddies said I was screaming so bad I was just half outta my mind. Next thing I knew I woke up in the hospital with my head all wrapped up."

Sack let the silence fill the space between them for just a moment before speaking. He kept his voice low. "It was the same for me. I got blown off the ship and a buddy pulled me outta the water. Woke up in the hospital without my arm." Tim nodded but didn't say anything more.

Sack waited and then decided to ask, "Why you going to Texas?"

"They got a big burn center there. Guess they got a lot of guys coming out of Pearl and the battle lines with burns and stuff. Sorry about being rude. I just can't figure out whether I'm better off alive than dead. Everybody looks at me like you did. Can't blame them."

Sack felt a wave of guilt. "I'm sorry about that but I was just surprised. People look at me, too. I'm gettin' used to it some. How come they ain't got no bandages on you or nothin'?"

"Doctors said that it was better to let it get some air. They're going to try to cut some of the scar tissue away. Supposed to make it better. I don't know. Can't make it look worse I guess. What about you?"

"Guess they can't do much for me. They said they was going to put on some kind of fake arm. Suppose I'll have a hook or something. Don't know yet. Mostly I'm going to Texas cuz I got a girl there that I was seein' before the war started. We was plannin' on gettin' married. Don't know now."

Tim looked at him. "You think maybe she won't want you because of the arm?"

"Yeah. I haven't exactly told her what happened. Figured I'd see her and then find out."

Tim looked at him, the left corner of his mouth pulled up slightly. "That's your plan?"

Sack laughed. "Not much of a plan, huh?"

"Nope. Look, maybe you should tell her so she knows what to expect. I been married and I don't think my wife would want to see me the first time without my arm and not know."

"You're married? I been hopin' to get married. Guess I'll find out when the time comes, huh?"

"Guess you will. What's your girl's name?"

"Carmen. We both worked pickin' grapes in California and then I left and joined the Navy. I been writin' her but I haven't heard nothin' since right before we got bombed. How about you. You talk much to your wife?"

Tim turned his face back and leaned it against the window. "No, we aren't talking much. I told her what happened. Figured it was best to be honest. We were only married for a few weeks when I shipped out. You know, we met and one thing led to another, so we just got married. I thought it was going to work pretty good but she wrote me that things had changed and it was best if we just let it go. I can't blame her. She'd have to look at me every day. I can't even look at me every day."

They both sat silently for a few minutes listening to the sound of the wheels against the tracks. Finally, Sack spoke up.

"I'm sorry about your wife."

Tim looked over without trying to hide his face. "If you don't mind, I'd just like to be alone. But I appreciate you coming by. Maybe later tonight you can come by again?"

"Yeah, I'll do that." Sack got up and walked back through the train to his seat. He couldn't get the conversation out of his mind. Sooner or later he would find out what was going to happen to him and Carmen. Maybe it was better to just let it go. He turned his face into his pillow, staring out into the endless blackness of the Texas night.

~

Three days passed slowly at Brooks Army Hospital in San Antonio. Sack sat fidgeting on the edge of his bed in a large ward of patients. Almost everybody in his section was an amputee of some sort. Some men were lying on beds with bandages still seeping blood from recent surgeries, blank expressions on their faces. He could only imagine what was going through their minds; probably not that different than what was going through his. Would he be able to make it in the outside world? Would he be able to work? Most important, would Carmen still want to be with him?

He had talked to a nurse when he arrived, who told him that a Red Cross worker would be up to see him in the next day or so, and that the worker would get information to his girl. So he waited. The hours passed too slowly and they passed too fast.

He looked up when a nurse came by. "Are you Billy Pritch? We just got a call at the nurse's station that you have a visitor. Are you expecting somebody?"

"No, ma'am. At least, I don't think nobody knows I'm here just yet. Who is it?"

"They said that there were some Mexican people at the reception desk who asked to see you. Do you know any Mexican people around here?"

"Well, just my girl, but she doesn't know I'm here yet."

"Somebody knows you're here because they're waiting to see you. Do you want me to call down and say you're coming?"

Sack hesitated. "Yes, ma'am. I would appreciate it." Sack pulled the robe around him. "Where do I go?"

"I'll have one of the aides take you down." She motioned for a young man to come over. "Please take Seaman Pritch down to the visitor's area."

As he walked from the ward, he looked around at all the young men lying in the beds. Most of them couldn't walk; most were missing a limb. He looked at the empty sleeve pinned up to his shoulder. It was time.

Sack followed the aide down to the elevator and through the hallway to a large area where a number of patients were talking to civilians. As soon as he walked in he saw Carmen standing with her father and brother. She looked just like he had seen her every time he thought about her. She walked toward him while José and her father waited a distance back. Tears were already evident on her face as she moved closer. He looked over at her father, unsure of what would be acceptable and yet not really caring.

Soon she was in front of him. Her small hand moved slowly across his face, the caress like the down of a feather, her dark brown eyes welling with tears as she gently touched his arm where the stump was. He felt himself pull away slightly at the ripple of pain that came with even her light touch. Carmen took care of all of his uncertainty by placing both her hands on his face and kissing him. He could feel the soft warmth of her lips, reminding him of the last moments they shared by the canal on the ranch so long ago.

CHAPTER 20

February 11, 1942
Washington, D.C.

Secretary of War Stimson sat looking at the increasing pile of paper on his desk. His assistant secretary, John McCloy, was sitting in a leather wingback chair, waiting for him to say something. McCloy could see that the pressures of the war were taking their toll on Stimson. His already austere face had deepening lines in it. His graying eyebrows were furrowed, and crested eyes held dark bags under them. An unruly shock of gray hair hung down over his forehead. His neatly trimmed mustache showed the gray also. McCloy thought, *Even his skin is turning gray. The Japanese problem isn't helping any, either.*

General DeWitt kept pushing for them to take more action but he didn't seem to be at all aware of the serious political consequences for the President. DeWitt had proposed a plan that was already being evaluated by the Army Chief of Staff's office. DeWitt's restrictions on Japanese movement were getting more and more severe. Already they couldn't travel more than five miles from their homes. The Secretary was rightly concerned that DeWitt wanted to lock up Germans and Italians as well as the Japanese, and now Stimson was expecting him to make a recommendation. Congressman Leland Ford of California was elevating the Jap problem to a national level, and so was Earl Warren, the California Attorney General.

McCloy sat quietly waiting for Stimson to finish signing documents. Stimson was going to ask for his advice. *Even the mayor of Los Angeles is calling for relocation of the Japanese. There is tremendous political pressure on this. Something has to be done.*

He had thought about it. He didn't like DeWitt, but that didn't mean he was wrong. Bendetsen, DeWitt's man in Washington, said that Governor Olson's plan of moving only noncitizens wouldn't do much good because it would only move old people. *Bendetsen may be a little too ambitious for his own good, but he has a point. It's not the old people that we have to worry about.*

Stimson looked over at McCloy. "So what is the status of this Japanese issue?"

"Mr. Secretary, Colonel Bendetsen has recommended creating military areas that can be used to keep anyone we want out as a matter of military necessity. Bendetsen thinks this is legal and I think he has a point. Anyway, he recommends we get an executive order from the President that will allow you to designate what the military areas are. We then order evacuation from those areas of everybody that we think needs to have permission to be in there. We would deny permission to any Japanese, avoiding any political problems. We will let the Germans and the Italians kind of slide by."

Stimson leaned back in his chair and put his hands together over his chest. He seemed lost in thought for a few moments. "What do you think?"

"I think that the decision has to be made by the President. The big issue is, what to do with the Japanese who are American citizens. We have to get some guidance from the President on this."

McCloy reached into a file folder on his lap, removing a stapled memo. "I've taken the liberty of drafting a proposed memo for the President. If you approve we can send the memo with your revisions, if any, up to the White House right away."

McCloy handed the proposed draft to Stimson, who took it and began to read.

Stimson looked up from the memo. "This recommends we ask the President if he's willing to move Japanese who are American citizens and whether we should move all of them in Los Angeles, San Diego, and Seattle, or just the ones around critical installations. You're talking about over 70,000 people. You know, John, the Japs—their racial characteristics are such that we cannot understand or trust even the citizen Japanese. The Nisei, who are the second generation naturalized Japanese, are more dangerous. That's what Earl Warren is saying out in California."

Stimson put the memo down on his desk and rubbed his eyes. "You think I should get this to the President, or do you think it will provide talking points for a discussion with the President?"

McCloy responded. "Well, both. I think you should take it over to the President and let him look at it while you flesh out the position of the War Department. At least then we'll make the President aware of the political ramifications, and he can make the policy determination."

Stimson nodded his head. "I agree. Let me call the President and find out if he has time to see me today."

Stimson moved the memo around on his desk and buzzed his secretary. "Please contact the President's secretary and see if he has time to see me. Tell her that it's urgent and it involves the Japanese issue. I have a memo that needs to go over to the White House immediately. Thank you."

He waited quietly until he heard his secretary's voice over the intercom. "Mr. Secretary, the President will be unable to see you today, but his secretary has indicated that he does have time for a telephone call tomorrow. Would you like me to place one?"

"Yes, please contact the President's office and set up a telephone call."

After a few minutes his secretary came back on the intercom. "Mr. Secretary, the President will be available for a telephone call at 2:00 p.m. tomorrow. Will that be acceptable?"

"Yes, set up the call, thank you."

~

All through lunch the next day, Stimson ruminated on the issues that he had to address with the President. In some respects Roosevelt was a hands-on leader, and in other respects he seemed to delegate a great deal of authority. Right now, the President was preoccupied with military and naval strategies. It was difficult to get his time on domestic issues, but this was urgent. The newspapers on the West Coast were becoming increasingly critical of the administration regarding the Japanese situation. The columnist Walter Lippmann wrote more than one article about the so-called "Japanese problem," and there was a Mutual Radio commentator named John B. Hughes who claimed that 90 percent of Japanese American citizens were still loyal to Japan and willing to die for the Emperor.

Stimson looked at an advance copy of Walter Lippman's nationally syndicated column that was going to run soon in the *Los Angeles Times*. The headline was "The Fifth Column on the Coast." He looked down at the column and noted the portions that staff had underlined.

> *"What makes it so serious and so special is that the Pacific Coast is in imminent danger of a combined attack from within and from without . . . .The peculiar danger of the Pacific Coast is in a Japanese raid accompanied by enemy action inside American territory. . . . Japan could strike a blow which might do irreparable damage if it were accompanied by the kind of organized sabotage to which this part of the country is specially vulnerable. . . . The official approach to the danger is through a series of unrealities. There is the assumption that it is a problem of "enemy aliens." As a matter of fact it is certainly also a problem of native-born American citizens. . . . The Pacific Coast is officially a combat zone; some part of it may at any moment be a battlefield. Nobody's constitutional rights include the right to reside and do business on a battlefield. And nobody ought to be on a battlefield who has no good reason for being there . . ."*

Stimson put the article down and shook his head. *Where did these newspaper people get these things and these ideas?*

At 2:00 p.m., Stimson's secretary buzzed him on his intercom. "Mr. Secretary, the President's secretary is on the line. The President is available to take your call."

Stimson picked up the phone. "This is Secretary Stimson."

The response was immediate. "Hello, Mr. Secretary, I will put you through to the President."

No matter how many times he made these calls or visited the Oval Office, Stimson still felt awe when he heard the words "the President will see you now" or "the President will take your call." In Washington, access was power and there was no question he had access. The issue was whether he had influence.

He heard the rich, warm voice boom over the telephone line. "Henry? How are you? I'm sorry I wasn't able to see you personally today. I've been meeting with generals and admirals all day long. The Philippines are going to be lost, I'm afraid. MacArthur can't hold on for much longer, even though he keeps saying he will die there. You know Douglas, he never makes a small gesture when he can make a grand one. We just need them to hold on, keep the Japanese tied up there so they can't spend their resources elsewhere. You understand, I know."

Stimson smiled ruefully. He was Secretary of War, but Roosevelt relished the role of Commander-in-Chief, and more often than not the generals returned to the War Department and informed him what the President had already decided.

"I understand you want to talk about the Japanese problem?"

"Yes, Mr. President. You have our memo I hope?"

The President didn't answer immediately. "I am familiar with the issues, yes."

Stimson waited a moment, but the President didn't say anything else. He never said more than he had to. Stimson decided to move forward. "I am sure you have seen an advance copy of Lippmann's new column?"

"Yes, yes, Lippmann has decided he should be making war policy for us now. Everybody is a general and has ideas about how we should fight the war, right, Henry?"

"Yes, Mr. President, but this problem is quickly getting out of control. General DeWitt out on the West Coast has been pressing for us to do something about the Japanese out there."

"Henry, this DeWitt isn't much of a politician, is he? I keep hearing that he wants to round up all the Germans and Italians as well as the Japanese. Well that isn't going to work, you know. I've already signed a proclamation on this. What do you think?"

"Mr. President, I think we have a problem involving the Japanese American citizens as opposed to the enemy alien Japanese, the ones that live here but were born in Japan. The military commanders think that we need to do something to control the Japanese who are citizens. They think they are a real threat. We need guidance from you on whether to move Japanese American citizens out of restricted areas, but that would involve a large number of people. In Los Angeles, San Diego, and Seattle alone that could be over 70,000 people. We're also discussing doing something a little smaller, say just moving them away from critical installations like airplane plants, but that is a little more complex."

"What's the position of the Justice Department?"

"Well, sir, Justice is opposed and takes the position that if this is done, then the Army needs to do it. I don't think Secretary Biddle has any stomach for this." Stimson waited for the President to make some comment, but there was a long silence over the telephone.

Finally, the President responded. "Look, Henry, it seems like this matter has been talked to death by all of our best people. Do what you think is best. Just be as reasonable as you can. A lot of hard decisions are going to have to be made to win this war. I have confidence in you, Henry. Is there anything else?"

"No, Mr. President, thank you for your thoughts."

"Not at all, Henry. Maybe you can drop by after 5:00 sometime this week. Give my secretary a call. Good to talk to you."

Stimson hung up the phone. Even in time of war, the President kept his cocktail hour. Some people said that was when the President made most of his political overtures. It was a special honor to sit down while the President of the United States mixed a martini for you, but it also meant that you were being warmed up for something. He was the best politician Stimson had ever seen. It was not lost on him that the President had more or less sidestepped the issue and left it to him.

He pushed the intercom switch. "Please have Undersecretary McCloy come and see me."

McCloy soon walked into Secretary Stimson's office. "You asked to see me, Mr. Secretary?"

"Yes, John. I've talked to the President. I'm afraid he didn't give us anything too specific. Just told me to do what's best. I've decided to move both the enemy alien Japanese, the Issei, and the American citizen Japanese from areas critical to the war."

"You mean that we're going to move them all off the West Coast?" McCloy's face showed his recognition of the magnitude of the decision. "You know, we have a number of generals that don't think there's any possibility of invasion on the West Coast."

"Well, I think the major issue is sabotage. It's like anything else. If nothing happens people will say it wasn't necessary, and if something happens they'll ask why we didn't do anything. I'm not going to take a chance. As for the Germans and the Italians, I've decided that we're going to wait on them. We'll do it on a case-by-case basis. For now, we need to get started on the Japanese. Talk to the Army about this. The Justice Department is going to resist this, but we need to move forward."

"I'll get started on it right away." McCloy stood up and walked out of the Secretary's office. He sat down at his desk and pulled a pad of paper in front of him. McCloy reached for his pen and started to make some notes. Plans had to be made, an executive order prepared, and it all had to be kept quiet until they were ready. He pressed the intercom button and told his secretary to get Colonel Bendetsen on the line out in San Francisco.

"Colonel? Yes, McCloy here. We have carte blanche to do what we want as far as the President is concerned."

~

February 17, 1942
Washington, D.C.

Assistant Attorney General of the United States James Rowe walked down to Attorney General Biddle's office. He had put a lot of time into drafting a memo to the President based on the rough draft that the Attorney General had prepared.

Biddle was standing by the window, looking out on another gray Washington day. He looked over when Rowe walked in. "Jim, have a seat. I keep getting indications the War Department is pushing the President to make a decision on the Japanese. I think they are going to try to relocate all the Japanese, including American citizens. We have to get something to the President quickly."

Rowe shook his head. "Sir, I just can't believe the President is going to approve of mass incarceration of American citizens. There is no reason for this. Even Hoover agrees with that and everybody thinks he's the toughest cop in the country. Have you seen the column from that guy McLemore of the *Los Angeles Times*?"

"You mean the one who said if I could run for office in California I couldn't even win the post of third assistant dog catcher, and that I was handling the Japanese 'menace' with all the severity of Lord Fauntleroy? He's not the one with the responsibility. I am. Well, we may already be too late on this. If the President has made a decision, we wouldn't necessarily know about it. I think we'll have to assume that he still has an open mind. What do you have?"

Rowe handed over the memo and watched carefully while Biddle reviewed it. The Attorney General paused over the words. *I have to make the effort. Somebody has to tell the President what he needs to hear.*

Biddle looked up from the memorandum. "This is exactly what the President needs to hear. We need to get it over to the White House right away. Will you take care of it personally?" He reached for his fountain pen and scratched his signature on the memo.

"Let's hope this does some good before this whole thing gets out of control."

Biddle sat at his desk and turned to look out the window on a quickly darkening Washington.

～

Franklin Roosevelt was still at his desk working when his secretary came over the intercom. "Mr. President, I have an urgent memorandum from the Attorney General."

"Bring it in, please."

She walked in and handed him an envelope from Attorney General Biddle marked URGENT. Roosevelt opened the heavy bond paper envelope and looked at the memorandum regarding the movement of Japanese American citizens. The President carefully refolded the memo and placed it back in the envelope. He took off his glasses and wiped them with a handkerchief.

His secretary came back on the intercom. "Mr. President, will you need me to stay for a reply to the Attorney General?"

Roosevelt paused for a moment, the weariness showing on his face. "No, there will be no reply." His decision had already been made.

CHAPTER 21

February 17, 1942
Calwa, California

The sun shone weakly through the winter mist hovering over the Bagdasarian ranch. Fog still laid over the vines, but it was not the dense blanket of January, when the vines were just a shadow in the mist. Soon, the vines would begin to sprout spring leaves. Already the ground showed the first signs of weeds pushing up. Shig was sharpening a disc in anticipation of controlling them. The round wheels were honed like a knife's edge to cut into the ground and turn the soil. He enjoyed pulling the disc between the rows, turning the winter-rested earth. Weeds quickly became a problem in the vineyard rows, and he wanted to get a start on them. He looked forward to the activity of spring.

Aram walked into the equipment shed and interrupted his work. "Shig, have you seen the new restricted areas?" He waited for a response, but none came. The orders coming from the military now restricted Japanese movement to areas within five miles of their residences. He stood there a moment longer while Shig continued filing the disc.

"The government says that Japanese who aren't American citizens are going to be restricted. I don't think you'll be able to even go into Fresno. I think this is only the beginning. I want you to know that Esther and I will help you in any way we can."

Shig put his file down and looked directly at Aram. "I have read the restrictions. I do not intend to go any further than church, but I do not intend to be treated like a criminal either. I appreciate all the help that you and Esther have offered. We will not forget it. We are going to have a meeting at the church to discuss this. I think we are going to hire a lawyer. I don't know, but I am not going to let my family and friends be treated this way."

"Be careful. You don't know who's listening when you talk. There are people out there who want all the Japanese in jail. Just be careful, that's all."

Aram and Esther were not that far removed from what had happened to their parents in Turkey at the turn of the century, when millions of Armenians had been killed by Turkish troops. The memories that had been pounded into his head as a boy reminded him that people could never be complacent about either their rights or their safety. He couldn't help but think that if the Japanese didn't stand up for their rights, they would be the victims of oppressive action. Not like what happened to his family years ago, but oppressive nonetheless. He knew his long-time foreman would consider his words. His silence was not a rejection.

Shig changed the subject. "Isamu has heard from José Duran. He said they got a letter from that Pritch boy in the Navy." Shig shook his head, his face showing a sad weariness. "He lost his arm at Pearl Harbor. Isamu said he is still in the hospital and they are going to discharge him from the Navy. I was thinking that we may need some help around here, with so many young men in the service."

Aram lowered his head. There were still reports coming in about the carnage at Pearl Harbor. There were very few families who did not know someone there. He had a vague memory of the Pritch boy, but he seemed to recall that he was a good worker for a young man. He wanted to do something for those who were fighting. After all, they were fighting for his family too. But he had to be practical.

"He lost his arm? I hate to think of these young men being so badly injured. What are these boys going to do when they come home?" Aram was dubious about letting the Pritch boy have a job, but he also felt a responsibility to him.

He voiced his reservations. "I don't know if he could farm. You think a one-armed man can handle this work?"

"I think a one-armed man is probably better than no man at all. I feel badly for the boy. I don't know what else to say."

Aram shook his head. "Well, if the boy wants to work, I suppose we can find something for him to do."

"It seems that the Pritch boy has been courting Carmen Duran behind her father's back. I do not approve of ignoring what Pedro wanted, but young people are different now. They think our ways are old-fashioned."

"Pedro will get used to it, I guess. Tell Sammy to let Pritch know that if he wants work, we will give it to him."

Aram started walking out of the shed and then turned. "Shig, remember what I said. Be careful. There are a lot of stupid, angry people out there." Aram turned and walked away. Shig picked up the file and started working again on the disc. The slow, sliding pressure of the file against the steel gave him satisfaction. He liked work that showed its results after patient effort.

Shig drove to the Shiraga store on the way to church. Mas came right out. Obviously he was waiting just inside the door. Mas walked out to the car and got in. "You have heard this order the government made? What are we going to do? Already I cannot get cash from the bank and now, you and me, we cannot move around so good because of the government order."

"Mas, I think this is only the beginning. There are rumors that the government is going to put people like us in jails or in some kind of camps. I don't believe that, but I think we must be prepared. Let's just wait until we hear more tonight." They rode in silence the rest of the way.

When they got to church, the parking area was already filled and the meeting hall was packed with men talking in hushed voices. Everyone stood around talking and waiting for something to happen.

What they heard was that any kind of civil disobedience was not going to help them. They needed to go home, obey the law and wait.

Shig heard murmurs of resignation in the room. The truth, he knew, was that the situation was even worse.

～

February 28, 1942
San Francisco, California

Mike Masaoka sat nervously in the offices of the Japanese American Citizens League. Presidential Executive Order 9066 had been all over the newspapers. Signed by the President, it gave authority to the military to move anyone, but that didn't mean that they would, especially if the House Select Committee Investigating National Defense Migration came up with different recommendations. The Army had not said they would move them all. *Nobody had said that.* The restrictions were not good, but at least they were still free to live in their homes. *There is still hope. Perhaps we can convince these people that relocation is not a good policy. Then the Army will listen. The government will listen.*

General DeWitt had summoned Masaoka and Saburo Kido to his headquarters, but both were unsure why. *Maybe he wants to listen to our point of view? We can talk to him, get him to understand.* They left the JACL office by bus for the appointment, avoiding unnecessary gasoline use. Both kept speculating on why DeWitt wanted to see them. Certainly he did not expect them to agree to the proposals made by Governor Olson.

In each man's mind were the events of the night before. Two days earlier, the Army appeared on Terminal Island in San Pedro, California. They hung up posters giving every Japanese orders to be off the island by midnight. Most people left when they received the order earlier in the month. It was total chaos. People, mostly simple fishermen and their families, sold possessions that had taken a lifetime to acquire for pennies. But Terminal Island was in the main channel to the Port of Los Angeles and very near the Long Beach Naval Station, so it had been deemed a sensitive military location. Despite frantic phone calls, there was nothing the Citizens League could do. Cooperation, they decided, was the best course.

The two men arrived at the offices of the commanding general and looked around with trepidation. It was clear from their surroundings that they were at a seat of considerable power over their lives. They waited quietly until a military aide came to get them, and then walked into the room.

General DeWitt was dressed in his uniform jacket and tie. The three silver stars gleamed from his collar points and his shoulder epaulets. He looked at them from his seat behind his desk. When he stood up, Mike was surprised that he wasn't tall. But he rose with command authority and stood facing them. He did not introduce himself and he did not extend his hand. Mike and Saburo looked around at the others in the room. All of them were officers. The visage of the military men in the room was not friendly. Mike began to have a premonition that what was to come was not good.

General DeWitt placed his hands on his desk and leaned forward, looking straight at the two men standing in front of the massive expanse of mahogany.

"Gentlemen, you've made appearances on behalf of your people and you were called in today as a courtesy to tell you what is going to happen. I want to make it very clear that I do not intend to discuss the proposed course of action nor will my officers engage in a negotiation regarding it. I want you to hear it before you read about it." With that, the general walked past them and out the door of his office

A ranking officer stepped over to face them. *"It is my responsibility to inform you that in the next few days the Office of the Western Defense Command will issue a public proclamation. In that proclamation it will be made clear that all enemy aliens and non-aliens of enemy alien descent will be ordered to leave the western half of California, Oregon and Washington as well as a portion of Arizona. The order will be clear that your people will be given the opportunity to move out voluntarily. I want to be clear on this; if they do not move out voluntarily then the Army will move them into temporary locations until a more permanent location can be determined. We would like your people to cooperate but I must make it clear that lack of cooperation will not change the result."*

Saburo and Mike looked at one another. Mike was overcome with the magnitude of what he had just heard. It was expected that their parents' generation, the Issei, would be scrutinized, but now they were talking about citizens with the same rights as the other men in the room.

Mike spoke up. *"Excuse me, but you mean Japanese American citizens when you refer to non-aliens of enemy alien descent? You mean American citizens will be included in this?"*

Mike looked around to see if there was anyone who would disagree with what had been said. All he saw were silent faces and guarded eyes. He felt compelled to say something.

"I cannot speak for all Japanese living in this state. I don't represent all Japanese living in this state. We must talk to the leaders of our organization before we respond. We will need some time."

*"Of course. But remember that the order will issue within the next

few days whether or not you respond."* The two men turned and walked slowly from the room.

They took a taxi from the Presidio, but neither man had much to say. Mike felt sick to his stomach. Saburo spoke first.

"We can't agree to this. We can't lead our people in this direction."

"But, Saburo, how are we going to stop this? If we refuse, then people will accuse us of disloyalty."

"Perhaps, but where is the loyalty to us as citizens?"

"Where's our loyalty if we refuse?" It only took him a moment to realize that was precisely the argument that Earl Warren had made. It was a trap no matter what they decided. If they refused they were disloyal and should be interned, and if they agreed they were prisoners by consent, but prisoners nonetheless.

Mike looked at the president of the League. He blinked hard to hold back the tears that welled up from deep inside. What had happened on Terminal Island was going to happen to them. *It is just a matter of time.*

~

March 18, 1942
San Francisco, California

Colonel Bendetsen looked around his office suite in the Whitcomb Hotel. His uniform jacket was carefully hung with the new silver eagles on the epaulets, the symbol of his promotion as the youngest full colonel in the Army. The office was a better accommodation than the Presidio. His offices were down the hall from Milton Eisenhower's, the new Director of the War Relocation Authority, who oversaw the civilian relocation administration. Bendetsen already concluded he needed to be cautious in his dealings with Eisenhower. His brother, Brigadier General Dwight Eisenhower, was the Assistant Chief of Staff of the Army.

Bendetsen looked at his desk and the already mounting paperwork. His job was the key to ensuring that the Army controlled what actually happened, regardless of any civilian involvement by Eisenhower. The military already made the major decisions—his job was to ensure that the task of removal and enforcement was carried out. Once the Japanese population was safely contained, he wasn't really interested in the day-to-day operations of concentration camps. He was only interested in keeping them there.

With the Japanese evacuated from Washington's Bainbridge Island, Los Angeles wouldn't be far behind. Already preparations were being made to build a relocation camp at a place called Manzanar, out in the Owens Valley. Hundreds of Japanese volunteers were going to build it. The first group of volunteers would start in a few days. The irony of it rolled around in his head—*Japs building their own relocation center*. He stood, straightened his tie, and put on his uniform blouse. All the agencies needed were waiting for him in one of the hotel's conference rooms.

Bendetsen walked into the conference room with a sense of purpose—first impressions were key to what he intended to say and do. Already the room was filled with a pall of blue cigarette smoke as the military and civilian representatives in the room watched him. He could feel all the eyes on him. He closed his hands—they were warm and dry. He was ready.

"Gentlemen, I am Colonel Karl Bendetsen, commander of the Wartime Civil Control Administration of the Western Defense Command. You will be working with me in our task of evacuating the Japanese population from the Western Coast of the United States. This will be a formidable task. Some of you have questioned its necessity. Let me say that the highest levels of government have already answered that question. We are not here to reexamine that policy decision, we are here to implement it."

As he spoke he could feel the rapt attention in the room. It was almost hypnotic in its feeling. He turned to the map on the wall. "Gentlemen, here is the new boundary for the Japanese." He reached up, forcefully drew a black line down the western portion of the United States, and looked out at the audience for the intended reaction. He could see them staring at the line. "Gentlemen, everything west of that line will be controlled. All Japanese will be moved into secured locations of our choosing. Eventually all of them will be moved out of California. First, they will be moved from their homes into assembly centers based on voluntary evacuation. After voluntary evacuation efforts are no longer fruitful, they will be moved by necessary means into assembly centers. Then they will be moved to permanent relocation camps. These relocation camps will provide housing, schools, and medical facilities. These are not prisons, but there will be security forces to ensure compliance. I expect that this detention will last no more than three or four years—until the war is over. After that, there will be no reason to maintain these institutions."

Bendetsen turned to the blackboard and began sketching out the basic field organization. "The Army expects this to be done rapidly. We are at war and this is part of the defense of this country. Get your people on the job as fast as you can. If you are unable to meet the Army's expectations, then I recognize that a few more days may be necessary. You will receive appropriate paperwork to facilitate your implementation. I will leave the details to my able staff to complete. We are under some pressure to issue orders regarding the evacuation, and we are already scheduled to proceed in the State of Washington with Los Angeles to proceed shortly after."

He turned and left the room. He knew all eyes were on him.

⁓

The next day, Bendetsen issued the movement order to the Western Defense Command. He looked up as his secretary knocked on his open door. "Colonel, I have received confirmation that the verbal order has been read to all the sector commanders. Here's your copy."

Bendetsen set the order down on his desk. 15,000 Japs would be moved to Santa Anita racetrack within the next three weeks. San Diego and the Tanforan racetrack in San Francisco were also on schedule, as were fairgrounds in Sacramento and the San Joaquin Valley. The problem of personal belongings had been perplexing, but he finally decided that they could take only what they could carry. Storage space would be provided at their risk. All else would be sold or abandoned.

Bendetsen smiled with no small sense of satisfaction. Since he was the Assistant Chief of Staff of the Civil Affairs Division, by these orders, every sector commander would have to go through him to do anything. Nothing went to DeWitt except through him. *We will move them all*, he thought. *If they have one drop of Jap blood in them they are going. Now it begins.*

CHAPTER 22

April 20, 1942
Calwa, California

Sack and Carmen tried to find a comfortable place to sit in the hard bed of the truck. When they arrived at the bus stop in Fresno it was late, and they didn't want to waste money on a hotel. Carmen suggested they just start walking and hope to find a ride. Before long, they heard the rattle of the truck as it came up behind them. Sack stuck out his thumb and looked in the open window of the truck as it stopped beside them. The driver was an older man, his face crossed with lines etched by the sun, a battered straw hat pulled low on his forehead. A woman, her reddened bare arm resting out the window of the truck, took up most of the front seat as she and her husband smiled at the young couple.

"You folks need a ride?"

"Yes, ma'am, we could sure use one. We're headed toward Calwa, if that's the direction you're going in."

The man spoke up. "We're not going that far, but we are going near the fairgrounds."

"Anywhere closer than here is okay with us. We sure appreciate the ride."

The wife motioned toward the truck bed. "Get in the back. Sorry about the picking boxes back there. Just move them over and find a spot."

"Thank you, ma'am. My wife and me, we're real grateful." The wife couldn't help looking at Sack's empty sleeve. "You lose your arm in the service? Our boy, he's in the service right now."

Sack no longer minded the stares or the questions. "I lost it at Pearl Harbor. I was on the *Arizona*—got blown clean off and when I woke up my arm—well, they had to take it off. Got burned real bad." He shrugged.

The husband nodded to his wife. "You two get in. We'll take you to Calwa. It's not that far for us."

Carmen smiled her thanks. Both of them were exhausted— but there was an excitement in being so close to home. They watched familiar land-marks go by while the truck made its way to the Calwa post office.

The husband stopped and leaned out his window. "Where from here?"

"You folks can just let us out here. We're fine to walk the rest of the way. Don't want you to waste no more gas and all, what with the rationing."

The husband nodded. "You take care of yourselves. My wife and me, we're real sorry about your arm. We worry all the time about our boy."

Sack could see the man becoming emotional. "I'm sure he's fine, sir. We appreciate the kindness."

He and Carmen climbed down from the truck bed and pulled off their suitcase. Carmen went to the wife's side of the pickup. They talked to one another for a moment before she rejoined her husband by the side of the road.

Sack looked down at the tiny woman who was now his wife. "What'd you say to her?"

"I told her I would say a special prayer for her son, just like I did for you." Sack nodded. He was still getting used to her way.

They walked the last half-mile to the road leading to the Bagdasarian ranch and turned in at the mailbox.

Setsuko saw them first, walking past the main house toward their home in back, by the work shed. She called to Shig, "They are here." She wiped her hands on the towel by her sink and walked out to greet them. "Hello, Carmen, Billy. We read your letter, but it did not say when you would be here."

"No, ma'am, Mrs. Miyaki. I didn't know when the Navy would let me out. My arm and all." He nodded toward his empty left sleeve. "We was real grateful for the job. Carmen and me, we got married, and the job—it will be a real help to us."

Shig looked out the window when he heard his wife call out. He walked slowly to the young couple, but he couldn't keep his eyes off the empty sleeve. When he told Isamu to write and offer a job, the injury didn't seem all that real to him.

Sack could tell that Mr. Miyaki was staring. He knew more or less what he was thinking. "Don't worry, Mr. Miyaki, I can work. You'll be real surprised what I can do. You learn to make do."

Shig nodded. He knew he was being impolite but his mind was on so many other things. He tried to remember his manners.

"How are you, Sack? You are married now?"

"Yes, sir. We got married a couple weeks back and then when the Navy let me go, we took a bus from Texas to get here."

Shig stuck out his hand and was satisfied with the firm grip. "Setsuko has made a place for you where Carmen and her parents lived. It's over here." He led the way toward the side of the equipment shed, where there was a small living area with two rooms attached.

Setsuko was apologizing as they walked, but Carmen smiled. After all, she had lived there with her parents and José.

They walked inside, but the familiar smell of the peppers and drying herbs was gone. Only a faint musty odor met them when they walked through. Still, it had a bed and a stove. It was a beginning.

Setsuko turned to them. "The blankets on the bed, they are our wedding gift to you. We hope you can be happy here." She looked around and began to find hints of dust she had missed. Setsuko looked up apologetically. "We did not know when you would be here. There is much dust in the air."

Carmen took her hand. "It is a wonderful place. Thank you for the gift. We're grateful."

Sammy came through the door while everyone was talking. Before he could say anything, Shig asked him if he was finished helping Toshi with the watering. "We just finished, Papa. All of it's done." He wiped his hands on his pants and walked over to Sack. He tried not to look as he stuck out his hand. Sack reached out and put his arm around the younger man's shoulder.

"I'm real grateful for what you did—the letters and all. Me and Carmen, it meant a lot."

Sammy felt his face redden. "That's okay. I'm just glad you got them." He stepped back and laughed. "I can't believe you're married."

Sack also laughed. "Yeah, we got married right after her father said it was okay with him."

Shig smiled. "Knowing Pedro, I would guess he did not make it easy for you."

"No, sir, but once I got through it all and he said okay, well, he's treated me real good since then." Setsuko nodded her head several times. "I am sure Esperanza had something to do with that." Carmen laughed.

Setsuko took the younger woman's hand. "We have food in the house. Let me prepare dinner for you. You can tell me about your wedding."

Sammy followed them out the door as they walked toward his parents' home. "Sack, you were on the *Arizona*? What was it . . ."

His father turned and gave his son a sharp look. "There will be time to talk of that, but not now."

Sammy looked over at Sack and was relieved to see him wink. After all, Sack was the first person he knew who had really been in the war. He wanted to know what it was like.

~

Sack woke up early, feeling a little disoriented when he looked around the room. It took him a minute to realize he was at the ranch and not back in the hospital ward. He laid quietly in the bed, savoring the first light of morning. He had always enjoyed the time between night and morning. He closed his eyes and listened to the rhythmic breathing of the woman next to him. He still couldn't believe that she was his wife.

Sack rolled over onto his left side, ignoring the slight discomfort in the stump of his arm. Carmen moved slightly, and he placed his hand on the curve of her hip. She moved over and he could feel her warmth brushing up against him. He waited a little longer before getting up. The Miyakis had been very kind, providing a late dinner. Sammy and Toshi wanted to talk more, but he and Carmen had been so tired. All they wanted to do was sleep.

Sack got out of bed as quietly as he could and dressed without turning on the light. He wanted to let Carmen sleep. It was hard to sleep on the bus, and he knew it would take a few days for them to catch up. It was a little easier for him since he was used to moving around with his family.

He hoped that he would see them soon. Maybe in the next month or so, as the field workers moved down from the north.

He walked out into the light just as the sun was beginning to warm the day, just on the cusp of spring. The trees were budding but winter still kept the branches well-defined, not yet hidden behind the coming leafing of spring and summer. He could see the grape vines with their buds just beginning to burst. He and Carmen had come at the right time. It wouldn't be long before the ranch was in full swing. He had watched it all his life. He didn't hate it and he didn't love it. It wasn't what he wanted out of life, but with his rehabilitation time he had learned the virtue of patience.

Shig walked out of his home and came across to the room where Sack and Carmen were staying. They both exchanged greetings, but Sack could see that Shig still was uncomfortable about the empty sleeve. He kept trying not to look at it and that just made it more obvious.

"Mr. Miyaki, don't worry about it."

Shig looked startled. "Don't worry about what?"

"Don't worry about my arm. It takes a while but folks get used to it. Look, it doesn't bother me no more. I don't spend a lot of time thinkin' about it."

Shig stood silent for a moment. "Sack, I'm sorry about your arm and I'm sorry about the way you lost it. What is bothering me is difficult to explain."

Sack looked at the older man. "Is this cuz it was Japanese that done it? Is that it?"

Shig's face showed his discomfort as Sack continued. "You folks known me a long time. You helped me get a job. What they done, they done. Far as I'm concerned, you didn't do nothin' 'cept give me a job. Carmen and me—we're real grateful."

Shig nodded. "Aram will be out in a while. We need to talk to him."

"Everything's all right, ain't it?"

Shig could see the sudden worried look. "Everything is fine. But things are not so good here. I don't know how long we're going to be able to stay."

Sack frowned. "I don't understand."

"Maybe you haven't read the papers but Japanese are being forced out of their homes all over California. Setsuko and I—we don't know what is going to happen. But you should not worry. You have a job no matter what happens to us. Aram and I talked about this. We want you and Carmen to have a place here as long as you want to work." Shig could see the confusion in the young man's face.

"I don't pay much attention to the news and things, Mr. Miyaki. I don't know what you're talkin' about. But you folks always been nothin' but good to me and my family. If I can help you, I want you to know you can count on me."

The older man gave a weary smile. "I am afraid there is very little you can do for Setsuko and me. Soon enough it will all be decided for us."

~

Mas heard the sound of pounding coming from the area outside the store. At first he feared more vandalism, but when he looked out he saw a young man in military uniform nailing a flyer onto the telephone pole near the road. He came out to see what was going on. The young soldier avoided his gaze. The soldier was Tommy Campbell, the son of Bill Campbell, who delivered the milk in Calwa. Mas had known Tommy since he was a boy, when he used to ride with his dad on milk deliveries. He heard that Tommy had been drafted. He looked thinner, more muscular.

"Is that you, Tommy? What are you doing?"

The young man looked embarrassed. "Look, Mr. Shiraga, I'm just doing what I been told to do. I'm sorry." He finished putting the flyer up and hurried over to an idling Army truck. Mas waited until the truck left to look at the flyer. He didn't have to get very close. It was the order of evacuation for all Japanese. He and his family had five days to report to the Fresno fairgrounds for relocation.

PART
III

CHAPTER 23

May 11, 1942

Fresno, California

The spires of the fairground race track grandstand rose up sharply against the blue morning sky. The grassy area in front of the track was just beginning to show the green of spring but instead of stands with steaming food, the grounds held tents and men in uniforms carrying papers to tables set up near the entrance. Women from a local church were pouring coffee. The chill air still lingered in the morning hours. Summer had not yet come to the Valley as the Miyaki family got out of their car. Aram and Esther drove behind them in his truck. There was a silent winding line leading up to the gate of the Fresno fairgrounds. Sammy's eyes were not fixed on the Japanese waiting to enter. His eyes were fixed on the young soldiers standing at the gate and down the line carrying rifles with bayonets, the steel blades glinting in the sunlight.

Aram and Esther got out of the truck and waited for the Miyaki family to gather their possessions. Aram could also see the soldiers as he untied the rocking chair from the truck bed and placed it gently on the ground, near the rest of the family's bundles.

Toshi helped *Obasan* from the car. She promptly walked over to her rocking chair and sat down. She had said almost nothing when her son told her they had to move. Shig moved near his mother, his eyes following her slow rocking motion as she stared out at the line of people. He tried to keep it from her, to not worry her, but he knew she understood. He felt tears gather in his eyes as he took a deep breath. He leaned down and spoke softly in Japanese. "Mother, we will have to move into the line." He looked around. "Toshi will help you."

Obasan looked up at her son, the tissue-thin skin under her eyes tinged with the dark weariness of age. She moved her gaze back to the line of people, each carrying two bags of possessions, her mouth barely moving as she whispered, "*Shikata ga nai.*" *It cannot be helped.* Shig lowered his head and stared at the dry ground. There was no choice here but there was no honor, either.

Aram swallowed hard, forcing himself to keep his emotions under control. "Esther and I will visit you as soon as we can."

Shig shook his head, acknowledging his friend's concern. "Remember, the southwest corner of the ranch is sandy, you have to watch the water because it does not hold it well. And the boy, Sack, he will take care of things if you show him."

Aram just nodded quietly.

Setsuko stood by the car, looking at the small pile of possessions she had carefully selected to take with them. She turned to Esther. "Please take care of my roses?"

Esther didn't have Setsuko's green thumb, but she would do the best she could. They exchanged a close hug. Esther reached into her pocket and took out a small object wrapped in tissue paper. She handed it to Setsuko, who opened it with care. It was a broach she had always admired.

"I cannot take your broach."

Esther held her hand. "You will bring it back to me when you come home."

Toshi helped his grandmother to her feet and picked up some bags, while Shig carried the rocking chair and led his mother to the line.

Soldiers were inspecting the families' belongings. Finally, they reached Shig. A tall young man looked at the chair. "I'm sorry, but you can't take that in with you. Only clothing and small personal possessions are allowed."

Shig looked up at the young soldier. "This is my mother's chair. She does not understand what is happening. If she has her chair, she will be all right."

The young man raised his voice to be more commanding. "I'm sorry, sir, but I can't let you take in the chair."

Shig looked for a long time at the young man, his eyes narrowing until only the blackness of the iris showed. "I am taking in the chair."

Sammy had never heard his father speak in that tone of voice. The soldier stepped back and went to another soldier who appeared to be in charge. The two men looked over at Shig as they talked, then the older man nodded and walked over.

The older soldier looked straight into Shig's face. He could tell that others in line were watching. When he had been given this assignment, he was fine with it. After what the Japs did at Pearl Harbor, he didn't have any sympathy. But now these people seemed like folks he had grown up with. They looked tired and worn, shuffling forward with their small bags. He looked at the tiny, reed-thin woman holding onto Shig's arm. At last, he spoke.

"I'm Sergeant Davis. You keep the chair, okay? But I can't promise that you'll be able to take it with you when you leave."

Shig nodded his thanks and the sergeant walked away. The young soldier came back and mumbled that he was sorry, he was just doing what he had been told. He looked in Sammy's bag, a baseball bat sticking out of the end.

"That's a weapon and I'll have to keep it."

Sergeant Davis was listening. "Let him keep the bat. If they wanted to bring in a weapon, they could do it very easily. Come on, Johnson, use some common sense, will you?" He looked over at an elderly Japanese man in line wearing an Army uniform from World War I, standing ramrod-straight with a look of defiance. "This is bad enough as it is."

Sammy picked up the rocking chair and followed his parents as they slowly guided *Obasan* through the gate. He didn't look at the guards who stood at the edge of the opening. He kept his head up like his father. He didn't look back.

～

The Shiraga family waited patiently as the line slowly moved past the men taking down information and giving instructions. As they got closer, they could hear numbers being given to each person and a housing assignment. A Japanese man stood next to the table. Mas didn't recognize him but he had heard him speaking to some of the people in Japanese, giving instructions and translating.

A soldier with two stripes on his sleeve looked up at him. "Name and address?"

"Mas Shiraga. I live in Calwa. I have a store there." The man looked down a list and made a notation.

"This your family?"

"This is my wife, Satomi, my children, Freddy and Betty."

"Are those their real names, or do they have Japanese names?

"Those are their real names." It was becoming increasingly difficult for Mas to control his anger at the tone with which he was being questioned. Just that morning he gave the keys to the store to Luis and Maria. They offered to run it for him until his family returned.

He looked down at the soldier writing in a large book. The dust was beginning to hang in the air from all the shuffling feet. He could taste it drying in the back of his throat.

The corporal wrote down a number next to each person's name and handed a copy to Mas. "These are your identification numbers. Don't lose them."

Mas nodded that he understood.

"This is your housing assignment. It's the best we can do for right now. Give it to one of those boys over there and he'll show you where it is."

Mas motioned for his family to follow. He handed the housing assignment to one of the young Japanese standing near the gate.

The young man looked at the paper, then smiled. "I'll show you where you've been assigned, Mr. Shiraga." He didn't look much older than Freddy as he walked quickly through milling people to the south side of the racetrack.

"Is this your job?" Mas asked.

"My family got here yesterday. Everybody calls me Jimmy. I volunteered for this. It was better than just sitting around."

Freddy couldn't restrain himself. "What does our room look like?"

The boy hesitated before answering. "It isn't exactly a room. They're building some barracks, but not everybody is going to be able to move into them because there aren't enough. I'm sorry, but you folks are going to be living over there."

Mas looked at the long building with doors every ten feet, the shed roof giving scant shade to the front. The graying wood showed through what was left of the white paint, blistered from the sun and rain. He could not see anything through the cracks in the board walls, but he did not need to. He had been to the fair before. He knew what they were.

Freddy looked over. "You're taking us to horse stalls?"

Jimmy stopped. "I'm sorry. I know they've been cleaning them out. There's cots you can pick up at that building over there. They'll give you a bag so you can make mattresses. We put hay in ours but I took it out. I couldn't stop sneezing." He led them to a door with a number that matched the one they had been given, the powdery dust of the road between the stalls rising up as he pulled the door open.

Mas stood at the door. He could still smell the odor of hay and manure, regardless of the effort made to clean it out. He looked at the ground as he stepped through the entry, his family following quietly. The dim light revealed little other than the small size of the room. There was a light, the bulb shielded by a metal shade. He could hear Satomi crying. Freddy threw his things on the floor and began kicking at the wall. Betty moved close to her mother, looking around at the rusty nails in the walls.

~

Sammy walked toward the fence near the gate. He told Freddy that he would meet him at 5:00 p.m., after their families had gotten settled. He shuffled his feet through the floury dirt in the stable area, walking down the rows of stall doors that now held families just like his. People were sitting on suitcases outside the doors, smoking and talking. Everyone was subdued. The air of sadness was pervasive. A sense of resignation hung over the area, as thick as the dust he raised with his feet.

Traffic moved along Butler Avenue, bordering the assembly center. Sammy could see drivers and their passengers staring at the soldiers standing near the gate, rifles slung over their shoulders. His high school was only a few blocks away, and he could see the top of the auditorium in the distance. A few days before he had been on the other side of the fence, playing his last baseball game with his team. He didn't understand what coming inside the fence meant until now, when he looked out through the wire walls separating him from the world he had known only hours before. Freddy and Betty were standing by the gate when he got there.

"We're in a horse stall."

He said it as if he was telling them something they didn't already know.

Freddy didn't look any happier. "Yeah, we got the same thing. Mickey's family got into the barracks but his sister, Rose, said it's just wood covered with tar paper. They had to hang a blanket to separate them from another family. They don't have any privacy. I guess her dad couldn't work out the lease on their farm. Rose said they had to leave everything. Some neighbors stored their furniture, but I guess the farm is gone. At least we have Mr. and Mrs. Machado taking care of the store."

Sammy's face showed his surprise. He hadn't heard about Rose's father losing their farm. "Does Mickey know about the farm?"

"I don't think they've told him yet." Both young men remained silent for a moment. The reality of the situation beginning to sink in. For a few minutes they both watched the cars slowly passing by. The guards had already quit paying attention to them, deciding they weren't any threat.

Sammy and Freddy stood with their hands wrapped around the wire of the fence, their knuckles whitening as their grip tightened on the fragile barrier. Sammy pulled his hands off the wire, the steel chords ringing a sound as the fence shook. His words were hissed. "I hate this." The words hung in the space between them. They stood around quietly for a moment as a guard glanced over at the sound and then went back to staring at the traffic.

He searched for conversation and thought about his morning. "One of those guards tried to take my baseball bat. Said it was a weapon. I couldn't believe how stupid he was. Some sergeant finally told him to leave me alone. You got your glove?"

"Yeah, I got my glove and a few balls. What stall you in?"

"We're on the right side over there down in the middle. Why don't you come by tomorrow morning and we can figure it out. Can I speak to Betty alone for a minute?"

Freddy looked at them for a moment and then nodded. "Okay." He walked off leaving the two of them to watch the sun fall behind the trees in the distance.

Sammy took Betty's hand and looked around to see if anybody was watching. It still wasn't acceptable for people their age to show any kind of affection in public. She squeezed his hand and then let go. "Maybe we could meet here by the gate around the same time tomorrow?" He smiled when she nodded.

He took her hand and held it while they watched the cars passing on Butler Avenue, just outside the fence. Guards stood at the gate, talking and smoking. They carried rifles but it didn't look like they expected anything to happen. They called this an assembly center, but it was beginning to feel like a prison. Sammy walked Betty back to her family, then kicked the dust on his way back to his own.

His mother said nothing when Sammy walked through the door. She was sweeping, just as she had been when he left. The floor was clean, but the smell seemed trapped in the walls and concrete. His father and his brother Toshi weren't there.

Obasan was sitting in her chair, slowly rocking back and forth. Her eyes looked at him and he could see what he thought was the faint beginning of a smile. But she said nothing even in response to his greeting. He watched for some small sign that she heard him. All that he heard was the faint sound of the curved rockers of her chair pushing against the grain of the concrete floor. He looked at his mother. Setsuko simply shook her head and kept sweeping, pushing imagined dust from what was now their home.

~

The next morning, Freddy came by with his glove. Shig was standing in the front of their quarters. "Mr. Miyaki, is Isamu here?"

Shig looked up and smiled. It was good to see people that he knew. It made the whole experience a little less distasteful. "Isamu is inside. Are you boys planning to play some baseball?"

Freddy nodded. "We have to do something."

Sammy walked out when he heard Freddy's voice. "Where we going to play?"

"I heard Moon Kurima is in here too. Maybe we can find him and see if he wants to throw some balls."

"Moon's here? I wonder how many of the other players are here?"

Shig was listening to the two boys. "All the ball players are here. Everybody from around most of the Central Valley is here, already over four thousand people." He looked at the boys. "Right now, baseball is not important. We need to find out how long we're going to be here and see if we can get some kind of community organization going. We need leaders. We need somebody to complain about the conditions and see what can be done about it."

Neither boy said anything. Sammy's father was right. They were living in horse stalls and tar paper shacks. He looked over at his grandmother. *Obasan* was sitting in the shaft of light that came through the door with the morning sun, warming herself in a new place.

Sammy watched the motes of dust spin around her in the sunlight. The light seemed to go through her face with a translucent glow, the veins shadowing blue against the aging white of her skin. The last words he heard from her had been "*shikata ga nai.*" She said nothing more since they had come through the gate. He was so tired of hearing those words as he had walked up and down the path between the stalls. They came from every direction, and those words hung in the air, heavier than the dust.

CHAPTER 24

May 14, 1942

Camp San Luis Obispo, California

Technical Sergeant Young Oak Kim looked at his watch. It was 5:00 a.m., but it felt like he had just gone to sleep. He woke up automatically, but that didn't make it any easier. The motor pool for his unit was out of control. Cannon Company had fifty-three vehicles, most of which were heavy trucks and halftracks that were supposed to carry a 105-artillery gun. And he was the motor pool sergeant responsible for all of them. As far as he was concerned the halftracks with tank tracks in the back and tires in the front were almost worthless, a constant maintenance problem.

To make matters worse, the entire 17th Infantry Regiment was using his motor pool. They had vehicles spread from Santa Rosa to Ukiah, and now the unit had been moved from the Santa Rosa fairgrounds to Camp San Luis Obispo. At least the ocean-side Army camp had green-roofed barracks to sleep in. The smell of the new wood was a pleasant relief from the odor he had slept with for the last few months.

He laughed to himself, remembering that Sergeant Durham told him they would be responsible for guarding the coast all the way up to Oregon.

"Ah, Bull, what's there to guard? You and I both know the Japanese aren't going to invade San Luis Obispo or any place on the coast." It was one of the few times he had ever referred to Durham by his nickname. He noticed that Durham didn't seem to mind.

"Well, that's a decision for people with stars on their collars. We ain't got none, so just keep the trucks ready to move." And he had.

The only break Kim had received occurred when Captain Simmons had called him into the charge of quarters. It wasn't very long ago that Simmons had been a lieutenant; now he was the commanding officer of Cannon Company. Simmons congratulated Kim on getting married and offered him a weekend pass to go into San Francisco where his new wife, Ida, was in nurse's training. Weekend passes were in short supply, and he used them to take Ida to Los Angeles and visit Japanese friends who had been moved to Santa Anita Racetrack.

Simmons asked whether the internment created problems for him, but Kim acquiesced. It wasn't his decision, even if he didn't agree with it. He just wanted to see his friends.

Simmons nodded and his young face took on a more serious look. He told him they were going to be moving the unit out in another week over to the desert for training. He wanted all the equipment accounted for and ready to go. Kim thought the Army was preparing them for desert fighting. That meant Africa.

The visit with Ida at Santa Anita Racetrack made a sobering impression on him. People were living in cleaned-out horse stalls. It was one thing for a soldier to make do with those living conditions, but those people weren't soldiers. The experience left him with a sense of anger. The only reason those people were there was because they were Japanese. But Kim kept his mouth shut, glad to have the distraction of the upcoming move to the desert.

Captain Simmons seemed to have a lot of confidence in his ability to keep things moving, although he himself wasn't so sure. It might have made more sense to move the tracked equipment by train, but they were going to take the roads. He was sure they would the tear hell out of both the roads and the equipment. Kim shook his head and sighed. Orders were orders.

By the time he got down to the line of vehicles, Durham and Simmons were already looking over the convoy, making sure all men and equipment were in place. At the rate these big vehicles moved they were going to be on the road for several days, and everybody knew it.

Kim walked up to the two men quietly talking about the logistics of the day's move. "Everything look okay?"

Simmons looked over and smiled. "Everything seems fine, Sergeant. Let's get the men ready to roll. Kim, these halftracks going to work all right on the roads?"

"Yes, sir. They'll probably work better on the road than off. I don't think they'll throw too many tracks as long as we stay on the roadway."

"Good, let's saddle up."

"Yes, sir."

The cool ocean air of Camp San Luis Obispo quickly gave way to the inland heat as the convoy moved to the desert area. Rolling hills, coastal oak, and pine trees turned to miles of alkaline soil dotted with scrub and tumble weeds, the desert sun drawing more and more energy from the men and machines. By the time they got to the train stop near Needles, the men were exhausted. The convoy pulled off the road, and Kim and his crew climbed into the back of their halftrack to bed down. They were too tired to eat and, besides, it was cold rations anyway. He wasn't in the mood for another can of baked beans and ham.

It wasn't long before sleep came and then morning. Kim was up and moving before most of his men. He could hear the officers coming down the line of the convoy ordering the men up. Better to at least get some hot coffee in his stomach before everybody else had the same idea.

~

It was another long hot day moving slowly toward the training ground. They moved into a flat area to set up a makeshift motor pool. Already halftracks were breaking their treads, the long steel-tread strips unraveling from their sprockets like loose thread. It was going to be a long training session. Rumor was they were going to do war games with Patton's boys before they shipped out for North Africa. That was okay with him. At least they would keep moving, and so would the time.

Kim watched the sun begin to set. In some ways Needles was a beautiful place, not like the coast or the city where he grew up. It was strange the way the flat tans and browns of the desert looked almost lavender, and then purple, as the shadow of dusk moved over the hills. He pulled his coat tighter around him. It was also strange how the heat of the day was replaced with a chill as the sun disappeared. He sat with the men for a while and then climbed into the back of the halftrack. It wasn't long before he fell asleep, dreaming about fighting in Africa with Patton, dreaming about Ida, dreaming dreams he wouldn't remember in the morning.

CHAPTER 25

May 18, 1942

Fresno Assembly Center

Fresno, California

Sammy and Freddy walked back from their baseball practice with Coach Zenimura. Sweat and dirt coated both of them, but cleanliness would have to wait until their turn in the communal showers. Taking showers in large groups had been a difficult adjustment, and the loss of privacy was particularly hard on the women. It wasn't as difficult for Sammy and Freddy. They were used to showering with other boys after high school baseball practice. But it was one more thing that weighed down the morale of the camp.

Decisions were rapidly made to establish a sense of community within the camp. Schools were set up. Teachers began classes for the younger children. Community camp leaders created activities to keep people busy, taking their minds from the memory of homes and businesses now out of reach. In a matter of days Coach Zenimura had scrounged lumber from around the camp and put volunteers to work, building baseball diamonds on the empty grounds. Now the barren dirt was scraped and shaped into baselines and pitching mounds, with rough spectator stands and a wooden backstop. Sammy and Freddy had worked with the other young men, dragging boards across the infields to make them smooth, while their fathers built the stands.

Freddy fished into his back pocket and pulled out a sheet of paper. "You seen the camp bulletin?" Sammy took the paper and looked at the page.

* BULLETIN

FRESNO ASSEMBLY CENTER Fresno, Calif.

May 18, 1942

MORE COOPERATIVE SPIRIT

Everyone is vitally concerned in the smooth and efficient functioning of the Assembly Center. The health of each individual is one of the important factors which will contribute toward that end, and it will depend tremendously upon the sanitary conditions of the Center. It is evident to everyone that there are certain necessary tasks to be performed, such as maintaining the cleanliness of the lavatories. The people who are engaged in such activities are to be commended for their cooperative spirit in volunteering to help keep the Center sanitary and clean.

DO NOT CROSS OVER FENCE!

It should be definitely understood by everyone within the Assembly Center that no person is permitted to cross over or crawl under the fence for any purpose, even to retrieve a ball . . .*

Sammy didn't bother to read the rest of the page. He handed the bulletin back to Freddy. "What do they think we're going to do, run away?"

"I'd be more afraid one of those guards with a gun would shoot us. I think some of those guys are younger than us."

As they reached Freddy's quarters, Sammy noticed that both Mr. and Mrs. Shiraga seemed subdued. Mas came up to him and put his arm on his shoulder.

"Isamu, I think you need to go home. Your father is looking for you."

Sammy could tell something was wrong by the tone of Mas's voice. He hurried through dusty pathways separating what once had been horse paddocks, but were now carefully raked in front of each door. As he turned down the road leading to his family's quarters, he could sense subtle glances in his direction. The normal din of community hushed as he passed with nods of acknowledgment that a young person would not normally get. But he could sense something in their brief eye contact that wasn't fear, more like uncertainty.

As he drew toward his home he could see a small cluster of people gathered outside, faces he recognized from church. People separated silently and let him pass through the door. His father and mother were sitting quietly on their bed. His father's face was a mask blank of emotion, his eyes sunken and vacant. His mother's face was flushed, the tracks of tears still showing as she twisted the handkerchief in her hands.

Shig looked up at his younger son. "*Obasan*," he began, before his voice faltered.

Toshi spoke up. "Grandmother is dead, Sammy. She was sitting in her rocking chair and we thought she was asleep. Mom went to wake her to get ready for lunch. But she wouldn't wake up."

Sammy sat down on the floor and held his head in his hands. *How could Obasan be dead?* He had seen her in the morning when he left for baseball practice. She had given him a gentle smile. He had only taken a minute with her because he was in a hurry. He could feel hot tears coursing down his cheeks. *It's this place. Maybe if they had just left us alone, she would still be alive.*

Only one thought came to his lips. "Where have they taken her?"

Toshi responded for his parents. "The sergeant who talked to Dad at the gate when we came in got some men to help us. There are women dressing her now. They moved her to the . . ."—he faltered as he searched for the right word—". . .the stall across from us. Nobody knows what to do. I guess they didn't think about people dying."

The vehemence with which Toshi spoke caused their father to look up. Shig felt like his chest was going to explode. His head throbbed from grief and he kept breathing deeply, trying to maintain control in front of his family. His mother was gone. *She lived a long and honored life and her death should have carried dignity. It should not have ended in a place where horses were kept.* He could not help but think that if his mother had been left alone at the farm she would still be on the porch, rocking in the sun. He touched Setsuko's hand and bowed his head. He couldn't speak any more.

Finally Setsuko broke the stillness of the room. "We must attend to *Obasan*. I will go and help the other women. Toshi, please find Sergeant Davis. He is the one who helped us move her. Please find out how we will give her a proper burial. *Obasan* will not be buried here. We will take her to the cemetery in Fowler for burial. Isamu, please find Rev. Ishii so that *Obasan* may have proper words."

Both boys looked at their mother with some surprise. They had never heard her speak with such authority in front of their father. Sammy placed his hand on his father's shoulder.

"Papa, Toshi and I will take care of it."

His father looked up at his son. His eyes seemed to be looking at something that wasn't there. Shig nodded but that was all. Sammy looked back as he went out the door. *Obasan's* empty rocking chair sat in the corner of the crowded horse stall.

Sammy brought Reverend Ishii back to the stalls. He paused outside the family's room as the minister entered. There were already too many people in the small quarters. Sammy looked across the road at the faces of the women standing outside the room where *Obasan* lay. He hesitated and then walked through the small cluster of women and into the faint light of the unlit room.

Obasan was lying on a cot. Sammy walked over and sat in a chair next to her. *Obasan's* frail body was drawn into the straw filled mattress, barely rising above it. The tissue-thin skin laid against her face in gentle creases, her lips only a narrow line. Her blue-veined hands gently crossed her chest. He had never noticed the delicacy of her hands, even though she had been the wife of a farmer.

Sammy paused before reaching out and covering her hands with his, the brown hand swallowing the small fingers of his grandmother. He could feel the tears come up from deep inside, the burning sensation of a grief he had never felt before. "I will not forget you, *Obasan*."

Sammy did not know how long he sat next to his grandmother. The sound of other people startled him. Sergeant Davis stood at the door with two men that Sammy did not recognize. Mr. Toshiukii, the pharmacist, was with them.

People came out of their quarters and watched as men from the funeral home carried *Obasan's* covered body down the dirt path toward the front gate. The faces of people who knew the Miyaki family were the same as those who did not; tightly drawn stares, eyes signaling their resentment. Even if *Obasan* was not their loved one, she was one of them. To be carried down a horse path was not the ending befitting an honored mother. Shig, Setsuko, Toshi, and Sammy followed behind, the dust stirring with their shuffling feet.

~

The next morning Sammy woke up to the gentle creaking of his grandmother's rocking chair. His father sat in it, staring off at the door. Sammy slipped quietly out of his cot and walked over to his father. Shig did not respond to the movement. Sergeant Davis and Mr. E.P. Pulliam, the assembly center director, had arranged for Shig to go to the funeral home today to make arrangements for *Obasan*'s funeral. A soldier had been assigned to drive him.

Sammy watched his father slowly rise from the chair. He felt like he had to say something. "Do you want me to come along?"

Shig looked back with immense sadness in his face. "No, I will do this alone. I will be back by this afternoon. I think tomorrow we will have *Obasan*'s funeral."

Sammy watched his father's heavy steps move slowly down the dirt road between the now-occupied stalls.

~

The day of the funeral, Sammy and Toshi rose early. He could hear his mother rustling around. The two young men dressed quickly. Both boys put on their white shirts and waited for instructions. The rituals of death were not something they had come to learn. It all seemed strange to them. The family gathered and walked to the headquarters office for their passes. Sergeant Davis had called Aram, who waited at the gate.

Aram shook his head as the family walked to his car. "I'm sorry about *Obasan*." Shig simply nodded and kept his words to himself. They rode the ten miles in silence to the small cemetery in Fowler, just south of Calwa. They could be out until 5:00 p.m. It would be enough time.

Shig said very little as they rode past ranches with budding grapevines. He found himself studying each ranch with a critical eye. It had once been his function to take care of such a ranch. Within a matter of days, all the security he had known in his life had been taken away—his job, his home, and now his mother. He could feel a weight pressing down on his shoulders.

When they arrived at the cemetery Reverend Ishii was standing by the open grave. Esther waited with Sack and Carmen. A young soldier kept a respectful distance. He would drive Reverend Ishii back after the service.

The words were simple, befitting *Obasan*'s simple life. She had devoted herself to her family, and now her family stood near her resting place to say goodbye. Sammy watched his father place his hand on his mother's coffin and speak softly to her picture resting on top. He could not hear what was said, the words in Japanese lost to him. He could see tears drop from his father's lowered face. His father stepped back and they prayed together, watching the polished wood coffin slowly lowered into the ground.

Aram and Esther had brought roses from Setsuko's garden. Shig and Setsuko laid the flowers by the grave and silently shared their last thoughts with *Obasan*. Sammy and Toshi watched as workmen began scattering soil into the grave.

There were very few words shared during the ride back. Aram offered to take them to the ranch for lunch, but Shig politely refused. He promised Sergeant Davis they would return right after the funeral. He would keep his word.

When they arrived at the Assembly Center, Aram watched as they walked through the gate in single file, each presenting a pass to the guard. Shig turned to look through the fence. Aram stood on the other side and raised his hand. They didn't have any more words left, not even goodbye.

CHAPTER 26

May 20, 1942
298th Hawaii National Guard
Schofield Barracks
Honolulu, Territory of Hawaii

Yuki and Tug spent another day guarding another beach while kids played in the waves. They were both exhausted from the heat and boredom, as well as from an increasing sense of dread. They had heard from some of the mainland families that their sons in the military had been removed from their units and sent to places in Arkansas.

There was rising concern within the unit that something might happen to them, especially after all the Japanese boys had been removed from the Territorial Guard. Tug's mother had a cousin in San Francisco who received an evacuation order and was now living at a racetrack under armed guard. Everybody knew about Bainbridge Island in Washington. Almost all of them had family or knew someone on the West Coast who had been moved to some kind of detention center. The two men walked toward their barracks to shower and get ready for dinner.

"Yuki, I think maybe we could get put in some kind of camp."

Yuki shook his head. There was almost no conversation with his friend where this didn't come up.

"Look, Tug, half the people in the islands are either Japanese or Chinese. What're they going to do, lock everybody up? Besides, why would they take us out of the military? Who's going to guard the islands? Face it, we're all they got right now."

"Maybe so, *brah*, but they got all the ammunition. They could just decide to make us prisoners or something. I think we got a problem."

"You need to stop getting worked up about this. If something happens, then we'll deal with it."

"Yuki, you saying you're not worried too?"

"No, I'm saying that there's no point in putting all my energy into worrying about something I have no control over."

They walked by First Sgt. Ka'ne, who was standing in the company compound watching a work detail clean the area. He called out. "Hey, Yuki, come on over for a minute."

Yuki walked over to Ka'ne. The Hawaiian sergeant had heard whispers from men in headquarters that General Emmons planned to separate the Japanese boys out of the units. It was hard to keep secrets from the sergeants. All the paperwork went through them. It was still only a rumor, but his sources were almost always right.

Ka'ne pulled him over to the side of the compound and looked around to see if anyone was nearby. He leaned in close to Yuki, keeping his voice low. "Yuki, listen up. I don't know much of anything, you know, but I hear some things around. You got family over on Maui, that right?"

"Yeah, Joe, you know that. My mom and dad moved to Lahaina almost a year ago."

"I probably shouldn't say nothin' but I'm getting a funny feeling, you know? I think maybe you should go talk to your mom and dad. Maybe keep this between us?"

"What are you saying? Is something going to happen?"

"Yuki, I told you. I don't know anything. Just think maybe you want to talk to them, okay? If you want a pass, come see me and I'll get it for you. Just say your mom sick, okay?"

Ka'ne walked back to the work detail. You could hear him yelling all over the company compound. "Asses and elbows. That all I want to see. You boys better make sure we got a clean company area. Pick up those cigarette butts."

Yuki stood by himself for a minute and then walked by the work detail. Ka'ne didn't look up, so he kept walking into the barracks.

～

Yuki obtained the pass in the morning. Coehlo, now a captain, never said a word. Ka'ne only said, "Just two days, you understand?"

Yuki hurried out the door to catch the noon boat for Lahaina. He stood on the bow, catching the salty breeze and the fine spray of water that blew up from the bite of the bow into the sea. He breathed in the cool air and savored its taste. It was good to see the water again, from the deck of a boat instead of the beach. He could see Maui off in the distance.

When he walked up the path to the small house overlooking the ocean he could see his mother, Chiyeko, hanging his father's clothes on the line stretched from a pole to the house. He stopped for a moment and watched her perform a task he had seen a thousand times. She moved slowly and deliberately, shaking out the clothing and then reaching into her apron for a clothespin. She swayed as she worked, listening to some inner song. Finally he walked quietly up behind her. "Mama?"

She threw up her hands and turned immediately. "Yuki, Yuki, why did you not say you were coming? So good, so good to see you home." She placed her arms around his neck and pulled him as close as she could. She looked thinner than he remembered, and her face a little more weathered. She ran her small hands over his face, and he could feel the palms roughened by years of work. "Your father is out with the boat trying to catch dinner. He will be so happy to see you."

His parents moved to Lahaina to live in the home of his mother's parents after they both died. With his father's fishing and their well-tended garden, they got along on his retirement pay from the Honolulu Street Department.

"So, Mama, will you do my wash?"

He laughed when she pushed at him. "You bring wash home from the Army?"

"No, Mama, I only brought clean clothes." He hugged her one more time.

They walked over to the small porch in the front of the house. The house wasn't much to look at, a wide porch with board walls, but it had a sound roof that kept out the rain, and it overlooked the water and the waves. Even a painting could not create a better view.

His mother's voice pulled his attention from the water. "I will get you tea?"

"Mama, maybe just some water. It's too hot for tea." She looked at him until he relented. "All right, some tea would be very good, thank you."

His mother smiled and walked inside. "Yuki, come inside with me while I make the tea." He followed her in and sat while she heated the water.

"It is so good to see you. Your father will be very happy. It has been a long time."

He let the gentle rebuke pass without comment. "Mama, it's difficult to get away from the Army long enough to come over here. But my sergeant gave me a few days of leave and I thought I'd surprise you." His mother couldn't stop smiling as she bustled around her small, tidy kitchen, preparing tea for her son.

He decided he wouldn't say anything about the concerns everybody had. It was easier to visit and let them decide what to ask. She poured the steaming tea into small china cups. He waited until she sat, and then took the first sip while she watched. He knew she wouldn't drink until he had.

"As always, Mama, the tea is very good."

She smiled and lifted her cup. Together they sat, sipping the delicate warm liquid silently and watching one another, savoring the moment of reunion.

Hikosuke Watanabe came slowly through the door with fish wrapped in newspaper. It took him a moment before he realized there was someone else in the kitchen besides his wife.

"Yuki! Why did you not tell us you were coming? I would have been here when you came."

"I didn't know until this morning. I can only stay for two days, but my first sergeant let me have the time." He stood and walked to his father.

The men embraced one another. "It is good to see you, my son. You look fit."

"He looks thin, I think."

Yuki looked back at his mother. "You always say I look thin."

Chiyeko beamed while clucking her tongue in a show of concern over her son's weight. "We will make a special dinner."

Yuki laughed. "All your dinners are special, Mama. You know that."

~

After dinner, Yuki and his father walked outside to the porch. The moonlight spread over the water, glistening silver into the distance. Yuki looked up at the sky, the stars standing out against the blackness. It wasn't like Oahu, where the lights shut out the blackness of the sky and dulled the stars. Here the stars seemed so close.

He settled into a chair, staring up, his mind wandering. There was a small decanter of sake on the table between them. He waited while his father poured two cups and handed him one. "I know you, my son. There is something you are keeping inside. Is that why you are here?"

Yuki sipped the warm wine, pausing before he answered, watching the nighttime waves breaking on the shore, the phosphorescent foam slowly making its way up the beach with the tide. The water seemed to fold against the beach instead of crashing, the sound barely audible.

"Father, I don't know the answer to your question. I came because I wanted to see you and Mama, but I was encouraged by my sergeant to take this time. I believe he was trying to tell me that I might not have another opportunity to visit. Things are very bad for Issei and Nisei in California and Washington. We've heard rumors that Nisei in the Army have been detached from their units and sent to Southern states away from the coast. The papers say that our people have been moved by the government against their will and are living in horse stalls at racetracks in California. Some of the men in my unit think we'll be moved away too. I don't know. But I do know that if this happens, we won't see one another for a long time."

Hikosuke sat quietly while his son spoke. When Yuki finished he waited, giving the silence between them the opportunity to bring the right words.

"My son, we have heard some of these things too. We never know what the next day will bring. Our people have survived many thousands of years. This will pass and we will still be here. Do not question who we are loyal to. This is our country and we must do what our country asks. So must you. *Kuni no tame ni—for the sake of our country.*" His father lifted his cup to his lips and drank. Yuki nodded to his father and drank also. They sat quietly in the dark, sipping the slowly cooling wine and watching the waves rolling against the shore.

~

At noon the next day, Yuki walked down to the dock with his father and mother. He spent the morning with his mother telling her stories of the baseball games and what he did in the Army. He left out the concerns that he had expressed to his father. The delicate soya-flavored fish and sticky rice his mother had prepared were a welcome change from the repetitive diet of the military. His mother stood quietly looking up at him with glistening eyes. He was afraid he couldn't look at her for very long without becoming emotional. In his heart he knew that this might be the last time he saw them for a long while. In her eyes he saw that she knew this, too.

He could feel the hard lump in his throat when she pushed a cloth-wrapped package into his hands. He knew what was inside and would wait until he was on the boat to eat the pickled vegetables and sea-weed-wrapped rice.

His father stood quietly, his hands at his sides. "Yuki, you must be careful. You must do your duty." Yuki embraced his father and then turned to his mother. He placed his arms around her small shoulders and she grasped him tightly. He leaned down and kissed her on the cheek. "*Kuni no tame ni,*" she whispered. "You have always brought us great pride." He turned and boarded the boat, standing on the side as it pulled away.

Yuki watched until he could no longer make out their faces standing on the dock.

～

Yuki arrived at Schofield just before midnight. He walked quietly into the barracks after checking in with the nighttime duty officer. He felt like he had barely fallen asleep when he heard the men around him stirring and Tug shaking him awake. "Yuki, come on, we got duty." He slipped on clean fatigues and just had time to tie his boots before the morning formation.

Captain Coehlo stood in front of the men, waiting for them to quiet down before Ka'ne called them to attention. He waited until the platoon sergeants accounted for the men, and then he told them to be at ease. Already there were looks exchanged between the men. Something was different. Coehlo's voice focused their attention.

"First Sergeant Ka'ne will be calling out names and I want each man to fall out and report to Lieutenant Halder over by company headquarters. Any man whose name isn't called will remain at this location for further instructions." Ka'ne stepped forward and began calling names. It didn't take very long before it became obvious that no Japanese names were being called.

Finally, the big Hawaiian was finished. The Japanese men looked at one another and the reality of the situation became evident. He ordered them to close ranks and stand at attention.

Coehlo stepped up as close as he could to the first rank, looking at the men before he spoke. "Men, I have received orders from regimental command that all members of the Hawaiian National Guard who are of Japanese descent are to be detached from their units. This means every man in our 298th and every man in the 299th infantry regiments that are on the outer islands. My orders state that you will be transported to separate billeting here at Schofield Barracks. You will turn in your weapons to the supply sergeant prior to being transported. I want you to report back here in one hour with your gear packed, and your equipment ready to be turned in to supply."

With a voice cracking from emotion, Coehlo paused and then spoke. "We've served together for a long time. I didn't have a choice in this. All the men of Japanese descent are receiving the same instructions as you are right now. Please get your gear and reassemble." Coehlo turned and walked back toward company headquarters, leaving Ka'ne to supervise.

Tug turned to Yuki. "I told you they were going to do something to us. They're taking our rifles and equipment. We gonna be put in some kind of jail."

"Let's just get our gear. Maybe it won't be what you think." But Yuki knew it would be exactly what Tug thought. The men walked to the barracks. Angry words could be heard as they gathered gear and stuffed it into canvas barracks bags. They took their rifles and equipment to Supply and waited in line while each weapon was checked against its serial number and then secured. Kazo Suzuki slammed his rifle down on the desk in front of the supply sergeant, daring him to say something. As soon as it was over they returned to the company common area with their barracks bags, while Ka'ne watched quietly from the side.

Ka'ne told the men to board the idling trucks nearby. Yuki watched out of the back of the truck while they crossed Schofield. He could still see the trenches, fresh wounds to the once-groomed parade ground. He had sat in those trenches on the evening of December 7 prepared to fight. Yuki kept his face toward the outside of the truck. He didn't want anyone to see the tears coming down his cheeks.

When the trucks stopped, the first men out could see the compound. There were tents already made up inside an area surrounded by barbed wire. *Haole* soldiers were on the far corners of the compound perimeters. They were sitting idly behind sandbagged bunkers but the barrels of machine guns jutted up from the edge.

Yuki stared at the strands of barbed wire attached to posts stuck into the ground. He looked at the open gate. *Soldiers sleep in tents. Prisoners sleep behind barbed wire.*

CHAPTER 27

June 2, 1942

Schofield Barracks

Honolulu, Territory of Hawaii

Yuki looked around the theater for a seat. All of the men were trucked over on short notice and nobody knew what was going on. Some of them had thought they were finally being moved to a more permanent detention center, but when they saw the building was used for a theater they relaxed a little.

As they got out of the trucks, Tug started asking questions. He could tell Yuki seemed very focused. "You know something, Yuki? Like when we gonna get out of this shithole?"

"Maybe sooner than you think. I talked to Ka'ne. There's rumors all over the place. Word is they're going to make us some kind of special unit. But nobody's saying anything." He could see that he had their interest now.

Tug looked disgusted. "You believe that, Yuki? If we gonna be so special, how come they got barbed wire around us?"

"All I know is that they want everybody in one place. Ka'ne says the rumor is that they're going to make up a whole battalion—all Nisei."

Tug was still adamant. "Then why take our rifles and our other gear? I think we gonna go to camps, just like my cousin over in California."

"All I know is what Joe said. He says it's going to be okay. Look, I thought you would be glad to hear this. At least it's something to hang on to."

Everyone was shuffling around trying to find a seat when they heard a voice from the stage area, yelling to get their attention. They looked up to see a master sergeant they didn't recognize bellowing for them to quiet down. Immediately the room quieted and they each found a seat, looking at one another and wondering what was going to happen next. When he called them all to attention they snapped straight up and stood as Lt. Col. Farrant Turner and Maj. Jim Lovell, Yuki and Tug's high school coach, walked up the steps to the stage.

Colonel Turner came up to the microphone. He was forty-five years old, his hair already turning gray and his waist thickening. He had graduated from the Punahou School on Oahu and from college on the mainland. He served in World War I as a captain, and was a National Guard officer when the unit was activated.

Born and raised in the islands, he had fought to gain command of the battalion. He knew that General Emmons thought he was too old to be a battalion commander and that it was only his community support that had decided the issue in his favor. But he knew the boys in the unit. And he wanted to make an impression.

"At ease. Please take your seats."

Major Jim Lovell stood next to Turner. He coached baseball and football in Honolulu. Many of the boys staring back at him had been on his teams. Ramrod straight and muscular from constant physical training, Lovell stood off to the side while Turner looked out over the sea of brown faces waiting for him to say something. At least he was a familiar face to the boys from the 298th. It wasn't hard for Yuki to notice the shiny gold leaves on Lovell's uniform.

Turner started to address the men. *"First of all, I know you've been wondering why you were removed from your units and taken to the area where you've been. I want to make it clear to you that there was a reason for that decision. I want to apologize for any discomfort you have had over the past few days and I want to assure you that all of this is going to change.

*"It certainly comes as no secret to any man here that we're at war. We all saw what happened on December 7 and some of us even lost friends and family there. The attack by the empire of Japan has made it hard on you and your families. I know that. The Army knows that. Maybe we haven't handled this situation very well. I'm hoping that is all going to change starting right now.

"A decision has been made in Washington at the request of General Emmons of the Hawaiian Defense Command to create a new unit called the Hawaiian Provisional Infantry Battalion. All you men are going to be placed in that unit, an all-Japanese infantry battalion."*

Turner waited to see the reaction of the men. He could see most of them looking at one another with smiles on their faces. Some were grinning. Some weren't.

"It will be my privilege to be the commanding officer of this unit. Major Lovell, who many of you already know, will be the executive officer. Most of the officers from your old units that are of Japanese descent, as well as some of the white officers, will be transferred into the new unit along with you. If I have anything to say about it we're going to be a combat unit. And we're going to be different from anything the Army has seen before. I intend for this to be the best damned fighting battalion in the Army." The cheering and foot stomping overwhelmed anything else he had to say for the moment.

Turner looked at Lovell, who was grinning from ear to ear. Lovell held up his hands for quiet. Turner had everyone's undivided attention.

"Okay, now for the bad news. Most of you have never been off these islands. You have families here, friends here. Some of you are married. I was born here and my wife and children are here. Major Lovell was a coach at McKinley High and Roosevelt High where a lot of you men went. He has a wife and daughter here. Well, we're going to be leaving all of them behind in the next few days. What I am going to say to you needs to be kept secret. The enemy is all around us listening. This is now a military operation and you won't have much time for anything. Most of you won't even have a chance to say goodbye to loved ones. This unit is shipping out in the next few days. We're being sent to the mainland for more training as a fighting unit. What that means is that when we're through training we're going to be sent into battle. I don't know where and I don't know when. I don't know how many of us will be coming back. But all of you know what we're fighting for. We're not just fighting for pride, we're fighting for the home that we have made here in Hawaii. We're fighting for our way of life. I know I can count on you."

~

Yuki spent the rest of the day making sure the men in his squad readied their equipment. He shook his head in frustration. These guys were slow. He pulled his equipment out of the tent and set it nearby. Men all over the camp were doing the same thing. Some were already striking their tents and folding the stiff canvas so it would be ready for pickup.

A few radios were still plugged into the electrical cables running through what was left of the camp. The interruption of the music for a special bulletin caught everyone's attention. Midway Island was under attack. That meant only one thing—Hawaii was vulnerable. Work slowed to a standstill as men listened for any piece of news.

By late afternoon, the tent compound was disassembled. Yuki and the other sergeants already received their instructions and were getting their men on the trucks outside the barbed wire compound. Everybody got into a rough line and they walked to the waiting trucks. Radio broadcasts repeated the same small bit of news over and over again, interrupting with air raid instructions and civil defense communications. The men walked with a heavy step as they climbed into the trucks. The reality of leaving was before them.

By the time they got to the dock it was almost dark. The men all looked up at the ship tied to the dock, with gangplanks bridging the gap between dock and ship. Yuki could see her name in the thin light still remaining before the blackout—the S.S. *Maui*. He pulled his men into line behind him and they started to board the ship.

Tug was still talking, as usual. "Hey, we got no leis. How we gonna toss leis into the water to make sure we return home?"

Some of the men muttered their agreement. It was a long standing tradition in the islands. You took your lei off as you left the islands. It would float back to shore as a symbol that you, too, would return. Tug looked around. "No lei, bad luck."

Yuki looked back. "Forget the leis. We don't even know where we're going. None of us even been on a ship before. Just relax."

Tug moved to the side and Yuki could hear the hollow sound of something banging against Tug's side. "What've you got with you?"

Tug reached back and pulled out a ukulele. "What we gonna do without music."

Kazo looked over at Tug and spoke up before anyone else had a chance. "More bigger problem. What we gonna do if we have to listen to your music all the way to mainland?" The others laughed as they moved slowly up the gangplank and into the unfamiliar territory of the ship.

~

Yuki could feel a change in the noise of the boat as the low rumble of the engines began to rise in intensity. There was a shudder and the sense of movement, even though they were all in one large area with no openings. They were definitely moving. He sat up and put on his boots. "I'm going to go see what's happening." He hopped off his bunk and walked to the stairs to the upper passageway leading to the deck.

He heard heavy footsteps behind him and looked back to see Tug following along. "You might need help."

Yuki nodded. Just standing in the open area of the passageway made him feel like he had been set free. They could feel the air movement from the passageway doors leading to the deck as they walked out.

Most of the people at the ship's rail were Army and Navy wives being moved out of Hawaii on the same ship as the Hawaiian Provisional Battalion. Yuki and Tug managed to find an open spot at the railing. Looking out at the dock, they could see others watching the ship. If their departure was supposed to be a secret, then it was a secret shared by several hundred people who crowded to the edge of the dock and watched the widening separation as the *Maui*'s tugs pushed her out into the channel.

Yuki and Tug looked behind them as more and more men came through the passageway. *How long would it be before I see these shores again?* Each man kept that thought to himself as he tried to etch into his mind the rising mountains behind Honolulu, as he pulled the last of the island air into his lungs.

~

As soon as the first word came down into the hold that the mainland had been sighted, Yuki, Tug, Kazo, and the rest were up on the deck, craning their necks to see as much as possible. None of them had ever been to the mainland and some had only seen their own island from a short distance out to sea. This land stretched as far as they could see in both directions.

The sky was crystal clear and the sun made the water dance with light as the *Maui* moved toward the entrance to San Francisco Bay. Barrage blimps were up to provide cover for the convoy, but it was the Golden Gate Bridge that held their attention. They all stared at the orange span stretched across the harbor. The two massive towers rose up on either side, dwarfing the *Maui*. Their heads moved back and forth from the towering bridge to the sight of fabled San Francisco. Yuki stared at a stone tower on a hill that alone was bigger than any building in Honolulu.

Tugboats moved to nose the *Maui* into a berth at the Oakland docks. Their eyes stayed fixed on the buildings on both sides of the bay. The whole expanse was larger than anything they had ever seen.

Yuki looked at the men swarming the dock as lines were thrown. Tug noticed it first: Everyone was white. This was a different kind of place.

His attention was brought back by Lieutenant Mizuta of Company B. Mizuta walked along the deck, letting the men know that they needed to get their gear packed. They were not going to disembark until after dark, and he expected every man ready. Already those on the dock were looking up and staring at the brown faces lining the deck. Everyone went below quickly to wait out their final hours on the gently swaying ship.

Darkness came slowly for the impatient men. The troops moved quickly, partly to get ashore but partly to get into the fresh air and out of the fetid atmosphere in the hold. B Company moved into position on the dock while the other companies did the same. Yuki had his squad in order and they waited while the HQ staff looked over the assembled battalion. Each company announced that it was "all present or accounted for," and Colonel Turner nodded as he listened to the company commander's report.

Turner walked to the front of the assembled ranks. "All right men, there are several things you need to know. First off, when we get to our destination your families will be notified that you are here and safe. Any letters that you have will be mailed once we reach our destination. From this time on you are the 100th Infantry Battalion, Separate. I need you to move onto the trucks waiting here to take you all to the trains. Company commanders, you have your instructions. Form your men up and move them out."

Yuki and the rest moved to a waiting truck. The drivers stood outside looking at the small brown men climbing into the backs of the covered trucks. It wasn't hard to hear the comments from the drivers.

"These guys are all Japs!" The men stared straight ahead, but Yuki could feel himself bristling at the comments. All of a sudden he heard their captain, Clarence Johnson, say, "Private, these boys are all Americans. You have a problem driving them?"

"No, sir, but they just ain't what I expected, sir."

"Yeah, well I don't think you're what they expected either. So get us to the train." Johnson had just established himself with his company.

B Company moved on board a darkened train. The engine was belching smoke from the coal-fired boiler, settling around the boarding area. Most of the men had never been on a train, and the choking smoke was hard to breathe. First a ship and now a train. They moved inside and found seats.

Tug started to pull up a shade when Mizuta told him to keep it down. "No shades up unless we tell you. Just settle in and get comfortable. We're going to be on this train for several days. May as well just get some sleep. And you"—Mizuta pointed at Tug—"don't even think about taking out that ukelele. These boys need sleep and I don't want to listen to it right now. There will be plenty of time for noise later."

~

Yuki couldn't help wondering how much longer they would be stuck on the train. At first it was a novelty. But after a few hours it was almost as unbearable in the train car as it had been in the hold of the *Maui*. He couldn't get used to the constant smell of sweating men and cigarette smoke mingled with the ever-present odor of engine smoke. It was a difficult combination for a young man used to clean breezes off the ocean and flower-scented air.

It was clear now that all the men from what was now called the 100th were not on the same train as Yuki and Tug. At least two other trains took the rest. Even Mizuta didn't know where they were going. The drawn shades were an increasing source of agitation, and most of the men pulled them up to get a look. Mizuta frequently walked through the car, ignoring the cracks of light coming through.

When they stopped at the border of California and Nevada, the men were unable to contain their curiosity and raised their shades to look out. What they saw was unlike anything they had ever seen: Brown as far as they could see; stretches of sand; dry, wooden-looking brush; and railroad workers laboring on track repair.

Tug grabbed his friend's arm. "Yuki, you hear what some of the boys call us? We the One Puka Puka now." Tug laughed. "We not the 100th Battalion anymore. Make it more Hawaiian, right?" He repeated the words again, "One Puka Puka. I think that more better."

Yuki leaned back and closed his eyes. Maybe there was going to be another stop soon. The last one hadn't been so bad. Red Cross workers had come on the train with coffee and doughnuts. *The One Puka Puka? That was a good name for Hawaii boys.* Puka meant "hole" in Hawaiian, and it also meant zero when it was in a telephone number. *Yes, the One Puka Puka—that was okay.* He dozed off to the sound of the train car.

～

Four days later, the shades were up all the time. The desert gave way to mountains. The mountains gave way to flat expanses of grassy plain, which in turn gave way to rolling green hills. Yuki looked out at the forests that dominated the scenery for the last several hours. It wasn't anything like home, tall trees reaching a hundred feet in the air and lakes and ponds that had geese and ducks in them. Everywhere they looked there was no ocean in the distance, only trees on the horizon and more fields. There were tall round buildings that they seemed to pass all the time. One of the boys said they were for grain. And the cows. He had never seen so many cows in his life.

Yuki watched the dusk settle in and then felt the train begin to slow. Tug was snoring beside him and startled awake when the train stopped. Tug stretched over Yuki's shoulder and looked straight into his face. "Yuki, look. They got guard towers out there. That fence got barbwire on it."

All over the train, men were beginning to raise their voices. They moved over to the side to see the fence and the unmistakable watchtowers. The thought that they had come all this way to be imprisoned was more than any of them could bear. Yuki slumped back against his seat. How could he have been so wrong? He looked over at Tug, who just stared at the high wire fence.

For thirty minutes everyone sat in relative silence, occasionally punctuated by expressions of anger at how they had been tricked. The old man said they were going to be a fighting unit. Yuki could feel the confusion inside him.

The lurching movement of the train as it started forward again caused everyone to tense up. Yuki watched as the train moved past the barbwire fence line and into open country again. But now the feeling of tension and fear was throughout the car. They had seen it. They didn't know that the train had stopped at a stockade for German prisoners of war.

After less than an hour, the train came to a stop and the lieutenant walked into the car. "Okay, get your gear. This is it! We're moving off the train. Line up with your squad leaders and let's get off this damn thing."

He didn't have to ask twice. Everyone was pulling out what little gear they had and pushing toward the train car door. Their legs were stiff from lack of use. Every man just wanted off.

The air outside was cool and smelled fresh. Not like Hawaii, but fresh, like clean clothes. It was already dusk, and the light was fading quickly. Yuki looked around for the source of the sounds that were all around him. He had never heard birds like that before. Little bugs glowed in the dark, dancing all around them. It wasn't long before men began slapping at their faces as bugs settled on them, pulling blood out and making red bumps. The men were looking at one another with expressions of amazement.

Captain Johnson walked to the front of Company B, looking up and down the ranks to make sure everyone was there. He turned to his platoon leaders. "We got all of them?" He walked to the front of the company.

"Okay boys, we're here. And that sound you all hear—those are what these folks call cicadas—crickets. You'll get used to it. And the bugs that glow, they're called fireflies. Those other bugs that are biting you—they're called mosquitoes. Welcome to Camp McCoy, Wisconsin. This is going to be our new home."

CHAPTER 28

June 19, 1942

Fresno Assembly Center

Fresno, California

The room held the rising heat of summer. Everybody knew that the real heat had not yet begun. The heavy, still air settled in the wooden walled stalls where it became trapped, bringing out the smell of horses. The only ventilation was the door. Sammy kept his shirt off as long as possible. Eventually he put on his white shirt and carefully combed his hair in silence. Today was supposed to be a day of celebration, but the most treasured member of the family would not be there to share it with him.

The death of *Obasan* had a profound impact on him. It had made Sammy realize that life was not forever. He had not thought about that before and was seeing the effect on his family. His father spoke very little in the weeks following *Obasan*'s funeral. Grandmother had always been a part of their life and now she was gone. He never realized how difficult it was to hold a picture of someone's face in your mind. Even now, so soon after her funeral, he could not see her clearly.

He looked at his mother and father dressing with as much privacy and modesty as the small room permitted. He couldn't imagine not having them. It seemed that those moments alone with *Obasan*, as she lay in the stillness of death, changed him somehow. He began to realize that he needed to help his family as a man, and not as a boy. He just wasn't sure yet what was expected of a man. He hoped that with time it would come to him.

He cleaned the dust from his shoes as best he could. Arrangements had been made for the high school seniors in the Assembly Center to graduate. It wasn't going to be anything like what he had expected, but his parents insisted that he go. Freddy's parents had done the same. They all walked over to the bleachers near the grandstand to the racetrack.

A small platform had been set up with chairs in front of it. All one hundred forty-four of the seniors had practiced earlier in the afternoon. But there would be no valedictorians, no graduation parties. Those were the parts that he had anticipated, and they, too, had been taken from him.

"Good evening. I am Dr. Hubert Phillips, Professor of Social Science at Fresno State College. I'm here to make a few brief remarks before all of you receive your diplomas this evening. Congratulations on your graduation from high school." The man seemed to lose his train of thought for a moment as he looked out at the solemn young faces staring back at him. The entire assembly center turned out for the graduation. The strangeness of the moment was not lost on him. These people were prisoners and yet they were having their own graduation, just like thousands of other young people all over the state. He looked down at his prepared remarks that, he hoped, would make the situation a little better. Now, as he looked at the faces of the young people staring at him, he doubted his words would have any effect at all.

*"We are making history tonight. This is the first commencement of its kind ever held in the United States. But making history is not new to you, for whether you know it or not, you have been making history the past few weeks in that you are the first American citizens who, as a group, have had your liberty restrained and your usual routine of life interrupted without formal charges of crime or disorder being made against you. It is a thrilling experience to make history. If one can keep his perspective, if one can see things in the large; if one can distinguish between real causes and protests that are advanced as causes; and above all, if one can control his emotions and think calmly and coolly. Had things continued in their normal courses, all of you who will receive diplomas here tonight would have graduated in twenty-three different classes in twenty-three different communities of this state. In that case you would have been shown all the honors and dignities that the other members of your class received. Many

of you would have received those scholarship honors, along with your diplomas tonight. You graduates, Americans in every sense of the word, have been caught in an accident of history. Loyalty makes itself known quietly and no other group has had so much contact with you as your teachers. They believe in your loyalty. Their belief is part of the reason that you are here tonight. You can be resentful, cynical, and bitter or you can be understanding, calm, long suffering . . ."*

Sammy sat quietly listening to the speaker. His mind drifted to what would have been, a party thrown by his parents like Toshi had. He was ashamed for feeling sorry for himself. He looked to the side. Everybody else was in the same position. He could sense movements of boredom as shirts and blouses stuck to the backs of the graduates. Freddy looked over at him. It was clear that he was resentful. His face didn't hide it.

The speaker raised his voice.

". . . Americanism is over and above color or racial characteristics. It is an ideal that was never realized by the forefathers of this country. It is a dream which they hoped would come true—a land of equal opportunities and rights as set forth in the Declaration of Independence. You can still help make that dream come true."

Phillips sat down to rousing applause. He listened quietly as one of the graduates, Haruo Kawamoto, spoke on a topic listed as "The Rights We Defend." Then another graduate, Mary Kishiu, spoke on her chosen topic, "We Face the Future." Phillips could not help considering the poignancy of the moment, these young people still finding optimism in what he could only contemplate as a dreadful and bizarre situation.

Dr. Phillips paused while the names of the graduates were read from a list. Mr. Pulliam, the Center manager, presented diplomas to the students, sent by each of their schools. Each graduate walked up to the platform when his or her name was called. Sammy walked up to the edge of the podium and then across to Dr. Phillips. The balding man shook his hand and congratulated him while the audience applauded. Sammy grasped the small bound diploma. He would look at it later.

The graduation ceremony did not last very long, and all the graduates filed out quietly when it was over. They sought out their parents and family but there would be no pictures. Cameras were not permitted.

Toshi waved Sammy over as he looked around to see if any guards were watching. He pulled a camera out of his bag.

Setsuko looked up and her eyes widened. "No, Toshi. Cameras are not allowed." She looked around, frightened that her son would be arrested.

Toshi waved off her concerns. "Just get together as fast as you can. I'll have the picture over before anyone knows." He saw Freddy watching. "Get over here, Freddy. I'm only going to do this once."

Freddy scrambled over and stood next to Sammy while Toshi took the picture. "I'm not using a flash bulb so I don't know how this is going to turn out. Just hold still." He aimed the camera and framed the picture. Maybe someday it would be a good memory. He snapped it quickly and put the camera back in the bag.

"Hello, boys." Sammy and Freddy turned around at the sound of the deep voice they had heard so many times on the ball field. Coach Hubbard was standing there. He reached out and shook hands with each of them. "I watched from the bleachers. Had a hard time getting in this place but I told the soldier at the gate that I was a baseball coach for you boys."

He reached into a folder that he was carrying. "Here's your varsity letters. Thought you might want them. I'm just sorry you couldn't get them at a school assembly with the rest of the team." The coach seemed to be reaching for words. He finally just handed over the green and gold letters.

Sammy and Freddy took the cloth letters and stared at them. Sammy looked up at his coach. The letter meant more to him than the diploma. "Thanks, Coach. I'm glad you came." Freddy took the letter and nodded his thanks, staring down at the heavy woven cloth.

Hubbard looked embarrassed. "You two earned those letters. All the boys talked about it. They wanted to make sure you got them." Hubbard shook hands with Shig and Mas, who had been watching quietly.

"You got good boys here. I'm real sorry about all this." It was obvious Coach was uncomfortable with the situation. He nodded to the two boys. "You take care now. Stop by and see me when this foolishness is over." He walked back toward the front gate.

Freddy stayed quiet during the ceremony. The speeches had only made him angrier. He twisted the letter around in his hands and looked over at Sammy. He couldn't seem to control how he felt. The varsity letter seemed to represent everything that was wrong. Right now he didn't want to talk to anybody. He turned and walked away.

Sammy stood there, watching Freddy leave the graduation area. He looked down at the varsity letter in his hand. There was a time when the piece of cloth would have been sewn on a sweater that he could wear to school. There would be no sweater now, no graduation dance, no moment to walk by the underclassmen and swagger. None of that would ever happen. He rubbed his fingers across the nubby cloth, feeling its texture. He turned and started walking when his eye caught green and gold in the dirt. Sammy reached down. It was Freddy's letter.

CHAPTER 29

July 19, 1942
Needles, California

K im got his crew up out of the shade of the truck. The tank-like treads in the back made a convenient spot to rest their backs. There was another radio call about a thrown track and they had to go find the disabled vehicle. He looked at the map coordinates and then herded his men into the back of their truck. They moved out all the benches in the back and set up their tools. It was where they worked, slept, and ate. For all intents and purposes it was home as long as they stayed out in the sand practicing desert maneuvers.

"Let's move it. We got a halftrack broken down about a half hour from here." He climbed into the cab and pointed the direction to the driver. "That way." For some reason, it always surprised people that Kim seemed to know instinctively where he was going. He couldn't explain it either, but Captain Simmons relied on his sense of direction to find the unit. Wherever it was. He never seemed to get lost.

Kim picked up a can of grapefruit juice that was halfway finished, left over from what passed for lunch. He discovered that the unsweetened juice quenched his thirst better than anything else. He was grateful to be riding in the cab. The metal bottom and sides of the halftrack were like an oven, and the men were slow to move back in.

He leaned out the door. "Come on, let's move it. We got a broken track out there." He waited for the inevitable grumbling to stop and heard the slap on the back of the cab when all the men were in.

The broken halftrack was mired in the sand near a gully. Kim got his crew out and surveyed the problem—these vehicles threw a track all the time. He couldn't figure out what use they would be in an actual combat situation, but that was not his problem. His problem was making sure they worked. He ordered one of the men to throw down a thick wooden pole to pry under the track. He couldn't understand why they didn't just train the men to fix their own halftracks. He worked without thinking much about what he was doing. He had to get a letter written to Ida tonight and he used his concentration to compose what he would say.

After they came in from the day's maneuvers, Captain Simmons told Kim they needed to talk. Kim hoped Simmons was happy with his work. He didn't want to disappoint him. Simmons had been his lieutenant at Basic and pulled him into Cannon Company when he took it over. Kim appreciated the confidence.

Kim washed up and then walked over to the Cannon Company headquarters tent. He waited at the open flap and cleared his throat to catch Captain Simmons' attention.

"Kim, come on in. I'm glad you came by. I've been wanting to talk to you for a while now. Have a seat." Kim moved over to the canvas stool that passed for a chair and waited for Simmons to tell him what he had on his mind.

"Kim, I want you to know that I think you have exceptional ability. That's one of the reasons I asked for you to be assigned to my company." The young captain waited to see if the usually taciturn Kim would respond. Kim just sat looking at him, his face expressionless. "I have some papers I want you to sign."

Kim looked at the small sheaf of papers on Captain Simmons' desk. "What are they?"

"It's an application to Officer's Candidate School."

"Where? To the Ordinance School?"

"No, to the infantry school. I think you would make an excellent officer and if you're agreeable, I'd like to recommend you for OCS." Simmons once again waited for Kim's reaction. He didn't expect to see much. Kim never showed much difference in facial expression, no matter his mood. But it did seem that he was a little taken by surprise, his eyes opened wider than normal.

"An officer? Captain, I wasn't allowed to be an infantryman when I finished Basic. Do you really think they're going to let me be an officer? I mean, why would I go to infantry school?"

"Kim, I've talked to some of the other officers and we all agree. We think you should go to OCS. The Army is going to need a lot of good leaders to get us through this war. You're too smart and too well-educated to be an enlisted man."

"Well, if I've got to compete against all these other sergeants who've been with the regular units, I'll never make it to Fort Benning."

"Don't worry—you will. I was your second lieutenant in charge of your Basic Training and I know you have the capabilities to be an excellent officer. You can do this. I've prepared the application forms and they're right here. I want you to sign them and I'll get the process started. You're going to have to go through a couple of interviews, but I don't think you'll have any problem."

He pointed to the bottom of the application and held out a pen. "All you have to do is sign." Simmons continued to hold the pen out, waiting for some response.

Kim looked down at the forms and back up at Captain Simmons. "You really think I have a chance at this?"

"Look, your testing scores are very high and clearly are well within the standards for an officer. Your leadership ability is excellent, and your ability to know where you are is uncanny. Sign the papers and we'll get started."

Kim took the pen from Simmons' hand. "All right, Captain. Nothing to lose, I guess." He signed his name.

"You're going to have to take some tests, so I'll tell you when you need to stay in from the field. Go get something to eat and some sleep. We've got a long day in the field tomorrow. The way I hear it, Patton wants his boys to go through more training before they ship out."

Kim stood up. "Captain, I appreciate this. Thank you for giving me a chance."

"Nothing to thank me for, Sergeant. Any chance you got, you earned. Good night."

"Thank you, sir, good night."

Kim turned and walked out of the tent into the cool evening air. *An officer?* It was more than he had hoped for. It was also unexpected. He had only set his sights on being a combat soldier. He never dreamed of this. He smiled to himself, forgetting the resentment he had held in for so long about not being given a chance. Maybe all that was behind him. Now he would have something to write Ida about.

~

Kim spent the morning carefully preparing himself for the interview process. He polished his boots and straightened his uniform as best he could. He walked into the large tent where the interviews took place and looked around. There were a lot of sergeants in the room, and almost all of them were senior to him. He went over to the clerk who was signing people in and put his name down.

"Just take a seat, Sergeant Kim, and I'll call your name when they're ready. This is probably going to take a couple of hours, so make yourself comfortable."

He found himself a metal chair and looked around, watching as one man after another went in. It seemed like the process took forever and nobody came out looking happy. It didn't inspire confidence in him.

"Sergeant Kim? They're ready for you now."

Kim walked in and looked at the three officers seated at a long table.

"Sergeant Kim, take a seat please. Just relax. We have a few questions."

A major sat in the middle. Kim didn't know him, and he braced himself for the first question.

"Sergeant, please give us your name, rank, and tell us about the job you currently are assigned and your schooling."

"Sir, my name is Young Oak Kim, Tech Sergeant. I graduated from high school in Los Angeles. I am currently the motor pool sergeant assigned to Cannon Company."

"You like working in the motor pool, Sergeant?"

"To be honest with you, sir, I want to be in a combat unit. Being in the motor pool is all right but I want to be in the field, sir." He hoped that didn't sound like he was dissatisfied with the Army or his assignment but it was the truth. He didn't see much of a reaction. A few more questions and it was all over.

"Thank you, Sergeant, we'll let you know."

He got up, saluted, and walked out of the interview area. It hadn't taken more than fifteen minutes, far shorter than the others.

~

Kim had been told to see Captain Simmons at Cannon Company HQ. He figured it was to let him know he hadn't made it to OCS. He completed three interviews and none of them had been longer than fifteen or twenty minutes. It seemed to him that they were just going through the process. He was just sorry that he had let Captain Simmons down after he put so much confidence in him. Simmons' repeated assurances that he was doing fine hadn't helped. Nobody seemed really interested in asking him tough questions. Just the same thing over and over.

He walked through the open tent flap to Simmons' office.

"Sir, you asked to see me?"

"Sergeant Kim, come on in." He walked in and saluted.

"Kim, you still want to be an officer?"

"Yes sir, but I don't think the interviews have gone very well."

"They went well enough, Sergeant. You've been accepted to OCS. You should have your orders in a few days. Congratulations. In a few months you're going to be a lieutenant." Simmons held out his hand.

Kim took it, looking at Simmons with some uncertainty. "I made it, Captain? I mean, they never asked me many questions. I figured they were just going through the motions."

"I told you not to worry. Look, they just wanted to make sure you could carry on a conversation and had the composure and ability I said you did. There was never any doubt."

It was obvious that Simmons was happy for him and Kim allowed himself the beginning of a smile. "Thanks, Captain. I don't know what to say."

"You don't have to say anything, Sergeant. Just be the officer I know you can be."

Kim stood at attention and saluted. "Yes, sir, thank you, sir."

Simmons laughed. "You're welcome, Sergeant."

~

Kim carefully packed his uniforms and few personal possessions into his barracks bag. He was scheduled to leave on the 1:00 p.m. train out of

San Luis Obispo and he wanted to say goodbye to a few friends, and to Captain Simmons, especially.

Durham walked in before he finished packing. "Kim, thought I'd stop by and say goodbye. You'll make a better officer than a mechanic." He laughed and put out his hand. "Wanted to tell you thanks for all your help with my papers and such and let you know I wish I could go over with you. They're not going to let me fight. I'll be lucky if they let me stay in, what with my vision and all. Anyway, somebody's got to stay here and make sure you boys get trained up right. Look, I'm glad we're both leaving as friends. A man needs friends, you know."

Kim knew how difficult that statement had been for Bull. "Thanks. I'll do the best I can. You taught me a lot."

Durham stared at Kim before responding. "Maybe we both taught each other something. See you around the Army." Durham seemed to search for something more to say and then coughed. "Hey, I got you a ride to the train station so you won't have to take the bus. Be over at the motor pool at 11:00. I got a driver waitin'."

"Thanks, I'll be there. I'm going over to say goodbye to Captain Simmons."

"I'll see you."

"See you, Bull." Durham turned and walked out of the barracks. Kim thought for a moment about how strange their path together had been. Even though they started out as antagonists, they were parting as friends.

～

Kim got off the train in Columbus, Georgia. The first thing he noticed was the humidity. It was like breathing in a shower. He looked around at the unfamiliar pine trees and the red earth. Not much to write home about. He saw a master sergeant standing on the platform near the station with a sign that said "Fort Benning." He picked up his barracks bag and walked over.

"I'm Sergeant Kim. Supposed to report to Fort Benning for OCS training." He waited for a response but didn't get any. The sergeant looked like he had fought every battle in the First World War and maybe even some before that. His face was creased and lined in every direction and looked like water-stained leather. Kim had the distinct impression that the sergeant didn't care and, what's more, wasn't impressed with officer candidates going to Benning.

"Yeah, you and every other sorry-ass clown gettin' off'n this train. Just stand there near the wall while I get all you wannabes together. Got a truck to take you to Benning." He resumed looking at the people getting off the train and held his sign in front of him.

Finally, a group of about fifteen men gathered near the sergeant. "All you wannabe shave tails get on that truck over there. I'll be along shortly." There wasn't any question that the sergeant took some measure of pleasure in handing out disrespect to the candidates. Kim figured he was just trying to get his licks in now, while he still could.

When they got to Fort Benning, Kim got off the truck with the rest of the men. The same sergeant that met them at the train walked around to the group.

"My name's Master Sergeant Peel. You boys call me Master Sergeant Peel for right now. When this is over, most of you will still be calling me Master Sergeant Peel and I may be calling one or two of you sir. The rest of you will be outta here and back in the ranks. Now get in line over there by the Company headquarters. You sign in and the clerk'll give you a meal card and start your processin'. Be back here at 3:00 p.m. this afternoon. We got ninety days to turn you into what passes for officers in this Army and I'll be helpin' to decide whether you make it or not. It would be real bad if you started out pissin' me off." Everybody looked at one another while Peel just turned and walked off. Kim reported in as directed.

At 3:00 p.m. Kim made sure he was in the company area for formation. He saw Peel standing and looking at all the men moving into the area. He noticed was that he was the only Asian in the group. Peel immediately yelled at all of them to form ranks, and they quickly gathered into some semblance of order to wait for instructions.

"All you men listen up. I want you to form up accordin' to the first letter of your last name. All the A's over here, the B's here, and so on. If you know the first letter of your last name then you got the makins' of an officer. Now move it."

The commotion and chaos was unbelievable. After a while things settled down and the men stood in about twenty clusters, asking each other what their names were so they could make sure that at least they were standing in the right group with two or three others.

Peel walked down the line, looking at the groups. He stopped.

"What group you in, soldier?"

"T, sir, I mean Sergeant. My name's Thompson."

Peel leaned in until he was right in Thompson's face. His voice was quiet, but everyone could hear it.

"Well, Thompson, I didn't tell you that you could call me Sergeant did I? What did I say you could call me?"

"Master Sergeant Peel."

"That's right, I told you to call me Master Sergeant Peel. You don't have permission to call me just Sergeant. Is that clear?"

"Yes, sir, Master Sergeant Peel."

"Better. The other thing Thompson is—don't call me sir. I'm not a sir. You should know that. I don't want to be a sir. I want to be what I am, which is a master sergeant, and I have a feeling that you're never going to be a sir, Thompson. And I already know you'll never be a master sergeant."

He turned to the man next to Thompson. "What's your name?"

"Schultz, Master Sergeant Peel."

Peel looked over at Thompson and then turned to Schultz. "Well, Schultz, why are you standing with the T group instead of with the S group?"

Schultz looked over at Thompson with growing pity. "This is the S group, Master Sergeant Peel."

Peel looked at the seven other men standing near Schultz. "All you men's names start with S?" Everyone nodded and waited for what they knew was coming next.

Peel turned back to Thompson. "Well, Thompson, I said if you knew what the first letter of your last name was you had the makins' of an officer. You evidently thought your last name was Shithead. Now get your sorry ass over in the group what's name starts with T."

Peel looked around. "I'm going to give you all just one minute to make sure you're in the right group. After that if anybody can't figure out what group they's supposed to be in then I'll make sure his ass is back on the truck headed for home. Any questions?"

The master sergeant looked at the group like a sleepy crocodile and waited for the mumbling and nervous glances at one another to subside. Nobody else moved. Peel nodded. "Good, I guess we got us a start then."

Kim looked cautiously out of the corner of his eye at the three men standing next to him. All of them were doing the same thing. Peel divided them up into groups of four as he moved down the ranks. When he got to Kim he looked him up and down, focusing on the stripes on Kim's arm. Then he smiled. His smile left the uneasy feeling that he would just as soon have you for lunch than look at you. "What's your name, boy?"

Kim had been through this before. If you just kept your mouth shut and didn't let it get to you, it would be fine, but he wasn't going to back down, not on the first day.

"Kim, Master Sergeant Peel. *Sergeant* Young Oak Kim." He put the emphasis on his rank and looked directly back at Peel.

"You plannin' on being an officer, Kim?"

"Yes, Master Sergeant Peel."

Peel didn't take his eyes off the young Asian man staring back at him with narrow black eyes. He nodded his head. "We'll see. You got four men in your group, including you. You boys will be a team. You bunk together, eat together, and shit together for all I care. Everything you do, you do it together. You got it, *Sergeant* Kim?"

"Yes, Master Sergeant Peel."

"Good." Peel moved on down the line, dividing them up as they counted off. There were at least 200 men in the ranks. When he was finished, he stepped back.

"All right, you got ten minutes to get to know the men in your team. Smoke if you got 'em, but make sure you police your butts. For all you *officers* out there, that means pick up them butts off the ground so's workin' soldiers don't have to."

Kim turned around with the other three as they walked over to the shade by the barracks. The tallest of the group looked at Kim. "What's your name other than K?" He spoke with a heavy Southern accent.

"My name's Kim, Young Oak Kim. Yours?"

"Kyle, they call me G.G. Where you from, Kim?"

"California—L.A. Where you from?"

"Why I'm from right here in Columbus, Georgia—God's country. This here's you boys' lucky day cuz my family's right here, and we got someplace to go eat besides this mess hall soon's they let us out of here. How about you, what's your name?"

"Kloch, Joe Kloch. From Massachusetts."

Kim had almost as much trouble understanding him as he did understanding Kyle. He wasn't used to the way these boys talked.

Kyle continued on. "And you, what's your name and where you from?"

"Koontz, Bill Koontz, from Wisconsin. I was in the newspaper business. How about you fellows?"

Kyle said he was in the family banking business. Kloch said he was just going to school and decided to try the Army. They looked at Kim. He shrugged. "I was in the grocery business."

Kyle pulled on his cigarette, then stripped off the ash and put what was left of the butt into his pocket. "Well, boys, I guess we're a team. So we better learn to like each other cuz I don't think we're going to get any sympathy from Master Sergeant Peel. Anything any of you boys are good at? I didn't come to OCS because I like gettin' my ass chewed."

Kim looked around at the others. "I'm pretty good with maps and directions and I'm a pretty good shot."

Kloch laughed. "You're good with maps? Good, because I'm a city boy and I get lost unless there are street signs. I'll just watch where you're going." They all laughed and started moving back to the formation to wait for more instructions.

CHAPTER 30

September, 1942
Calwa, California

Four months had passed since Shig and his family moved to the fairgrounds. Other than the funeral for Sammy's grandmother, Sack had not seen the family. People around town were divided on the issue. Some thought all the Japanese should be locked up and some thought it was unfair. Since the move to the fairgrounds there hadn't been much in the papers about it. Not that he read the papers much. But he had heard talk that the government was going to move all of them to camps in different parts of the country. There was nothing he could do about it. But he sometimes thought about the unfairness of it all. He bore no ill will toward anybody, even when others made comments assuming that he should hate the Japanese because of his arm. He didn't want to hate anybody. It was Shig and Sammy who had given him this opportunity. They hadn't been responsible for what happened at Pearl Harbor. Still, when people made derogatory comments about Japs, he didn't speak up. He knew that wasn't right either.

Sometimes he helped Mr. Bagdasarian take care of the nearby ranch of Tom Kitihara. Aram had promised to help keep it up until the Kitihara family could return home. Helping out made Sack feel better about the whole thing. Being out in the vines was peaceful. He preferred it to the company of most people.

Sack walked out in the fields. It was late afternoon and the sun had soaked into the ground all day. Now the heat radiated up from the smoothed dirt between the rows, where the wooden trays rested. He paused and turned a bunch of grapes that still showed too much green on the underside. The drying fruit had a distinctive odor that men who worked the fields could easily recognize. It was a heavy odor, an earthy, sweet smell. The bunches by now had turned a dark rose amber color. The summer had been cooler than normal and the drying was taking longer than usual. Soon they would be dry enough to go into sweatboxes, where they could cure and finish turning into dried fruit with just enough moisture to give a soft but slightly firm feel.

He reached up and pulled a bunch off a vine that the workers had missed. He separated out the few that still were firm before dropping the rest of the bunch on the ground. He slowly chewed the overripe fruit and let the juice rest on his tongue. The tannin in the skin of the grapes gave a dryness to the sugary sweetness. He swallowed and hoped that the sugar level in the drying bunches was as good as what he had just tasted.

Sack looked at the sky, worried about the risk of an early rain spoiling the crop. Rain could cause mildew and easily ruin a promising harvest. The sky overhead was clear with just a few wisps of clouds. It didn't look like rain, but the air carried the hint of moisture. He looked over toward the mountains that shimmered through the late afternoon heat and he could see clouds building up against them.

He started back toward the rooms where he and Carmen lived. It had not been easy running the crews. He was more used to working on the crews than being boss, but Mr. Bagdasarian worked with him until he felt comfortable. Within the next few days he would run crews into the field to start picking up the drying raisins.

This would be his first harvest as a foreman. He was beginning to feel a sense of ownership over the ranch, but he fought the feeling. He was just a temporary replacement, but he already knew it was going to be hard to leave when Shig came back. Years spent working the fields for other men had taught him to simply accept what he could not control. Now that acceptance was a part of his character.

Sack walked into the room through the open door. What little breeze there was moved through the room and brought some relief. He took his hat off and wiped his forehead across the line left by the hat brim. He went over to the sink and washed as Carmen moved dishes to the table. The swell of her belly was a wonder to him, a source of ceaseless amazement. Carmen's face seemed to radiate a softness that he noticed more every day. He wished his parents could see it. Perhaps they would be here by November for the pruning of the vines.

Carmen felt his arm reach around her and gently rub her belly. She looked back over her shoulder and gave her husband a kiss on his still wet cheek. "You need to dry your face, *mijo*."

He laughed. "I can't dry my face off and put my arm around you at the same time, darlin'."

Carmen shook her head at his poor humor. "There is a letter from José." She pushed the rumpled envelope toward Sack and returned to the stove.

Sack pulled the thin sheets from the envelope and read the neatly printed script. "He says that Camp Blanding is in Florida and that it rains all the time. He's in the 36th, which they call the Texas Division." Sack laughed. "He says maybe he should have listened to me and joined the Navy. Wants us to name the baby after him but only if it's a boy."

Even though her back was to him, Sack could tell Carmen was smiling because she was rubbing her belly. She always smiled when she did that. He caught himself reaching over to scratch the arm that wasn't there. Phantom pains, the doctor called it. Sometimes in the dark it was like nothing had changed.

He sat silently for a moment. "I went to the store today with Mr. Bagdasarian, the one that the Shiraga family ran? Anyway, Luis Machado and his wife are running it now. There's a lot of folks doin' that, runnin' ranches and things for those folks. I heard in Fresno some people just locked their houses and businesses and drove to the fairgrounds, left their cars and everything right there."

Carmen stood at the stove, swaying slightly back and forth. "Mr. and Mrs. Miyaki, they are nice people. I am sorry for them."

"You know, I read in the paper that the government is talking about movin' all the Japanese to places outside California. What they're doing to those folks, it ain't right. But some folks say it's for their own good. Say they'll be safer. Don't know how anybody is safer cuz they're locked up like that. Guess the government knows what's best, but somehow it don't seem right."

All his life Sack had been on the move, following the crops with his family. The field workers kept to themselves and looked to one another when they needed help. His father taught him that you didn't forget it when a man gave you a hand when you were down. When he needed help, the Miyakis had been there for him. He couldn't do anything in return except take care of the fields.

He got up slowly from his chair. "Got a few more rows to walk, check on a few places where the bunches are still lookin' a little green." He put on his hat and walked back outside. He glanced over at the Miyaki home. The roses were blooming. Esther kept them trimmed and Carmen made sure they were watered. Sack pulled his hat low over his eyes and started walking.

CHAPTER 31

September 15, 1942
Fresno Assembly Center
Fresno, California

Shig and Mas walked back from the mess hall with bundles of paper in their hands. A meeting had been called by Mr. Pulliam, the administrator, for the long-rumored news of where they were going. Michio Toshiuki, the pharmacist, told them he thought they were all being sent to Jerome, Arkansas. He was asked to set up the hospital there, and had already left his wife June and their two daughters at the Assembly Center. Everyone assumed that was where they would be. Now it was not so clear. Both men knew this was not going to be easy to share with their families, especially with the boys so close. Not to mention the growing relationship between Sammy and Betty that still made both fathers uncomfortable.

Mas spoke quietly. "Do you know this place, Arkansas?"

Shig didn't hide his uncertainty. "I just know that it is in the southern part of the country. I've heard it is hot there, but they have farms and grow cotton."

"Why are they sending you to this place, Manzanar? We should stay together."

The sadness was evident on Shig's face. "I don't know why we are going there. We're not the only family going to Manzanar. And some are going to a place in Arizona, others to another camp in Arkansas not far from you. It could be worse, I imagine."

"How could it be worse?"

"I have heard there are camps in the north states. At least it doesn't get too cold where we're going. This Manzanar is in the desert, so it must be hot."

Shig stopped when they got to Mas's place.

"We will talk later."

He walked slowly, not eager to deliver this news. There was a smell in the air that caused him to close his eyes and inhale. It was the smell of drying raisins. So many times he stood in the fields and looked at the slatted trays as the sun leached the moisture from the drying fruit. The smell hung heavy over the entire valley this time of year. He was going to miss it. He pulled it in one more time and then walked on.

Everyone was waiting when Shig walked through the door. They all knew why the men went to the meeting. They looked with trepidation at the papers Shig carried in his hand. "We are being sent to a camp at a place called Manzanar. It is to the east of us over the mountains in the high desert. That is all I know."

Toshi spoke up first. "I thought we were going to Arkansas? Why are they sending us to the desert?"

"Most people here are going to Arkansas, but not everybody. Some of us are going to Manzanar and some to Arizona. We must accept the decision."

Shig looked at Sammy. "I have spoken to Mas Shiraga. They're going to Arkansas. We will not be together."

Sammy stood and pushed his way past his father. The anger on his son's face was evident but not unexpected. It would take time for him to accept the decision. Best to wait until his anger subsided.

~

Sammy found Freddy sitting in front of their stall. Freddy looked up, anger and frustration evident on his face. Like Sammy he had begun to fill out, his body more muscular, his face more angular.

"Why the hell are we going to different places? I hate what's happening to all of us. I feel like a cow being herded around. I don't feel like a person."

Sammy looked at his friend. "I don't know. Where's Rose going?" It was unimaginable that they would be, for the first time in their lives, separated.

Freddy looked up. "I saw her father. They're going to Arkansas with us."

Sammy heard the door to the Shiraga's room being opened. Betty was standing there looking at him. He could see the tears on her face. "My father says there is nothing to be done," she said. She put her hand on his shoulder. "But we still have time. Mama said that nobody knows what will happen until it happens. Maybe something can be done."

"Nothing can be done," he said. "Don't you understand?"

She backed up at the vehemence in his voice.

Freddy looked up. "It's just crap—that's what it is. Face it, they're going to treat us like garbage until we do something about it. I'm sick of just doing nothing. We should protest. We need to fight back."

Sammy could sense Betty's fear at her brother's comments. The lack of control over their fate made them all more insecure about what could happen if they rebelled. The three stood silently by the Dutch door to the stall. The top half was open. Mas and Satomi could hear everything, but they didn't come to the door. They felt no different than their children.

⁓

Sammy watched his parents quietly packing their few belongings. He could sense the sadness with which they moved, a sadness he shared with them. While he detested the horse stall, it had become familiar. Rumors swirled around the rooms about what the new camps would be like.

He stood and walked over to the door. "I'm going to go over and see Freddy and Betty. I want to say goodbye tonight. We probably won't see them in the morning."

His mother looked up like she was going to say something, but then stopped before any sound passed her lips. She only nodded. His father never looked up. Both Sammy and Toshi had watched his spirit start to lose its sharp definition in the days since *Obasan*'s death. Slowly, the whole process was eroding him. He was not the only father who was beginning to show the burden of their situation.

Sammy walked out the door into the late afternoon sun. He looked up and down the dusty road separating the small stable homes. People were gathering outside, but there was a listlessness to it all. There was no sense of adventure or excitement—just the dread of the unknown. He walked slowly down the road toward Freddy's place.

They had been friends for so long that their minds worked in tandem. Freddy walked out the door just as Sammy arrived. He looked at his friend standing there, waiting for him to say something—both of them not knowing who would speak first, or even what they would say. Sammy broke the silence at last.

"Look, I have an address for the place in Arkansas. I wrote down the place to write us at Manzanar. Here." He handed over the rumpled slip of paper with the addresses on it. "You write me, okay?"

Freddy looked at his childhood friend and saw that he had changed. He hadn't noticed it before. Sammy's face had taken on a firmer look, and his shoulders and arms were bigger. He had felt his own body changing too.

"I'll write. I know I'm not much good at that—letters and things—but I'll write." Freddy moved forward and reached out with his hand. Sammy took it and they stood for a moment, waiting for one of them to make some further move. But it never came.

Sammy looked over at the door. "Betty here?"

"She's waiting inside. I'll get her."

Betty walked out and looked at the young man waiting in the road. There was no frame of reference for what she was feeling. She didn't want to lose someone she had known all her life.

Sammy spoke up. "Want to go for a walk?" She nodded and extended her hand.

Sammy hesitated before taking her hand in public. It would mean something to people watching. They both knew that. It was as much of a public acknowledgment of his feelings as he could make. They walked down the road and over to the fence near Ventura, the avenue at the northern end of the Assembly Center.

When Sammy stopped, she looked at him, her eyes showing a recognition of the unspoken thoughts they both had. "What will happen to us?" she asked.

He stood there, trying to say the right thing, unsure of what it was. "I don't know. I don't know what's going to happen." He couldn't seem to say what he was thinking, that his feelings for her seemed deeper than before. When he looked at her he thought about the future, even if he didn't know what that future was.

Betty leaned in close to his cheek and rested her head against the side of his face, sensing what he was thinking. "My mother said time would make our decisions for us."

Sammy put his hand against her back, feeling the warmth come through the thin blouse. "I'm not very good at this. I'd like to say something but I don't know ..." He felt his awkwardness and knew it showed. Betty's eyes were beginning to brim over with tears, and Sammy brushed them away. He leaned forward and kissed her in a way that was different from anything they had done before.

~

The morning came slowly, ending the sleepless night. Shig and Setsuko lay awake as did their sons. All over the Assembly Center families were lying in their beds, sharing the same uncertainty. Shig rose with his family and began checking to make sure they had packed everything. It was not difficult to inspect the small quarters that had been their home these last several months.

Shig stood at the door and took one last look at *Obasan's* rocking chair, sitting by itself in the corner of the room. He allowed the stillness of the empty chair to tear at him for one more moment. Then he turned and led his family as resolutely as he could. The Miyaki family gathered their bundles and walked out the door.

~

It didn't take long for the buses to reach the trains waiting for them. The Shiraga family moved quickly onto their assigned car. Young soldiers standing outside the bus moved back. Nobody said very much. The shades on the train remained drawn. Mas took one last look around as he boarded, one last glimpse until they reached Arkansas.

~

Sammy and Toshi crowded onto their bus. Shig and Setsuko found their own seats nearby. They weren't going to be taking a train. Mr. Pulliam said the bus ride would last seven or eight hours. Sammy didn't spend his thoughts on where he was going. All he could think about was where he had been, and who he was leaving behind. He never had felt such a great sadness—not even when *Obasan* died. He moved his head over to the window and pressed his cheek against his reflection. He no longer recognized the eyes staring back at him in the glass.

CHAPTER 32

October 1, 1942

Manzanar War Relocation Camp

Independence, California

The hours on the bus spread out over the day and into the late afternoon. For several hours they saw nothing but the stretch of barren, gravelly land intermittently dotted with scrub vegetation. For the last hour Sammy could see a huge mountain dominating the others and growing in size as the bus moved toward it. By the time the bus reached the road leading off the highway, the sun was beginning to move behind the top of the mountains to the southwest and shadows were falling across the flat landscape.

The bus moved up to a small stone building where a guard appeared. He walked around to the front of the bus and waited for the driver to open the door. The sudden temperature change from the outside air was startling and pulled Sammy's attention away from the tall barbed wire fence that ran down both sides of the entry and away in the distance. He couldn't see beyond the guard towers, but it didn't matter. He knew why they were there.

The bus pulled forward and traveled to a line of batten-board wooden buildings with walls covered by black paper. Several guards came out, with rifles and bayonets exposed on the barrels. There was still enough sun for the light to flash off the sharpened lengths of steel. There was no menace in the movement of the guards, but their rifles carried the message that they were in control and the people on the bus were not. They were instructed to move off the bus and form a line of family clusters, moving toward a building with an open door and wooden steps.

Sammy heard his father give the family's identification number from the Assembly Center. The clerk handed Shig a sheaf of papers and directed them to another station administering shots. A nurse explained the typhoid shots and that everyone would get a quick physical to check for TB or other respiratory illnesses. It didn't seem to take very long and Sammy felt like he never stopped moving, even when being examined by a doctor.

It was after the physical that Sammy saw soldiers looking in their bags. He turned to Toshi, whispering, "I think they're looking for things that are forbidden. Do you have your camera?"

"It's in my bag, but I have it wrapped in dirty clothes. Maybe they won't want to look."

The young soldier was obviously bored and not very concerned by the time he got to Toshi's bag. "You got anything in there like cameras?"

Toshi surprised Sammy by how casually he responded. "Hey, if I had anything they would have taken it in Fresno, but you can look if you want. All I got in here is some dirty clothes and some baseball stuff."

The guard peered into the bag and moved back at the smell.

"Okay, move on through." The family moved forward while more clerks handed each of them empty mattress ticking and two Army blankets, repeating over and over that tomorrow they would be able to fill the mattresses.

Finally, the group moved into what looked like a mess hall, where sandwiches and drinks were handed out. Both boys grabbed two sandwiches and sat with their parents to eat what was going to pass for dinner.

Shig spoke up. "We are in a barracks—ten, fourteen, three. The clerk said that after we finish eating someone will come to get us and lead us to our room." They sat and ate quietly, waiting.

Soon, a sergeant with a side arm walked to the front of the mess hall and asked for attention. "Welcome to Manzanar. I'm going to call off names, and I want the head of the family to raise his hand so we know who you are. We have some young men here who will help you find your rooms. Tomorrow you will receive further instructions, but I'm guessing all of you are pretty tired and just want to get settled." As they heard their name called, Sammy saw his father raise his hand until a slightly overweight young man came over. "You the Miyaki family?"

Shig nodded. The round faced young man in front of them was no older than Sammy. With a quick smile, he seemed comfortable with his surroundings. "I'm Akiro Morita. My family lives over in Block 10, barracks 8. You're in Block 10, barracks 14, room 3—or 10-14-3. I'll take you there and help you get settled in." He looked at the Miyakis and smiled. "We got a lot of things here that we've been building for a couple of months. You folks came here pretty late. Where you from?"

Sammy spoke up. "We're from Calwa, near Fresno. Where you from?"

"Me? I'm from L.A. Most of the people here are from L.A., but we got people from Stockton and Washington State—all over, it seems. Nobody has been able to figure out why they put us here instead of closer to home. Or at least someplace warmer. But I'm kind of used to it by now. My family and me got here the first part of April."

He looked at Sammy and Toshi. "Either of you guys play baseball?"

Sammy nodded. "I play."

Akiro smiled. "Well, we got some pretty good ball players here and some pretty nice fields. Tomorrow I'll take you over. Maybe we can work up a game or something."

He looked apologetic that he needed to get them up one more time. "We need to get moving. It's getting dark and the road is a little rough." He led them out of the mess hall. There was a chill to the wind and Sammy could feel the sting of sand hitting his face. Akiro looked over and seemed to know what he was thinking. "Wind blows all the time. You get used to it."

Akiro led them down a road lined with row after row of tar paper-clad barracks until he came to a sign that said "Block 10." As they got closer they could see the barracks number on the side. "You're in with another family, I think they're named Doi, from Washington. They got a boy a little older than you. His name's Tommy. He's a pretty good ball player too."

Shig stopped. "We are sharing our room?"

Akiro looked at Shig. "Yes, Mr. Miyaki. Almost everybody shares a room here. They're supposed to be building some more barracks so people can have their own."

A single light bulb hung by a cord from the ceiling. The unfinished pine board walls still carried the smell of pitch. Sap from the green wood seeped through knots and crevices in the wood. Akiro walked over to the couple who rose when the Miyakis came in.

"Mr. and Mrs. Doi, these are the Miyakis from Fresno. They've been assigned here." He turned to Sammy. "I'll see you around tomorrow. We'll go see if you can really play." He smiled and walked back out the door.

Setsuko stood looking at her silent husband and the three strangers staring back at them. "I am Setsuko."

"I am Fumiko and my husband Nobuo—he goes by Ben—and our son, Tommy."

Ben looked at his wife and took over the introductions. "Let us help you get settled. Tomorrow, perhaps, we can find a way to make a wall to give you some privacy." He seemed apologetic about a situation over which he obviously had no control.

Shig bowed. "I'm Shig and this is my wife Setsuko, our sons, Isamu and Toshio." Sammy nodded. Toshi didn't say anything. He was becoming increasingly sullen and sarcastic about their situation, making everyone in the family uncomfortable. His outbursts began to draw attention back at the Assembly Center.

Ben nodded at the introductions and bowed slightly. "It will be good to now know who our neighbors will be."

Setsuko looked around the room. The walls were bare—just boards with no insulation. There were some knotholes where she could feel cold air whistling through. Fumiko caught Setsuko's look. Her voice was apologetic. "We have covered some of the holes with cardboard, but we did not have enough. Perhaps tomorrow we can go together and see if we can find more. I will go with you to get hay for your mattress."

"Please, do not be concerned. We are grateful that you have already started making it warmer in here." The wind moved through the eaves, causing Setsuko to shiver. She could hear the voices of people in the next room. She looked at her husband with a sinking heart. She turned and began to place the blankets on the metal-framed canvas cots.

Fumiko could see the sadness in the eyes of the woman who now shared the room with her family. She knew what she was thinking. Tomorrow they would go together and make the best of it. Hopefully, they could become friends. But tonight it was best just to rest. She knew that the new day would be even worse, as the starkness of their new surroundings became apparent. It had taken her at least a week to accept this place and now there was a family for them to also accept, strangers except for fate.

~

After miles of hearing the hum of train wheels against the tracks, Freddy no longer paid attention to the sound until it stopped. Word quickly passed through the car that they were in Little Rock, Arkansas. They were going to change to an Army train that would take them to their final destination. He couldn't wait to stretch his legs and walk on solid ground. Maybe he would get a chance to see Rose. Her family was on a different car, and they hadn't been allowed to move around to visit.

The guard spoke up and caught everyone's attention. "Get your stuff together cuz we'll be movin' in just a minute. Stay together cuz you're gettin' right on the next train." It didn't take more than a minute for most of the families to gather up their few possessions and start shuffling toward the door.

A shock awaited them as they filed out onto the train platform. The air held a warm dampness that hung on them as they moved around, surrounded by the musty smell of wet leaves. Everywhere they looked, Negroes were working in the station, pulling luggage onto carts. One of them looked over at Mas with a puzzled expression on his face.

"Where you white folks gawn to?"

At first Freddy wondered what the black man was saying. Then he realized—here, they were the white people.

Mas shook his head. "We don't know."

The black man shook his head and kept pushing his luggage cart. "Sure are a lot of ya' all."

Freddy and Betty followed their mother and father up the step and into another train car with the shades drawn. He wondered when he would see the sunlight again.

Two and a half hours later, they felt the train slow to a stop. After a few minutes an older soldier came into the train car and held his hands up for attention. "This is it. You're in Denson, Arkansas, and this is the Jerome Camp."

Mas stood and helped Satomi to her feet. They walked to the front of the car and waited for the people ahead of them to move off the train. It was a slow process. People were stopping as soon as they got off the train and looking around, backing up everyone behind them. Freddy could hear men yelling for people to move forward. He felt like he was in some kind of bizarre fire drill back at school. Betty held onto the back of his shirt as they walked down the steps onto a wooden platform.

Mas turned to make sure Freddy and Betty were next to them. The line of people moved forward across a paved road that ran along a fence line, toward an open gate. As he got closer he could see the barbed wire and guard towers. Guards with fixed bayonets stood along the way urging people to move forward.

Freddy felt Betty's hand holding tightly to his shirt, keeping step with him. He put his free arm back to reassure her. "Don't worry, nobody's going to hurt us. Hold on to me. I won't let you go."

Freddy scanned the crowd for Rose but there were so many walking together. He couldn't see that far ahead or behind him. Never in his life had he felt the coldness in his stomach that he felt right at the moment they walked through the gate.

Mas followed the instructions he had been handed, along with their housing assignment. Block 44, barracks 3, room 2. It took them an hour to find their barracks, toward the back of the camp near a copse of trees. The ground looked so different. Red, heavy soil covered their shoes and clung to their legs and pants as they walked. Mas reached down and scraped some of the dirt into his hand. "Much clay in this. It will not be easy to grow things." He brushed his hand off on his pants, leaving a rusty streak on the cloth.

Already some families were inside the barracks, which were merely a series of long open rooms. There were windows and doors, but no individual apartments or much in the way of partitions between the rooms. The air was close, heavy with the smell of tired, unwashed people. The red clay from outdoors had already stained the bare pine floors with the rusty footprints of its occupants.

There were eight families to a barracks and more than one family to a room. The lack of privacy and the undignified arrangement took what optimism they had left. Mas led the family to a room marked as 2. There was a family already in it that he recognized, the Saitos, who had lived down the road from them at the Assembly Center. At least they were familiar faces. He nodded but said nothing.

George and Mary Saito watched while Mas and Satomi set out their few possessions. It was not seemly to interrupt at this time. They waited until the Shiraga family had a chance to adjust. Mas moved forward and smiled.

"You are Mr. Saito from the Fresno Assembly Center?" George smiled in return and nodded. "And you are Mr. Shiraga?"

"Yes. Is everyone in this barracks from Fresno?

"I think all of us are from the San Joaquin Valley, but I am not sure." He introduced his wife to Satomi. "I think we will get to know one another very well, particularly if we do not find some way to make a wall." He tried to smile. "When we pick up the filling for the mattresses, perhaps we can find some material for a wall. That is the best we can do for now, I think."

Freddy dropped his bag in the corner, near a metal-framed cot. He sat on the edge of the cot and looked around the room. The white light of the single bulb gave the room a harsh glare, drawing out the shadows in the rough wood walls. He looked down at the floor and sighed. The cracks in the floorboards were allowing outside air into the room. They didn't have to share the horse stall, now they had to share this. Freddy looked up at this father standing in the middle of the room. The lines that had once wrinkled the corners of his eyes now drew down the sides of his face. He could already feel this place slicing out slivers of his soul.

CHAPTER 33

November 26, 1942
Calwa, California

Sack finished his breakfast and started to wipe his mouth with his sleeve. He thought better of it when he saw the look on his wife's face. He put his arm back down on the table, picking up the napkin and wiping his mouth. "Sometimes it's just hard to remember, Carm. That's all."

She smiled at his discomfort. "I want our child to have good manners. If his papa uses his sleeve to wipe his mouth, then he will too."

"So sure it's gonna be a boy, are you?"

"I can tell by the way he kicks. Mrs. Bagdasarian also says it will be a boy." She reached down and placed both hands on her swollen belly. The women at the store all said the baby would come in March.

Carmen hadn't seen a doctor, as it wasn't their way. She had been born at home with one of the neighbor women helping her mother, just as one of the local women would help her. Maybe a doctor would come, maybe not. She did not fear having her baby at home. She only regretted that her mother was not here to help her. But she had no pains so far, no bleeding or other bad signs.

She reached for her husband's hand and placed it on her belly. "Feel him kick. He is going to be a strong boy, like his papa."

Sack held his hand on his wife's stomach and felt the baby moving around. "Just want our baby to be healthy, Carm. Life's tough enough for kids without sickness problems too."

If his mother was here, she would know what to do. He wished there was more he could do to help. His family had not had much luck getting help from town doctors. Money had always been an issue. Now, even though he had some money to pay, there was another problem because Carmen was Mexican. Some doctors in the area didn't treat Mexicans, and it didn't make any difference that she had his name now. The hospital would treat her, but they had no way to get there.

He looked up at his wife's face and could see the tenderness there. He moved his hand away and put it on her cheek. "I have to go to the shed and work on the equipment. The tractor's been actin' up some and I told Aram I could fix it. I'll be out there if you need me. You just take it easy." He kissed his wife's cheek and walked out into the chill November air.

The San Joaquin Valley didn't lose its heat until the end of October. By November it was a cold that set into the bones. Sack needed to keep moving in order to stay warm outside. It wasn't so much the temperature as it was the dampness in the air. He stamped his feet, but the dust no longer puffed up. He started to walk across the yard to the shed where the tools and the tractor were kept.

He heard the tired engine of a car moving down the road on the other side of the Bagdasarian's house. It was an old vehicle, and it ran rough. It needed work, that much he could tell, before he saw the rusty black car roll into the yard near the shed. He remembered that car. He had ridden in it most of his life and it never sounded much better than it did now. He stood quietly by the shed waiting for his parents to arrive. He could just make out his mother's face through the grime on the windshield.

Frank Pritch wasn't what most people would call a big man. He was more of a raw-boned man, lean with ropy muscles, face permanently sun-burned red and showing lines that looked far older than his age. His neck carried deep-set grooves that made the skin look like quilting, and his big hands hung from sleeves with cuffs too big even for his workman's wrists. He had the same reddish hair as his boy, going to gray here and there, and he combed it back with his fingers as he stood looking at his son.

There was no expression of shock on his face as he took in the mea-sure of his boy's empty sleeve. He just nodded in the tired way of a man who has seen misery many times in his life. He started right off as if they had just seen one another the day before. "Heard about your arm, son.

Some of the pickers saw your mama and me up north way and tole' us you was here. They said you was foreman now. That so?"

Sack couldn't help realizing the weariness of his father's greeting. No hello or small talk, right to the point with no gilding on it. As pleased as he was to see his parents, he couldn't help feeling a flash of resentment that they hadn't been in touch with him sooner. But that had always been his father's way.

"Yeah, Daddy, that's so. Where you been? You didn't write me or let me know where you was."

Frank Pritch shook his head and looked at Sack with his crooked smile. "Boy, you know I can't write and neither can your mama. Figured we'd see you when we'd see you. Heard you got married to a little Mexican gal."

Sack waited before he answered, watching his mother come around and start walking toward him. She didn't say anything, but Sack could see the sadness in her face as she looked at her only boy. She looked much older. The gray took most of the color from her hair, and her skin was not as tightly drawn around her face as it once had been. Her complexion had taken on a coarser texture, giving up its youth to the harshness of her life. His father always said his Mae was the prettiest bride he had ever seen. But years in the fields were no easier on the people who labored there than the sun was on the fruit they laid out to dry. He smiled as she made her way toward him. She reached for his face and hugged him.

She didn't let go, just pulled him in tighter. "Billy," using his given name, "we wanted to come back sooner but things been hard this year. Work was hard to come by for your daddy and me. We didn't have money to fix the car and we been trying to get enough so we could come down here. Hard to get tires what with the war and all and gas rationin' don't make it easy to get very far."

He stepped back from his parents and smiled. "I got married to a pretty girl, Mama—Carmen Duran. You 'member her. She was the girl I used to talk to when we worked here. She's been real good to me, Mama. We been real happy." He decided to wait before telling them that his wife was going to have a baby. He reached out and hugged his mother again, pulling her as close to him as his arm would allow. He could feel her thinness sinking into his chest.

Frank reached around them both. It was as close as they had been for a long time, much longer than before Sack left for the Navy. Frank Pritch had never been a man of many words and even now, looking at his son's empty sleeve, he didn't have much to say. He reached inside himself for the only thing he could find:

"We missed you boy, God knows we missed you." Sack looked at his father and, for the first time in his life, saw tears moving into the dry crevices of his face.

Sack nodded slowly. He took his mother by the arm and led his parents into the warmth of what was now his home.

CHAPTER 34

December 6, 1942
Manzanar War Relocation Center
Independence, California

Sammy kicked at the thin crust of snow on the ground while he walked with Tommy and Akiro. All over the camp they could see small clusters of men and women standing away from the barracks and other buildings. Everyone was talking about the same thing and nobody wanted to be overheard. Even if you had what passed for a wall in the barracks, you could always hear the conversations in the next room. If you tried to listen, you could even hear the whispers. Private conversations were no longer uttered inside the barracks room. Rumors were all over the camp that informants were giving information to camp authorities about dissenters. That was why people were standing in the cold in order to talk about the night before.

For weeks there had been rumors that people in the camp administration and those handling food storage were stealing sugar and meat. Everyone knew that with rationing going on everywhere, including inside the camps, foodstuffs like sugar were easily sold on the black market. Whispered accusations soon took the form of truth. It all boiled over into violence.

One of the cooks, Dick Miwa, had been more and more vocal about conditions in the mess halls, and he publicly accused the assistant director and the chief steward of stealing from the camp warehouses. There were mixed reactions to his accusations. Some people thought *he* was wrong, some people thought *he* was foolish to say anything, and some people thought *he* was heroic.

His charges added one more layer to the festering dissension that seeped through the camp. Two groups had begun to silently form within the community. For some time there were groups of people, mostly non-citizen Issei and Kibei, the latter having been born or raised in America but had gone back to Japan for education, who bitterly opposed the Nisei members of the Japanese American Citizens League. Some believed the JACL were collaborators with the administration and informants for them. Some were left-wing groups and some were just Issei, Kibei, and Nisei opposed to the administration and opposed to the JACL for reasons including general distrust to outright blame for supposed cooperation in the evacuation.

The night before, Frank Matsuda, a Nisei and leader of the JACL, was beaten and sent to the hospital. That he had been assaulted was a cause for much talk. Miwa was arrested for suspicion of being part of the assault, along with several others, and taken to the county jail in nearby Independence.

The unrest had been a long time building. Many of the national JACL leaders were in Utah and not detained in the camps. The JACL leaders had held a convention in Salt Lake just the month before and Manzanar had sent two delegates, including Fred Tayama. The convention had urged that Nisei be allowed to volunteer for the draft, and this had stirred anti-JACL feelings into a frenzy. Leaders of the opposition, like Miwa and Harry Ueno, head of the Manzanar Mess Hall Workers Union, had bitterly opposed the JACL. Ueno also had been arrested for "questioning." Threats were being made against Tayama, journalist Togo Tanaka, and others from a shadowy group calling itself "The Blood Brothers."

Sammy leaned in close to Akiro. "You've been here since the beginning. Do you think those guys beat up Matsuda and Tayama? Why would they do that? The JACL is right about us getting into the Army."

Akiro looked around before responding. "A lot of people don't think we should go in the Army. After all, why should we fight? You think it's right that we fight and our families stay in places like this?"

Tommy added. "The only reason we're here is because people don't trust us."

Sammy snapped back. "The only reason we're here is because we're Japanese. You don't see any Italians or Germans here, do you?" He immediately regretted the way his words sounded. Tommy's face showed his hurt and confusion.

Sammy softened his voice. "Look, I want in the Army because it's the best way for all of us to get out of here. We join the Army, we prove our loyalty in the only way we can. It's the best way to show that we're just as good as everybody else."

Tommy walked slightly ahead of the other two and turned his head back.

"We shouldn't have to join the Army to prove we're as good as everybody else. We should be able to join the Army because we're no different than anybody else." The two others nodded their heads in agreement.

Tommy stopped and pulled on Sammy's arm. "My parents, they're concerned about us being together. They say that your brother, Toshi, is one of the troublemakers. People are saying he's in with the Blood Brothers."

Akiro pulled in close, watching Sammy's face for any sign of agreement. Sammy's head seemed to pull into his jacket, as if it would help him hide from the whispered accusation that his brother was part of the dissenters. He had heard it before. His parents had, too. Toshi hadn't denied it, and had even expressed his agreement with the dissenters. Now, his parents wavered between shame and concern for their oldest son. His father didn't share the view of the dissenters. He wanted nothing to do with any conflict. He told Sammy repeatedly to do his work and stay away from trouble. But Toshi's increasingly sullen behavior and apathetic work in the gardens made his feelings clear. He refused to discuss any of his activities with anyone. Which caused more people to talk.

Sammy lowered his voice to a whisper. "I think we need to be careful who we talk to and who we're seen with. I'm going to find my parents. Maybe you should do the same."

"Too late." Tommy was pointing to a crowd of men who were walking toward one of the barracks buildings. "That's where Miwa lives."

They followed from a distance, mindful that people could be watching. As they got closer, they could hear men demanding that Miwa and Ueno be released and returned to the camp. Men were shouting now that Masuda, Tanaka, and others were *inu*, dogs or spies. Lists of names were being read by different men, some of whom Sammy recognized. But what concerned him more than anything was that Toshi was standing with the men yelling.

Sammy turned to his friends. "I'm going back to our room. Maybe you should both go home, too."

He started walking away, but not before he made eye contact with Toshi. He could see a look he had never seen before on his brother's face. It was more than fury. It was hate. He broke away from Toshi's gaze and walked as quickly as he could back to his room. Tommy followed closely behind. Sammy knew Tommy would tell his parents what they saw. There were no secrets at Manzanar.

Shig listened calmly to what Sammy told him. That Toshi was involved in the unrest did not surprise him. He felt it coming, the anger in his son. It was hard to blame him for his discontent and resentment; he was still a young man and raged against what he could not control. He watched his younger son very carefully for any sign of that rage. The path that Toshi had chosen was bad enough. It would be worse if he led his younger brother down the same path. It would also bring harm and shame to his family, and he knew that he must think of his family first.

"Isamu, put on your coat."

Sammy followed his father back out into the cold, now made biting by the constant wind. Both father and son pulled their coats closer at the throat and walked a safe distance from the barracks. Groups of men and boys were running toward the front of the camp. Shig steered his son toward the back, away from listening ears.

"Isamu, we must consider the situation. What Toshi is doing will end only in pain for him. I think there will be more trouble. Will we fight against armed troops? Is fighting going to make our situation better? I think we must find our way with words and not with violence. I do not want you to listen to Toshi or the others who have let their anger control their heads."

Sammy listened quietly. He did not agree with Toshi, but was still sympathetic. Toshi was wrong to disregard their father's wishes, even if he could not help questioning his father's submissiveness.

Sammy could hear the resignation in his father's voice. "He will take his path. I have told him all I can, just as I am telling you." Sammy nodded. The father and son continued walking in silence, broken only by the crunching of the thin crust of hardened snow on the ground.

~

Tommy knocked on the wall separating his family's room from Sammy's. It was their signal to meet outside. Akiro was waiting for them near the latrines, and his whispered voice carried excitement.

"People are at the front of the camp near the police station. The director brought Miwa back, and they have him at the police station jail. I heard they're going to try to bust him and Ueno out." He looked at his two friends to see their reaction.

Sammy crouched down and pulled his coat around him to cut the chill against his body. "Look, my dad said there was going to be trouble. I'm staying out of it."

Tommy didn't say anything.

Akiro stayed silent for a moment and then blurted out, "Toshi's there. I heard he's with a bunch of men who are going to look for Masuda at the hospital. Those guys want to kill people."

Sammy let out a long sigh. If there was trouble, he couldn't abandon his brother but he wasn't going to join him, either. Finally, he spoke.

"All right, let's go down there but we won't get involved, okay?"

There was silent assent. What little moonlight there was lit the pathways between the barracks. Lights at the ends of the paths brightly defined anyone who ventured out into the main roadway. The three young men started toward the front of the camp, staying as much in the shadows as they could. They saw searchlights near the front and heard angry voices shouting as they neared the police station. They stopped near the edge of a building that fronted the open area around the camp administration buildings.

The boys could see a large group of people facing the camp police station. Loud, harsh voices were shouting for the release of Miwa. Soldiers kept their backs to the building. Armed with rifles and shotguns, they were slowly stepping back from the mob, a wall blocking any further retreat. A machine gun was set up with sandbags in front, its barrel tilting, menacing in its presence. Sammy could see the crowd pressing in closer, insulting the soldiers and waving their fists.

Suddenly, the soldiers threw tear gas canisters. The gas cloud settled quickly into a haze over the protesters as people began to run. It was then that Sammy saw Toshi with a group of young men. He watched his brother and the others stop, turning in the direction of the soldiers. It happened so slowly that Sammy could see each face before they seemed to merge into one writhing mass, turning slowly at first and then all at once. The angry assemblage began moving back toward the soldiers. Sammy saw the rifles come up. It was hard to hear over the yelling and screaming, but there was no mistaking the sound of gunfire.

Sammy could see men lying on the dirt and pavement in front of the soldiers. One soldier kept yelling "Cease fire!" over and over again, so some of the soldiers pointed their rifles at the ground. Everybody was screaming but nobody was moving.

Sammy leaned over to Akiro. "Where's my brother?"

Akiro kept his gaze on the men lying scattered on the ground. Some were moving, others were still.

"I saw him at the beginning but I can't tell where he is. I don't know."

Tommy grabbed Sammy's shirt. "Toshi's over there. See him? He's the one holding his shoulder."

Sammy saw someone his brother's size being helped by several others. A dark stain grew over his shoulder. The light caught his face, and Sammy ran across the open area to find Toshi leaned against a wall. His face was ashen, his right hand covered with blood.

"Sammy, get away from here. Go on, run."

Sammy grabbed his brother. "No. We'll get you back to our place. Dad will know what to do. Come on!"

With the help of Tommy and Akiro, Sammy reached around his brother's waist and helped him as quickly as possible back to their room. He didn't know what else to do. As they moved through the shadows, they could hear more shouting and a burst of rapid fire from a machine gun. People rushed past them in every direction, running and shouting, faces moving in and out of the shadows, staring briefly at the four men and then moving past them to their own quarters.

They half-carried Toshi into the room. By now, others in the barracks were gathering, asking questions about what had happened. Already hysterical rumors were spreading about people being killed.

Shig and Setsuko saw Toshi. There was no hiding the blood. Sammy heard his mother make a small noise of shock. "Sit him on the bed." She grabbed a small cloth that she had been embroidering and folding it into a compress, pressing it against her son's wound.

Shig watched his wife's effort to stop the bleeding. He placed his hand on her shoulder. "He is hurt too badly. We must take him to the hospital." Sammy saw the tears gathering at the corner of his father's eyes. So much sadness and grief. Sammy did not know whether his brother was right or wrong but right now, it didn't matter. It pained him to see the sadness his brother's actions had brought to his parents.

Setsuko shook her head. "We cannot take him to the hospital. He will be arrested."

Shig knelt next to his son and put his hand on the side of his face, looking into Toshi's eyes. "If we do not take him to the hospital, he will die. What is done is done. I want our son to live." He helped Toshi to his feet. "Isamu, will you help me?"

Tommy's father, Ben, had been standing back. He came forward and put his arm out helping to lift Toshi up. "Fumiko will stay with Setsuko. I will help you take Toshi to the hospital."

The three men got Toshi to his feet and helped him walk, while Tommy ran to get help. Fumiko helped Setsuko to a chair and stayed to comfort her.

～

Shig sat in a chair inside the door of the camp medical facility. At least one man died in the melee. Others had been brought in for gunshot wounds. Soldiers were already there when the three men brought Toshi in for treatment. Toshi was being cared for, but he was under arrest. He had sent Sammy back to carry the news to his mother.

Shig looked down at his hands. His fingernails still bore streaks of Toshi's blood, the dark rust stains a silent reminder of his son's decision. He lowered his face into his hands. He knew his son would live. What he didn't know was whether he could live with the fact that his son's blood had been shed for him and all the others. What he didn't know was whether that was a decision he should have made, instead of his son.

CHAPTER 35

December 14, 1942
Calwa, California

Sack and his father sat on wooden stools in the equipment shed. Both men were looking at the engine parts they had removed from the old John Deere tractor. Once, the tractor had been green and yellow. Now the yellow was more of a dingy tan and the green had powdered to a dull finish mottled with scratches from many seasons in the fields. Unlike a car with a shiny paint job or a lush interior, both men appreciated the tractor for what it was—a workhorse—its beauty captured in its strength and endurance. Farmers took care of their tractors, and the tractors took care of their livelihood. The scrapes and scratches were simply character marks made by the passing seasons. She still had years left in her. Besides, with the war still raging, there was little chance of replacing her.

Much of what Sack knew about machinery he learned from his father while helping repair their car. Many parts that others might throw away Sack could salvage, squeezing a little more use out of them. The tractor parts were no exception. The two men worked without much conversation. Frank didn't talk much in a social setting. When he was working, he talked even less.

Aram had permitted Sack's parents to stay in one of the storage rooms off the shed. Sack and his father covered the drafty areas and made the room as comfortable as possible. His parents only used it at night, spending most of the day in Sack's small living area. Aram offered to let Sack and Carmen use the Miyaki's house since it was empty, but Sack didn't feel comfortable with that. It made him feel like an intruder. His parents both agreed that it should be left as it was. In many respects the shed room was better than most of the places they stayed over their years following the harvest. Sometimes they had wintered in tents. At least this room was dry and out of the cold.

"Daddy, Carmen and me got a letter from Sammy Miyaki. They're in some camp to the east—place called Manzanar, near Independence."

Frank nodded. "Know the area. Went through it once to pick apples. Not much there as I recall. Pretty hard country."

"Yeah, well Sammy said there's lots of wind but he and his daddy, they been working in the fields I guess, trying to get in some kind of truck crop, onions and things like that. He says he's hopin' to get in the Army if they'll let him. What you think about all this?"

His father rocked back on his stool and looked up toward the rafters, moving his mouth as if he had a wad of tobacco in his cheek. Mae had long ago insisted that chewing tobacco was not a habit she was going to abide in any man who wanted to kiss her. He gave up the habit but still pushed his tongue into his cheek like he did back then, to catch the flavor. It was one way you could tell he was deep in thought.

"I figure Shig was pretty good to me and your mama. I never had much truck with folks what looked down on other folks. Maybe cuz I spent so much of my life knowin' there was folks lookin' down on me. Seems like this ain't no different. Those folks didn't do nothin' to us near as I can figure. Guess I just don't think it was right, what been done to them, but it's like anythin' else—when it's over they'll move on, and the folks what done it'll move on up. Way it's always been, far as I'm concerned."

Sack looked at his father in a different light. Frank was not given to deep thoughts or philosophizing, but there was an intensity to his statement that pressed his thoughts home to Sack. He nodded to his father, acknowledging his statement. Yes, that was how he felt too.

Frank looked over at his son. "You know, boy, for a foreman you ain't doin' much to warm this place up. I'm colder 'an a witch's heart. Let's go inside. Maybe get that wife of your'n to make us one of them tortillas. Kinda like them, you know."

Sack laughed and wiped his hand on the grease rag by his stool. "I guess we can do that. But just you remember that I'm boss so I get to decide when we take a break."

"Well, you decided?"

"Yeah, let's take a break. I could use one of those tortillas too."

Both men walked quickly from the open area of the equipment shed to the door of Sack and Carmen's set of rooms, feeling the interior warmth as they made their way to the sink to wash up.

Carmen and Mae were sitting at the table by the stove, pulling rags into strips. Carmen looked up from her work.

"Your mother is teaching me how to braid a rug." Mae was twisting rags into braids and linking them together in an oval pattern. Everything was made useful, even rags.

"Carm, Daddy and me was wonderin' if you could make us a tortilla and maybe with some butter?" Sack reached for the coffee pot sitting on the stove and motioned toward his father to find out if he wanted a cup. He poured two and set one near his father.

Mae looked at her two men with some disapproval. "You men be need'n to wash up if you want to sit in here. Look at your clothes and hands. You gonna come in here like that when the baby comes?"

Sack was gratified by how quickly his mother and Carmen had bonded. The two women worked easily together, almost like mother and daughter. Mae didn't miss a beat when she saw her son's new wife, a virtual stranger to her except for the few glimpses she had of Carmen during the picking season. Now she fussed over Carmen's aches and pains and occasional bouts of nausea, looking forward to a new generation.

Sack noticed a letter sitting on the table. His wife could see his eyes drawn to the open envelope.

"A letter from José. He says he has finished with his training. He thinks his unit will be leaving soon."

Sack picked up the letter and pulled out the two sheets of paper with the cramped scrawl of his brother-in-law. José's unit had been sent to a camp in Massachusetts. It looked like he was going to be trained on a Browning automatic rifle, a BAR he called it, a small machine gun. It also looked like José was being trained to fight Germans. Sack knew that meant North Africa. He put the letter down.

"Says he misses Mexican food. Guess they don't serve that in the Army." He looked over at his father. "José's in the Texas Division, the Alamo regiment. Wears a T patch on his shoulder."

Sack's father looked at his son. He could hear something in his voice that told him Sack was concerned.

"That boy will be all right. You just hold on to that."

Sack nodded. He carefully refolded the letter and put it back in its envelope. It would join the bundled pile of other letters that he and Carmen received. They liked to reread them at night.

Every time he thought about José going into a fight, he could feel his arm and the burning sensation as he went into the water at Pearl. He could also remember the lines of bodies on the grass. There were still nights when he woke up in a cold sweat, thinking they had carried him off with the dead. He understood as well as anybody why José went into the service but he also understood better than most the possible consequences.

He still thought about Bufe down in the cold belly of the *Arizona*. Those boys, his friends, were still there. He had seen the pictures, the superstructure sticking out of the water that washed over the submerged deck. He didn't like to think about it, Bufe being down in that hold with all the boys from the band. *At least he was with other sailors. Not by himself.* It was some small comfort.

CHAPTER 36

January 5, 1943

Fort Benning, Georgia

Kim woke up before reveille. Most of the men in the barracks were still sleeping, but waking up earlier than everyone else had become something of a habit with him. He could hear some of the men snoring. Some were just breathing heavily. They had all been out the night before, celebrating their last day as officer candidates. Today, what was left of the original class would graduate. Fewer than fifty percent had made it through, and every group lost at least one or more men except the four K's, as they called themselves—Kim, Kyle, Koontz, and Kloch.

He lay quietly in his bunk waiting for his head to clear, then reached into his boot by the bunk and took out a small knife. He had waited a long time for this, and he wasn't going to do it until he knew he would graduate. With light coming from the bulb over the barracks door, he could just make out the etched names in the frame of his bed. He wondered how many of those were still alive.

Carefully, he cut his name into the metal of the bunk—YOUNG OAK KIM, 1/5/43. When he was finished, he leaned back on his pillow. Now he was one of them. Now he, too, would go out and meet his fate just like the others in this bed before him.

Bill Koontz was in the bunk next to him.

"Kim, what the hell are you doing? If Peel sees that he'll kick your ass all the way to the CO's office."

"Peel isn't going to do anything. This afternoon, we'll be second lieutenants. I'm leaving my mark here, just like the other guys before me.

Besides, I like Peel. I'm going to give him my dollar and take my first salute from him." It was a tradition. A new officer made sure his first salute came from a noncommissioned officer he admired. Then he gave that sergeant a silver dollar.

"No matter what anybody thinks, I learned some things from him."

"Yeah, like how to be an asshole."

"No, like how to be an officer. It's his job to be an asshole. Maybe he taught us how to stay alive. Come on, Bill. Let's get up. Today we put on a butter bar and we're officers."

"And gentlemen."

The rest of the men were starting to stir in anticipation of reveille. The door to the barracks slammed shut and Peel stood there, looking at the men in the barracks. The empty bunks from the men who washed out were a testament to his diligence.

"All right, lieutenant dick heads, everybody up. I need you all bright and shiny for graduation and receipt of your orders. Get these bunks made up and turn out in fifteen minutes. No PT today, Captain's orders. Too bad. You boys need a few more orders from old Master Sergeant Peel." He started to laugh. "Don't think when you put that yellow butter bar on your collar today that you know more than I do. You'll never know more than I do. I just hope you know enough to keep yourself and your men from getting killed. Just listen to your sergeants. Now move your sorry asses!"

The air was brisk but clear when Kim walked outside with G.G., Joe, and Bill. They formed up and marched to the parade ground for graduation and congratulations. But it was the receipt of orders that was on everybody's mind. Each man wondered where he would be going. They all knew they'd get at least a week's leave, then report for duty somewhere that needed officers. And the way the war was going, it was most likely that they would be replacement officers for men killed in combat. It was a sobering thought.

Kim watched each man go to the podium when his name was called out. The colonel shook his hand and received a salute, then handed him his orders. Finally he heard his name and walked as smartly as he could to the podium.

"Congratulations, Lieutenant Kim."

"Thank you, sir." He saluted and waited for the colonel to hand him his orders, but the colonel looked over at the captain who shook his head with an expression of confusion.

"I guess there was some kind of mix-up, Kim. We'll get it straightened out."

"Yes, sir."

Kim walked off the podium and looked back as Joe Kloch's name was called. The colonel handed Joe his orders. Joe saluted and then shortly joined Kim back in the ranks. As carefully as he could, Kim looked around. Everyone had orders. Everyone except him.

By the time the ceremony was over, he realized he was the only one without orders. Each of his friends were reading where their new duty station was. All of them were joining field units. Some of the units were still stateside but a few of the men were ordered to report to Fort Dix, New Jersey, for transport to units already in action.

Kim walked over to company headquarters and saw Peel standing by the clerk's desk.

"Master Sergeant Peel?" He waited for a moment and then saw Peel smile as he rose to attention and saluted. Kim grinned and returned the salute.

"Lieutenant Kim, what can I do for you?"

Kim reached into his pocket and took out the silver dollar he had obtained in anticipation. Carefully he placed it into Peel's hand.

"First of all, Master Sergeant, I want to say thank you for the training." Peel stood looking at him, quietly, and waiting for him to finish.

"You're welcome, Lieutenant. I could tell the first day that you were going to make it. You looked me straight in the eye and you weren't afraid."

Kim laughed. "Well, Master Sergeant, I knew there was only so much you could do to me and it wasn't anything I was afraid of. Look, Master Sergeant, I didn't get any orders and I came to see the Captain. Maybe somebody misplaced them?" He looked at Peel, waiting hopefully for an answer.

Peel didn't say anything for a moment. "Lieutenant, your orders never came. They weren't in with the rest, and I know the clerk and the exec been lookin' for 'em. I don't know what to tell you. This never happened before since I been here. Maybe Captain Timmins knows somethin'. Go on in. He's in his office. I got to get ready for the next group comin' in a few days. More little officer wannabes for old Peel to thin out the herd.

I'll see you later, Lieutenant. Good luck." Peel walked out the door of the headquarters office.

Kim nodded and watched the grizzled sergeant walk out of the room. He opened the door and stuck his head in. "Captain Timmins, may I come in?"

"Certainly, Lieutenant. You want to know about your orders, right?"

"Well, yes, sir. I thought maybe there was some mix-up and you knew what I was supposed to do?"

Timmins looked at him for what seemed like a long time before he responded. Finally, he shook his head.

"I don't know what to tell you. I'll try and find out. I have the clerk working on it, but your orders didn't come in with those of the rest of the men."

"Well, sir, what do I do? I don't have any place to go. I was hoping to see my wife. We got married while I was in Camp San Luis Obispo and we only got to spend a few days together. She's going to be here day after tomorrow. I don't know what to do."

Timmins' eyes showed his sympathy. "Look, Kim, I understand but there's nothing I can tell you. I do know we have to make the place ship-shape—you know, get it all cleaned up for the next group, which will start in a week. So you can stay here a whole week before we have to figure out where to put you. Can you get hold of your wife?"

"No, sir. Ida's on her way by train. She'll be in Columbus in the next day or two. Sir?"

"Yes, Lieutenant?"

"Did I maybe do something wrong? Is that the reason I didn't get my orders?"

"No, Lieutenant, you did very well—one of the best in the class. That isn't the problem. Go on back to the barracks and see your buddies. Just move in there for a while and we'll figure it out. Okay?"

"Sir? I need to know. Is it because I'm different than the others?"

Timmins looked at him and then slowly turned his chair toward the window. "Different, Kim? What do you mean, different?"

"Sir, I mean different, like when I got into the Army they wouldn't let me be in a combat unit because I was—well—different. I don't like to say it, sir."

"This is the Army, Kim. We'll have a place for you or you wouldn't be here. Go back to your barracks, Lieutenant. We'll work on this."

"Yes, sir."

Kim walked back to the barracks, where the rest of the men were packing their gear and laughing about what they were going to do in their new assignments.

Kyle came over when Kim walked to his bunk. "You got it straightened out? You got orders?"

Kim shook his head. "No, G.G., no orders."

"It's not right. There's something wrong here. Didn't they tell you anything?"

"Nope. Captain Timmins just said the Army would have a place for me, so I guess I just wait and find out."

"Where you gonna stay?" The rest of the K's started to gather around him.

"Don't know. Ida's supposed to be here in two days. I guess they'll figure something out. The Captain said it's never happened before, so I don't know."

G.G. looked at the others. "Look, Kim, why don't you come down to Columbus and stay at the hotel?"

"Well, thanks, G.G., but for one thing, I can't afford it, and have you ever tried to get a room in Columbus, Georgia? There are people sleeping in the lounges and all over the place—there's no room. It would be crazy to even think about it."

G.G. started to laugh. "Naw, I told you, boy, my family has the influence in Columbus. I know people and my daddy knows people. You stay here tonight, and I'll get back to you tomorrow."

"Well, I don't think anybody can help out with this except the Army. But thanks for the thought."

"Boy, you just have a little faith in old G.G. I'll see you tomorrow."

~

The next day, Kim was sitting on his bunk reading when he heard the barracks door open. G.G. was standing there, grinning.

"Well, I told you not to worry. Your lucky day was when you hooked up with old G.G. I got you a room. I not only got you a room, I got you a nice room and it ain't gonna cost you an arm and a leg. Told you I could do it. Now you and that wife of yours got a place to stay. Come on, my car's outside. We going to town so I can show you around Columbus."

Kim got up and grabbed his barracks bag. "Give me a hand with this trunk." They each grabbed an end to the olive-green trunk and carried it out to the car.

~

Kim was standing at the station when Ida got off the train. It had been over four months since he had last seen her, and even then they had only had a few days together. He forgot how good she looked. She stepped down from the passenger car and looked around until she saw him wave. Barely five feet tall and petite, her black hair was swept back under a hat that matched her coat, her face round and porcelain in complexion.

Even though it wasn't seemly for them to show affection in public, he was no different than the other young men in uniform holding their sweethearts. Kim grabbed her suitcase and stood for a moment while Ida admired him in his uniform with the shiny yellow bars. Even though they had known each other since they were children, he couldn't overcome his awkwardness around her. He wasn't one to be very romantic. That wasn't the quality she expected in him, or what she admired about him. She could always sense his discomfort with intimacy.

"You look very handsome."

Kim's face reddened. "And you look very—beautiful." It was all he could think of to say out loud. It was easier for him with less personal conversation.

"One of the men I trained with got us a nice room in town. Let's see if we can catch the bus. Maybe you want to freshen up after the train ride."

"It was a very long ride, but I would really like something to eat."

"Sure, we'll go to the hotel and drop your things off first."

The next morning he got out of bed as quietly as he could manage. No matter how hard he tried, he could not sleep past 5:00 a.m., and the soft bed took some getting used to. He moved over to a chair and watched his wife while she slept. It seemed unreal to have spent the last months in the field, training and crawling through the dirt. And now he was here with her. As much as he wanted to stay with her, the military life seemed right for him. He was eager for it to begin.

Kim called Benning every day, waiting for orders that still hadn't come. Finally he and Ida came in one afternoon from walking around the town, and the desk clerk told him that he had a call from Fort Benning. His orders were in.

Ida waited while he made the call and watched his face for emotion. She never saw any but, then again, his expression never changed much regardless.

"I've been assigned to the 100th Infantry Battalion at Camp Shelby, Mississippi."

"What kind of unit is that?"

"I don't know. All I know is that it's an infantry outfit. Must be something new. I need to go to Fort Benning and pick up my orders. They said the 100th is moving from Camp McCoy in Wisconsin, where they've been training, to Camp Shelby. Anyway, I have more than two weeks before I have to report, so what do you want to do?"

Ida had been thinking about what she might do after her husband got his orders. Her friend that she had roomed with during nursing school, Janet Nishimura, was sent to a camp in Jerome, Arkansas. They had last visited when Janet was at the Santa Anita Assembly Center.

"Janet—I would like to visit Janet."

They had both talked about the Japanese evacuations on the West Coast and the fact that Janet and her family were now at this strange place in Arkansas. Many of the friends they had grown up with were now in relocation camps. This was hard for either of them to accept. Both Ida and Kim had a vivid recollection of the horse stalls the Nishimura family had been living in at the racetrack.

Kim nodded to his young wife. "We'll visit Janet. I have to get permission to go there because I'll be traveling on orders, so I need approval for a delay in route to Shelby, Mississippi. I don't think it will be a problem. I'll go to the fort and get my orders. See if I can work everything out. Maybe you can take a walk around town."

Ida shook her head. She would wait in the room. This was a different place and she did not feel comfortable walking around without her husband, especially with the attitude toward people who looked Japanese. On the long trip from California she had seen people staring at her and whispering. Some even came up and asked her if she "was a Jap." She had politely explained that she was Korean, but was ashamed later that she had even answered the question.

~

Lieutenant Kim and his wife managed to obtain tickets on the train for Little Rock, which was only a bus ride from Jerome. It was a long and uncomfortable trip. There wasn't an empty seat all the way from Columbus to Little Rock, so Kim stood most of the way so Ida could sit on their suitcase. His Army trunk was in the baggage car. All he carried with him in the passenger compartment was his barracks bag. He didn't mind standing. His officer's uniform made him proud and he knew Ida was proud of him, too. He could tell by the way she kept looking at him and brushing his shoulder, as if to straighten out wrinkles that weren't really there. There were a lot of men standing, most of them in uniform, but they looked away when they saw his yellow bars. It would be different, now that he was an officer.

By late afternoon the bus slowed to a stop in front of a gate with a guard at the entry. Barbed wire was strung in both directions. Kim immediately saw the tower with the guard in it—and the machine gun. Night was falling and the lights were coming on. Barbed wire stretched as far as he could see. His eyes moved back up to the tower that stood fifty feet in the air. He could see the soldier manning his gun and watching. They both turned to one another and Ida put her hand on his arm. He could see the concern in her face. This wasn't a camp. This was a prison.

He walked to the entrance and rang a bell beside the gate.

A young Army private came out and looked at the two of them. "No visitors," was all he said.

Kim waited for a moment and then looked at the guard. "Excuse me, Private, is that the way you address an officer?"

The young man stood for a moment, appraising Kim's uniform and the bars on his collar and shoulders, and then straightened to a semblance of attention.

"Excuse me, Lieutenant." He kept looking at Kim and then raised his hand in salute.

"Sir, no visitors are allowed. You folks will just have to go back to wherever you came from."

Kim returned the salute. "How are we supposed to get back to Little Rock, Private? I'm an American Army officer and I'm here. I demand to be allowed inside."

"Well, sir, I have my orders. What am I supposed to do?"

"You're supposed to go talk to whoever gave you those orders and get him out here to talk to me."

The private looked at the Asian man wearing an American officer's uniform, the confusion clear on his face. He shrugged.

"Okay, sir, but it's going to be awhile."

"I have time, Private, so make that call."

"Yes, sir, all right, sir." He turned and walked back inside the gate and into the guard shack, where he spoke to another guard. Then he picked up a field phone and spoke. After that, he just stood inside the shack while Kim and his wife stood outside the gate.

After about an hour and a half, a sergeant came up to the gate and looked through at the two of them.

"What can I do for you, Lieutenant?"

"You can let my wife and me inside, Sergeant. We have people inside we would like to visit. Nishimura—check the name—Toshiro Nishimura and his wife and their daughter, Janet."

"Well, sir, we don't allow no visitors. Ain't nobody been in this place 'cept the folks that's supposed to be here."

"Is this a prison, Sergeant?"

"No, sir, it's a relocation camp for Jap—ah, Japanese people."

"Well, if it isn't a prison, then the people inside should be able to have visitors. Maybe you could get an officer down here?"

"Yes, sir, but it's going to take some time."

"Look around, Sergeant, we don't have any place to go. I know you're just doing your job, but we want to come in."

"Yes, sir."

It was another fifteen minutes until a civilian came out.

"Can we help you, Lieutenant?"

"Yes, sir, I'm Lieutenant Young Oak Kim and this is my wife, Ida. We would like to visit our friends who are in this place."

"Well, no visitors are allowed, Lieutenant."

"Is there a regulation to prevent visitors?"

"No, but—well, we just never had any visitors before. You really want to come in here?"

"We have friends here."

The man, obviously some kind of civilian supervisor, stood looking at him, weighing his decision.

"All right, I guess it's okay, you being in the Army and all. Come on in. We'll have to sign you both in and then we'll send somebody over to the Nishimuras' room and they can walk you back. I'll warn you now, it isn't going to be very comfortable. And it's going to be crowded."

He motioned them through and they walked to the wooden head-quarters building, signed in and waited. After fifteen or twenty minutes, Janet Nishimura walked through the door. Ida stood and embraced her friend.

"Ida, how did you get here? You wrote and said you would try to come, but we didn't really expect you."

"Young Oak and I—we were able to come on his way to his new post. He was able to get permission to take some extra time so we wanted to come. This place . . ."

"I know—it's not what we expected, either. I'm sorry I never wrote back, but it is very difficult right now to get mail out. Come, come. Everyone is waiting to see you and Young Oak."

She led them outside, where the Nishimura family and a large group of their friends were standing. Everybody was talking at once and admiring Kim's uniform. Both he and Ida found it a little overwhelming until Mr. Nishimura took some control.

"There will be time in the morning to ask Lieutenant and Mrs. Kim questions. They must be very tired. Let us get them back to our room so they can rest."

Kim noticed the walkways were covered with what looked like packing box boards. The ground was muddy and the makeshift walkways allowed them to keep their feet relatively dry. Both Kim and Ida were appalled at the tar-paper, board-and-batten accommodations. Communication wire was strung across the room and blankets hung from it, held in place by clothespins. The blanket was all that separated the Nishimuras from the other family in the room. A single bulb hung from the ceiling. The draft through the room was evident and the people in the room kept their coats on.

Immediately, Kim began to apologize for increasing the already crowded conditions. Janet stopped him. "Please, do not apologize to us, Young Oak. It is we who must apologize for not having more to offer. But this is what we have for now. My parents offer their bed, but please take mine."

"We won't take anybody's bed. I'll sleep on the floor, and perhaps you and Ida can share." He looked at the narrow bed with the thin mattress. He would just as soon be on the floor anyway. Janet and Ida were already talking about everything that had happened since they had last seen one another, the train ride to Little Rock, the guards, the food.

Kim's attention turned to Janet's father. "How is it here, Mr. Nishimura? I have difficulty even believing this is happening. It doesn't seem like this can be legal."

"We have stopped thinking about whether it is legal. There is no point. We are just trying to get settled and make our life as comfortable as possible."

"Are most of the people here from Los Angeles?"

"No, most of the people here are from the San Joaquin Valley and Fresno."

Kim could not conceal his surprise. "Fresno? Why would they send people here from Fresno?"

Toshiro shrugged. "Why would they send us here? There is no reason to it. Many of our friends are in the Manzanar camp in California and some in Arizona. Here, let the women talk. You must be tired but many would like to talk to you. Perhaps we could go to the mess hall and sit with the other men, share news of the outside?"

Toshiro was right. Kim was very tired but these people were in far worse condition, and it would be a source of great pride to Mr. Nishimura if he could bring a visitor from the outside, an Army officer, an Asian.

"Of course, Mr. Nishimura. I'll follow you." He turned to Ida. "I'll be back after a while. You two have a lot to catch up on."

As they walked to the mess hall, Kim looked around. "I don't see any soldiers. Where are the guards?"

"Oh, the guards don't come in here. They are only at the gate. Did they bother you?"

"I think they were a little confused by my uniform and rank. They didn't seem to know what to do with us. I'm not sure if they could figure out whether to salute me or shoot me."

Toshiro gave a rueful laugh. "Inside, we don't see them very often. We can't go outside so they just do what they do and we do what we do. It is better that way, I think. We have all learned to get along."

Kim nodded and kept his thoughts to himself.

~

Kim woke in the early morning. He could hear the steady breathing of his wife next to him. He could also hear the sounds of the family separated by the blanket wall. It had been six days since they arrived at the camp and still he struggled with the reality of it. Guards with machine guns in towers along the wire walls. Citizens watched over who had committed no crime. He was an American Army officer, sleeping in a room with American citizens living in a place surrounded by barbed wire and guarded by Army troops.

He rolled over and moved closer to Ida. He could feel her warmth through her nightgown. The outside air leaked through the board-and-batten walls with impunity, and the floor gave little resistance to the damp earth chill coming from the crawl space beneath the barracks.

So many young men had come up to him and asked what it was like to be in the Army. What was it like to be an officer? What was it like to be an Asian in the Army, when there was so much hostility? He realized that he hadn't given it much thought. He had been so bent on getting through it that he had given very little consideration to the uniqueness of his position. He realized that now. He did not really think of himself as a role model. He never lived his life for others; but here he was a person to be admired. As much as he hated to admit it, he just wanted to move on. He wanted to get to this new unit. He wanted to be part of the adventure of his lifetime.

Others in the room were starting to stir. Toshiro was also beginning to get out of bed and fumbled for his shoes. There was a rush in the morning to get to the common-area bathroom. Toshiro was no different than most men his age, and it was difficult for him to make it through the night without a visit to the bathroom. Kim followed him out the door, and they walked together across the muddy common area separating the barracks in their section. There was already a line and some of the men who couldn't wait moved behind a small stand of trees to relieve themselves.

As soon as the men saw Kim, they started to ask questions. There had been much speculation about where he was going to be assigned. Rumors spread over the camp that an all-Japanese unit was being trained up north, but nobody had much information. Letters coming into the camp asked about the unit but the details were vague. Since he didn't know anything about the 100th, other than its designation as a separate battalion, he hadn't been able to offer much in the way of answers. Still, it was an intriguing possibility. Despite the traditional animosity between Japanese and Koreans, he had always gotten along well with Japanese people. He had grown up on Los Angeles's Bunker Hill with Japanese neighbors and playmates.

"So, Lieutenant, how much longer will you be able to stay here?" The question came from a young man named Freddy Shiraga, who made it a point to talk to him whenever he could.

"I have to leave in another two days, Freddy. I need to report to my unit. It's moving to a new location, so that's why I got the extra time to come here with my wife."

Freddy nodded. "Lieutenant, you think we will be able to join the Army? My best friend, he's at Manzanar, and they signed a petition to let them join the Army. A lot of the guys here want to join, too. You think that's going to happen?"

"I don't know, Freddy. If the rumors are true about the unit I'm joining up with then the Army is going to take Japanese in, but I don't really know."

Freddy looked down at the ground for a moment while they moved forward in the bathroom line.

"Lieutenant, I'm not sure I want to join the Army."

Kim looked at the young man, not that much younger than himself. "Why?"

"Well, I guess it's because of all this, the camp and everything else. Why should we fight for the government when they put us in here?"

Kim stood quietly for a moment. He could tell others were listening for his answer and he wasn't really sure what to say.

"I guess the answer would be that this is your country and your country is at war. Sometimes governments do things that aren't right or that people don't agree with, but we still have to remember that it is the country and our families we are defending. Governments change, policies change. I understand why you would feel resentment. I resent this and I can leave anytime I want to. Look, Freddy, you'll just have to do what you think you can live with for the rest of your life. For me, being in the Army is the best way to protect my family."

Freddy's furrowed brow showed his concentration and confusion. It was going to be a hard decision for a lot of these young men. If they were ever permitted to make that decision. Most seemed to take the attitude that this was their country, even though what it was doing was wrong. Any anger was mostly kept inside, away from the observation of others.

Kim watched as Freddy moved away from the line and walked slowly toward one of the barracks. It occurred to him that Freddy was the same age as many of the young men he would soon be commanding. They would have questions, too, and he needed to have answers if he was going to lead them.

The realization that he would soon be making decisions for young men that weren't much more than boys weighed heavily on him for the first time. He had been taught at Benning that the first thing a leader said in combat was "Follow me." The reality of what that meant was becoming clearer, day by day, as he moved closer to his assignment. If he was to lead, then he had to convince the men they should follow him.

~

The guard at the gate saluted. They had all heard of the Asian Army officer who was spending his leave inside the camp. Kim returned the salute.

He and Ida walked through the front gate of Jerome. He heard the wood gate shut and the scraping sound of boots against the gravelly red earth, walking back inside. He looked up at the wooden towers hiding machine guns. The barbed wire of the fence glinted dully in the winter sun. The barbed wire was now behind him. And so were the people he had come to call friends.

CHAPTER 37

February 1, 1943
Office of the Secretary of War
Washington, D.C.

It was late in the evening, but lights were still on at the War Department. Assistant Secretary of War John McCloy walked directly into Secretary Stimson's office. The week before, based on the successful training of the all-Japanese 100th Infantry Battalion in Mississippi and the increasing need for troops, Secretary Stimson authorized a press release on the formation of the all-Japanese 442nd Regimental Combat Team.

General DeWitt and Colonel Bendetsen strongly opposed the formation of a new unit on the basis that it would undermine the rationale for the creation of the camps. According to Bendetsen, if the Japanese were in camps because their loyalty was in question, then how could the government justify using them as soldiers? To answer part of their objection, loyalty questionnaires were created that would open the possibility of people not only volunteering for the Army, but also leaving the camps to help in the war effort outside of the West Coast.

The War Department publicly announced Stimson's statement that *"It is the inherent right of every citizen, regardless of ancestry, to bear arms in the Nation's battle. When obstacles to the free expression of that right are imposed by emergency considerations, those barriers should be removed as soon as humanly possible. Loyalty to country is a voice that must be heard, and I am now able to give active proof that this basic American belief is not a casualty of war."*

Stimson indicated to McCloy that they were going to have something very public on the Japanese combat team, and he was anxious to hear what it was. Stimson smiled and, without a word, held out a letter. McCloy could immediately see the familiar White House stationery.

*WHITE HOUSE

February 1, 1943

My Dear Mr. Secretary:

The proposal of the War Department to organize a combat team consisting of loyal American citizens of Japanese descent has my full approval. The new combat team will add to the nearly five thousand loyal Americans of Japanese ancestry who are already serving in the armed forces of our country.

This is a natural and logical step toward the reinstitution of the Selective Service procedures which were temporarily disrupted by the evacuation from the West Coast.

No loyal citizen of the United States should be denied the democratic right to exercise the responsibilities of his citizenship, regardless of his ancestry. The principle on which this country was founded and by which it has always been governed is that Americanism is a matter of the mind and heart; Americanism is not, and never was, a matter of race or ancestry. A good American is one who is loyal to this country and to our creed of liberty and democracy. Every loyal American citizen should be given the opportunity to serve this country wherever his skills will make the greatest contribution—whether it be in the ranks of our armed forces, war production, agriculture, government service, or other work essential to the war effort.

I am glad to observe that the War Department, the Navy Department, the War Manpower Commission, the Department of Justice, and the War Relocation Authority are collaborating in a program which will assure the opportunity for all loyal

Americans, including Americans of Japanese ancestry, to serve their country at a time when the fullest and wisest use of our manpower is all-important to the war effort.

Very sincerely yours,

Franklin D. Roosevelt *

McCloy looked up from the letter and smiled.

CHAPTER 38

February 1, 1943
Camp Shelby, Mississippi

Lieutenant Kim looked out the bus window as he rode from Jackson, Mississippi, to Camp Shelby. It was getting close to dusk, and he hoped he would make it to his new assignment before nightfall. The countryside here wasn't that much different from Georgia. Pine trees made up most of the landscape, which was heavily forested but still featured the same reddish earth.

Walking out of the camp and leaving the Nishimuras and other people he and Ida had befriended had been difficult. He could still feel the shudder that passed through his body when he looked at the guard towers, and the armed soldiers who saluted and called him sir when he and Ida left. Ida had cried for hours, riding with him as far as Jackson, where they said their goodbyes before she returned to California. It had been a bittersweet moment. They had spent very little time together since getting married, not counting their time together inside the crowded camp at Jerome. He knew it was not likely they'd see each another again for a long time. Realistically, he knew that they might not see each other again at all. He was nothing if not pragmatic. That was the way of war. Ida knew that and so did he.

In the rapidly fading light he could make out the lights of what was obviously a military installation. It was only a moment before the driver called out, "Camp Shelby." He looked down at his watch, which read 4:30 p.m. He was here at last.

It took a while to get through processing into Shelby, but he finally made it onto the bus that dropped off men at different points around the camp. It had been raining a short time before and puddles of water and mud were everywhere. He was used to mud. It seemed to him like the Army never put a camp anywhere without a lot of mud.

The driver stopped and turned his head. "This here's the 100th, Lieutenant."

A building at the end of a wooden board walkway held a sign on it that read "100th Battalion." He picked up his suitcase and barracks bag and got off the bus. He had left his trunk with Ida, too hard to transport. The thin gravel on the edge of the roadway barely kept him from sinking into the slick reddish mire. The whole area looked like something built in a swamp. He stood in the fading light of dusk, noticing the board walkway that covered the mud in front of the battalion headquarters. Not much to look at.

Kim took a deep breath, straightened his back and moved as quickly as he could to the door, struggling under the awkward weight of the barracks bag and suitcase. He entered and stepped immediately into a puddle of water on the floor. He felt a drip on his uniform and looked up at the still-leaking ceiling. He approached the orderly sitting behind a desk, the spongy floor giving against his weight, boards soaked to softness. The dark-skinned, angular-faced private looked up at him, his almond-shaped eyes narrowing even more as he scrutinized the officer in front of him. It seemed unusual, as Kim hadn't seen many Japanese in the military in the last few months.

He took out his orders and travel papers. "I'm Lieutenant Young Oak Kim. I'm to report to the commanding officer of this unit."

The private looked at him curiously and then blurted out, "The battalion is doing field training, Lieutenant, sir. They're not expected back tonight. Maybe tomorrow."

Kim looked around, trying to figure out what to do next, not wanting to appear like the situation confused him.

"Is there another officer in charge?"

"Yes, sir, Captain Kometani is here. Do you want me to get him?"

"Yes, Private, that would be fine." He could not help considering the sensation of command. He never felt it before.

Kim stood quietly while the obviously befuddled private left him and went to get the officer he had mentioned. Kim looked around the outer office of the battalion HQ. He could feel cold air moving through the room, the walls exuding dampness and the odor of mildew he had gotten used to at Benning. *Everything damp all the time. Damp from the rain in winter, damp from the humidity in summer.* He hadn't felt completely dry since he arrived at Benning.

He looked up when the private walked back in the room. "Sir, Captain Kometani is over at the officer's quarters. He said for me to bring you over. You can follow me, sir. Just leave your gear and I'll see that it gets to you."

Kim had some difficulty following the conversation with the private. He was speaking English, that was clear, but he had a peculiar way of slurring his words and dropping out his T's and H's. It wasn't impossible to understand, or even unpleasant. Just different. Lilting in a way, almost like he came from a foreign country and was learning English, even though he understood everything said to him. He kept close to the private and followed to the officer's quarters.

The man sitting in the commons room stood up when Kim walked in. He had the face of a bulldog and a barrel chest—and was Japanese, too. Maybe the rumors were true? Had the Army sent him to some kind of all-Japanese unit?

"Lieutenant, this is Captain Kometani." Kometani put out his hand and looked searchingly at Kim's face, with an expression that also seemed confused. Kim stiffened his posture and saluted.

"Sir, Lieutenant Young Oak Kim reporting for duty, sir."

Kometani's face moved into an expression that passed for a smile. He drew back his hand and casually returned the salute. "Lieutenant, you say your name's Kim? That right?"

Kim nodded. "Yes, sir."

Kometani nodded his head in a thoughtful manner. "You Korean, Kim?"

"Yes, sir."

Kometani's face betrayed his confusion. "Where've you come from, Lieutenant?"

"Sir, I just graduated from Fort Benning, sir. Before that I was a sergeant in the motor pool in a unit at Fort Ord in California."

"And the Army sent you here?"

"Yes, sir, Captain."

"Did you ask to come here?"

"Sir, I didn't ask to go anywhere. I graduated and I didn't get my orders like the other fellows, so I waited for a while and then I got orders to come here."

Kometani's face still showed confusion. "So where were you when Pearl Harbor was attacked?"

Kim paused, as he hadn't expected that question. *What difference did that make?*

"I was in San Francisco, sir, on a two-day pass, going to see my girl-friend. She's my wife now, sir."

"And after the attack?"

"I went back to Ord and then over to San Luis Obispo, where I pulled guard duty and helped run the motor pool, sir. Then I did desert training until I was accepted to Officer Candidate School, sir."

"Well, Lieutenant Kim, in case you haven't figured it out by now, this unit is all Japanese." Kometani waited to see if there was any reaction, but there was no expression at all on the face of the young lieutenant in front of him. "Our motto is 'Remember Pearl Harbor.'"

Kim still hadn't changed his expression, but his mind was racing. He couldn't help thinking that there was some irony in the motto. He stood and waited for Kometani to make some further comment.

Finally, Kometani spoke up. "Find yourself an empty bunk, Lieu-tenant. I'll call over and have them send some blankets. The battalion is out in the field and won't be back until tomorrow, at the earliest. When they get back, our CO, Colonel Turner, will want to see you. He'll talk to you about your assignment.

"I don't think we can offer you anything to eat at the moment. Maybe if you go over to the mess hall they'll have something. When you get yourself a bunk, come on back. We can talk."

"Yes, sir." Kim picked up his suitcase and barracks bag that had been brought in while he was talking to Kometani. He started down the hall, looking for a place to sleep. He wasn't really hungry. Everything that had happened so far had killed his appetite. Besides, it was a lot to digest—an all-Japanese unit in Mississippi.

He looked down the hallway until he found an empty bunk—no blankets, just a bare mattress. He sat his gear down. Left everything in it. No point in putting it in a locker and finding out he had taken somebody else's space. Besides, he wanted to get back, talk to Kometani and find out more about this place.

Kometani was still sitting in the common room looking at a magazine when Kim walked back in. He glanced over at the Lieutenant.

"You going to eat?"

"No, sir. I'll just wait until breakfast."

"Suit yourself. So, Kim, where you from?"

"Los Angeles, sir."

Kometani's face took on an amused expression at the formality. "Look, Kim, everybody calls me Komi here. The officers, that is. I'm not really a combat officer; I'm a dentist. Went to the University of Southern California as a matter of fact, so I know L.A."

Kometani saw the confused expression on Kim's face. "I know, you're wondering why a dentist is in this unit, right? Look, all the boys in this outfit except a few of the officers and sergeants are from Hawaii. They let me in because I know a lot of the boys and their parents trust me. You might say I'm kinda like a liaison with their folks. They trust me to make sure that the *haoles*, the white people, treat them right. Understand?"

"Yes, sir. I thought the rumors about an all-Japanese unit were just rumors. My wife and I, after we got my orders, we went to visit friends over at the relocation camp in Jerome, Arkansas. They talked about the rumor, but nobody seemed to know anything."

Kometani clearly looked surprised. "You've been inside Jerome? What's it like?"

"Well, it has gates and guard towers with armed troops. It's kind of like a prison, I guess, and then not. I mean, I stayed inside with friends of my wife. Most of the people are from California, the San Joaquin Valley, and from the assembly center they had at Santa Anita racetrack. I guess it just made me feel bad, sir. The people live in rooms similar to these barracks, but there are a couple families to a room and they have to make some kind of wall to have any privacy. The food is a lot like Army food but they're not used to it. I was glad to get out of there but I felt real funny, you know? I can't describe it any better than that."

Kometani nodded and kept watching him. "Look, Kim, the old man, Colonel Turner, he's been told that you're here. He'll be in tomorrow morning around 8:00 a.m. You report for duty then. Just go back to the headquarters building where you first came in."

"Yes, sir." Kim hesitated. "Captain, could I ask a question?" He waited until Kometani nodded.

"You looked surprised when you saw me. So did that private when I checked in at your HQ. Is that because I'm Korean?"

Kometani looked at him, his face expressionless. "Kim, maybe you ought to ask Colonel Turner about that. But for right now, I guess I'd say that it takes our people a while to get used to outsiders. Why don't you go get settled in. It's late." Kim looked at his watch and realized he was more tired than he thought.

~

Kim woke up at 5:00 a.m. It took him a moment to remember where he was. The disorientation came from moving to so many different places in such short periods of time. He lay in bed for a few minutes and thought about where he was and what was going to happen. Obviously Kometani had some concerns about the fact he was Korean. Almost every place he'd been in the Army, he'd started out as the only Asian and he had to work to make people comfortable with him. Now everybody around him was also Asian, and he could still sense the discomfort. The thought that Asians from one culture would have reservations about Asians from another seemed almost incomprehensible to him, especially after the problems he had with white people, and then being promoted by them. *Well, I have to fit in someplace. May as well be here.*

He rolled out of the bunk and turned on the light. The night before, he set out his uniform and polished his boots; good impressions were important. Besides, he wanted to get in line at the mess hall. He was hungry.

At 7:50 a.m. he walked over to 100th HQ, picking his way carefully across the wooden board walkway and trying to keep mud off his boots, at least until after he had reported to the CO. Another private was sitting behind the desk when he walked into HQ. He looked up with a quizzical expression.

"Can I help you, Lieutenant?" The same lilting accent as the private from the night before.

"Yes, Private. I'm Lieutenant Kim and I need to report to the battalion commanding officer, Colonel Turner. Is he in?"

"Yes, sir, he's in. I was told to expect you. I'll let him know you're here."

His first impression of the man sitting behind his desk surprised him. Turner had to be well into his late forties, maybe into his fifties, fairly old for a battalion commander. He had gray, almost white hair, and he didn't look very intimidating.

Kim moved to the front of the CO's desk and stood at attention, saluting.

"Sir, Second Lieutenant Young Oak Kim, reporting for duty, sir."

Turner returned the salute, looking at the slender young man in front of him with the flat expression and hooded eyes. There was something different about him.

"Relax, Lieutenant." Turner sat in his chair for a moment and seemed unsure of what to say. He then looked Kim directly in the eyes and searched for any kind of reaction or expression. "You're Korean, aren't you?" It sounded more like an accusation than a question.

He continued staring. Kim remained, standing stiffly in the position the Army euphemistically called "at ease," his feet spread apart shoulder-width and his hands clasped firmly in the small of his back.

"Yes, sir."

Turner pursed his lips and looked down at the orders for Kim lying on his desk.

"Look, Lieutenant, maybe the War Department made a mistake here. Japanese, Koreans, I imagine they think there's no difference. This is an all-Japanese unit, do you know that?"

"Yes, sir, but I didn't know for sure until I got here last night."

"Well, I'll get the staff to work on your transfer. We'll have you out of here without a problem." He continued watching Kim's face, no change of expression, just the same stare from under the heavily lidded eyes.

"Sir, why a transfer?"

"I told you, Lieutenant, this is an all-Japanese unit."

"Yes, sir, I understand that, sir, but what difference does that make? With respect, sir, you're not Japanese."

Turner ignored Kim's comment and shuffled the papers on his desk, searching for the right words.

"Look, Lieutenant, I'm sure I'm not telling you anything you don't already know. Japanese and Koreans, well, they haven't gotten along very well historically. You have to know that." He could see Kim's posture get a little straighter, but still no change of expression.

Kim then spoke very deliberately. *"Sir, I think you're wrong. These men in this unit, they're American soldiers and I'm an American soldier and we're both going to fight for America. I would like to stay with the unit, sir."*

Turner sat back, startled and a little taken aback. He hadn't expected this reaction, and he began to take a new measure of the young lieutenant standing in front of him.

"You know, Kim, we've had other officers come into the unit. Some were Chinese, some Korean, some white; they didn't want to stay. We have a process in place. If you don't want to stay, it's no problem. It won't reflect on your record."

"Sir, I would prefer to stay." His tone was even and his voice never changed, except that there was something else behind it. Something that Turner caught, but couldn't quite put his finger on. *Determination, perhaps?* Something that made this young man different.

Turner stared at Kim for what seemed like a long time. He looked down at the personnel jacket in front of him. Finally he moved his tongue across his lips, then spoke.

"All right, Lieutenant Kim, you can stay. You're going to be assigned as a platoon leader in Company B. You report to Captain Clarence Johnson, the company commander. Johnson will give you your specific assignment. Go on out to the clerk at the front. He'll give you directions. We'll try it out for a while, maybe give you a chance to get used to the men."

Kim nodded. "Yes, sir, thank you, sir." He snapped to attention and saluted, waiting until it was returned. He stared for a brief moment at the gray-haired lieutenant colonel and kept his thoughts to himself. *The men will have to get used to me, too.*

He turned and walked out of the office.

CHAPTER 39

February 15, 1943
Manzanar War Relocation Center
Independence, California

Sammy sat on his bed, listening to his father and Toshi talking about the loyalty questionnaires circulating throughout the camp. After the riot and his questioning, Toshi had been released, but he was now under constant watch. He was speaking out all over camp against the questionnaire. All people over the age of 17 were required to answer. The camp director made it clear that men would be allowed to join the new 442nd Regimental Combat Team that had been announced by the War Department, or leave the camps to work in places other than the West Coast, depending on how the loyalty questionnaire was answered.

The news of an all-Japanese combat unit caused much excitement in the camp and much dissension as well. Whether it was right to have a segregated army unit, whether anybody should volunteer when their family was in a camp, and whether the actions of the government should be met with civil disobedience, were all topics of heated discussion. Everywhere Sammy went in the camp, people were talking and arguing. Not a room in the camp was silent on the issue, but now, with the loyalty questionnaire, there was something new, something worse. Father against son, brother against brother, sister against brother. Sammy could hear loud talking between Tommy and his parents through the thin wall that separated them. Worse, his father and Toshi were also arguing.

Shig sat with his head down as Toshi railed against the questionnaire. "Father, listen to what they are asking. Don't you understand what this could mean?" Toshi held up a questionnaire. *"Question 27 says, 'Are you willing to serve in the armed forces of the United States on combat duty, wherever ordered?'* Question 28 says, *"Will you swear unqualified allegiance to the United States of America and faithfully defend the United States from any and all attack by foreign or domestic forces, and foreswear any form of allegiance to the Japanese Emperor or any other foreign government, power, or organization?"*

"Don't you understand what could happen? You and Mom aren't even allowed to be citizens in this country. If you say 'yes' to these questions, will you be allowed to stay here? What's going to happen to you? Will you have a country? You are still a citizen of Japan—give that up and what's left if you are not a citizen of this country? These people don't want us. Why do you think we're here? I am not going to answer 'yes' to these questions. I'm not going to be an *inu* for the government." Toshi's face had grew red from anger, and spittle gathered at the corners of his mouth.

Shig did not raise his voice, but there was no mistaking his tone. "You will not speak to me like this. I am your father and it will not be tolerated. Your mother and I have listened to the talking all over the camp. What people do is their decision. This is our country now. You do not understand that Japan offered us nothing when we left. Japan offers us nothing now. *Umi-no-oya-yori mo sodate no oya. Your adoptive parents are your real parents.* This is our country now."

Toshi threw the questionnaire on the floor. "If this is my country, then why am I in here? No Germans are in here. No Italians are in here. Just us. I say no."

Toshi sat down on a bed and stared at the floor while his father looked at him. Shig barely whispered. "It is for you to decide."

Toshi turned and looked at his younger brother. "Well, what are you going to do?"

Sammy, too, had listened to the endless talk and argument in the camp. He had made his decision.

"I am going to volunteer for the Army. I've made my own mind up. I've told Mom and Dad."

Toshi's mouth curled down. Contempt was on his face. "You will be a 'yes-yes' boy then?" Being a "yes-yes" person had become the derogatory term for people who signed yes to questions 27 and 28. Being a "no-no" was worn as a badge of defiance.

Sammy stared directly at his brother. "If you think by being a 'yes-yes' boy that I'm weak, then I have nothing more to say about this. You do what you have to do." Sammy looked at his parents and could see tears in his mother's eyes.

"I'm going in, Toshi. I'll help you if I can but if you don't sign this, and with what they know about you and the riot, they're going to arrest you. I'm not doing this because I'm afraid of punishment. I'm doing this because it's what is right for me."

Toshi stood up and walked toward the door. "You're going to regret this. You watch. They aren't making white boys take a loyalty oath to get into the Army. You're going to end up taking some white boy's place in a labor battalion or worse, on the front line."

After pausing for a moment, Toshi realized where this conversation was taking him. He softened his voice.

"You do what you have to do, brother."

With that, he looked at his parents and walked out the door.

Sammy was surprised. There were no more tears from his mother, no angry words from his father. They both simply sat on the bed and let the room fill with silence, broken only by the endless wind of Manzanar seeping through the cracks in the walls.

~

Freddy walked with his parents and Betty over to the administration office to sign the loyalty questionnaire. The whole family discussed the decision they made: They would sign together. The Shiraga family would be a "yes-yes" family. Freddy felt deeply resentful of the questions, but had already decided he would volunteer for the new all-Japanese Army unit. He thought a lot about what Lieutenant Kim said when he visited Jerome.

His father listened to Freddy while he gave his reasons for his decision. In the end, Mas simply looked at his son and said, "It is the decision I would expect from my son." No other words about it had been exchanged.

Freddy sat in the recreation hall, listening to the Army captain talking to him and about fifty other young men about volunteering for the 442nd. He talked about how well the 100th was doing in Shelby, Mississippi. Mostly, he talked about how they would benefit from volunteering for service. He said there were a lot of questions out there about them, and they could answer many of them through volunteering.

Freddy raised his hand. "Captain, if we join, will we be able to come back and visit? What about our parents? What will happen to them?"

The discomfort of the military officer was evident. With his round glasses and thinning hair, he looked more like a lawyer than an infantry officer. His slow response didn't change that impression.

"Ah, well, I'm not in charge of the camps, so I can't speak for the policy here or in any of the camps. All I can say is that I am not aware of any restrictions on travel for men wearing the uniform of an American soldier. Except, of course, travel restrictions on leaving their base, obtaining passes, and things like that. I haven't heard anything about your parents not being provided for. I know that there are those questionnaires people here have been asked to fill out and I've heard the same rumors you have, that if people are approved they may be allowed to leave the camps on work permits. I can't answer any better than that."

Freddy persisted. "Will our parents be allowed to go home?"

"If by home you mean back to the West Coast, I'm not in a position to know the answer to that. I'm sorry. Any other questions?"

He was met by stony silence. The captain waited uncomfortably and pulled at his tunic while he looked at the faces in the crowd. He couldn't blame them. Here he was, asking them to fight while their families were imprisoned. He could only imagine how that must feel.

Continued silence brought the meeting to a close. He called for volunteers to step forward and sign up. At first nobody moved, then a few looked around. The sound of metal folding chairs pushing against the wooden floor filled the room. Several young men walked over to a table where a sergeant was waiting with forms.

Freddy didn't look at anyone as he moved between rows to get in line. Some people moved their feet to get out of his way. Others kept their feet out in front, making him climb over. Not everyone was going to do this and of those who did, Freddy knew some were going against the wishes of their parents. He was grateful for his father's support.

He stepped to the desk and signed where the sergeant's finger pointed. When he looked up, the sergeant was smiling.

"Congratulations, son, you're in the United States Army."

Freddy smiled back and accepted the handful of papers.

The sergeant added, "You'll be getting your orders to report in the next few weeks. You made a good decision."

Freddy nodded and moved to the back of the room, where Rose was waiting.

He had talked to Rose about his intention. She had been accepting, but quiet. Now she took his hand as he walked out of the recreation hall and into the cold winter air. They walked along the back of the hall, looking to find some privacy.

He felt like he had to say something, but he wasn't sure what she expected. He was excited about the prospect of the Army and he was torn with concern about his family, but his feelings about Rose were still ambiguous. He cared about her, at least as much as a friend could, but he knew that he wasn't ready for any kind of commitment, especially now with him leaving.

Rose broke the silence. "Did they tell you when you will leave?"

"That sergeant said I would get orders in a few weeks. I'm not sure where we're going, but they said the 100th is in Mississippi, and that's not too far away. If we go there it won't be so bad. Maybe I'll be able to visit. They didn't say."

He hadn't thought about that part, visiting. If they weren't allowed to leave the camp, were they going to let them come back as soldiers and visit?

Rose turned and faced him. She could tell he was searching for words, but he remained silent. She decided one of them had to make an overture.

"I'll write to you and when you come back we will start where our letters end."

He looked at the round face and black eyes staring at him, shining as tears gathered but did not fall. In that instant he realized how many times he looked past her instead of looking at her. He had never thought of her this way, realistic and strong, maybe stronger than him. In that one moment he knew that he wanted to come home to her. She had set a path he could follow.

~

Sammy listened to the rhythmic sound of his parents breathing. The beginning of dawn came through the window, the cold gray light barely illuminating the few items of furniture in the room. He got out of bed quietly, dressing in the early morning chill.

Sammy walked out of the barracks, stepping down onto the gravel between structures. The ground was frozen solid and the gravel didn't give way against his shoes. He pulled his coat tightly around him and walked to the edge of the living quarters. In the distance he saw the fence line. He could make out the posts that marked the edge of his world. He could not see the wire in the dim light, but he knew it was there. It was always there.

The mountains rose up against the flatness of the high desert like splinters thrusting through sand. The sun was beginning to warm the peaks, purpling the snow that brushed the tops. He could feel the wind biting his face.

Toshi was gone. The guards had taken him to a separate barracks. He was going to be sent to Moab, Utah. They took all the men they could identify who stood up to the guards.

Sammy walked as quietly as he could, the rocky soil crunching under his step. He'd made his decision. Toshi had made his. They would go separate ways. He didn't agree with what Toshi had done, but he couldn't bring himself to disagree with it, either. There were Japanese Americans living in freedom on the East Coast and in the middle of the country while he and his family were imprisoned, their loyalty questioned. He wondered if anybody ever thought about how that didn't make sense.

Sammy watched the sun edge up, making the rosy color of dawn slowly seep back into the earth. *My parents are right. It is not a question of proving my loyalty. This is my country.* He turned and walked back to the barracks, the thin winter sunlight falling on his back and the wind still biting at his face.

~

Freddy walked to the fence and put his hands around the cold wire. The guards no longer paid any attention when people came up to the fence. The sun had finally broken through the overcast sky, giving some warmth to the end of the day. He looked across the roadway to the railroad siding where they had come in by train. It seemed so long ago. Soon he would be leaving this place.

He debated endlessly with himself over whether he had made the right decision in joining the Army. Many had refused and he couldn't blame them. *Was it because I didn't have the courage to refuse?* In the end he decided that if joining the Army proved his family's loyalty, then that was reason enough.

He was never a deep thinker like Sammy. He always did what came to him in the moment. He wasn't angry when he signed the enlistment papers, but he resented having to prove something that shouldn't be in question. This was his country. He felt his grip tighten around the icy wire of the fence, his knuckles whitening. This was his country—but it was his parents' country, too. He was willing to fight for his parents. That was enough of a reason for him.

Freddy pulled his hands from the fence, listening to the metallic vibration of the wire. The sun was almost setting on Jerome as he walked to the barracks.

CHAPTER 40

March 28, 1943
Calwa, California

Fog hung in the low spots around the ranch, but now the Valley chill lingered only until late in the morning. The sun broke through the mist earlier and earlier in the day. Soon it would be full spring. Already the vines were starting to bud, and Sack and his father took to walking the furrows in the morning to make plans for the thinning as the buds began to push out from the canes, providing the basis for the new crop.

It was always a wonder to Sack how something as old and gnarled as a grape vine could sit gray and lifeless all winter and then begin to push out new growth, year after year. It reminded him of elderly people who could still offer up valued wisdom from bodies bent with age. You had to look beyond the outside to appreciate the hidden vibrancy of the inside. There was a harsh beauty about the twists of the wooden trunks that reminded him of the effort these plants went through, pulling their lifeblood from the soil.

His thoughts were broken by his father.

"Boy, your mama says that wife of your'n is most ready to burst. She says any day now that baby's gonna come. You ready?"

Sack looked at his father with a sober expression.

"I guess so. Were you ready?"

He let out a long sigh and smiled. "Guess I was ready." Frank looked at his son with subdued pride. "Maybe it don't make no difference."

Frank stood for a moment and shoved his tongue to the side of his cheek. He looked down at the ground, then up into his son's face.

"I figure you turned out to be a better man than me and you make sure that baby is better'n you. I figure if that happens then your mama and me, well, we did good."

Sack could hear his father's voice break just a little before he finished talking. He looked at his father and nodded.

"You did right by me, Daddy. You and Mama, don't worry."

He looked up when he heard the sound of the bell outside the empty Miyaki house. That was the signal if Mae or Carmen needed them at the house. They both started moving as quickly as they could.

When Sack walked in the door, he could see Carmen on the bed. Her face was already bathed in sweat. He looked at his mother, who just smiled and said. "It's her time. Frank, get Mrs. Bagdasarian. Billy, we got your baby comin'."

Sack stood out in the equipment shed with his father, where the women told them to wait. Sack walked back and forth over the hard-packed dirt floor of the shed. His father sat sharpening one of the furrowing discs and watching his son pace. "Don't worry. Your mama's delivered lots of babies for other folks. She knows what to do." He knew that his son was listening only partially, but hoped it made him feel better.

Sack didn't hear anything. His mind was focused on his wife and his baby. He found a place to sit while he thought about how to communicate with God. What little religious training he had came from itinerant preachers and tent revivals that his mother dragged him to attend. He was never a strong believer but he was never a doubter, either. He didn't think much about God. He was too busy most of the time trying to figure out how to get through his life, and, now, the lives of those he was responsible for. He had always thought that God probably didn't think much about him either. He struggled with his thoughts, trying to make an introduction to a being he could not visualize.

At last he found the thought he wanted to convey: To bring his wife through this and to bring their baby safely into the world. He didn't want to make a promise that he couldn't keep. He decided that his commitment to take care of Carmen and the baby was enough. His father watched in silence. He knew what his son was thinking. He said the same prayers long ago.

They waited four hours before they heard Mae call out to the shed. Sack ran back to the front door where his mother stood, wiping her hands. He could see the blood on her arms and it terrified him, the only reassurance being her smile.

"Come see your wife and the boy she brought you." Mae stepped aside as her son rushed into the room. Carmen was lying on the bed and he could see that the sheets were still damp from perspiration, but her face looked soft and almost rested, even with her hair falling in tangles around her face. The small face beside her was almost hidden by the blanket wrapped tightly around him. He opened his eyes for just a moment, black as coal, like his mother's. She looked up at her husband, who reached down and stroked her head.

"You all right?"

She nodded. "I'm just very tired. Your mother says the baby is perfect."

Sack looked over at Mae and Mrs. Bagdasarian for reassurance. Both nodded. Sack looked at the small face. He said to Carmen, "Well, I reckon he looks like you."

He gazed at the tiny red and wrinkled face, black eyes barely open, thick black hair matted and sticking up in places. He touched the tiny hand and felt the fingers grab his hand, barely long enough to hold his finger. He was perfect.

Carmen pulled the baby close to her, nuzzling his cheek. Sack watched his son yawn, the tiny mouth opening and drawing in the air of his new home. He reached over and put his hand on Carmen's face, the empty left sleeve brushing his son as he reached across to his wife, reminding him that he would never hold his boy in the air and watch him laugh.

Sack leaned down and kissed Carmen. "Thank you." She looked at him, black eyes shining. Her face showed the strain of birth. Tiny ruptured blood vessels splotched her skin. She pushed herself up and cradled the baby, lying him in his father's lap. He felt his son move inside the blanket. Sack decided to make one more silent commitment. His boy wasn't going to go off to war if he could help it. His son was going to have a long good life, a better life than his father.

CHAPTER 41

April 13, 1943
Manzanar War Relocation Center
Independence, California

Sammy didn't sleep most of the night. Today he would be leaving for the Army. The whole of Manzanar rocked in turmoil about the impending departure of the volunteers. Some people yelled that he was a traitor. Others congratulated him and his parents for his decision. But hanging over it all was the pall of Toshi's removal from the camp to Utah.

Sammy dressed and went outside into the cold spring air. It wasn't long before Tommy joined him. At least the two of them, along with Akiro, would be together. It wasn't as easy going off as he had thought it would be. The excitement of anticipation was beginning to wane. The day before, all the young volunteers had gathered for a photograph. Everyone looked so serious that it was unsettling. There had been very few smiles. They all wore their best clothes and ties, if they had them.

It was time to start walking toward the front gate. The bus would be leaving at 9:30. Sammy placed the last few personal items in the bag that his mother had made when they went to the Fresno Assembly Center. Shig and Setsuko stood quietly watching their son as he picked up a small packet of food his mother had prepared.

"Isamu, there are some pickled vegetables, some bread, a hard-boiled egg that cook made for you and the others." He could see his mother's eyes were wet, but she did not cry.

His father stood nearby, his face stoic, but the lines coming down from the corners of his eyes looked deeper and his face looked tired. It was evident that he, too, had not slept.

He put his hand on his son's shoulder. "Isamu, what you are doing, it is the right thing. This is our country. I do not want you to share the bitterness that Toshi carries. This will pass and we will survive. Do not worry about us. You have honored our family."

Shig stepped back and extended his hand. He had never done that before. Sammy realized it was an acknowledgment that he was a man, someone his father would now treat as an equal, at least as equal as a father and son could ever be.

The Miyaki family walked out the door. Tommy and his parents were already outside and they all started toward the gate, where they would meet the bus. The slowly moving procession gained numbers as other families joined.

When the families reached the gate, they could see the buses waiting outside and the men in khaki uniforms standing by them. Sammy turned to his parents and hesitated. He thought about this moment a lot. He wanted to look at them, to burn their image into his mind. He was torn between the excitement of going off to something new, and the realization that this might be the last time he would ever see his parents. There was silence as the finality of the moment rested on everyone's shoulders. The talk around them had now softened to murmurs between parents and sons.

Setsuko leaned forward and said, "*Kiyotsukete itte irrashai.*" *My son, go with care.* She placed her cheek against his.

Shig put his hands on his son's shoulders and held them there as he looked directly into his eyes. Isamu could see that his father was struggling. He reached out and hugged him, holding tightly, first to him and then to his mother.

Sammy walked through the gate along with Tommy, Akiro, and the rest of the volunteers. It was the first time in almost a year that he had been outside the camp. As he boarded the bus he looked back as the crowd of parents pushed up to the gate, their bodies straining against the wire as they stretched as far through the barrier as the strands of steel would allow, hands reaching, waving goodbye.

~

Jerome War Relocation Center, Arkansas

Freddy stood outside the barracks and waited for his parents and sister to come out. Rose was standing next to him and he appreciated the fact that his parents had given them a few minutes to be together. She stood there quietly holding onto his hand, waiting, like she always did. He had come to learn that her quietness was filled with thinking. She was always aware of what he was going to do, while she remained a mystery.

Rose looked up at him. "Freddy, I know some of the people have said things to you and your parents about volunteering. They have said things to my family also, because of Mickey. Don't pay attention to any of it. You're doing the right thing." She stood quietly for a moment. "I will think about you and pray that you're safe. Promise me that you will come home and I will believe it."

Freddy could feel himself thrown off balance. *How can I make such a promise?* He stood for a moment, thinking about what she asked. He knew he wanted to come home to her. He looked into her black eyes.

"I'll come home, I promise."

He could see tears sliding down her cheeks and he reached out to wipe them away.

"I promise."

He looked up when his parents came out. They had already said their goodbyes from the privacy of their room.

Mas walked the few steps to where his son was standing. "It is time."

The five of them walked along the main camp road toward the gate. Soldiers stood by while young men walked through it, casting looks back toward their parents standing at the fence line. Freddy glanced at a young soldier manning the gate. In a few days, he would be wearing the same Army uniform as his parents' guards. He kept that thought in his mind as he walked to the other side of the fence, turning and watching the men in uniform close the gate and separate him from his mother, father, sister, and Rose.

As he looked out the window of the bus he held onto the last glimpse of his family, the tarnished steel braids of the fence framing their faces like lines between images in stained glass. It was the memory that would stay with him in the few quiet moments to come.

PART
IV

CHAPTER 42

April 18, 1943

Headquarters, 442nd Regimental Combat Team

Camp Shelby, Mississippi

The small group of men from Manzanar kept together, not so much because they were friends as much as they were familiar. People on the train stared at Sammy, Akiro, and Tommy when they got up and walked around. Sammy learned to bite his tongue rather than respond to the occasional whispers of "Japs" that he heard when he walked to the restroom. After the months at Manzanar, to be around so many white people was disconcerting. Sammy realized he was back being in the minority.

They changed trains several times before they got to Hattiesburg, Mississippi. Like so many men before them they looked at the covered trucks lined up outside the station with uniformed soldiers waiting. Sammy couldn't help noticing the differences. The soldiers weren't carrying rifles with fixed bayonets. They weren't guards, only drivers there to organize them.

Nobody had to tell them twice to move off the train. After five days in the cramped passenger cars, it was a welcome relief. Until they stepped outside. The cold air penetrated straight through their thin shirts. The men stood shivering as they formed up outside the station. It wasn't long before they were sitting in a truck rumbling toward Camp Shelby, the conversation and excitement quickly lapsing into the silence of each man's thoughts about what was to come.

As soon as the trucks stopped, the men got down as quickly as possible and moved into a line. Sammy followed the men snaking toward what seemed to be some kind of reception center. Sergeants were bellowing incoherent orders. Sammy stayed in line and kept his head down. Tommy stood behind him whispering about how disorganized everything seemed. Sammy looked over his shoulder and told him to be quiet. He didn't want to be one of those who was noticed.

For two days all they did was stand in different lines, getting shots and being handed papers. Eventually, Sammy, Akiro, and Tommy gathered up their papers with arms sore from constant inoculations and followed the men ahead of them toward a low building. Uniforms were piled up in their arms as they were told to remove their civilian clothes. After trading back and forth they managed to get together some uniforms that fit, except for the boots, which were always too big. It was fairly obvious that nobody cared. They had to move on and make room for more men crowding into the uniform line.

Sammy lined up in front of signs with letters on them. Each man walked to a clerk and gave his name and serial number, and the clerk in turn gave a barracks assignment. Sammy hoped to see Freddy, but the crowd was too big. For all he knew, Freddy was already there.

"Name? Last name first."

"Miyaki, Isamu."

"Sign here, Miyaki. You're in Company B. See those men by that tree? Go over there. They'll get you to your barracks. Keep your papers and don't lose anything. Next."

Sammy moved over and looked around to see where the others ended up. He felt a tug on his arm and turned to see Tommy.

"Akiro and I go someplace else, I guess. We're in Company D. We'll see you later."

Sammy nodded and watched them walk away.

A sergeant looked at the eleven men standing around. His practiced eye took in the assortment of men in poorly fitted uniforms. He had fought in the trenches in France during the first war. He wasn't going to fight in this war. He knew he was too old. His job was to train a new generation of soldiers. The doubt on his face wasn't concealed as he looked over the short and skinny young men.

"Okay, you men are all assigned to Company B. Try and stay together. This is the Army, not some school dance. Try to act like soldiers." He turned and started walking while the men scrambled to grab their clothes and papers, trying to keep up.

Fifteen minutes later, the sergeant pointed at a shabby-looking building with peeling paint and wooden stairs, with steps made of boards cupped by weather and lack of maintenance.

"This here's Company B. Go on in and find yourself a bunk. Your sergeant will be along, so try to get your gear together. There are men already in there, so don't take a bunk that belongs to somebody else. I don't want to come back and hafta' break up more fights between you boys. Already had three fights today between them boys from Hawaii and you new men, so watch yourselves."

He turned and walked off, leaving them to look at one another and then start up the stairs. Cold air blew through the cracks in the walls like an open window and the hutment stoves, similar to a potbelly wood stove, weren't efficient or big enough to keep the barracks warmed. It was almost as cold inside as it was outside.

There was a dice game going on in the corner and the men playing looked over to see the new faces, but didn't move. Sammy heard somebody with a strange accent say, "New guys, mainland boys I think."

Sammy looked around the room. There was a heating stove at both ends and rows of bunks. A few had bare mattresses, but most had blankets and pillows on them. All of a sudden he heard a voice. "Sammy, over here, we got some bunks." He looked in the direction of the familiar voice and saw Freddy standing, grinning.

"What took you so long? I've been here for three days already."

"California's further away." He walked over and put his hand out. Sammy could feel emotion swirling inside him. He had missed his lifelong friend terribly, and still the feeling was unexpected. It took him a moment to realize how much the friendship meant to him. No matter how long it had been, the separation hadn't changed anything.

Both of them hesitated for a moment, unsure of what to do, especially in front of strangers. Freddy reached out, grabbed Sammy's hand and then hugged his friend.

"You okay?"

"Yeah, you?"

"I'm okay. Let me set my stuff down."

Freddy pointed at a footlocker. "Put your things in here for right now. They'll be in here pretty soon to get you guys some blankets and pillows. I'll make sure nobody takes your bunk. Sit down."

Sammy looked around. "All these guys from Jerome?"

Freddy laughed. "No, most of these guys are from Hawaii, volunteers like us." He lowered his voice. "They're real different than us. Just watch yourself. I've already been in one fight. I don't know what their problem is. They stick together so the guys like us from the mainland, we been sticking together too. Just don't say too much or they'll start kicking your ass."

Sammy kept glancing at the darker-skinned men who were all grouped at one end watching the new men come in. "Aren't they Japanese like us?"

Freddy let out a little snort of derision. "Not like us. You'll see. So what was Manzanar like?"

Sammy shook his head. "Not as nice as the Fresno fairgrounds. Out in the middle of the desert, but not as hot like you'd expect it. Just flat and dry with mountains in the distance. Tar paper walls. Two families to a room. Wind all the time and so much dust in the air that you could taste it. It was cold when I left, colder than here. I hated leaving my mom and dad there. How about Jerome?"

"It was cold there too when I left, but it rained a lot. Tar paper buildings, but better than the horse stalls in Fresno, I guess. The dirt was red, heavy like clay, and when it got wet it stuck to everything. When it was hot, you'd sweat all the time from the humidity. I don't think I was dry all summer long, day or night. Mom and Dad seemed to have accepted it. I never could. Doesn't seem right somehow, you know."

Sammy nodded. "Toshi couldn't seem to adjust. He's somewhere in Utah. Dad doesn't talk about it much. Toshi says he isn't going into the Army, not unless they let Mom and Dad out and maybe not even then. He's doing what he thinks is right, I guess, but Dad doesn't agree with him. Neither do I. He almost got himself killed in a riot."

Sammy waited, hoping that Freddy would mention his sister, but he didn't. Finally, Sammy couldn't stand it.

"How's Betty?"

A faint smile flickered over Freddy's face. "She's okay. She gave me a letter to give to you." He held out a creased envelope.

Sammy took it and put it in his pocket. He would read it later.

"How's Rose?"

Freddy looked over to the side. "She's fine. I don't know. I think she feels more serious about things than I do. I'm just not sure what I want."

Sammy could hear some of the Hawaiians talking about *katonks* and looking in their direction. "What are they talking about? What the hell is a *katonk*?"

Freddy didn't look at the Hawaiians. He leaned in toward Sammy and lowered his voice. "A *katonk* is the sound a hollow coconut makes when it hits the ground. That's what the Hawaiians call the men from the mainland. Some of the mainland guys call them *buta* heads, means pig-headed. They started that *katonk* crap right after we got in here. I just ignore it and most of them leave me alone, but some of the guys been getting into fights. Better if you just keep your mouth shut."

Sammy shrugged. "Hey, I got a letter from José. He's in the 36th Division out of Texas. Said they're sending his division to North Africa. Guess he's gone by now."

Freddy looked around. "Well at least he's doing something besides sitting around. Guess we'll be in it soon enough."

Sammy started packing his uniforms in the trunk at the foot of his bed. He reached into his barracks bag and felt his hand brush against a nubby piece of cloth. He hesitated before pulling it out.

"I brought something with me that I thought you might like to have."

He held out the green and gold varsity letter that he had picked up from the dirt the night of their graduation. Freddy took the heavy woven cloth and held it in his hands, slowly turning it, brushing his hand across the letter. He looked at Sammy, his face almost expressionless, his eyes squeezed into tight lines.

Sammy smiled slightly. "I figured maybe you lost it."

Freddy nodded his head. "Guess it means more to me than I thought. Like some friends."

~

The training at Shelby was a lot tougher than Sammy or Freddy anticipated. The 442nd had to live under the shadow of the 100th from Hawaii, which was at the end of their training. Occasionally they would see the Hawaiian unit when some of its men would stop by the barracks to visit the 442nd members who had volunteered out of Hawaii. It was easy to envy the good-natured banter between the toughened men of the 100th and the new trainees in the 442nd.

The men of the 100th had already created a reputation by taking on the men of a Texas division that had trained with them in Wisconsin, before transferring to Mississippi. After a string of racial taunts, thirty-eight men from the Texas division had been hospitalized. The Texas troops badly underestimated the small brown men with extensive judo training. When men of the 100th walked through the 442nd training area, they had a swagger that the new men respected.

Sammy and Freddy weren't in condition for the kind of training the Army was providing. The commander of the 442nd, Colonel Charles Pence, had been toughened on the battlefields of France during World War I. He had every intention of making sure his troops could stand the rigors of battle. Tall and square-jawed, he kept constant watch on the men.

At first both Sammy and Freddy thought they had gotten lucky. Their drill instructor turned out to be Kazuo Otani, the soldier they had first seen at the baseball game in Fresno, when Moon pitched. They quickly found out that familiarity didn't mean friendliness. The first time Freddy referred to Sergeant Otani by his first name, he found out that being from the same area wasn't going to make any difference to Otani, at least as far as training was concerned. Still, when nobody else was around, Otani tried to help them out. Sammy and Freddy understood that Otani couldn't look like he was playing favorites and, if anything, would make it tougher on them in front of the rest of the boys if there was the slightest indication that they were getting special treatment.

~

After two months of constant marching and field drills, their bodies began to toughen. The cold air they felt on arrival was replaced by the heat and humidity of summer. It was late when they shuffled into the barracks, their bodies dripping. Company B had been out in the field working on all day on basic maneuvers. They only had a few hours in their barracks to clean their equipment and get a little relaxation before lights out.

Sammy was sitting on his bunk and looking at a blister on his foot when he heard someone come up behind him. "What's the matter I-sa-moo, you got a blister?" He didn't need to turn around. He knew who it was. Only one person called him by his given name, drawn out like that.

Mickey stepped around and stood in front of him. "How you been, buddy? It's been a while." Freddy was standing behind Mickey, grinning.

Sammy jumped up and grabbed Mickey. "What're you doing here? We all heard that you were in Minnesota somewhere doing some kind of training." He stepped back when Mickey's three stripes caught his eye. "You're a sergeant?"

Mickey nodded. "Yeah, I'm at a special school there. I'm here looking for recruits. We're testing some of the guys in your unit."

Freddy and Sammy walked outside with Mickey and sat down, look-ing at the fireflies and trying to brush away the mosquitoes. Mickey kept his voice down.

"Look, I'm not supposed to say much, so you guys have to keep your mouths shut. We're looking for men who can speak enough Japanese to be trained as translators and document examiners. We're at Fort Savage over in Minnesota. It's kind of a dump but it was the best that we could do, after we got kicked out of the Presidio when the exclusion orders came down. Just like you guys, I guess. In some ways I'm sorry I wasn't there to help my parents and sister and in some ways I'm glad. It was bad enough when we had to leave the Presidio. I don't know how I would have felt if they had made me go to the fairgrounds."

Sammy wasn't sure what to say. "You heard about the farm, your mom and dad's place? I guess your folks lost the lease when we all had to move."

"Rose told me. Mom and Dad haven't said anything. Rose writes all the letters for them."

Freddy changed the subject. "So you going to stay there at Savage or what?"

"Right now they have me and a couple of the guys out recruiting. I'm hoping I get a chance to get out of Savage. The lieutenant said that maybe after this trip I can go out to a field unit somewhere, probably in the South Pacific or Southeast Asia, but I won't know until I get orders. How about you guys? I never went through all this. They pulled me out of Ord and I've been in school or looking at papers since."

Both young men filled Mickey in on their training regimen, carefully exaggerating the difficulty and hardships they were faced. For the rest of the evening, the men sat around talking about what June would be like back home. The hard-edged resentment of the relocation camps began to blur as they told each other about baseball games and family life. They watched the fireflies dancing in the shadows cast by the moonlight on the trees, the crickets layering the sounds of the darkness, their conversation lulling into periods of silence while they enjoyed the moment of being together again. As they sat on the barracks steps, it reminded them of the summer evenings growing up they had so casually taken for granted. But they also realized that their lives had changed dramatically. Each had begun to view the world as larger than the dusty little valley town in which they had been raised. The idea of home being a specific place was being replaced by the idea of home being where their parents were—and the constant awareness that they could not yet return to the Valley of their youth.

CHAPTER 43

June 11, 1943

Headquarters 100th Infantry Battalion (Separate)

Camp Shelby, Mississippi

Kim walked across the Company B compound toward the barracks. The unit had come back from maneuvers in Louisiana just two days before, and the old man gave the boys a few days to rest up. As far as Kim was concerned, rest was over. The men needed to be kept battle-ready. He went over the lessons of the Louisiana maneuvers in his mind.

It was one of the largest military exercises in history. Whole divisions moved across terrain, practicing battle tactics. The entire time the 100th had been assigned to be an offensive unit, moving against others assigned to defense. Unlike the other units, the 100th had to march to different positions, constantly moving, but they had been successful almost every time in capturing the enemy's flag. Even though the men resented the lack of rest, they relished their small moments of victory. But as far as Kim was concerned, victory came because of training. And training had to be constant.

He had come to learn more about the other young officers in the unit, and he had come to a greater understanding of what the outside world was like. He never even carried the slightest interest in politics. To the extent that race played a role in keeping him from doing something, he merely accepted the situation without much resentment or rebellion.

But nights spent around campfires while on maneuvers in Louisiana had changed his perspective.

First Lieutenant Sakae Takahashi spoke up on some of those humid evenings, talking about the divisions between whites and the Japanese, Chinese, and Hawaiians in the islands. He said that this war was about more than just the country being attacked by some enemy. It was about how things needed to change. He would talk for hours about how change wouldn't come without power, and how power in a democratic society came from becoming a political force, not from forcing people to accept political ideology at the point of a gun. The men were fighting for their future and when they got home they needed to go into the political system. If they wanted change, they had to lead. Even Lieutenant Candy Tanaka joined in about what needed to happen.

Kim just listened. But now he thought about the world and how he had been controlled by the way things were. He had spent much of his life depending on his own inner strength to guide him and push him forward. He began to give more thought to the very inequities that created the unit in which he now served. He found the entire concept disquieting, because it forced him to look beyond his world. He knew that in military terms he needed to see the larger view that a field commander would have of a battlefield, instead of the immediate view of a lieutenant following orders. That, in and of itself, was an epiphany for him. Now he thought about how things should be.

The men of the 100th were glad to be back from Louisiana. They were used to a level of humidity, but they hated the swamps. There were no snakes in Hawaii and some fool was always grabbing a snake and bringing it into camp to scare everyone, which it always did. As time wore on the practical jokes continued, but the men began to display a more determined and serious attitude.

The news from North Africa and the South Pacific was not good. Americans were being pushed back by the Germans and the Japanese. Europe was firmly in the control of Hitler's armies. They knew they were nearing the end of their training and that soon the unit would be committed in some way to the larger war effort. Sooner or later they were going into action. Catching some time to relax and have fun was becoming more and more important, as soon there would be no time for it. The newspapers carried casualty reports that brought the reality of war closer.

Letters from home told of rationing and shortages. Sergeants told wide-eyed young men what it was like to crawl through mud made of dirt and blood. Yuki and Tug listened carefully to every word. They didn't know which lesson would be the one they would soon need to know.

The 100th and the 442nd trained separately, but occasionally there would be baseball games between the men of the two different units. As the One Puka Puka neared completion of its training, they began to look at the men of the 442nd in a paternalistic fashion. They had been through the worst the Army could throw at them, and the 442nd was just beginning.

Yuki was watching one of the perpetual dice games being played in the corner while one of the other boys stood at the door, watching for an officer or a sergeant. As usual, Tug was down on his hands and knees with a handful of money held tightly, while he egged the game on and tried to increase his pile of cash. Yuki turned to Kazo, who was watching with him.

"Well, what do you think of G.I. Kim?" The young Korean officer had become notorious for driving his men through repeated military exercises and training. G.I. Kim was one of the more polite names that some of the men used for their second lieutenant.

Kazo looked thoughtful and shook his head back and forth. "He's tough, that's for sure, but we won in Louisiana and I liked that. I'm thinking better for us with him on our side. He's not very friendly, but he is Korean, you know."

Yuki nodded. He, too, had begun to acquire a grudging respect for Kim. He trained them hard, but their company did better than the others. He made them learn to be more self-reliant and if they failed, he didn't spend any time blaming anyone. He seemed to know what he was doing. But Yuki still found the way Kim never raised his voice to be unnerving—like nothing bothered him.

Tug looked up. He had been listening to the conversation. "Kazo, you like G.I. Kim? You know, maybe he's better than some of the *haole* officers, but I get tired running my ass off all the time."

Johnny Kitahara was getting ready to throw the dice and started laughing. "You got a lot of ass to run off. I don't think you lose very much. Besides, Kazo's right. I think we're better off following Kim up the hill when the time comes." The others listening nodded in agreement.

Tug looked around. "Maybe Kim is an okay guy, but I would like to rest once in a while. Other companies get rest, but Kim just keeps pushing." Yuki nodded. When other companies were taking some slack time, Kim was always looking for more training. But when they got into combat, it was training that would keep them alive

~

Colonel Turner gathered his officers in the meeting room of the 100th. The moisture-laden air of late July barely seemed to move, even with the slowly turning overhead fan. He carefully surveyed the officers staring at him, eyes expectant. Rumors were already traveling. He cleared his throat and began to speak.

"Well, I have good news. We've passed the combat inspection and the inspector general's office has verbally communicated to me that we are being certified as combat-ready. While I haven't gotten the official orders yet, I have been informed that we will be deployed for embarkation by mid-August. Basically, we have a little over two weeks to get everything together."

Turner looked around the room to gauge the reaction. Every officer was staring straight at him, the impact of the moment apparent on their face. Major Lovell broke an extended silence.

"Sir, the boys have been asking about the colors and the unit motto. There are a lot of strong feelings about what the Army has proposed. I guess "Be of Good Cheer" makes sense to somebody in Washington or wherever they think of these things, but, well, it doesn't seem very aggressive. Frankly, nobody likes it and that unit patch with the red dagger isn't much better. We have a good design with the *ape* leaf and the yellow-feather Hawaiian battle helmet. It would mean a lot to the men if they could have what they picked out."

Turner looked around the room at the officers nodding their heads in agreement with Lovell. He smiled.

"I talked to the folks in Washington about this and they've agreed. The unit motto will stay "Remember Pearl Harbor" and the unit patch our boys designed will have the yellow helmet and the *ape* leaf for good luck, like the ancient Hawaiians believed. I thought we would bring it out and show the colors when we tell the men that we're going."

Lovell appreciated Turner's efforts to support the men as much as possible. "Thank you, Colonel. I know the men will appreciate it. So what are they going to be told and when?"

"Tomorrow. Have the men stand battalion formation. We'll show the colors. We won't tell them where they're going, just that we're deployed as a combat unit." He looked at the silent faces still staring at him.

"Gentlemen, we're going to North Africa. The 100th is going to fight Germans. We are assigned to the Fifth Army under the command of Lieutenant General Mark Clark. I was told he was the only one that would take us. Rumor is Eisenhower turned us down. Everything else, we'll find out when we get there. We leave on the 11th of August. Any questions?"

Nobody said a word.

"All right, dismissed." He turned and looked at Lovell. "Jim, I want you to stay a moment. We have a few more things to discuss. We've got a few boys who haven't signed up for G.I. insurance. Do you know the reason?"

Lovell shifted uncomfortably in his chair. "Colonel, as I understand it, their parents are in Japan and they don't think the government will pay them if something happens."

Turner's mouth turned down in a frown. "Jim, you tell their company commanders to get them in and have them sign the papers. If something happens to them, the government will pay. The boys have enough to worry about without being concerned about whether their parents will be taken care of. I've been asked whether we really want to take the Kibei who went to school in Japan and some of the others that Army Intelligence has questions about. I told them that we're taking every man who has trained with this unit. They've done their time and I trust them. Make sure that the boys know that."

"Yes, sir."

~

The 7:00 a.m. formation moved much more quickly than usual. Lieutenant Kim stood with Company B, Second Platoon, waiting for the battalion to be addressed by Colonel Turner. Every man thought today they would get "the word." Yuki stood with his squad and glanced out of the corner of his eye at Tug standing next to him. He felt like the men were ready. Captain Johnson stood at the front of the company formation. It felt different, more serious. This was not going to be some pep talk.

Colonel Turner and Major Lovell walked to a small platform placed in the center of the battalion line as the battalion was called to attention. Turner didn't tell the men to stand at ease. He stood for a moment looking down the line of officers and young men who had sailed with him from Hawaii over a year before. They were boys then. Now, they were well-trained soldiers. He wanted them to know that. He waited until the unit colors with the feathered helmet and ape leaf was unfurled, the words "Remember Pearl Harbor" emblazoned across the flag. He wanted the men to see their flag and their unit colors. Finally, he told the men to stand at ease and watched them snap their hands behind their back with military precision.

"Men, there are two things I want to tell you. First, I'm proud of all of you. The 100th has passed all of its inspection tests and we have been certified as combat-ready." He paused to allow the stirring in the ranks to quiet down as the men glanced at one another with looks of satisfaction. "Second, we have received our orders for deployment. The 100th is going into combat. This is what you have prepared for. I believe you're ready and I want you to know that I have faith in you. We have been away from our home for a long time. It will probably be a long time before we see the islands again, but when we come home—and we will come home—we will do so knowing that we have proven to everyone our loyalty, about our resolve—we will have shown them that we lived up to the motto, 'Remember Pearl Harbor.'"

Turner waited for the cheering to stop. Even though the men were in military formation, this was their moment. He held up his hand and waited for the men to resume standing at ease. "All men will receive a ten-day furlough, which your company sergeants and commanders will authorize. Don't go too far away and don't get into too much trouble. In ten days you need to be back here, ready to go. Good luck to all of you."

~

Two weeks later, Sammy and Freddy watched as men from the 100th trickled into the barracks of Company B, saying their goodbyes to the

Hawaiian boys in the 442nd. One of the men who went by the name of Yuki grinned as he walked by with a heavyset private everyone called Tug. The heavier man called out, as he walked out of the barracks, "You boys will get your chance. We try leave some Germans for you to clean up."

Scattered laughter mixed with good-natured jeering until the two men walked out the door, then there was silence as each man wondered whether he could joke when his time came to march to battle. The next day Sammy stood by the road in front of the company common area, watching as the last of the 100th's trucks pulled away with its cargo of men, their voices carrying only faint shadows of their usual swagger.

CHAPTER 44

August 20, 1943

Fort Kilmer, New Jersey

The men of the 100th stood in clusters, nervously smoking or lying on barracks bags staring at nothing, trying to pull a memory of home or a girl clearly into their mind. Everybody was wide awake, even though it was after midnight. Tug was one of the few men talking.

"Yuki, why we waiting until the middle of the night? Why can't the Army do anything during the day, after you get some sleep?"

Yuki looked over. "Maybe in the middle of the night nobody will be able to tell that we're all Japanese."

Lieutenant Kim overheard the comment and turned around, looking at Yuki and the others. He didn't say anything, but the talking stopped.

Tug muttered under his breath, "Well, maybe not all of us, but the *haoles* can't tell the difference." He looked over at Kim and grinned. Kim just shook his head.

Each man carried his primary weapon, his field pack, and two barracks bags. The amount of equipment weighed almost as much as they did. They struggled with their loads as they boarded trains with shades drawn and rode to New York, where they got on ferries for the ride to the waiting ship.

By now it was coming on afternoon, and even the harbor air moving through the windows of the ferry was hot and sultry. Yuki and some of the other men walked to the railing of the ferry and looked across the bay. They stared at the towering figure rising up from the harbor water, raising her torch, the glint of the gilded flame flashing in the August sun.

The dull greenish-copper folds draping the statue seemed to ripple as the heat rose through the air. Yuki stood at the rail, silent for a moment, looking at the water frothing at the bow of the ferry and across the harbor, the barely perceptible movement of life in Manhattan. He could imagine people were walking around, eating and laughing. It was hard for him to envision the war while people simply sat under umbrellas in the midday sun. It struck him that war was different for those at home. He could see the tops of trees in Battery Park on the Manhattan shore, where people would eat their lunch and read about the losses in distant countries, places where he would soon be.

Tug looked over at Yuki as Kazo and Johnny pointed at the troop ships looming at anchor. Staten Island was ringed with ships of every description painted a dull gray, broken only by rust streaks revealing their age. Men were everywhere, crawling over decks and working on the docks, manhandling boxes and the machines of battle. The battalion slowly walked down the gangway from the ferry, adjusting their field packs and weapons constantly, their uniforms chafing as the heavy packs rubbed stinging sweat into backs worn raw by the straps. They looked at similarly burdened men who stared back at them with the familiarity born of the same situation. The sound of boots drummed and scuffed the groaning gangway as the 100th made its way across the heavily timbered dock, the afternoon sun leaching up the smell of creosote.

Like the men marching with him, Yuki looked up at the gray slab side of the troopship they were boarding, the S.S. *James Parker*. Word came filtering down the line that it had once been a banana boat, engendering nervous laughter from those who thought it was a joke and those who thought it wasn't. They made their way down into the hold and stored their equipment as best they could in the stacked bunks, hoping to escape the close confines and stale air as soon as possible and return to the deck.

Yuki, Tug, Kazo, and Johnny crowded into a small open space on the rail, giving them a last glimpse of the New York skyline. They stayed there as tugs began nosing the *Parker* out into the harbor along with numerous other troopships, the *Parker*'s aging engines throbbing, rumbling the deck under their feet. The men were silent. Any relief from the movement of air was overcome by the heat of the others packed at the rail. They remained transfixed at the verdigris statue and the Manhattan skyline, trying to hold the details in their minds, another memory to take out and relive in the long days to come.

Down the railing, Lieutenant Kim stood with several of the other young officers, but his mind wasn't on the skyline. It was on what lay ahead: the battlefields, where his measure would be taken and where the men standing at the rail would depend on him, not just for his orders, but for their lives.

~

For two weeks the *Parker* rolled through the waves of the Atlantic, wallowing in the sea and plowing forward, hiding inside the ring of convoy escorts that slowed to keep the plodding troopships safe from enemy submarines. The men spent their waking time on deck, trading their bunks in shifts, and looking forward only to fresh air and the diversion of cards, dice, and movies.

Yuki stood near the rail, trying to catch as much fresh air as he could so he wouldn't have as far to run when he threw up. Even though they only had two meals a day, he was grateful because it gave him less to throw up. He wasn't the only one at the rail. At the end of almost two weeks he saw Lieutenant Kim down the railing from him. Kim spent almost as much time out here as he had, and it had been one of the first opportunities Yuki had had to get to know the young Korean lieutenant.

Yuki looked over at Kim, the misery evident on his face. "Lieutenant, how much longer? I never been this sick. I think I've thrown up more than I eat."

Kim looked back and managed a weak smile. "I don't know, Yuki. I think we're almost there. The sailors say that they've seen birds, so we should be getting close. All I know is that I want to be on land." Yuki nodded. He could understand.

~

On September 2, word passed through the ship that the shoreline of Africa was on the horizon. Yuki managed a quick look at the smudge of distant coastline, the blue sky rippling in the heat. It was the smell that reassured him they were really near land. The air was different, not the clean salty air of the open sea, not like Hawaii with the scent of flowers, but weighed down with the odor of heat and rock.

It only took an hour for all the men to disembark from the *Parker*. Turner wanted to get his boys settled and then go to Mediterranean Base Section Headquarters to get their assignment. He still didn't know where they were going.

Yuki, Tug, Kazo, and Johnny rode in a truck convoy, along with the rest of the battalion, to an area that was only dirt and rock. They were told to get off and form by company. The moving air provided little comfort; it was heavy with heat and dust that carried grit into everything. Men immediately went to dripping canvas water bags to fill already empty canteens. The water was brackish and barely drinkable, even though it had been heavily chlorinated. It was so alkaline that when they tried to wash, the Army soap wouldn't make bubbles.

As usual, Tug was talking, even though the rest of them tried to keep their mouths closed to keep out the dust. The encampment was on a rocky pile of sand without a tree in sight.

"Yuki, you know what they call this place? Called Goat Hill. Why they call it that, you think? Not even a goat would live here. I don't see any goats. All I see are sand fleas, I got bites all over."

Kazo and Johnny sat down on their barracks bags, waiting for orders. It was too hot to move unless someone told them to. The sweat dripped down faces only partially shaded by the heavy steel helmets that were already too hot to touch. Nobody took them off. They were the only shade available, the barren landscape of dirt and scrubby vegetation offering no promise of any comfort except a place to sit.

~

The next morning, word came for Colonel Turner to report to Fifth Army HQ. He waited at his jeep for Major Lovell to join him. Lovell was still weak from the voyage on the *Parker* and hadn't looked forward to the ride in the jeep. His stomach was churning, and his legs felt like his body was still rocking from the wallowing of the ship.

At Fifth Army HQ, they were told that they were to report to the 34th Division, "The Red Bull," under the command of Major General

Charles Ryder. Turner and Lovell were pleased. The 34th had already fought at Kasserine Pass and at Tunis. They had been through battle and survived.

As soon as they arrived at the 34th's encampment, they began to relax. The division was bivouacked in a forest of cork trees, with plenty of shade from the oppressive heat. They walked into General Ryder's head-quarters and were taken immediately to his office at the back of the HQ tent. Ryder didn't waste any time with long introductions. He was a West Point graduate and had already commanded a battalion in World War I. He stood with military authority, looking far younger than his fifties. He looked at Turner and Lovell, motioning for them to sit.

"Colonel Turner—Ferrant, Major Lovell, you're here because I asked for you. I heard you had a unit that didn't have a place to go and that you wanted to fight. I need men who want to fight. Eisenhower took one of my battalions to be his personal guard for his headquarters. We're going into Italy within the month and the 34th is a big part of General Clark's plan."

Ryder looked at Turner and Lovell for a moment then spoke in care-ful, even tones. "You think you can trust your boys to fight?"

Turner looked straight back. "Absolutely, sir."

Ryder nodded his approval. "That's all I wanted to know. You move your boys into our area and out of that shithole I hear they have you in. Welcome to the Red Bull Division, Colonel. The division motto is 'Attack, Attack, Attack,' and that's what we're going to do. As soon as your men get settled in, I want to meet with you and all your officers. We have work to do."

"Yes, sir."

Turner and Lovell stood and Ryder extended his hand. "Get your men here quickly, Colonel." Turner and Lovell saluted and walked out the door. General Ryder's clerk hurried by them at the sound of Ryder's voice, yelling he had a memo to send out.

"Get this down for all my commanders. *The 34th is being joined by the 100th Infantry Battalion, a Japanese American combat unit. These men are Americans, born in Hawaii. They are not to be referred to as "Japs." They aren't asking for any special consideration and none will be given to them. They will take their turn in battle rotation like the other units in the 34th. Each commander is directed to communicate the con-tents of this directive to his men."*

~

Yuki and the rest of the men were relieved to get word they were leaving Goat Hill. It didn't take long to dismantle the tents and pack everything for movement. Within two days they were on their way. A murmur of excitement went through the ranks as the shaded tents of the division bivouac appeared in front of them. As they approached the camp, they heard music. The 34th Division band was standing by the road as the 100th's convoy rolled by. The sunlight caught the polished brass of trumpets and trombones. But it was the drums beating that gave each man a sense of home. All the men were waving and the men of the 34th were waving back.

Ryder called a meeting of all the officers in the 100th. "I asked for the 100th because I heard you wanted to fight. Well, that's what we're going to do. Officers must provide leadership. That's what I expect of you. The Germans are tough fighters, don't make any mistake about that, but we've learned a lot about their tactics. In a few days I'll be speaking to all of you about what the plans are for the 34th. You can count on this: Within the month you and your men will be in combat. You'll see men you've served with go down next to you, but you need to keep fighting. No matter what happens to your unit, no matter how tough it gets, you need to keep fighting. I'm going to meet with all your men tomorrow. I want the 100th turned out tomorrow morning to start training. That is all."

~

The next morning, the battalion assembled and for the first time most of them saw a general officer stand and address them. Ryder stood front and center on a platform. Two silver stars were on his helmet. His fatigues weren't the sharply creased battle dress of a man who led from behind the lines or behind a desk. They were the uniform of a man who wore them alongside his men. Ryder looked out over the sea of brown faces intermixed with the sun-reddened faces of white officers.

*"I am Major General Ryder, commander of the 34th Division. In this division everyone will earn what they get and get what they earn. This is the Red Bull division and our shoulder patch is a red bull's head against a black background. You can wear that patch when you earn it.

Once we get into combat and you prove you're capable, we'll be happy to give you the right to wear it. Nobody gets that patch until they have demonstrated they can uphold the expectations of the 34th. After you have gone through battle like the men in this division have, then you can sew on that patch and wear it on your shoulder just like I do. The division motto is 'Attack, Attack, Attack.' Your unit motto is 'Remember Pearl Harbor.' Keep both those mottos in your minds in the days ahead. Welcome to the 34th."* Ryder stood for a moment and looked over the men of the 100th battalion, then he walked off the raised platform.

Yuki, Tug, and the others in Second Platoon looked over at Lieutenant Kim. Everybody, including Kim, was smiling. They were now a part of something much bigger than themselves.

CHAPTER 45

September, 1943
Salerno, Italy

The rumble of the engines of the U.S.S. *Frederick Funston* slowed to a dull thrum. The men in her hold could feel the vessel pitch and roll as she kept enough power to maintain her position offshore as one of four ships assigned to the 34th Division beachhead. The officers were yelling for men to check equipment before they came upstairs. The stench of seasickness vomit mixed with the sour smell of the close quarters. Salt air rushed down into the hold as the hatches opened to the deck. Yuki looked around at his squad to make sure everybody was in line. Tug's face was impassive, his mouth shut, his nostrils flaring as he inhaled heavily in the warm stale air, humid with the breath of hundreds of fast-breathing men. Yuki could see them swallowing repeatedly, trying to hold down the gorge that rose to the back of their throats.

The men of the100th shifted uneasily, trying to keep their balance against the pitching of the ship, a task made difficult by their heavy field packs. Down in the hold they couldn't see what lay topside, and they couldn't hear anything except the yelling of crewmen and the rustle of nervous men and equipment. By now they knew the beach was supposed to be secure, but they had never trained for an amphibious landing. The closest they had come to moving through water had been in the swamps of Louisiana. Now they were going to hit a beach.

When the order came for them to move topside, they surged against the stairwell like a writhing, living thing, each focused on the back of the man in front, forcing their leaden legs to move forward. As they came up from the dim hold they blinked against the sudden light, their nostrils catching the sharp odor of gas blowing forward as the light beachward wind caught the fumes from the ship's single smokestack.

The sky was gray and dark, closing in on the swarm of men moving across the deck toward the rail. Swirling black clouds hung over the dull brown hills behind the beach. There was a distant rumble that seemed like thunder, but nothing flashed across the darkened sky. Officers kept yelling for the men to move forward as they struggled to keep their footing on the mist-slick deck, their minds distracted by the realization that the distant growling rumble was the sound of heavy artillery, voicing the anger of battle. Somewhere out there, men were dying under fire.

Lieutenant Kim and the men of Second Platoon, Company B, moved across the deck of the *Funston*. Slowly and carefully they followed the rest of the men of to the ship's rail, their eyes on the landing beach and the allied planes that circled overhead steadily, the dull drone causing them to look up to make sure the planes were theirs.

They were assigned to secure the Salerno plain, for movement up the Italian coast toward Rome. They had to secure Naples and then hold it against any German counteroffensive. They were almost two weeks behind the initial landing force which had finally pushed the Germans back to the Volturno River, some twenty miles from the beach. Every man knew that the Germans were off the beach but no man believed it until he had walked across the sand on the other side of the breaking waves.

Yuki and Tug climbed over the ship's rail and down the rope ladders, swinging out from the side of the *Funston* as the ship slowly rolled in the ocean swells. For once the usually cheerful and talkative Hawaiians were silent, marking their steps carefully down the rough rope ladders and into the landing barges rolling next to the ship's hull. Every man was acutely aware of what could happen if he fell between the side of the landing craft and the side of the ship. The barges slowly plowed their way toward the shore and dropped their bows so men could jump into the surf. The beach began bustling with activity.

Major Lovell climbed down into the landing barge carrying Second Platoon. He stood toward the front, smoking his pipe slowly and watching the shoreline. The landing craft ran up on a sandbar farther out than the others and dropped its bow. Lovell looked back, then raised his arm and jumped into the water, holding his rifle and his tobacco pouch high. Kim turned and gave the arm signal to follow on him.

Following his lead, the rest of the men struggled to maintain balance as they approached the bow and jumped into the crashing surf. Yuki watched as the men ahead of him went in and went under in water that was deeper than anticipated. Lovell was a tall man, the water reaching his chest. For most of the others, their faces barely cleared the water. Lovell grabbed one man and held his face out as he moved toward shore. Kim kept slogging forward, yelling at the men in his platoon to keep moving—they would find solid footing—while looking for stragglers foundering in the water.

Yuki and Tug moved out of the surf, soaked to the skin, and found themselves a place to sit as the rest of the platoon gathered nearby. Troops were massing all around them, and more barges were off-loading jeeps and heavy equipment. In their lightweight uniforms, the men began to shiver in the chill air blowing off the sea. Kim assembled the men and joined the rest of Company B as they all marched inland, the seawater-soaked boots rubbing their feet raw until they reached a bivouac area where they would spend the next two days.

Kim's body felt like a coiled spring, as the anticipation, the distant sound of battle, all of it closed in on him. His men were no different. All the troops and their officers were chafing at the lack of direction. The low-rumbling barrages of heavy artillery kept every man from grabbing more than a few minutes sleep. No man knew whether it was the sound of their guns or those of the enemy—they hadn't yet learned to distinguish the signature sounds of the weapons. Day turned into night and night turned into day and then night again, the darkened sky illuminated by the muzzle flash of the long guns and the bursts of shells.

After two days in the inland holding area, Turner had Lovell assemble the officers. Kim left his platoon and walked with the other lieutenants to the command quarters. It was almost dark and everyone strove to keep down the light. Inside, Turner's face took on a yellow cast in the low light from the kerosene lantern's low light on the map table. He looked around the room and waited for the others to settle down.

"I have a communication from Major General Lucas. He's told all his field commanders that we're here, and that we are an all-Japanese unit, in order to avoid cases of mistaken identity. Tomorrow, the 100th will be going to the front lines.

"There isn't a lot I can say to you that I haven't said to you before. Everybody is watching the 100th to see if we can handle it. They're looking at the men to see if they are going to fight. I know our men are going to fight. But when we get out there, I want you all to remember to take care of my boys."

Kim walked back and found a place to lie down. He wasn't ready to sleep. All he could think about was the test that lay ahead. All around him men were breathing quietly, their eyes half-open as their minds kept somewhere between sleeping and waking, their thoughts filled with the knowledge that their officers had come back to each platoon with serious expressions on their faces. They knew tomorrow was the day.

~

At daybreak, the unit moved into trucks and started climbing up mountains that rose sharply from the coastal plain. Steep drops edged roads cut into the sides of the mountains. The weather started to turn, and what passed for road soon became mud in the heavy downpour. Thunder and lightning masked the constant sound of artillery, whose register reminded them hourly that they were at war.

On the second day they passed through villages that were nothing more than rubble, crushed walls that had once sheltered families and bounded fields. The fetid smell of war hung heavy, and now the human wreckage of war filled their gazes as they rode past ruin after ruin. The first signs of death confronted them. The sweet, gut-churning smell of decay lingered heavy in the air. The roadside was littered with draft horses and other animals used by the Germans to move equipment through rough terrain, their insides leaking from bodies bursting from the bloat of death. The animal carcasses were not the only dead machines of war. The men stared silently at blackened German tanks shrouded with the same smell.

The outskirts of each night's encampment was ringed by hungry men and women. Then there were the children. Tug spent part of his time gathering candy bars and leftover food from the men. Each man gave what he had. Another smell came drifting over their convoy, the acrid tincture of gun smoke. The rumble of artillery became louder and sharper. They were moving closer to battle.

~

The next day, Second Platoon was sent out to confirm reports of a German soldier hiding nearby. The men cautiously encircled a shattered farmhouse, their rifles held out in anticipation. They probed the collapsed pile of stone and timber until Yuki's squad heard the muffled cries of a man waiting to surrender.

The German came out with his hands raised, his eyes rapidly blinking in the light. The first thing he said was that his father was Irish. His limited English was hard to understand, but it was clear he was attempting to identify with Americans. He kept staring in confusion at Yuki and the squad, the small-statured soldiers dressed in allied uniforms, their oversized steel helmets shielding eyes that were not round.

He kept asking if they were Chinese. One of the men responded that they were Japanese. The German's eyes widened, as he asked if Japan had switched sides and betrayed Germany. The men laughed as they prodded their captive to move to the rear of the unit for interrogation, telling him they were Americans.

~

Shells fell sporadically while the men moved forward on the Chiusano road, near the village of Castelvetere. The road began to turn from heavy mud into sucking mire, slowing progress as more rain fell. Yellow grass bordered the undulating roadway, the countryside brown from the heat of summer and now sodden with the first real rains of fall. The bulk of the German forces had moved back to the Volturno River but left mobile artillery units to delay the advance of the allied forces, harassing them with fire and then falling back. Their objective was to make any forward movement as slow and as expensive as possible.

The rain fell in sudden heavy bursts and long slow drizzles. All the men in Second Platoon were shivering, and the chill air left them miserable. Company B took the lead. They moved forward on foot for three miles while rain dripped down their ponchos, seeping into every opening in their clothing. The rubberized garments held in body heat and perspiration so that the men were almost as wet inside as they were outside. The sound of machine gun fire stilled the advance, leaving behind any thought of comfort.

Kim halted his unit for a moment to assess the direction of the machine gun. There was a hill which the road followed in a curve that ringed a shallow valley. Somewhere, the Germans were sweeping the elevated road with gunfire. There was more than one machine gun. Kim could hear at least three, with their staccato sound interrupted by the explosion of 75mm German shells. He looked back at his men and singled out Yuki and his squad to follow.

On their left, Third Platoon, led by Second Lieutenant Paul Froning, moved toward what he thought was the sound of one of the machine guns, but he was pinned down quickly, his men scrabbling through the wet ground for cover. Sergeant Takeba stayed close on Kim as he led the men forward.

Kim leaned over to Takeba. "Froning is stuck. There's not a hellava lot he can do." He could see that Froning was actually moving away from the guns, probably because he couldn't get a clear view in the massive field of fire being laid down by the Germans. He could see Third Platoon trying to set up mortars frantically, but they were close to the trees. Kim talked to himself: "They need to get clear of the trees with those damn mortars. If a round hits those trees above them, they're gonna kill themselves."

Artillery rounds landed near Third Platoon, and Kim looked along the ridgeline where he had taken Second Platoon. He was out of contact with Captain Suzuki, the Company B commander. He could locate where a German machine gun was by its sound and the fiery streaks of tracers and yelled out, "We're going to move down into that gully and try to flank them." He signaled back to his men to move with him.

Yuki repeated the command. There was no point in yelling. The 75s made a loud ripping sound as the German artillery attempted to find targets behind the squad. The noise was louder than anything they had ever heard before. Shells were raining on either side of them. Yuki could feel the concussion move him as the blast of air from the impact buffeted the squad. There was dirt flying all around them as they felt the stinging of sand and rock from the shell impacts. Yuki kept his eyes on Kim, watching him move forward, with Takeba glued to his side.

Kim kept motioning forward, into the fire coming furiously at his position. He was surprised by his feeling of focus. He hadn't expected that. It was like everything around him was happening slowly. He could see it all and even though he could hear the sound of the guns it was a curiously muffled noise, something only in the background.

All of a sudden his focus was drawn to a German soldier standing less than fifty feet away, with a machine pistol pointed directly toward him and Takeba.

"DOWN, EVERYBODY DOWN!"

Soon the men were flat against the ground, scraping with their fingernails to make a hole, to find a way to dig their bodies into the ground and out of the sweep of the machine guns. Yuki could hear his men screaming to get down. Tug raised his head and could see Yuki looking up to find the location of the guns. He screamed, "YUKI, GET YOUR ASS DOWN!" He couldn't even hear his own voice, only a ringing in his ears from the concussion blasts.

Burned powder and the sharp smell of ozone filled the air, leaving a bitter taste in the mouths of men gasping for air. Tug kept gulping air trying to keep calm, trying to make the irrationality of the situation something that he could accept. Ahead of him he could see Kim inching toward the sound of the guns. Tug could feel an intense burning in his bladder. He had never wanted to urinate so badly. It was the sound of the guns. He clinched his legs together and kept scraping at the rocky ground. The men around him were doing the same thing—digging, digging furiously.

Kim could see Froning leading a squad along a ridge where the Germans were firing. He was pinned down by enemy fire and his men were moving frantically to find cover. Kim realized he had to move behind the machine gun emplacements or they would all be ripped to shreds. He crawled behind the bushes off the ridge and into the gully that separated them.

By the time they moved to the rear flank, the rattle of machine guns stopped. Only the sound of thunder broke the silence. Someone found the German machine guns, or the Germans ran when they realized Second Platoon was flanking them. Each man looked up and then began to crawl forward, looking for their leaders.

Kim stood up and waved the men on to join him. When he looked back, he realized they were ahead of the rest of the unit. They crossed over to the second ridge, where Third Platoon had been pinned down, and now they walked back, waiting for their hearts to stop pounding. It was then they saw an image that remained with them for many days to come: a rifle, stuck bayonet first into the ground, with a helmet placed gently on it. A cluster of soldiers stood or knelt next to the silent weapon.

Kim led his file of men past the mark of a fallen soldier. Lieutenant Froning was standing, his arms hanging limply at his sides. Captain Suzuki was kneeling down, and Doc Kometani was sitting next to a man crumpled on the ground. It was Joe Takata.

Kim slowed for a moment. Yuki held his gaze on the half-opened eyes of his baseball teammate, Takata's skin had already turned into a chalky pallor against the blood streaking his face. Word passed all along the line of men. Tug closed his mouth and looked away, sharing his thoughts with no one, his memory of Takata a flashing image of his grin as he walked to the plate.

Kim kept the men moving forward even as some stumbled, their eyes on the fallen man rather than the rocky ground. Yuki could see Doc's bulldog face twisted in anguish, his grief openly displayed, mirroring those of the men walking by. Takata was one of his players for Asahi, a star, one of his boys. Doc was the one the parents entrusted with their sons. That was why he had been allowed to join the unit.

But it was the look on the face of the other officers, mouths half-open, eyes wide, that showed they had never expected to lose any men. These looks of confusion on the faces of the men who gave orders troubled Yuki greatly. He looked up at Kim. There was no confusion on his face. Just determination. His voice was still the same, level sound of authority. For the first time that morning Yuki realized Kim wasn't wearing a helmet, only a knit beanie.

Yuki watched Tug walk slowly in the column. The rain dripping from his helmet left streaks in the dirt on his face. Tug looked up and the anguish in his eyes was evident. He whispered, "Yuki, I was afraid. I never been afraid before. Now Joe ..." His voice trailed off.

Yuki understood. "I was afraid, too. You weren't the only one. Only man out there that wasn't afraid was Kim. Now we've been through it.

We know what it's going to be like. You did okay today, Tug. Don't think any different."

By noon, word moved throughout the battalion. Joe Takata had volunteered to get the guns and led his men to the flank of the gunfire. He had gone down firing as a piece of shrapnel from a shell explosion hit him in the head. His men said he was able to tell them where the German guns were located before he died. The 100th had won the right to wear the Red Bull.

~

The men didn't have long to rest. They received orders to move several miles up to the village of Chiusano. Yuki and Tug sat near a tree, confused and quiet, waiting for the signal to move out. The death of Joe Takata was hard to reconcile with the feeling of euphoria they both felt for having survived the fight. They were pulled from their thoughts by the sound of Kim's voice ordering the platoon to move. He led them below the road, amidst trees and bushes. While nobody was relaxed, they knew they were concealed, away from the open area of the road. They saw Captain Suzuki move up to Kim.

Taro Suzuki had taken over for Clarence Johnson when he was transferred to Ordnance. He was slightly shorter than Kim, in his forties, old for a company commander. His age showed in the weariness around his eyes.

"Kim, I want you to move your platoon up on the road. Keep the men eight, ten feet apart on both sides of the road. We have to move forward and clear those machine guns."

Kim looked at Suzuki impassively. "Taro, you want us to get back up on the road? If we get up there, we're going to be out in the open. There's a bend ahead of us. If I were the Germans, I'd be down in a covered position waiting. You can see them from here." In the distance, the German tanks had positioned themselves to cover the roadway.

Suzuki drew back and then straightened. "I said for you to get your men up on the road and move forward."

Kim's voice remained level. His aide, Takeba, stood watching. "No, that's stupid. You're asking me to commit suicide and kill my men."

"That's an order—this is a division order to go on road march."

Kim shook his head. "Road march? You're supposed to quit doing that when you've met the enemy. Look, it's smarter for me to go across the valley and attack the Germans over there." He pointed and said, "We cross the valley instead of following the road around it. It's got to be two thousand yards across the valley, but if we follow the road it looks like at least five miles in the open."

Suzuki looked at Kim, clearly angry. "That's an order."

Kim stared back at the captain. "Well, I'm not going to do it." Suzuki stood facing him, his face taught with emotion. After a moment he turned on his heel and stormed away, back toward the battalion command post, his face flushed with fury.

Yuki and Tug stood close enough to hear the exchange. Tug leaned over.

"Gonna be trouble. Kim gonna be in shit now."

Yuki kept staring at Kim. "Yeah, maybe so, but all I know is that I'd rather be down here walking through cover than up on that damn road." His head turned when he saw Suzuki returning with Colonel Turner, Major Lovell, Major Jack Johnson, and Doc Kometani, all walking toward Kim.

Turner walked directly to Kim. "Lieutenant, you received a direct order from Captain Suzuki to move up on that road. I expect you to follow it."

Kim looked at the Colonel. "Sir, you know the moment I go around that bend and head down there, the Germans are going to open fire and I'm going to get men killed. Why do I need to do that?" He stood looking at Turner, Lovell, and Johnson, while Doc kept shaking his head.

Turner looked up at the road and across the valley. He could see what Kim was talking about, but he also had a division order.

"Well, you either do it or I'm going to court martial you."

The men around Yuki and Tug were all focused on their lieutenant. They could hear the raised voices. But they could also see that the road was wide open. Kim didn't raise his voice. "Go ahead and court martial me." The Colonel looked back at Lovell and started shaking his head, then he walked away with Lovell, Suzuki, and Johnson following him.

After five minutes, Doc came back to where Kim was standing. Kim could see the agitation on Doc's face and he was breathing heavily. He got very close to Kim and looked over at Takeba, who stepped back a short distance. Doc kept his voice low.

"You know, you may be right. It may be a stupid order but if we court martial you, that's going to be on the record and everybody's going to remember that more than anything else. The 100th has a mission here, and we will have failed to prove we're good soldiers. Look, Kim, one man to another, obey the order. Even if it's stupid."

Kim had a great deal of respect for Doc, but he could not accept what he was asking him to do. Taking men into enemy fire was one thing when it had to be done. This was something else entirely. His mind turned over the training he had to follow orders, to let the senior officer decide. Finally, he looked at the dentist-turned-soldier.

"I'll do it because it's a division order. But I'm going to lose men and it's going to be on Turner and Suzuki's head." His face showed grim determination as he motioned for Second Platoon to follow him up toward the road. Yuki turned to the men in his squad. "We gotta move up to the road." He knew they had no choice. Orders were orders.

As Kim moved the platoon onto the road he heard the ripping sound of tank fire coming from the valley. Immediately Kim turned to the platoon and pointed. He could see chestnut trees down below the road that would provide cover from enemy fire. The tanks wouldn't be able to depress their guns enough to fire there.

"NOW! NOW! MOVE TO THE TREES!"

Kim raised his arm and began running directly across the gully and open area below the road, toward the trees and the direction of enemy fire. Yuki didn't hesitate. Kim made them practice this over and over again, running toward enemy fire, making them fire over you. He pulled his men with him as they ran down the gully by the road. Tank fire was coming over them. Yuki could hear the shredding sound the rounds made as they moved through the air. All he wanted was to get his men to the trees, to follow Kim and Takeba.

Yuki's squad collapsed under the trees, finding as much cover as they could, still breathing heavily and feeling the nausea that comes after a rush of adrenalin. Behind them they could see the last squad in the platoon hesitate and stop at the gully, instead of running in the direction of the guns.

German rounds began pouring into the upper portion of the gully, raining shrapnel down on the helpless men. Yuki watched in horror as tank rounds splintered the squad. The concussion of the shell impacts threw men into the air, tossed by the blasts of fire. Rounds kept pouring in until there was no more movement, just a brief space of silence. From the shelter of the trees, men could hear cries for help. The shattered, bloody body of Keichi Tanaka was visible on the rim of the gully. He was dead. The rest of the squad was either wounded or too paralyzed by fear to move.

Second Platoon dug in near the trees and waited as daylight began to fade. Tanaka's squad leader finally made his way out of the gully and down to the trees with what was left of his squad. Kim was leaning against a tree, watching silently as the corporal approached him and knelt down. The corporal ripped his two stripes off his uniform and held them out in his hand. Kim looked at him, black eyes staring from under heavy lids. Nearby men watched. Kim didn't reach for the stripes. He sat looking at the corporal. Finally he turned his hand over and the squad leader laid the stripes in his palm.

Kim led his platoon back to the unit over a ridgeline into the nearby village of Montefalcione, darkness concealing their movements. They found places to lie down and built a few fires to keep warm. Yuki sat with Tug, Kazo, and Johnny as they tried to pull warmth from the small fire. Tug was unusually quiet. Kazo broke the silence.

"I hear they gonna recommend Takata for a medal."

The others simply nodded.

Tug looked up. "Kim saved our asses today, you know? Tanaka, it shouldn't have happened." He looked at Johnny, who had been in the squad with Tanaka.

Johnny was quiet. He looked around at the faces of his friends, grateful to have lived through the day.

"When those shells starting hitting the gully I thought it was over, *brah*. I just keep my head down and hoped I lived. Nothing I could do, you know? We should have kept running like Kim said. It was a mistake but there were so many shells." He kept shaking his head. "Tanaka, before we went out, he said he was going to die today. You think he knew?"

Yuki looked at the faces reflecting the flickering fire. Nobody answered. They sat for a few more minutes in silence and then found a place to sleep, their bodies aching from the tension and adrenalin of the last few hours. It was the end of the first day.

CHAPTER 46

October, 1943

Near the Village of Alife, Italy

The 100th, now a battalion of the 133rd regiment of the 34th Division, pushed forward to the Volturno River, a twisting, turning rush of water which ran inland, snaking more or less along a parallel line with the western coast of Italy. The German forces had withdrawn the twenty miles to the river where they were entrenched, using the river as a defensive perimeter. Moving northward in as straight a line as possible meant the Volturno had to be forded again and again as it repeatedly crossed over the direct line of travel. To attack the new German lines meant that once more the Volturno had to be crossed— this time, under fire. The thought of wading again through the swiftly moving, freezing water was not a prospect anyone relished.

All day the battalion crossed open country toward the Volturno. The vineyards and orchards that once thrived in the pastoral countryside were now entanglements to be crossed, protecting the enemy that slowly withdrew while harassing the oncoming 100th with intermittent mortar and small arms fire. By midnight Company B sat hunkered down among the trees that clung to the river, waiting in the blackness of the moonless night for the order to cross.

There was no talking or joking around. The rushing water of the river was a constant reminder of what lay ahead. They could hear the German Nebelwerfer rocket launchers in the distance as other elements of the 133rd started crossing along the Allied front. The multibarreled, electrically fired rockets made a moaning sound as they were fired, rising into a shriek as they hurtled through the air. There was no mistaking the sound of the "screaming meemies." The pitch-black banks of the river were backlit by shell bursts and the staccato cracking of machine gun fire.

Company A led off while Company B moved into position. Kim's platoon waited with the rest of B Company for their sister company to move ahead. When they entered the water, the chill was immediate. Yuki could feel the icy water climbing up his legs as he moved his squad into the rushing river, Lieutenant Kim leading the way. Some of the men were knocked off their feet in the thrashing current and were pulled up by the others. Whispers moved up and down the line to keep their rifles above their heads. The heavy M1 Garand rifles weighed almost twelve pounds fully loaded, and their bulk made maneuvering in the swift water even more awkward.

Tug was already muttering, "Keep my rifle above water? I got enough problem keeping my head above water."

German machine pistol rounds punctuated the noisy splashing of the men, stitching small plumes of water as the German defenders fired down on them. Everyone moved as quickly as possible to the other side of the river, scrambling through the mud to get above the riverbank and into concealment, hearing the screams of men who were hit before they made it to the other bank. On the other side they shivered in their sodden fatigues and waited sleeplessly for the dawn.

~

After reconnaissance patrols spent the day probing German defenses, the 100th prepared for a night assault on the village of Alife. The open terrain in front of them was mined heavily. German defenders set up machine gun nests that forced any forward movement into crossing fields of fire. As darkness fell, Company A patrolled the flat ground above the river, with Company B behind it.

Picking their way through a tangle of abandoned gardens and splintered grape trellises, they approached a farmhouse that occupied the river valley. There was only a momentary creak as a door swung open. The unit was immediately caught in machine gun fire from inside the farmhouse. Yuki could see men falling all around as Company A was cut to pieces, the blazing streaks of tracer fire crisscrossing the killing ground. The men moving behind could do nothing.

Yuki's squad watched in frustration as they listened to the cries of screaming men. They could only keep their heads down and crawl forward, the incendiary trail of tracer bullets causing them to hug the ground as closely as they could, afraid to raise their heads into the stream of fire above them. Thirty men were down in seconds.

Colonel Turner stood in the 100th command post, listening to the sounds of battle and the reports streaming back. Kim could hear Turner's voice rising over the radio as he ordered mortar fire to protect his men. Kim knew orders meant nothing if you could not see. Men from Company A crawled back to the men of Company B, pushing themselves against the rocky ground as the enemy bullets followed the survivors falling back. Yuki could see other men from Company A moving forward to try to silence the machine guns. He could hear officers yelling for mortar cover, their voices barely rising above the roar of gunfire as the enemy defenders swept their guns across the ground.

Turner stood in his command post, clenching his fists in frustration as he listened to the urgent requests for help, the roar of battle in the background. He sent runners back to the 133rd command post asking for support. It didn't come. When he couldn't stand the losses any longer, he finally went himself.

Turner looked at Col. Ray C. Fountain, commander of the 133rd.

"Sir, I've sent a platoon off to the left of the German fire. I think we can envelop them and my men can move forward."

Fountain shook his head. "Pull your men, Colonel. I'm sending in 1st Battalion."

Turner started to argue, but then stopped.

"Yes, sir."

He went back to the 100th command post.

"Give the order for the men to withdraw back to the river and behind 1st Battalion."

He stood near the radio, listening as his officers gave the order to pull back as another unit was ordered to take over their job. He looked into the darkness outside the command post, flashes of light punctuating the blackness as flares lit the battleground. He rubbed his face, trying to push back the fatigue, his body aching from the pressure of command.

He could not help wondering if it was his fault, if he had lost men who should not have gone down. Turner's face was ashen, even in the dim light. These were his boys. He trained them. The thought rested at the back of his mind. *Was it me? Did I let my boys down?* The pinprick tingle of his rising blood pressure caused his neck to tighten. He turned to listen to the crackle of the radio, carrying the sounds of his men drawing back from the field.

～

At the first light of dawn, Company B moved forward with what was left of Company A, trailing down the road to the village of Alife, its ancient stone walls rising in the distance through the morning mist. Ten men were dead and twenty wounded in the futile assault the night before. The 100th was scattered all over the area, and the men still had not dried out from the freezing river crossing. Right before the village, they saw the massive German Mark II tanks. Someone fired a bazooka round and then another, knocking out a tank. Finally artillery fire pinned down the heavy machines and they moved back, giving the men a moment to breathe.

Second Platoon marched all day, drawing fire occasionally. Finally Kim and his men reached a bridge on the outskirts of the town. The shrill cry of screaming meemies began to shriek overhead as a rocket hit the bridge, the centuries-worn stone ripping apart. A man went down.

Yuki and the rest of his squad moved across the crumbling bridge. Ahead they could see the jutting stone markers of a graveyard, the encircling stone wall providing cover. Quickly, he ordered his men to move behind thin tombstones bearing names already washed out by time. The men spent no time dwelling on the graves. They pushed themselves against the mossy stones, trying to avoid the mortar fire raining down on their position. Other squads moved behind them, using the cemetery's stone walls to cover them from the fire chipping away at the hand-laid rock.

As he hid behind a grave marker, Yuki heard a voice. "What's the matter, boys?" Yuki looked back as Major Lovell pulled his pipe out of his mouth and tapped out the burning embers on a tombstone. Lovell stood up. The major pulled out his pistol and started walking up the hill leading into the village. The men slowly rose up and started following the lanky coach. The ripping scream of a rocket round broke through the machine gun fire. Lovell went down as his men pushed forward.

～

That night Yuki sat against a stone wall, the rest of the squad keeping close in the cold. The 100th lost men they had trained with for over a year. Some were dead. Many were wounded. So far, his squad had managed to make it without losing anybody. But they had lost Lovell. The Major had gotten them up the hill but now Yuki saw the price for what looked, to him, like nothing except a crumbling brick village and the crossing of two dirt roads.

He leaned back. Nobody explained why they had done any of this. He knew nobody would. He hoped there was a good reason for all of it. "I don't know if it was a rocket or a mortar. Coach caught part of a round in his leg. Some of the boys got him out. Damndest thing I ever saw. He just kept walking and shooting that pistol. Never saw anything like that."

Tug listened silently and thought, *Yes, that's something Coach would do.*

～

Three days after the assault on Alife, Lovell was lying on a cot in a field hospital. He heard rumors that Turner had been ordered by regimental HQ to send out a reconnaissance patrol. The patrol had reported no enemy sighted and, as a result, a platoon was ambushed. Lovell also heard from battalion staff that Turner was cracking. But he knew him. What was tearing him apart were the losses. He had seen the Colonel the day they lost Joe Takata. Every man lost took a piece of Turner with him.

The Major was half-sitting on his cot, his leg up and heavily bandaged. He was going to be shipped back to a rear area for more medical attention and recuperation. Lovell was considering his situation when Turner walked into the hospital tent. The Colonel had aged considerably, his hair was whiter, the lines on his face deeper. But it was the gray cast to his skin that gave him the look of a man who had already seen more than he could bear.

Turner nodded to Lovell. "Jim, how're you doing? They tell me you're going to be sent back for a while to get that leg fixed up, and then you'll be back in action. The unit's going to need you. The boys took Alife, you know. They followed you up that damned hill."

Lovell was cautious in his response. Something wasn't quite right about Turner's tone of voice. The Colonel's whole body seemed weighed down. His face carried a resignation to fatigue and age.

Lovell's words were measured. "Thank you, sir, I heard we took the town." He gestured toward his bandaged leg. "It isn't too bad, but the docs say it's going to take some time to heal. I'll be back real quick."

"Well, I'm glad you're okay." Lovell could see the emotion. Turner's mouth was trembling. "Look, I came to say goodbye. I won't be here when you get back. I'm being replaced." He paused, searching for the right words. "They think maybe I need some rest. I don't know. Perhaps it's for the best. We lost a lot of our boys . . ." His voice trailed off, and the two men stayed silent for a moment. There wasn't much to say. Lovell knew that Turner was not leaving his command by choice.

"Colonel, how many did we lose?"

"We lost 21 of our boys; the 133rd lost 59 and 148 wounded. We had sixty-seven wounded, including four of our lieutenants. Jim Vaughn got hit. I'm going to put him in for a silver star. I've got a lot of boys I want to put in for medals. Our medics, all our boys, they just fought their hearts out. I wish I could have done more for them."

Turner walked slowly out of the hospital tent as Lovell watched. He knew better than anyone that Turner made the unit work. They wouldn't have done as well as they had without his training and preparing them. His problem wasn't that he didn't care. His problem was that he cared too much.

Lovell lay back on his pillow and looked at the other wounded men in the tent. That was the problem with being a field officer. You weren't any good unless you cared about your men, and you weren't any good unless you were willing to order them to do things that were going to get some of them, and sometimes all of them, killed.

CHAPTER 47

October 26, 1943
Calwa, California

Sack's mother rocked quietly, her grandson finally asleep. She stayed up rocking most of the night, drifting between light sleep and wakefulness as the baby would stiffen and cry. She looked at the black-haired boy, his dark ruddy face and black eyes a contrast to her son. She moved the rocking chair slightly, swaying as her eyes slowly closed again.

Sack moved quietly past his mother in the early morning light. It was dawn. He had work to do, getting ready for the men to prune the vines in a few more weeks. He put a piece of wood in the stove to stir yesterday's embers and watched as the flame caught. Then he quietly closed the cast-iron door and stood close to pull in the feeble warmth of the stove.

He looked over at his mother holding the baby, her graying hair hanging loosely around her face. The years had replaced the youthful beauty he remembered with the marks of labor and sun, the finely drawn crinkles at the edge of her eyes from laughter now cut deeply into her cheeks, the soft white hands roughened and red. The chair rocked slowly, his mother trying to give Carmen some rest. His wife was exhausted. The baby had colic and had kept her up most of the night.

He still couldn't get over the fact that this little squirming bundle was his son. They debated over a name. Carmen wanted to name the baby after her brother José, but Sack couldn't really see his son named José Pritch. He wanted his son named after his father, Frank, so Carmen suggested Francisco. He couldn't see that, either. So they had settled on

Frank José. Sack figured Frank José Pritch was enough of a mouthful and when he was older, he could work it out for himself. Right now, they just called him Frankie.

Sack reached inside his coat pocket and took out José's letter. He hadn't shared it yet with Carmen. She worried so much. He struggled in the pale light to read José's cramped handwriting. They hadn't heard from him in a while. He and the rest of his unit had been training in North Africa after they shipped out in April. Then he had gone in with the 36th when they landed at Salerno. José only said that it had been rough. But Sack now read the papers. He knew. José said he had a good sergeant who got him off the beach. Thoughts of Smitty flashed across his mind.

Sack put the letter down. His hand was shaking. He refolded it carefully. He would wait a while before giving it to Carmen. She didn't need any more on her mind.

Sack squeezed the thin envelope in his hand and then slipped it into his coat. They would carefully bundle it away with the rest of José's letters. Sack walked over to the sink quietly, primed the pump with two quick downward motions, wet his hand in the running water and rubbed the bar of soap, waiting before putting his face in the ice-cold well water.

The oily soap took his mind back to the beach, the day that was always in the back of his mind. He could still feel the oily water closing in around him, the sea pulling at him, the noise blocking out the screams of dying men. Sack rubbed his wet hand across his face and reached for the towel. For some reason he couldn't put his face in the water this morning.

He never said anything to anyone about his memories, not Carmen, not even his father. Even when he looked at the irrigation water gushing into the furrows between the vines, he thought about it. They never left him, the memories of that day and all that he left on that beach.

Sack shook his head and rubbed the towel over his eyes to dry the tears that gathered at the thought. He had done his part. And now José and Sammy. He kept the towel over his face to muffle the sounds coming up from deep inside him.

CHAPTER 48

Early November, 1943
Headquarters, 442nd Infantry Battalion
Camp Shelby, Mississippi

Sammy and Freddy walked over to the Post Exchange, hoping to buy a few things before they went into Hattiesburg, the town outside Camp Shelby. Both of them began to break some of the barriers with the Hawaii boys, the *buta heads*, but the whole relationship was different. The Hawaiian boys thought the mainland boys were cheap and called them *manini*, which, Sammy learned, was a Hawaiian reef fish with a small mouth, so it could only take small bites.

The mainland boys thought the island boys were ignorant because they frequently spoke to one another in pidgin English that was hard, if not impossible, to understand. And even when they spoke in what passed for as regular English, they could be difficult to understand when they dropped words out of sentences, or threw in island words and said things like "Me go, you go" instead of "I'll go if you will."

They didn't seem very well-mannered. They were constantly running around in their bare feet and took their shirts off at every opportunity. It was difficult to get used to. Sammy avoided getting into fights in the barracks—he would always just walk away—but Freddy was constantly exchanging punches with somebody until one of the Hawaii boys, Bobby Nomura, took him aside and said that the Hawaii boys would continue to pick on him unless he just started to laugh and joke with them. They were going into town with Tommy and Akiro, but Sammy had also invited two of the Hawaii boys to go with them.

Freddy looked around to see if anyone was listening.

"Sammy, why do we have to go into town with those *buta heads*?"

"You mean Bobby and Stubby?" Sammy had made friends with Bobby, a soft-spoken island boy who had been a student at the University of Hawaii. He had also begun to warm to Bobby's friend Stubby Honda, a short, squat soldier who also had been at the university, although Sammy still wasn't sure how Stubby got into a university.

"Yeah, I mean they're okay, but most of those guys are like country bumpkins."

Sammy looked over with a wry expression. "You mean they're not sophisticated like us Calwa boys?"

"Okay, okay. Obviously you don't have a problem with them like I do."

Sammy stopped walking for a moment and looked over at his friend.

"What makes your problem with them any different than the problem the guards at the camps had with us? I figure there's no more reason for us to look down on them than there is for other people to look down on us."

Freddy started to say something and then stopped.

"Okay, you got a point."

Bobby, Stubby, Akiro, and Tommy were waiting for them when they got to the bus stop near the front gate. When the bus came, Stubby immediately headed for the back of the bus until Sammy grabbed his arm.

"Let's sit up toward the front."

Stubby looked at the back where several Negroes were sitting, watching them.

"What for? Back home all the guys sit in the back. Best place to sit."

Sammy kept pulling on him. "I'll tell you later; just sit up front."

For most of the bus ride they talked about the 100th. Both Bobby and Stubby had buddies in the unit. Nobody heard anything yet. Sammy and Freddy only met a few of the boys in the 100th before they left, and that had been through Bobby. There was a lot of speculation since they knew by now that the 100th had landed in Italy.

Stubby ended the conversation as the bus neared town. "My guess, those boys sitting on some beach over there catching fish. I bet they've not even fired their rifles except at some tiger or something."

Bobby looked over with a grin. "They don't have tigers in Italy. How'd you ever get into the University of Hawaii, anyway?" The other four started laughing.

Stubby was unaffected by the snipe. He grinned. "Same way you got in, through the back door."

When they got to Hattiesburg and got off the bus, Stubby turned to Sammy.

"Okay, smart guy, what's the reason we don't sit in back?"

Sammy walked a few steps away from the bus and waited for the others to join him. "The lieutenant talked to me about it. The Negroes are only allowed to sit in the back of the bus around here. If we go sit in the back, then they won't have any place to sit. The driver won't let them on the bus when the back is full, even if the rest of the bus is empty. We'd be taking the only seats they can sit in." He waited while Stubby looked at him.

At last, the chunky soldier nodded his head. "Okay, maybe you're right. Those people got more problems than we do."

They started walking down the streets of Hattiesburg, looking at all the stores and trying to figure out where to get something to eat.

Hattiesburg was a different world. There were "colored" toilets and "colored" water fountains. Already some of the men had gotten into trouble for drinking at the "colored" fountains. It was all very confusing. They heard the story about the boys from the 100th who took over a bus when the driver refused to let a Negro woman ride. They roughed him up and drove the bus around town, then abandoned it and walked back to the camp.

The movie theaters were even harder to understand. Back home in Hawaii, the balcony seats were considered the best. Here the Negro people were required to sit up there, while the Japanese boys couldn't. All Stubby said was that all the Southern *haoles* were crazy.

When they got back on the bus for the ride back to camp, most of the seats were filled and Bobby looked for a place to stand. The driver looked back and told a Negro woman sitting along the side to get up. "Let the soldier sit."

Bobby looked around and shook his head. "I'll stand. I don't feel like sitting."

The driver looked at him. "Suit yourself."

Bobby looked over at the woman who sat staring at him. She nodded slightly and he smiled. The irony of it all didn't escape him.

When they walked into the barracks, the usual dice game was not going on. Most of the men were sitting on their bunks talking quietly. Jackson, one of the Hawaii boys, looked over when Bobby asked what was going on.

"Sergeant Otani came by. He heard some reports about the 100th. It's bad, Bobby. A lot of boys gone. We don't know how many."

Sammy and Freddy moved over to their bunks and listened to the conversation. The Hawaiians were subdued. Some of them had family in the 100th. Bobby asked if there were any names yet. Jackson shook his head. "Just one name, Joe Takata. That was all Otani heard for sure. All he heard was that our boys got hit hard."

Bobby looked over at Stubby. They had watched Takata play ball.

The men tried to squeeze as much information as possible from those who spoke with Otani. Sammy watched the Hawaii boys. He didn't know Joe Takata. He probably didn't know any of the men who had been lost. But he did understand losing friends. He looked over at Freddy, who was lying silently on his bunk staring up at the mattress above his bottom bunk.

Jackson picked a letter up off his bunk, walked over, and tossed it in Sammy's direction. "You got a letter. I picked it up for you at mail call. Sammy looked at the letter. It was from Mickey, and had obviously come from a long distance. He held the thin paper carefully.

Mickey was now somewhere in the South Pacific and ended up in the same unit as Tony Machado. Neither of them could believe they were together. He thought it was funny to listen to the Japanese calling them "Yankees" and insulting American baseball. A lot of the letter was blacked out by censors, but it was clear that he had already seen action.

Sammy held the letter out for Freddy. "It's from Mickey. He's in the South Pacific somewhere. Now it's just us."

Freddy took the letter. "Don't worry. We'll be in it soon enough. The boys in the 100th are going to need some help."

~

Sammy and Freddy walked into the barracks after a cleaning detail to find some of the boys packing. Sammy walked over to Bobby, who was stuffing gear into his barracks bag.

"What's going on?"

Jackson looked up while he continued packing. "We going somewhere, *brah*. A whole bunch of us gettin' orders to go to Alabama because of the peanut crop."

Freddy looked confused. "They expect us to pick peanuts?"

"No, *brah*, they're using German soldiers from the Afrika Korps to pick peanuts and we're going to guard 'em. Can you believe it? We get to guard Jerry soldiers."

"Well, maybe that's not so bad," Sammy said. "If we're guarding German soldiers then we won't be marching around and crawling through mud, right?" A few heads nodded.

"So, what the hell, we go guard Germans. Maybe we can learn a little German—help us out when we start fighting them."

Some of the others began to nod also. A few even began to recognize that most of the time Sammy made sense, and he wasn't a bad guy for a *katonk*. Even his buddy wasn't such a bad guy, and he was a pretty good fighter. What Sammy kept to himself was the thought that he was an American soldier, guarding German prisoners, while other American soldiers were guarding his parents.

Sammy sat on his bunk trying to think of what to write to his mother and father. More and more rumors were coming in about losses in the 100th, along with some names. One of the boys in the barracks lost a cousin. Almost all of them lost someone they knew. He couldn't write his parents about that. Sergeant Otani let them know quietly that certain companies in the 442nd were being considered as replacement units for the losses in the 100th, and the company he and Freddy were in was likely to be going.

Every day new men were coming in, volunteers and draftees. They were just starting their training, and the men in Company B were already well into it. The 100th couldn't be backfilled with replacements from just anywhere. They had to have Japanese soldiers, and the 442nd was the only other Japanese unit. He couldn't write about that either.

Dear Mom and Dad,

Things are going pretty good here. Freddy and I have stayed together. Tommy and Akiro are in a different company but we see each other all the time. The training is getting easier but I guess it's because I am in better shape. I really miss both of you. I even miss Manzanar. This place is so different from the valley or the desert. I heard that now that they are drafting Japanese a lot of boys are leaving Manzanar. We are beginning to get men from all the camps but some of them don't have the same attitude as the guys like us who volunteered. It's hard to blame them. I heard from Mickey. He is with Tony Machado but he can't say where they are. I almost can't believe it. Two Calwa boys together like that. I don't know what it would be like if Freddy and I weren't together. Have you heard anything from Toshi? Freddy and I have been guarding German prisoners while they pick peanuts. They let those guys walk all over the place. Mom, I got the *senninbari*. I promise I will wear it. Don't worry about me. I'll be fine. I love you both.

   Sammy

Sammy folded the letter and put it in an envelope. His mother had sent him the *senninbari* for luck. About the size of a towel, the soft white cloth was covered with tiny balls of red thread. His father said that the red balls were stitched onto it by many hundreds of women. There was a nickel sewn into the corner. Sammy knew what it meant. *Shisen o koete, gosen ni naru.* If you have used up four lives, the death line, you get a fifth one. His mother meant for him to wear it under his uniform. Some of the other soldiers had *senninbari* from their mothers.

He held the cloth in his hands, a bit embarrassed by the superstitious meaning. "For luck," she had said. Sammy had a fleeting image of his mother the last time he saw her at the gate to Manzanar. She had been crying. He promised her he would come home. He carefully folded the *senninbari* and placed it in his trunk. He would wear it, just in case. Maybe it would help him keep that promise.

CHAPTER 49

November 5, 1943
Near the Village of Ciorlano, Italy

The 100th pushed north from Alife, first to the village of Santa Angelo. Like each of the towns they had passed, the houses of the ancient community sat close to one another, neighbors sharing walls with generation after succeeding generation. Its narrow streets created fear of ambush at every turn. None came.

The Germans were pulling back to the hills surrounding the river valley. Each day brought little progress as the 100th ground forward under artillery fire from the ridges looking down on them, and sniping from stone walls and abandoned farmhouses in front of them. Miles were marked by a man down, a man wounded. There was no rest. There was no respite. There was no silence from the relentless assault of artillery rounds and the screeching sound of the rocket guns as the Germans bracketed them from the heights. Each man struggled forward without knowing what was behind the next tree, the next wall.

Yuki led his squad forward, following Kim, following Second Platoon, following Company B, following the 100th picking its way through the olive groves and trellised grape vines that now harbored mines and booby traps.

The uncertainty of the march was heightened by the loss of Colonel Turner. They stood in ranks when he told them he was leaving. His hair was now white, but it was the pain on his face that each man saw. Tears streaked down battle-grimed faces. Who would lead them without the old man, without Coach?

Major James Gillespie transferred over from the 3rd Battalion of the 133rd. He was an up-from-the-ranks officer, and he understood how the men felt. They had lost their "Pop," but he also knew there was a job to be done. He let the men know he wasn't there to replace Turner. He was there to lead. It was small comfort that there was a new commander. The loss of Major Lovell set heavily on their minds.

On the dawn of the last day of October, the 100th moved into position over the village of Ciorlano when they heard sound coming low over the wintering fields. Six German Messerschmitts, fire streaming from their wings, came skimming through the morning mist. The men of B raised their eyes from the cold dirt as combat planes sprayed rounds across A and C companies, inflicting twelve casualties.

The men watched as the medics worked feverishly on the wounded, glancing up at the sky and then back to their bloody work, while stretcher bearers ran with the wounded to a hurriedly set up field triage tent. The unit was beginning to feel the losses, both in terms of men and emotion.

They pushed forward under low gray skies and mist-covered brush until they reached the heights near the village of Ciorlano and could look down on the Volturno again, twisting and turning through the killing fields of the river valley they had just crossed. The river had turned into a snake, crossing in front of them, swallowing them one by one. And now they could see it down below, glistening, waiting for them once more. They knew they would have to cross it. Again.

Lieutenant Kim walked with Taro Suzuki over to the 133rd Regimental Command Post. Col. Carley Marshall had taken over command for Colonel Fountain. There was going to be another crossing of the Volturno. Suzuki told Kim that Company B was going to lead the crossing.

Suzuki stopped right before they walked into the regimental CP. "Kim, we don't have any maps for this crossing. You've got a photographic memory for maps. I need you to look at the map and commit it to memory."

All the battalion commanders and company officers were crowded around the map board, listening as Marshall laid out the plan. In the dim light of the tent, Marshall twirled the heavily waxed tips of his mustache as he pointed at the lines and marks on the battle map. Kim was the only lieutenant present, and he knew better than to open his mouth. He simply listened and focused on the map. Even at Fort Benning, he had been able to look at the lines and grids on pieces of paper and see hills and valleys in his mind. To others, it was a maze of lines. To him it was a painting that only he could see.

The river ran in shallow tributaries around clustered islands covered with willows, joined by the narrow stream of the Sava River. The merging river courses spread out wide but ran only several feet deep. Kim had seen it through field binoculars: There was a small town set against the hills on the other side that would have to be taken, but first they'd march through open fields and olive groves and grape vines hiding mines and snipers. And then they'd cross the sinking mud of the river delta and move up the ridge, against the entrenched enemy. He knew where the Germans would be waiting. It was where he would be.

Marshall pointed at the map and began to speak. "The 3rd Battalion is going to cross the Volturno to move on the village of Santa Maria. The 1st will move on the hill near Santa Maria to give us high ground. The 100th is going to cross further downstream to the rear and left of the 1st. The 100th's job is to protect the left flank of the division. We know the Jerries have tanks and self-propelled guns down in the valley area, and they're using olive groves to hide in. Our reconnaissance of the area in the flats on the west side of the river shows it's heavily mined, with booby traps everywhere. Our artillery will start pounding the Kraut positions between 11:30 and midnight. As soon as the artillery stops, your men move out."

Kim stared at the map, mentally comparing it to what he had been able to see from their position. The entire 34th Division would push across in a line. His company would lead the 100th across as the point of the 133rd. From what Marshall was saying he could see there was a road that they had to find, and it would have to be found in the dark.

Midnight approached lit by the artillery bombardment on the other side of the river. Thundering guns of the 34th were attempting to break the enemy line and soften the advance. Second Platoon waited in the trees down near the river. Advance scouts had taken ropes across parts of the river, but some men could not use them as they advanced in a line instead of a file. The water was only a few feet deep at the crossing point, but that didn't mean there weren't holes in the bed that could swallow the shorter men in the unit.

Tug kept looking out at the rushing water. "Yuki, how many times we got to cross this damn river? I'm not a fish."

Yuki looked back at Tug and the rest of the squad. "You know, the captain didn't consult me before he offered advice to the colonel. Maybe they just don't realize how wet this is going to be."

"Yeah, maybe that's because they ain't gonna get wet." Yuki could hear snickering down the line.

The sound of artillery rounds hitting the water and moving up the other side of the river ended the conversation. They all hoped the curtain of fire would push the Germans back from the river. All of a sudden, the artillery silenced. Kim raised his hand and motioned the men to follow him. Yuki turned and gave a similar motion as they moved down the bank and into the freezing water.

Kim moved two scouts ahead of him to provide covering fire if they ran into any Germans. He was the one with the map in his head, and he needed to direct the men. He could see where the American engineers had marked off the river on both sides. He could feel the river rocks under his feet, causing him to slip and struggle to maintain his footing. The thumping of the 34th's guns sounded behind them. The ripping sound of their shells creased the air over them in the pitch-black night.

Water began rising in plumes along the line of advance, thudding explosions muffled by the liquid. Kim looked back at his men. Artillery rounds dropped in the area upstream from them. Rounds from American guns were falling short, where the men from the 1st crossed. Orders were screamed into the radio, held above the waist-deep water. Kim had to hold the advance as their artillery adjusted fire to move ahead of their units. The men stood as the swift current pulled at their legs, the icy waters sapping their energy. Every man knew that the longer they waited the more time they were giving to the enemy to entrench, to defend, to make them a target.

Kim heard the German self-propelled guns returning fire. Twenty minutes passed before he heard the call to advance. He moved quickly to the riverbank urging the men to move carefully up and onto higher ground. There would be mines. He knew there would be mines. It was what he would do if he held the high ground. He ran with his scouts to an area sixty or seventy yards from the river when his radioman hissed at him.

"It's the Captain. He says to stop and wait for him."

After a few minutes, Captain Suzuki caught up with Kim and his platoon. He looked around immediately.

"Kim, I think you're going in the wrong direction."

Kim shook his head in frustration. "Taro, you're the one that said I was going to lead. This is the way to the objective."

The Captain was shaking his head. "Well, I don't think it's this way on the map."

Kim could barely make out the Captain's face. They were under a canopy of trees, closing out what little light existed.

"Taro, we don't have a map. This is the way."

Suzuki looked at Kim. He had been through this before, when Kim became obstinate on their first day at Salerno. He wasn't going to make the mistake of being pushed by a junior officer again.

"No, you're going in the wrong direction. I want you to turn and go this way, parallel to the river."

Kim kept shaking his head. "I'm not going to do that. The objective is this way. You want to go that way, you go."

Suzuki stared at his lieutenant. "Okay, I've had enough. I'm not going to let you lead. I'll have Third Platoon lead." He turned and walked over to another group of men that Kim couldn't make out in the dark. Kim held his platoon up, watching the captain lead the other men away. There were mines out there. He knew it. He waited a moment longer and then raised his arm for his men to follow him as he slowly trailed through the heavy mist in Suzuki's direction.

The sound of explosions and screaming halted Kim's platoon in their tracks. Bursts of light cut through the blackness as boots stepped on hidden detonators. The ground ahead was laced with what the men called Bouncing Bettys, vicious explosive charges that sprang up waist-high and detonated. Kim heard the captain order the other platoons up. He led his men near where the rest of the company had stopped. Even in the dark, they could see at least seven men lying in the minefield. Suzuki was kneeling in the dirt.

Flares burst overhead, lighting the darkness in intermittent flashes. Kim could see enough of Suzuki's face in the white light of the descending flares to sense his anguish. He looked at the shadowy figures of the men still standing. They were frozen in place, afraid to move, afraid they might step on a mine. The cries of wounded men drew medics forward, picking their way through footprints barely distinguishable in the darkness, setting their boots where others had safely stepped before. Some of the men on the ground were not moving at all.

Kim and the other lieutenants worked their way over to the Captain. His knees were in the dirt. The eyes of the company commander searched the faces of his lieutenants, who stood watching him.

Finally the captain spoke. "Does anybody know where the objective is?" All the officers stood silently.

He looked over at Kim.

"You know where it is?"

"Yes, sir."

"You lead. I won't argue."

Kim looked around at the other officers nodding. They had all heard it.

"Okay, everybody look at your footprints and step into them as we back out."

He moved back until he was sure the men were out of the minefield and then headed in the other direction, following his mental image of the map.

They moved away from the river, through the trees until they came to a narrow dirt road. Across the road, the ground rose up. Kim and Suzuki moved toward the other side of the road. He could see stones piled up and a hedge separating the road from the embankment. Kim climbed through the hedge to the top of the ground on its other side.

"Captain, if you look in that direction over there . . ." He held his arm out, pointing. All of a sudden, the night air was shattered by the sound of machine gun fire. Kim felt a bullet graze his arm. He jumped backward. The captain scrambled back down the embankment and through the hedge. Kim rolled down the raised ground into a shallow gully no wider than his body and started to back through the hedge.

Before he could get his head up, he heard the Captain.

"OPEN FIRE!"

Kim heard the bullets from his own men whistling overhead. He pushed himself down against the ground as hard as he could. He heard men yelling, the thudding of bullets hitting the side of the gully above him. The sound of his own men screaming blurred into the roar of the gunfire until his mind had to shut it out to think. *What the hell are they shooting at?* The Germans were on the other side of the embankment. He was on the same side as his men.

Yuki and his men were firing as fast as they could. Men on both sides of his squad were screaming that Kim was down, that he had been hit. He heard the captain ordering fire. He looked over at his squad lying down and kneeling, pouring as much fire as they could at the top of the embankment. The sound of the enemy machine gun mixed into the vortex of fire, the blackness between the two sides lit by the strobe light-flickering of fire until there was almost no night. There was so much screaming and noise, Yuki couldn't think. Sergeants were yelling at their men to get the bastards that got the lieutenant.

Through the roar of fire, Yuki heard the order being screamed,

"FIX BAYONETS!"

He turned to his squad, hearing his voice crack as he made himself heard above the battle.

"FIX BAYONETS!"

The sound of sharpened steel being unsheathed broke the gunfire as bayonets were pulled out and attached to rifle barrels. As Yuki slid his bayonet onto the barrel of his rifle he sensed that the snap of the blade as it tipped his rifle was different than other battle sounds, in some ways more terrifying.

There was anonymity with a rifle. A bayonet meant a face-to-face fight with the enemy. Men were more afraid of that glinting steel knife than a bullet. You could see the blade coming at you. You would feel the ripping of the knife. You would gaze into the face of your enemy, knowing one man would die.

He ordered his men to prepare.

Kim kept his face shoved into the dirt. He heard someone scream, "BAYONETS!" He pulled out two concussion grenades and slipped the pins almost out, waiting for the firing to stop so he could lob the grenades over the embankment into the enemy machine gun nest. But he couldn't raise his head, and he was afraid to move up into a throwing position because of the fire coming into the top of the embankment.

He waited. He heard his men moving down. Then he heard the command.

"FIX BAYONETS! CHARGE!"

Shouts of *"Banzai!"* echoed around. Kim kept his head down and hoped nobody stuck him by mistake.

Yuki jumped up, screaming to his squad, "BAYONETS! CHARGE!" There was no time to think. Flare bursts lit the area as he rose up. Pulling his men with him, Yuki and the rest of the company rushed forward holding their rifles out, the flash of the bayonets catching the light between the shadows falling on them. Men behind them were still firing but the men in front surged against the hedge, slashing with their bayonets, forcing their way through.

Kim raised his head enough to see that the tracer rounds from the men still shooting were being fired up over their charging comrades. He raised up, pulling the pins and throwing the two concussion grenades over the embankment in the direction of the machine gun fire. The flash of light illuminated the men who had slashed their way through the hedge to reach their lieutenant. As Takeba reached him, Kim yelled, "I'm all right." He scrambled up the embankment where the men could see him, a darker image against the night.

Yuki looked up and heard Tug yelling, "That's the Lieutenant!" Yuki held his arm up and started up the embankment after Kim, following him over the top. The machine gun nest was right there, where the concussion grenades had been lobbed. There was no enemy. The Germans fled as the unit broke through the hedge, bayonets thrusting forward.

Kim looked around and saw the soles of two boots sticking out from under some broken branches. He kicked at them and a German soldier, dazed by the concussion grenade, jumped up and started running. He kicked at another pair of boots and when the owner jumped up the men in the company gained control of the situation. He waited until his platoon brought the two Germans back. He pointed at two of his men. "Take the prisoners back. We've got to move forward."

Yuki looked over at Tug and Kazo. The coppery taste of blood was in his mouth and he felt the cold sweat under his shirt. "*Brah*, I can't believe we did that. Who the hell yelled for us to fix bayonets? Like some kind of movie."

Tug shrugged. "Yuki, you starting to sound like me."

All the men in the squad waited for their hearts to stop pounding. Finally, Kazo looked around.

"Where's Johnny?"

Yuki looked down at the ground. He last saw Johnny in the mine-field. He looked up, making a decision. "Johnny will be okay. Come on, Kim's already moving. Get those bayonets off and back in the scabbards before you stick yourselves or somebody else."

He felt his hands shaking as he pulled the blade from the end of his rifle. Even in the darkness, it looked evil. The sound of the bayonet sliding into its sheath was different than it was before. Everybody turned and started walking. They still hadn't reached the objective.

CHAPTER 50

November 5, 1943
Somewhere Near the Village of Pozzilli, Italy

Kim led Company B through the night toward their objective, two nameless hills with the map designation of 550 and 610. The adrenaline of the bayonet charge had long since drained from their bodies, leaving legs leaden as they marched in the dark, trusting the man at the front. There was no talking. Each step added to the strain as eyes stayed on the ground, looking for mines. They saw what Bouncing Bettys had done to their comrades at the river crossing. Fatigue seeped into aching bodies as cold rain alternated with snow flurries, leaving the men shivering in their uniforms. Some of the men grabbed coats off of dead Germans and wore them over their own uniforms, glad for the warmth. It was 2:30 in the morning when they finally stopped near railroad tracks running through a cut in the valley floor.

Yuki settled in with the squad and dug into the side of the gully, trying to make himself as comfortable as possible. His whole body ached. It felt like he hadn't slept for days. The cold only added to the misery. Even Tug wasn't making much noise. Yuki waited for the question he knew would eventually come. He knew one of the men caught in the minefield was Johnny Kitahara. Yuki watched the medics working on him and made his face out in the cold light of a flare. He had also seen the medic pressing against the flow of blood from a gaping stomach wound, trying to gather Johnny's intestines back in while he pushed morphine into his leg.

Yuki struggled with leaving Johnny, but there had been no choice. It wasn't just his friend lying on the ground. There were men lying all over the minefield, some crying, some silent. The medics and the stretcher bearers would carry out the wounded and the dead.

Kazo slid over near Yuki and Tug. "Yuki, you know what happened to Johnny, don't you?"

Yuki blew out air in a long sigh. "Johnny got hit back at the river in the minefield. I saw him on the ground. I don't know if he's still alive or not. Medics were working on him." He stopped, looking at Tug as he debated trying to give an explanation that he needed more for himself than the others.

"We had to move out. I figured it was best not to say anything." He wasn't going to volunteer anything about the wound unless asked.

Tug was silent for a minute. "I figured something bad happen. You didn't say anything. Maybe Johnny isn't hurt bad. Maybe he's okay. Johnny been with us a long time, Yuki."

Kazo didn't say anything. He and Johnny were bunk mates back at Shelby. The other boys in the squad were listening as well. What was there to say? Everyone knew somebody that had been hit by the vicious, spring-loaded German mines.

Turtle Omiya, the great hitter who helped defeat the 34th Division players in North Africa, was down. He caught shrapnel in the face from a Bouncing Betty. Some of the boys said he was blind. Each man that heard about it remembered old Turtle standing at the plate, watching a fastball. Lieutenant Spark Matsunaga was hit at the start of the assault and now he was gone too. The men lay with their backs up against the edge of the gully, whispering about who got hit, wondering if they would be next. At last they settled in to try and take advantage of the lull and get some rest.

~

Before the first light of dawn the Germans initiated a heavy mortar barrage, shelling the railroad cut and forcing companies B and E to move out to escape the heavy fire. First Battalion made it partway up Hill 550 when the Germans pushed them back with their own bayonet charge. Twice German planes flew low over the area and dropped antipersonnel bombs. The entire unit was pinned down. They couldn't go forward and they wouldn't go back.

It was necessary to take the high ground in order to cover First Battalion. The German planes were taking a serious toll. The entrenched 100th took twenty casualties from the air-dropped mines and strafing runs. B Company pushed forward with the rest of the battalion into a grove of olive trees that, they hoped, would provide some cover from the German planes.

By 4:00 p.m. the battalion had arrived at the lower slopes of their objective. Advance scouts came down through the olive groves dotting the hills. Mines and booby traps were planted throughout the path of the advance. Light grew dim as the afternoon receded into dusk, obscuring trip wires. There was no choice. Men had to be sent through the minefield to cut a safe path. Lieutenant Key from Company E took a man with him, Kenso Suga, and moved ahead of the battalion carefully. They managed to cut trip wires and left strips of toilet paper to mark the path. Company B followed carefully along its path, led by Capt. Jack Johnson, who had replaced Major Lovell. Captain Suzuki stayed close on Johnson, with Kim leading Second Platoon through.

The explosion of first one and then several more mines halted the advance, the sound telling every man that ahead a mine had been missed in the dark. Kim heard the rapid series of explosions. He knew that one man had gone down and others had jumped to the side, triggering more mines. He halted Second Platoon and moved forward carefully.

In a matter of seconds Kim and the men in his platoon saw Captain Johnson hobbling back down the path. He was hit in the leg and bleeding badly. He moved past them, back toward the aid station. The men saw another man still on the ground, bleeding profusely from his arm. It was Captain Suzuki.

Kim crouched low and moved forward, followed by Second Platoon.

"Taro, how bad is it?"

Suzuki looked over at the young lieutenant, who had been such a difficult subordinate. "I don't know. I can't feel my arm; maybe I caught some shrapnel in a nerve. I can't keep going. Take the men forward. You understand?"

Kim squatted by his captain, quiet for a moment. He then spoke in a low voice.

"I'll see you when we get through here."

A medic moved into position and started putting a field dressing on Suzuki's arm. The two men held each other's gaze for a moment, neither sure what else to say. Then Suzuki reached into his holster and took out his .45 caliber pistol. He was very proud of it. He had been a champion marksman and this pistol was his favorite weapon. He always said he carried the pistol for luck.

He held the weapon out to Kim. "Here, I want you to have my .45."

Kim shook his head. "No."

Suzuki stared at him. "You take it. I want you to carry it for me."

Kim took the pistol from Suzuki's hand. "All right, Captain. We'll see you when we get back."

Suzuki nodded his head. "Take care of our boys."

"Yes, sir." Kim rose up and waved Second Platoon past him.

By now Second Platoon was the last in the battalion to reach the objective. They pushed forward until they were on high ground. The rest of Company B was in position, but it was growing darker quickly. Tracer fire from machine guns kept the men down. Kim hadn't been in position long when he received orders to report to Major Gillespie, who replaced Turner as battalion commander. Kim carefully directed Yuki's squad and one other behind him and moved as quickly as possible back to Gillespie.

When he got to Gillespie's position, he was shocked. The Major was seriously ill and could not even raise himself up straight.

"Kim, I'm sick as hell, got an ulcer and it's never been this bad." Kim could see the sweat on Gillespie's face and the pink pallor of his skin. Kim waited until Gillespie could talk. "You see all those tracers in front of us? We got machine guns pinning down any movement forward."

"Yes, sir, I saw them."

"Well, what do you think?"

"They're German machine guns. We got some in front and some behind us. They're on that hill next to us, firing down and they're on that ridge behind us, at least four or five nests I think."

Gillespie nodded and grimaced. "They're not supposed to be there, you know." Kim just stood there, waiting for the rest of it.

"Do you think you and your boys can knock them out?"

"I don't know, sir. All we can do is try. But I only have two squads with me. I'll go back to B Company and get another."

"No, you don't have time. It won't be long before daylight again. You need to move now—take those damn machine guns out."

"Yes, sir."

Kim walked over to Takeba and looked at his two squads. He turned to Yuki and the other squad leader. "Takeba and I will scout out front. The rest of you follow on us." They began moving forward in the dark. They crossed a ravine and moved farther up the hill, looking for the machine guns that were raking the 100th.

They had only been walking for twenty or thirty minutes when Kim heard a noise off to his right, coming from a gully just ahead. The sound was growing louder. Kim moved back to Yuki, whispering that a German patrol was coming down the gully. He needed Yuki to take his men and go to the other side of the gully. He would take the other squad to the opposite side.

"I want you to get grenades out. When I give the signal, throw the grenades. Move it!"

Yuki nodded and motioned to his men to follow him over. They quickly moved to the other side and lay down, waiting for the Germans to walk down what they thought was a covered position.

Kim waited until the German squad moved almost directly below them and then raised his arm. He never made a sound. Both squads lobbed their grenades into the German patrol before they were aware that they were being watched.

The brief blasts of grenade after grenade tore into the Jerry patrol. Dirt and shards of rock rained down as the upward force of the blasts sent airborne debris out of the gully, while the shrapnel ripped the Germans. It was a moment before anyone could clear the ringing from their ears. Moaning and cries of pain could be heard coming from the gully.

Takeba waited and then turned to Kim.

"Should we go down and see if there are any prisoners?"

Kim looked over at his platoon sergeant, and then at the men from the two squads waiting for his orders. The smell of gunpowder hung over the cut in the ground, mixed with the smell of loosened bowels and blood. The stench was inescapable as wisps of steam rose from the torn bodies, snow falling silently, already shrouding the men who lay still. He shook his head, his voice flat and unemotional.

"No. If they're dead, they're dead. If they're wounded, we haven't got enough men to capture anybody. Let's keep moving." They moved silently away from the gully, casting brief downward glances in the direction of the cries of the few men who were still moving. Soon there was only the sound of muffled footsteps as the two squads traveled farther up the hill.

Tug looked back at Kazo and the rest of the men behind him. He kept his voice low, the whispered words holding emotion. "You hear those Jerries in that ditch? They never saw us, *brah*. Never saw who did that. Made me kind of sick, you know?"

Yuki looked back at Tug and Kazo and shook his head for quiet. He could see the mouths of the men in the squad set in a grim line. If the situation was reversed, they all knew they'd be left lying in that ditch, with the snow falling silently on them. There was no decency in this. To both sides, the other side was only enemies to be killed. They had a job to do and it came before anything else.

The squads kept moving forward through the brush and rocks of the hill. Snow flurries added to the chill. All around them the brush and trees were rustling. Every sound was an enemy, a threat, a shadow soldier. Nobody knew what was behind the next tree. Or the next one.

Kim pushed his way through the brush, leading the patrol and taking the scouting position with Takeba. The clouds broke the moonlight into fleeting shards of light. The trees and brush moved in the air, which was blowing steadily. His eyes made out a shadowy movement. A bush? A tree rustling in the wind? He squinted to improve his distance vision, feeling Takeba right behind him, watching the area around them.

He then made out a figure moving toward them, a German soldier carrying ammunition canisters, his rifle slung over his back. The Jerry looked up and saw them, his face a startled mask. Less than ten feet away, the German dropped the ammo cans and pulled at his rifle. Kim reached for his holstered .45, the one Suzuki had given him only hours before. He brought it up and fired before the German could.

The .45 misfired and jammed. The German fired just as Kim pushed himself to the right. Takeba began firing. The sound of gunfire once again filled the silence of the night, the muzzle flashes blinding all of them. Kim looked up. The German was running. Takeba missed. Kim looked over at his sergeant. The German had missed, too.

Kim scrambled up and pushed Takeba back toward the squads. Both men felt their hearts racing. Their hands shook from the adrenalin and the realization that their safety was only a matter of fortuity.

The rest of the patrol hit the ground as soon as they heard the gunshots and then started crawling forward, meeting Kim and Takeba as they came back down. Kim pulled both his squad leaders near him.

"Keep moving. Keep the men quiet."

He looked up the hill, where he could see an open area without brush or trees. They moved as quickly as they could to the edge and crouched down, using the brush for cover. The thin crust of snow was trackless.

Kim moved next to the squads. He didn't see any Germans. He crawled across the frozen ground with Takeba and waited for Yuki's squad. They made it across. He turned just as his other squad leader, Jimmy Shimizu, stood up and started walking across the open area. A machine gun opened up and Jimmy went down. Yuki and his squad watched as Jimmy rolled and crawled near them, his leg trailing blood black against the snow.

Kim looked at Shimizu. They couldn't take a wounded man with them. There wasn't a choice and both men knew it.

"We're about a thousand yards from where we started. Can you find your way back?"

"I can make it."

"Why the hell didn't you crawl?"

Jimmy was clinching his teeth, but the men close to Kim and Jimmy could see the sheepish look on his face. "I didn't want to get dirty in the mud. Everybody else made it."

"Crawl, don't stand up. There's Jerries all over."

Shimizu nodded. "I'll make it."

Kim looked around for the place he'd put a machine gun, if he had one. He turned to Yuki and pointed at a brush-covered area.

"Go over and around those bushes. I think the machine gun is in there. Get behind it. I'll take the other squad and move toward it." Yuki nodded and signaled his boys to follow on him.

Kim crawled toward the bushes and pushed them apart, peering through the branches straight into the face of a German soldier. The German's eyes widened. Both men jerked their heads back. Takeba fired over Kim's shoulder. The other German gunners started firing just as Yuki

352

jumped into the machine gun dugout along with Tug and Kazo, swinging their rifles around and pushing the Germans down to the ground. One German started to struggle.

"Tug, you got him?"

"I got him."

"Kazo, keep your rifle on them." They pulled out seven Germans from the machine gun emplacement. Kim ordered two more of his men to take the prisoners down the hill for interrogation. There were still more machine guns to find. It would be dawn soon.

They started moving farther up the hill when they heard them. They found cover and watched as about fifty German soldiers walked past their concealed position. Yuki crawled over to Kim.

"Lieutenant, should we take them?"

Kim looked at the enemy walking up a path in front of them. "No, we don't have enough men. We need to get the machine guns."

He lay there, considering his options. He watched his men lying as quietly as they could as the Germans marched past. If they reached out, they could touch them. The battalion either needed to attack before the Germans dug in, pull back, or stay and defend. Any way he looked at the situation, there were major consequences to the battalion.

Kim turned to Takeba. "I've got to talk to Gillespie. You stay here with the men. I'll be back as soon as I can." He barreled down the hill.

Gillespie, still in considerable pain, listened to Kim's report. "Sir, we need to stay on the hill, the Germans are moving farther up to higher ground."

Gillespie didn't give any specific instructions other than, "Go back up the hill. Get the rest of the machine guns."

"Yes, sir."

Kim raced back up the hill and rejoined his squad. He knew the rest of the 100th was spread out over the hill, somewhere below his position. The night gave them cover, but the coming dawn would leave the battalion moving up in silhouette against hidden machine guns. They had to find them before first light. His men had to stand and fight.

When he got back to his squads, the men were pushing on stones left from clearing the area, probably by farmers. They crawled into the depressions left by the stones and tried to rest. The ground was too frozen for digging. They settled in and waited for dawn.

At first light the Germans attacked. From Kim's position, he watched the Germans set off smoke below their position to obscure their movement. The thick gray smoke fogged the entire slope of the hill below the enemy as the 100th slowed to a halt, unable to see where they were going, their line disappearing from Kim's vision. All of a sudden Kim's squads saw movement uphill from the wall of smoke in front of the stalled advance. At least seventy Germans could be seen and more were moving toward the men of the 100th, who were blinded and trying to find their way through the smoke.

Kim decided to let the Germans pass before opening fire. He could catch them from behind. He didn't know exactly where the battalion was, but he knew they had to be below the smoke the enemy laid down to conceal their front. What the smoke didn't conceal was their back.

He looked at Takeba and the other men, directing them silently. They lay out on the frozen ground, seeking whatever cover they could find, their rifles pointing toward the backs of the attacking Germans. It was one of the few times he raised his voice.

"OPEN FIRE! FIRE! FIRE!"

Tug fired as soon as he heard the order. He went through rounds so quickly that he startled when the magazine popped out. He fed in another. He felt spent casings hitting him as they ejected from Kazo's rifle. All the men fired as rapidly as they could pull the trigger. German soldiers started running, trying to find a direction away from an enemy that suddenly seemed all around them. Yuki watched impassively, squeezing the trigger again and again, enemy soldiers staggering as they were hit, falling, trying to find cover.

Gillespie was in position to hear the firing from Kim's patrol. He ordered a squad from F Company to flank the enemy and radioed 1st Battalion that the enemy was engaging. 1st Battalion opened fire, catching the enemy between two fields of fire. The enemy stopped moving and tried to gain order just as F Company swept up on them. The German advance stopped. Enemy soldiers were turning in every direction, looking for an opening in the scathing field of fire—any place where the bullets weren't coming from. There was no place to run.

The firing slacked off and the guns went silent one by one until the only sounds were the cries of the enemy, and the shouted orders from 100th and 1st battalion sergeants and officers. Yuki lay in his position, looking down the hill at the men on the ground. German soldiers rocked back and forth in the dirt, holding onto wounds, trying to keep their blood in, pressing down. He stood up and signaled for the rest of the squad to follow.

Kim was already walking down the hill toward the mass of dead and wounded men, the few not wounded raising their hands in defeat. As he walked past a soldier lying silent on the snow-dusted ground, the man jumped up and stumbled away, trying to run. He held a machine gun cradled in his arms. Yuki saw the German moving, blood covering his back. Someone opened fire, trying to cut the man down. Others fired at the same time. The mortally wounded soldier staggered and sank back to the frozen hillside, letting off a burst of fire from his machine gun as it hit the ground, his dead hand still on the trigger.

Kim was startled at the sound of the machine gun behind him. He felt the impact of something hitting him and then he stumbled forward, trying to regain his balance. He kept moving down the hill, ordering his men to contain the prisoners. It wasn't until after he stopped giving orders that he looked down. Blood was coming out of his thigh. He looked back. He'd been hit by a dead man. He didn't feel anything.

The rest of Kim's two squads and the men from the other companies wandered through the Germans, looking for wounded and taking prisoners. Yuki and Tug kept their rifles at the ready as they checked bodies for signs of life. It was Tug who heard it first, the sound of sobbing. Yuki looked over to where Tug and Kazo were staring. It was a German soldier. They walked over and knelt down around him. He was lying on the ground, grabbing at his chest. He was big and husky but his plump, young face told them he was just a boy.

Kim waited for the medic to finish securing a tourniquet on his leg and then walked over and got down on his knees, next to the wounded soldier. Tug pulled the boy's helmet off. His hair was blond and fell into his eyes. Yuki gently pushed the hair back. They could all see the blood streaming out of his chest and stomach, the stain growing fast on the dark uniform. The boy looked up at the faces of the men kneeling around him—faces of the enemy moments before, and now faces of men trying to help him.

He tried to talk. Kim leaned in. He didn't understand German, the boy's voice barely a whisper. He looked at the soldier's hand reaching for his pocket, trying to remove something. Kim reached into the boy's pocket and took out a wallet. He opened it. There was a picture of a woman and a man. Kim guessed it was the boy's mother and father. He looked down at the boy whose blue eyes were moving back and forth, staring at the faces of the men kneeling around him. Kim handed the wallet to Yuki and pressed down on the spurting wound, trying to hold in what was left of the young soldier's life, bloody froth foaming from his mouth as the boy's lips whispered something they could not understand.

Yuki held the wallet in front of the boy's face. He kept it there, the blue eyes staring up at the picture. After a minute Kim took his hand away. The whispered words and labored breathing stopped. Yuki gently placed the wallet back in the soldier's pocket. The men stood silent for a moment and then moved down the hill.

~

That night the battalion pulled back for, hopefully, a day's rest. The hours blurred into one long effort to survive. Even though the actual time actually confronting German troops had been brief, the long hours in between, waiting for the confrontation, had almost been more terrifying. It drained them all. Time had lost its meaning.

Yuki leaned back against what was left of a wall and felt his body for the first time in hours. He ached in every joint and felt the combination of dirt and sweat stiffen his uniform. All he wanted was a hot meal and a bath. Tug stretched out next to him and slowly the whole squad found places nearby. They hadn't lost any of their squad, but they didn't know what condition Kim was in. They all watched the medic put a tourniquet on the lieutenant's leg. Then he was taken away.

Tug started talking to no one in particular. "Old Kim is pretty tough guy. He'll be all right. I'm even thinking I'm going to miss him. Maybe I'll call him Samurai Kim from now on, instead of G.I. Kim."

Kazo started laughing. "You complained more about him than anyone. Now you like him?"

"I don't know if *like* is right. Hard man to like, you know, never says anything. Always just looks at you—like an alligator with his eyes just out of the water. But, I mean, he was there with us all the time. He was out in front, you know? Not like some other officers. He's eating what we eat and he sleeps where we do, no different."

Yuki listened. He had already formed his own opinions about Kim and they were based on respect. Kim was a leader and didn't ask his men to do anything he wasn't willing to do. That was good enough for him. But Kim was a tough man to figure out. He left those German soldiers in the ditch. He never flinched. Even Yuki felt bad, looking down at those wounded Krauts. But he had watched Kim with that young German soldier, the way he pressed down on his wound and stayed with him as he was dying.

Yuki saw Doc Kometani walking toward them. He started to get up. "Yuki, don't get up." Doc squatted down. "How are you boys doing?"

"Doing okay, Captain. It was pretty rough out there today."

Kometani nodded his head. "Major Gillespie says your boys did real good. I wanted to talk to you." Doc looked around at the dirt-caked squad of men. "Maybe some of you boys are worried about your lieutenant. He's going to be okay. It's a bad wound but it should heal up all right. They'll probably ship him back to Naples for treatment, but he'll be back. Your new company commander is Lieutenant Takahashi."

Doc was hesitating. There was something he was reluctant to say. He came out with it.

"Johnny Kitahara didn't make it. Our boys got him back to the aid station after the mine went off, when we crossed the river. He was hit pretty bad. I saw him and we talked a little bit before they moved him out from the aid station. Yuki, he asked me to write to his parents and tell them he was a good soldier. He wanted you to visit his parents. I think he knew he wasn't going to make it. He just said, 'Have Yuki tell my mom and dad.' Obviously, Johnny thought a lot of you. Maybe you can write them. I'll write a letter too but you were his friend. All of you were his friends. I thought you boys would want to know. I'm sorry. We lost a lot of men in the last few days."

As Doc got up, his bulldog face didn't show any of his usual energetic demeanor.

～

A memorial service was held the next morning. It was the first time they experienced a lull in the fighting and most of the men went, Christians as well as Buddhists. Chaplain Israel Yost talked about how much the men had given. Three officers and almost seventy enlisted men were dead. More than two hundred men had been wounded in action. Almost twenty-five percent of the 100th was dead or injured. The reality of the numbers fell hard on the silent assemblage.

The bespectacled and slender Lutheran chaplain spent most of his time helping out at the aid station, attending to the spiritual needs of the wounded men coming in from the field. All the men knew that it didn't make any difference to him whether you were a Christian or a Buddhist or a nonbeliever. He cared only that someone was there when needed.

He and Doc Kometani worked as stretcher-bearers and confessors to the men. Yost had earned the respect of the men, and they listened quietly while he talked of the brotherhood of war. They all knew that similar services were being held back home in Hawaii for the boys who had been lost. The grief was the same, whether it came from mud-encrusted men on their knees on frozen ground in a strange land, or garlanded men and women on their knees praying in volcanic rock churches and temples in Hawaii. In their prayers and in their tears, they were all the same.

CHAPTER 51

December 23, 1943
Calwa, California

The light outside the Shiraga store gave off a dull yellow glow, barely illuminating the M and S Grocery sign. Heavy fog settled over the Central Valley. It always arrived with the end of the year. The day had been weighed down by the lowering clouds of an overcast sky. The wood-fueled heating stove in the corner was going all day, trying to fend off the cold damp air penetrating the thin walls of the store.

As night fell, Luis could see his breath as he swept the aisles around the mostly empty fruit and vegetable bins. He turned off the light on the outside of the store. It had been a long day. People were buying what they could find in anticipation of Christmas. Luis managed to buy some meat from a few of his farmer friends, and he obtained as many winter vegetables as he could. Still, there wasn't much, and what he was able to provide was quickly sold. Eggs and milk were the easiest to get.

Hopefully tomorrow, on Christmas Eve, he'd be able to find more vegetables to fill the bins, perhaps some fruit. He'd saved two boxes of oranges. Something to fill the children's stockings. He smiled at the memory of Tony pulling his stocking down on Christmas morning, the red sock that Maria knitted to be hung once a year and stuffed with candy, some new socks, and always, at the bottom, an orange bulging out the toe.

Maria finished sweeping behind the counter. Both of them were looking forward to leaving for the evening. They never stayed in the store after closing. It was Mas and Satomi's home, not theirs. Every day when

Luis turned out the lights, he thought of his friend and his family. Maybe soon the Shiragas would be home. Tony would be home.

Luis put the broom away. He would take Maria home to start dinner and then walk to the post office. Maybe there would be a letter from Tony. It had been a long time, well over a month, since they received anything, and even that letter took over a month to reach them.

Luis walked the two blocks to the post office, the houses mere shadows against the rest of the darkness. Here and there a crack of light peeked out from behind drawn curtains. A few Christmas wreaths could be found on doors, their holiday message visible only in the daylight. Blackout restrictions and the cost of electricity made people careful. Very little light was shared with the pathways, and none fell upon the streets from porch lights that gathered dust in efforts to conserve. Even in better times, people in Calwa were careful with their money. With the war it was different. There were no street lights in Calwa.

In the dark, Luis's eyes adjusted enough to pick out the path he had walked so many times in recent months, looking for a letter. It had been so long. His mind moved to the fear that he kept suppressed. He shook his head. He prayed so hard. They lit candles. *No, his boy would be safe. He was all they had.* There was no letter.

The walk home felt longer. He caught the sight of a small banner hanging in a window, its two blue stars outlined in a sliver of light—two boys in the service. He shivered in the chill air. He passed by a window with a gold star. In the dark he couldn't see it, but he knew it was there. A son lost. He turned automatically up the path to his house, the familiar creak of the second step reminding him of his promises to Maria to make repairs. His eyes passed over the small piece of cloth in the window, another blue star. His boy.

It was still cold inside the house. He heard Maria moving in the kitchen. He regretted not putting wood in the stove that heated the front room before he went to the post office. He'd been in a hurry. He wanted so much for a letter to be there. He warmed his hands as the flame slowly built up while Maria made dinner. The rooms were small. It didn't take long to warm them.

He heard the knock at the door first. Maria came into the small front living room, wiping her hands on her apron. He looked at her and shrugged. He didn't know who it could be at this hour, almost

7:00 p.m. Luis pushed aside the curtain to see a young man standing on the porch, the darkness outlining the Western Union cap and uniform. He pulled the curtain closed and looked back at his wife. He waited until there was a second knock before he slowly moved to the door. The young man handed Luis an envelope, touched his cap, and said, "I'm sorry."

Luis held the envelope in his hand and watched as the messenger stepped down from the porch, looking back and quickly nodding his head before turning away. He closed the door and turned to face his wife across the room, her hands trapped in the air, her eyes fastened on the envelope he held in his hands. Finally, Luis opened it. He had difficulty reading the English words, but he already knew what they said. Tony had been killed in action almost a month ago. He reached for his wife. For the first time since he was a boy, he felt tears come down his weathered cheeks. Their son was gone.

The morning light didn't wake them. There was no sleep. They both shared tears and then Luis held his wife in the darkness, both of them wanting to believe that what they felt was only a dark dream, that they would wake up and today would be what yesterday was. Before word came. But there was no dream. The telegram was still there on the dresser where Luis had left it.

Luis and Maria got up and went to the store. People would need things. It was easier to work than it was to sit and stare at the walls of their home. During the day people began to drift in as the news spread about Tony, their handsome black-haired boy. People didn't know what to say. Some in the community had received the same telegram. They came by to share in their grief.

It was almost evening when the Marine chaplain came by. The young minister still felt uncomfortable in his uniform. He wasn't much older than many of the young men for whom he gave condolences. The daily sharing of overwhelming grief showed in his eyes. His teachers had only prepared him for the funerals of people who had lived long lives. They hadn't prepared him for this. Nothing prepared him for this.

He stood inside the door, waiting until the customers talking to Luis and Maria finished their awkward expressions of sympathy. He had seen it too many times in the last year, parents touching grieving parents while sheltering private relief that it was not their own son. He could forgive selfish hope. He had no children of his own, but he thought he understood.

The chaplain asked if there was a place they could sit. Luis and Maria listened quietly. He said that eventually the Marines would bring Tony home, but it might take a while. He waited for their questions, but they had none. He was relieved. There was so little he could tell these parents about what happened. He tried to comfort them, but he had so little time. He had other families to visit. It was Christmas Eve. Luis and Maria understood. They would see Father Kelly. They would light a candle. They would say a prayer.

The letter came four days later. Luis went to the post office when one of his customers came by and said that Luis had a letter. He rushed over thinking maybe it was from Tony, one last letter. Something to hang onto. It was from Mickey Hayashi. Luis took it home, and then he and Maria went to see Father Kelly for him to read it with them. They didn't want to be alone.

The priest held the letter in his hands for a long time, and then he opened it for them. It was not the first time he had opened such a letter. Every night he prayed that there would be no more letters, and every week brought a new one. Inside the envelope there was a folded letter addressed to Luis and Maria, the paper creased and limp. He knew what it was. He had seen them before. He carefully moved the folded letter behind the pages that held it and began to read.

Dear Mr. and Mrs. Machado,
By now I know you have gotten the news about Tony. First of all, I want you to know how sorry I am. He told me that he wrote you about me being with his unit. While we were together we became close friends. It was good to be with somebody that I knew. We talked a lot about home and I hope you know that he loved you very much. I wanted to write and tell you that I was with Tony when he got hit. He was very brave.

We were on an island called Bougainville in the Solomon Islands. We went in with a lot of Marines and it looked like we had pretty much broken the enemy. Maybe it has been in the papers but a lot of the enemy won't give up. They would rather die than surrender. It was November 28th. There were some Japs that had crawled into a cave and we were yelling at them to come out. I was doing most of the talking and Tony and some of the other guys were covering the front of the cave. We used flamethrowers to try and force them out when they wouldn't surrender. Finally three of them came running out and shooting. They had grenades strapped to them. We got two of them but one got close. Tony jumped on him and the grenade went off. I know he knew what he was doing because I heard him yell "grenade." He saved my life and the lives of two other guys. We were yelling for medics but he was really hurt bad. He looked at me and I told him I would tell you what happened. I know he understood. I could see it in his eyes. We promised each other that we would do that, tell each other's parents if something happened to one of us. He had a letter that he wrote you that he kept in his pocket. Most of us write letters like that in case something happens. I am sending it to you. I didn't read it.

I want you to know that we stayed with Tony and carried him off the hill. He didn't suffer very long. All the guys went down and volunteered to help with the burial detail. We buried Tony and made sure that his grave was marked real good. The officer in charge said that Tony would be sent home after we got control of the island. I am hoping that has happened. We had to leave. I know you understand that we didn't have a choice. I want you to know that I promise you if the Marines haven't sent Tony home that when this is over I will go back and bring him home myself. I wish I could say more that would make you feel better. All I can say is that Tony was a real hero. He gave his life to save his friends. The captain says he is recommending Tony for a medal, maybe a Navy Cross. He was a good friend. I hope this letter helps you, just so you know what happened.

Mickey Hayashi

Father Kelly looked at the still-folded letter that was enclosed with the pages from the Hayashi boy. The letters boys wrote in case they did not return. The letters young men wrote in hopes they would never be read. The paper lay limp in his hand, worn soft from being carried. The brown outlines of sweat stained the fraying pages. The creases from the folds were almost worn through and the priest held the pages carefully, afraid they would crumble.

The priest's mouth closed tightly as his face drew up into deeply etched lines. He looked at Luis and Maria staring back at him, their eyes red-rimmed from listening to what the Hayashi boy wrote. Now was not the time. "This is the letter from Tony. You should read this when you are ready. Perhaps when you are home. Perhaps you should go into the chapel. If you want me to read it I will, but first you need to be ready." He held out the folded pages.

Maria sat silently, waiting for her husband. Luis took the letter, holding it in both his hands. He looked down at the fragile sheets. For the rest of their lives, these pages would hold the last words of their son. He could not hear them now. All he could hear were the sounds of his boy when he had first lifted him up in the air so many years ago.

CHAPTER 52

January 17, 1944
Camp Shelby, Mississippi

Sammy sat on his bunk trying to write a letter to Betty. He was struggling with his words. He received a letter from Sack and Carmen telling him that Tony had been killed. The news had shaken him deeply. When he told Freddy, it was one of the few times he had seen his friend cry. Freddy and Tony were good friends. Neither of them had talked about Tony's death since. But he knew Freddy was hurting, even if he didn't say anything.

The death of his grandmother had been the first time Sammy was confronted by the reality of loss. But Tony wasn't much older than him, which hit closer to home. Sammy kept thinking about that, the unfairness of it. He had watched the reaction of the Hawaiian boys in the barracks when the casualty reports came back, looking at the names, finding friends and relatives. The barracks fell quiet as each man took time to be alone and think about lost friends. And the barracks fell quiet a lot in the last month. Casualty reports came frequently. Losses were heavy. But even though he sympathized with the men, he felt detached as he watched their grief. Now he felt the sense of loss that came with the death of someone he knew, someone who was young. Like him.

Bobby watched his two friends from the mainland. He understood how they felt. He and Stubby saw the casualty reports from the 100th as well, and they received letters from their parents telling them about the memorial services back home. The rumor throughout the 442nd was that the 100th was down almost five hundred men. They both knew some of the boys lost. Johnnie Kitahara had been a friend. Joe Takata was somebody they watched play ball. The heralded Asahi team had been decimated by the loss of many of its players. Bobby knew he would never watch another ball game without thinking about them.

As the casualty reports grew, their training became more real. What had been simply an exercise to get through now carried the realization that others, their friends, had been through the same training and now some of them, many of them, were dead. The excitement of being in the unit had long worn off. Talk in the barracks no longer centered on gambling and girlfriends. For weeks the rumors had been all over that men from the 442nd were going to be sent in as replacements for the losses of the 100th.

Then the word came down. All of B Company was joining the 100th as replacements. They were going to board a train in the morning. Sammy had gone over to visit Tommy and Akiro in Company D. He wanted to tell them goodbye.

The usual barracks noise was subdued as the men prepared to leave. Sammy and Freddy quietly packed their gear. There was no way to contact their parents or Betty and Rose. They couldn't make calls to report the unit movement. All they could do was write from the train. Freddy pulled his barracks bag next to his bunk. He sat down and watched as Sammy finished packing his equipment.

"I keep thinking about Tony."

Sammy stopped what he was doing. Freddy looked down at his hands, rubbing them on his pants leg.

"It's just that, well, I never thought much about dying. I don't think I'm afraid but I keep thinking about how it will be, what I'll do." He looked up at Sammy, his eyes searching for some recognition that somebody else might be thinking the same thing. "You know. What I'll do when somebody is shooting at me."

Sammy stayed quiet for a moment. He thought about it, too. What would he do when the time came, when it wasn't training, when it was real? More than anything, he wanted to do what was expected of him. If he was afraid of anything, it was that he might not be able to do it.

"I think about it too." He sat on the bunk across from Freddy. "Will I be able to do it? I think as long as we're all together, we'll do whatever we have to do. You and me, we'll be okay. We'll stick together like we always have."

Freddy nodded. "Like we always have."

~

The men in the barracks were up by 2:00 a.m. and shuffling down to the trucks for the ride to the train station. They were headed to Fort Meade in Maryland and from there they would move to an embarkation point for Italy and meet up with the 100th.

Bobby saw Sammy standing ahead of him. "Hey, Sammy, you hear anything from your buddy Otani?"

Sammy turned around. "All he said is what you already know. We're going to meet up with the 100th as replacements. He said that they're having a rough time and we should be prepared to go into combat as soon as we get there. You hear anything else?"

Bobby shook his head. "No, I guess we'll find out pretty soon what it's like. Maybe I'll just stay behind old Stubbs here for protection."

Stubby grinned. "You stick with Stubby, *brah*, that the best way to come home safe. I threw my lei in the water when we left. I know I'm going home."

Going home. Sammy checked his jacket pocket for the two letters he wanted to finish and send before they boarded the ship, one to his parents and one to Betty. He wanted to tell his parents that he loved them. He thought about all the things they did for him that he had taken for granted, that he hadn't appreciated. He spent the night awake, his mind wandering over things the he might never have a chance to say. He wanted his parents to know how much they meant to him.

The letter for Betty was different. He was sure. She was the one. He would put that in the letter while they rode on the train. Sammy wiped his eyes with his sleeve. Thinking of his parents and Betty, whether he would see them again. He looked around at the men in line. From now on they would be his family. The sergeants came out and ordered them into the trucks. It was time to go.

CHAPTER 53

January 24, 1944

The Village of San Micheli, Italy

Through the gray morning light and whispering flurries of snow, the ancient monastery of Monte Cassino dominated the winter horizon. The snow-crusted massive stone complex loomed high on a hill overlooking the convergence of the Rapido River Valley and the Liri Valley. Kim's binoculars swept the river valley. Across the alluvial plain was the town of Cassino. Its gray stone buildings tumbled down the slopes below the abbey, on the other side of the Rapido River. The 34th Division had been ordered to take Cassino, whose inhabitants had long since fled in the face of German occupation.

After taking San Micheli, the 100th stayed in reserve for a week, camped in an olive grove near the town. They began at Salerno with 1,300 men. Now only about 800 remained. Kim stood on the edge of a hill, the Liri Valley spread below him. Snow covered the muddy ground, the frozen flakes swirling lightly at first and then falling densely. He pulled his jacket closer. The uniforms and thin jackets simply weren't warm enough for this weather.

Kim had returned to the unit after weeks in the hospital in Naples. The new commander was Casper Clough, a West Pointer. Gillespie had been hospitalized because of the severity of his ulcers. Kim met Clough while the unit was engaged in a mountain assault taking the hills that led to this valley. When Clough saw Kim triangulate the location of enemy guns and call in precise artillery fire, Clough asked him to be the battalion S-2, the intelligence officer. Kim declined respectfully. He wanted to stay with his company. Kim finally agreed after Clough made it clear it wasn't a request.

Now Kim watched the men from his old company, resisting the urge to rejoin them. It wasn't the same. His platoon sergeant, Mas Takeba, was gone. Three days after he returned to the front, Kim had been spotting German positions on Mount Mojo. He moved by his friend Mas and lay down in the snow next to him to point out a machine gun position. Takeba's weight suddenly shifted against him. Even now, weeks later, Kim could still see the face of the man he was closest to in the unit, the trickle of blood from the machine gun bullet through his forehead slowly turning to red ice in the frigid air. He had to leave his friend there, in the snow.

When Yuki asked if they should go get him, he made the decision. Only more men would be killed if they tried. So he ordered Yuki's squad back down. The thought of leaving his friend on the frozen mountain returned to him again and again when he was alone. He chased the memory away and turned his attention to the valley below, raising his binoculars to make sure he hadn't missed anything in the dim morning light and falling snow.

The battalion received its orders to move against the German forces in the abbey above the town, used by the enemy as an observation post. They had to move past Cassino and take Highway 6, the Via Casilina— the road to the city of Rome—ninety miles ahead. Armies had passed this way for centuries, their men fighting and dying on this very ground.

Kim rested his binoculars against his chest. Right now the ancient abbey was only a monolithic pile of stone in the distance, clinging to a peak 1,500 feet above the valley floor. It was what lay between San Micheli and the monastery that chilled him. Once, the valley had been verdant farmland. Now it was the perfect killing field. Part of what intelligence reports called the Winter Line of German fortifications stretching across Italy, the area in front of him was named the Gustav Line, the most formidable fortification anyone had ever seen. It defended the most direct route to Rome.

The Germans had dammed the Rapido River, diverting its course and flooding the valley. The plain was knee-deep in icy water and freezing mud. To reach the highway, soldiers would have to push through almost two miles of flooded and sucking marsh riddled with concealed mines, cross an irrigation ditch at least four feet deep, travel a mud-covered corn field that was also full of mines, and then cross another irrigation ditch at least six feet deep. Then they would have to breach the old river channel, which was at least fourteen feet deep and had a bank of cement that rose above ground level to twelve feet in height. They then had to cross seventy-five feet of the shallow, swift river to reach the road on the other side, barricaded by double rows of barbed wire and sown with more mines.

On the other side of the river were German cement pillboxes. The assaulting troops would have to cross the watery killing ground without any cover from entrenched German machine guns and artillery. The Germans cut every tree, leaving only stumps, and leveled every building, leaving walls of four feet or less. Not an inch of ground existed that was not covered by German artillery or machine gun fire.

To Kim, the abbey was not a place of worship venerated by generations. It was a grim observer that sat immobile at the crossroads of war for a thousand years. And Kim knew that today, it would witness more death and destruction than its stone walls had ever seen.

For two weeks, the Thirty-sixth Division from Texas had been trying to cross the flooded plain to make the attack on Cassino. Already two regiments of the Texas Division had been all but annihilated, trying to move against the German defenses. They initially tried to cross upriver in rubber boats, but the German artillery bracketed the men as they rowed the shallow flood area, shredding the boats and the men as they struggled to return, many drowning in the frigid water or dying before they ever felt the icy bite of the river. The losses were staggering.

Now General Mark Clark, Commander of the Fifth Army, ordered the 34th Division, the Red Bull, to take Cassino. The 133rd Regiment was ordered to lead the assault. The regiment's 1st Battalion would take the right flank, the 3rd Battalion would take the center, and the 100th Battalion would take the left. They would attack abreast while the rest moved to the northwest of Cassino and encircled the entire area. There was no plan for what lay between them and the monastery, except to drag ladders through the water-soaked ground to breach the steep cement wall. Men would be sent ahead through the mud to cut a path across the minefields and mark it with toilet paper ribbons.

Kim raised his binoculars over the snow covered rocky slopes leading to the abbey. The only plan was to reach the other side. The attack would begin at midnight. He looked over at Clough. Both men knew they were being asked to do the impossible.

~

The 100th moved in the dark to the edge of an olive grove that skirted the crossing point. The cutting wind forced the frigid air into their fatigues, adding more misery to an atmosphere already heavy with dread. The unit moved forward into position and waited for the artillery barrage that would start at 11:30 and keep going until midnight, when the attack would begin.

There was no comfort in hearing the artillery barrage. Every man knew that when the big guns went silent, they would have to move across the open area to reach the highway. Every man knew that the enemy would know that, too. Every man knew they would have to make their assault under intense German fire. This was no surprise attack. Companies A and C would lead the 100th. Company B would be held in reserve.

The rolling barrage ceased, signaling the advance. As soon as the 100th moved into the sea of mud, colored flares ignited the sky, lighting up the men moving forward. Nebelwerfer rockets screamed overhead. The icy water numbed legs as Companies A and C pulled through the thick marsh, men slipping, falling, covering themselves with the frigid mud, soaked to their skin, keeping their eyes on the wall that could only be seen in the distance, with flare bursts overhead and tracer fire raising brown water plumes as rounds raked the mud around them.

Major Clough and Kim watched their men through field binoculars, observing the advance from the ruins of a house in the muddy plain, its broken walls no more than waist high. Keeping their heads just above the wall the command staff could only watch the attack, the skittering sound of machine gun fire hitting the walls of their observation post.

Suddenly, a mortar round landed four feet from them. The concussion staggered Kim and he looked down, expecting to see wounds. All he could see were shrapnel holes in his poncho. He looked around. His sergeant was dead. Major Clough had been hit in the hand.

Kim turned his attention back to the field while Clough received attention from a medic. As battalion intelligence officer, he was no longer leading his men at the front of a patrol. He had to stay back and advise the commander. He struggled with his desire to be with his men as he watched Companies A and C attempt to clear a path through the minefields.

Crouching and crawling in thick icy mud and water, sinking down almost a foot with every step, the soldiers in the front cleared a path about five feet wide and fifty yards long, marked on the sides with strips of toilet paper. Men were frantically but methodically scratching in the mud for mines and trip wire. They moved forward a few feet and then waited for a few more feet to be cleared. Both Clough and Kim could see their men sustaining heavy losses.

Withering machine gun fire could be heard as tracer rounds from the machine guns raked the muck where the men were crawling. Kim could see the sharp flash of light illuminating bodies flung in the air as mines exploded constantly. The bright explosive bursts marked the path the men were cutting through the mire, calling more German fire down on the men as they pushed, slipping and scrambling for any footing against the water-sodden ground. Flares lit the sky, illuminating the bodies of men dragging the wounded, leaving the dead.

After five terrifying hours Captain Fukuda led what was left of Company A to the wall of the dike, using the cement bank for cover. In the slowly breaking dawn Kim could see Fukuda's decimated command huddling against the wall, looking back at the men left on the plain, waiting for reinforcements before attempting to breach the wall.

Clough kept his eyes on the field. Kim heard him muttering to himself that the assault was insane. Nobody could successfully attack in force across this ground. It was like Pickett's Charge at Gettysburg or the Union assault at Fredricksburg against defended stone walls, both of which history recorded as military disasters.

The radioman caught Clough's attention. It was Colonel Marshall, the regimental commander. Kim was on the same frequency and could hear Marshall order Clough to commit B Company at dawn's first light—his old company, his men. Kim could see the look on Clough's face.

Clough stood silent for a moment, his head sinking down to his chest. Then he looked up and spoke into the radio. *"I refuse sir. It's suicidal to send men in daylight."*

Marshall didn't hesitate. *"Major, you are relieved of command."* Kim looked at his commander and saw his lips trembling. Clough said nothing. He was a West Point officer. He knew the consequence of refusing a direct order. He also knew that sending B Company across in daylight would be plain slaughter.

Clough handed the radio to his aide. Kim watched as Clough leaned back against the wall, oblivious to the wound to his hand, ignoring the sounds of the battle raging around him.

Lieutenant Colonel Moses, commanding the 1st Battalion, was on the same radio frequency.

Marshall, his voice edged with anger, spoke to Moses. *"Colonel Moses, you get those men across."*

Kim could hear the silence before Moses answered, his words respectful but clipped. *"Sir, I consider this an unlawful order. I'll carry it out but I'm going to personally lead those men. If I survive this attack, I plan to press court martial charges against you."*

Marshall hesitated. *"I'm sending my executive officer, Major Dewey, to take command of the 100th."*

Kim looked over at Major Clough, noticing the tears on the cheeks of his commander. He knew it wasn't because of the loss of the major's command. It was because of his men. As dawn broke Clough still remained, his back against the rubble, waiting for Dewey to relieve him.

Kim kept his binoculars on the battlefield, but he kept thinking about who was right. Of the three West Point officers, one had refused a direct order, one had accepted the order but intended to lead the men on a suicidal mission, and one had refused to reconsider his position, even though he couldn't see what was clear to his men. As far as Kim was concerned, Clough was right. *Any fool looking at the field of battle could tell what was going to happen.*

All day long, the few men at the wall held on. No one advanced. No one retreated. Kim watched the wall, sweeping the field with his binoculars and looking up at the abbey, silent and foreboding above the killing fields. Even if they took the valley and then the town, there was still the abbey. A thousand years of history. And if Kim had his way, it would be reduced to rubble.

It was evening by the time Dewey reached the battalion forward post. Only four men were still standing. Twenty-six officers and staff had been killed or wounded by the constant machine gun fire and mortar salvos. Major Dewey came into the walled area where Clough, Kim, and Major

Jack Johnson were waiting. Kim watched as Dewey looked at the area and then asked for briefing.

Dewey grabbed the radio. "Get me Colonel Marshall." He waited for the Colonel to get on the line. "Dewey here, sir. Colonel. I think we made a mistake. We should rescind the order and reinstate Major Clough as battalion commander."

"Forget it, Major. You have command. You make that attack."

"Yes, sir."

Dewey turned to Johnson. "Can you get one of the company commanders to come back and lead us up there?"

Johnson looked carefully at Dewey, not exactly sure what he intended. "Yes, sir."

Johnson turned to the radioman. "Send a messenger. Get Captain Fukuda from A Company to come back."

Fukuda finally made his way back to battalion command. Dewey looked at the mud-encrusted captain, who had now made the trip twice through the minefield and machine gun fire.

"Captain, can we do this—can we make it through to the hill?"

Fukuda looked at Johnson and Kim, then back at Dewey.

"Sir, some of us will make it, but not enough to hold the position."

Dewey nodded his understanding. "Thank you, Captain."

Dewey looked at Johnson and Kim. *"You know, I'm the one who came up with this idea in the first place—stupid, a dumb idea. Now I have to carry it out and I'm not going to send some unit there without personally going across myself. I'll get to the dike and send my orders back."*

Johnson shook his head. *"Major, with respect, that's not a good idea. It's too dangerous out there; you're in command."*

"I'm going."

Johnson looked at Dewey. *"I'm going with you."* Kim watched as Dewey, Johnson, and Fukuda made their way back in the dark through the path in the minefield, still marked by small streamers of toilet paper. Fukuda was leading the way, ahead of Dewey and Johnson. Kim could see the German machine guns firing randomly across the path. In the darkness the Germans couldn't see men crawling through the mud, but they could see the white toilet paper marking the path.

All of a sudden Kim saw a trip flare light up, and then an explosion from a mine. The German machine gunners zeroed in on the flare, raking the area with fire. Kim knew the commanders were down because Fukuda was ahead of the blast. He ordered medics to reach the wounded men.

"Make sure you pick up Johnson!"

The medics reached the wounded men quickly, both covered in mud and blood. They grabbed one of the men who looked like Johnson, based on his build. When they got back to the aid station, they could see they had picked up Dewey. The men went back and retrieved Johnson. Fukuda made it back to the dike.

Clough relocated to the aid station, leaving Kim in forward command. All Kim could do was wait for orders and watch his men try to hold on. He could feel the rising anger and frustration. He watched his men die doing what could not be done.

After an hour, Major Clough returned to the forward area. Kim watched him move to the wall and look out. He was calm, but the strain was clearly showing on his face.

"Johnson's dead. He lost too much blood. I don't know if Dewey's going to make it. I'm back in command. I have orders to commit B Company at dawn."

The look of resignation on Clough's face told the whole story. Kim stood there thinking about his old company, his platoon, being sent out into almost certain annihilation.

Clough picked up the radio. *"Captain Takahashi, I want you to take Company B across at dawn and link up with Companies A and C. Wait until we lay down a heavy smoke screen."* Clough waited for the response. *"All right, Sakai, good luck."* Kim watched his commander, his face taut, all emotion now gone. Somebody had to make the decision and take responsibility for it.

Company B had watched the battle from the olive grove. Yuki and his squad waited as Companies A and C committed themselves to the fray. The only men from those companies who returned were either dead or wounded. The night and then the day and then another night passed sleeplessly, waiting for the order.

Captain Takahashi turned to his platoon commanders and relayed the instructions. They would commit at dawn. They were going to carry two long ladders necessary to climb the cement dike wall. Takahashi looked out over the battlefield. His orders were clear. At dawn, artillery laid down a heavy smoke screen.

Kim watched from the forward command post as Takahashi and Company B plunged into the mud and freezing water. There was enough light now for him to see men sinking into the mire and leaning forward, as they pulled their boots out of the sucking mud to take one more step. Screaming meemies whistled across the field as artillery and mortar rounds began to fall. If he could see Company B crossing to reach the dike, then so could the Germans. Already the smoke screen was starting to blow away, exposing Company B to direct fire.

Yuki and his squad didn't move very far through the marked path before throwing their bodies into the mud and burying themselves deep into it or trying to hide behind tree stumps that had been cut down and left as tank impediments. To stand was suicide, to crawl was the only chance at survival. Yuki could hear his men grunting and swearing as they pulled on the breaching ladders. Other squads were pinned down as well, crawling forward slowly as mud splashed up from machine gun rounds and mortar blasts.

All around them, men from A and C companies lay still in the mud, some dead, some barely alive. Yuki kept looking ahead, urging his men forward, keeping his eyes on Takahashi and trying to close his ears to the sound of the wounded sinking in the mud. Cries of *okasan* were mixed with cries of "mother" in English. He'd heard it before, the last words of dying men. For a brief moment he recalled the young German soldier who had died in front of them, wanting only to see the photograph of his parents.

Yuki looked back to see Tug and Kazo struggling with the mud-encrusted ladder. "COME ON, TUG. PULL! GODDAMN IT!" He heard Tug grunting and the sounds of men screaming and yelling at one another as they tried to keep their bodies buried in the mud, trying to gain traction in the mire.

Tug felt the ladder growing heavier by the minute as fewer and fewer men pulled on it. He knew they weren't leaving it to him. They were being cut to pieces. He looked ahead for Yuki. All he could see were mud-covered men pushing forward as muddy water splattered down on them from mortar rounds. He couldn't see Kazo anymore. Everybody looked the same. Men caked in mud, squirming forward, trying to survive.

Yuki heard the men at the dike screaming at them to move. He had no energy to move. A hand reached out and pulled him forward as his aching legs pushed through the mud, trying to get to the safety of the wall.

When he reached the wall, Yuki realized that men from companies A and C had run out into the killing field and started pulling men in. He didn't know who pulled him to safety. All he could do was try to control the nausea that was overwhelming him. He heard Tug's voice calling to him, and he yelled back that he was okay. He was too tired to move. He couldn't see Kazo anywhere. The sound of the screaming meemies and German artillery drowned out everything. But he had no one to yell at. He had no men left.

~

All day long, the men clung to the cement wall of the dike. To move forward, they would have to go over the wall and expose themselves to direct fire. Then they would have to cross the river. No one had any illusions about what would happen if they went over the dike. They held tightly against the safety of the wall, waiting for dark, hoping no orders came to go forward.

Yuki sat with his back against the wall. He could feel the freezing mud crusting on his uniform. Tug moved over close to him and they sat huddled together, trying to share whatever warmth their combined bodies could muster. Tug kept looking out across the muddy plain. The bodies of men could be seen clearly. Some were still moving, slowly squirming through the mud, worming their way toward their comrades at the wall. Of those who could move, no man retreated. They kept trying to make their objective.

Night fell. The cries from the killing field became less frequent.

Tug whispered to Yuki. "Did you see Kazo? You think he's still alive?"

"I don't know. I don't know how *we* made it."

It was too much for Yuki to think about. His body ached with fatigue. He tasted the coppery film in his mouth. What little water he had, he shared with Tug. He sensed the movement of the men along the wall before he heard the whispered voices. Men were making their way out of the mud under the cover of darkness. A few, not many, stayed in the mud when the withering fire made going forward impossible. They were now crawling out.

It wasn't long before they heard Kazo talking to men along the wall, looking for his squad. Tug called out in a hoarse whisper. "Kazo, over here. Over here." Moving next to the wall in a low crouch, Kazo appeared made out of mud, covered head to toe and shivering uncontrollably. He crawled between Yuki and Tug to get some of their body heat. They could feel his body shaking and hear him trying to muffle his voice. Neither man said anything. They didn't want to humiliate him by noticing his crying, nor did they want to draw attention to the tears running down their own muddy faces.

On the other side of the killing field, Clough and Kim waited for orders. They already told regimental command they had no men left to go forward. Kim heard the crackle of the radio and listened as headquarters ordered the regiment to withdraw from the wall. He looked at Jim Clough, who had recognized from the beginning that the attack would be suicidal. Kim shook his head. Clough stood there looking at the radio, then turned to Kim.

"Order the men to withdraw. Bring our boys back."

The order passed down the wall to withdraw. Yuki could barely move his body. The cold was now deep inside him, stiffening his arms and legs, sapping his body of what little strength he had left. Some men were unable to control their bowels as their bodies gave in to exhaustion and diarrhea. Others simply stared blankly at the sea of mud they crossed, and the mounds of mud covering their crumpled comrades who had not reached the wall. Yuki grabbed Tug's arm. He looked back across the distance through which he and his squad had crawled. *Was it all for nothing?*

Kim watched in silence as the few men who had made it to the wall crawled back, pulling the wounded with them. The dead would have to wait. German guns fired sporadically as mud-caked men stumbled past him, trembling from the cold.

Kim raised his binoculars. Through the icy mist and haze of falling snow the ancient monastery of Monte Cassino still stood, its cold stone walls a silent sentinel watching the valley it had towered over for centuries, bearing mute witness once again to the blood-soaked ground slowly covering itself with a white blanket of snow. The abbey had survived countless long-forgotten wars, just as it had survived this day. Kim knew there would be another day. The brooding stone fortress guarded the road to Rome.

CHAPTER 54

February 8, 1944

Monastery Hill

Near the Town of Cassino, Italy

Major Lovell returned, recovered from his wounds. He took command of the battalion while Major Clough received treatment for the injury incurred during the futile assault across the Rapido River plain. When the 100th tried to cross the Rapido plain, they had 832 men. After the failed assault, they had 521.

The men of the 100th were moved back to a rear area to recover and regroup. There were no replacements to be found, except from kitchen crews and supply. They would wait for replacements from the 442nd. Sickness from exposure to the freezing water and mud had taken its toll. Men were down with fevers or incapacitated by diarrhea. Some medicated themselves with wine they found in an abandoned farmhouse. But the realization of how many men were gone took away their spirit. They waited for other units to break through where they had failed.

Slowly, after ten more days of fierce fighting, Allied forces moved to the foot of Cassino. Lovell received orders to join the attack on the town. He walked back to the 100th's makeshift headquarters and looked at Kim.

"The old man said he hates to have to do it, but he needs to use our boys in this attack. He called them fire eaters. We're going up the hill."

Kim could only stare at Lovell. The unit was a shell of what it had been, and the men were still struggling to get healthy.

"We should just go around it. We could leave the Jerries up there. Throwing more men against it doesn't make sense. They should shell that abbey and bomb the place to hell."

He looked at Lovell's stony expression of acceptance. There was no point in talking, Lovell didn't have any choice, either. Kim sighed with the same resignation already showing on Lovell's face. Both of them knew that Allied commanders had agreed the abbey would be spared. It was an international treasure harboring art and precious manuscripts, regardless of the fact that it also harbored the enemy who used it to direct their fire and guard the road to Rome.

"Our boys can do it, but I'm going up with them." Lovell finally said.

Kim shook his head vigorously. *"A battalion commander needs to stay back where he can see."*

"I know, Kim, but sometimes it's more important for the men to see him in front. You stay back to keep me advised of what's going on."

The battalion moved against Castle Hill, where old Roman fortifications still dotted the hillside that controlled the road to the abbey. The abbey sat high on its hill, waiting for them, the mist swirling around its untouched walls.

"Why don't they just bomb this whole place?" Tug's expression showed his resignation to what was ahead.

Yuki shook his head. "Stay with me."

They spotted German machine gun emplacements covered with steel roofs and connected by trenches. It was only moments before intense fire slowed the battalion's movement to crawling on knees and bellies. Radio calls asked for smoke as darkness fell. Eventually smoke shots were lobbed to cover their movement to Hill 165 nearby, as they forced themselves closer and closer to the monastery.

Even in the dark, the abbey filled the horizon, a black shadow rising up into the sky, lit by the muzzle bursts of German assault guns pumping shells down on the men. The hill's rocky face was crossed with terraces and what remained of gnarled grape vines, slowing the advance as men struggled to move up under the smokescreen's cover.

They were making progress when the wind shifted, exposing the men to full view of the enemy. Machine gunners in entrenched German positions rained fire down on the surging battalion, forcing them to find cover behind low terrace walls or rocks. There they stayed through the night and into the next day until Major Lovell again started moving up the hill, pulling the men with him, closer and closer, until they reached the wall of the fortress just below the abbey.

Enemy fire continued. Just down the hill, Yuki saw his battalion commander spin as he was hit in the chest. Pinned down at the edge of a gully, Lovell piled rocks up to provide cover, leaving his long legs exposed. The men below watched in anger as enemy rounds continually hit him in the legs, and everyone could see that Coach was down.

Yuki and Tug watched impotently with the rest of the men as German fire kept them from getting to Lovell. Sergeant Gary Hisaoka started digging a trench to get to the Major, lying almost twenty yards away. He made it almost ten yards before he jumped up and ran to Lovell, grabbing him and dragging him across the open ground to his shallow trench, then sliding him down to a litter. Medics pulled him back down the hill, treating his chest wound. His shin had been splintered by bullets. Everybody knew that even if he made it, he wasn't coming back.

~

Through four days on the hill, the German fire remained relentless. Wounded men lay in the open as enemy machine guns swept the rocky ground, preventing anyone from reaching them except in the dark. Medics crawled up to treat the wounded. Slowly, the already decimated ranks thinned even more.

Snow began to fall, then whip into a storm. The stony ground was frozen hard, and the men chipped away shallow holes where they waited. If a man had to urinate, he rolled on his side. If he had to defecate, he held it until dark. There was no place to go but into open, rocky ground completely covered by enemy fire. Yet the battalion surged again. Engineers ignited flamethrowers, spewing torrents of liquid fire into the German bunkers before them until heavy gunfire pushed them back. They edged closer and closer to the fortress wall below the abbey.

Kim watched the advance grind to a halt. He saw that men could not take the abbey, no matter how many men they had. Regimental command ordered them to withdraw. Kim took command as the men made their way back down the hill.

They had made it to the wall of the fortress, but the price was high. Coach Lovell was gone, and so were many Hawaii boys. Company A came down with twenty men. C Company had only twelve or thirteen, leaving the average strength of the 100th at fifteen men per rifle company still standing. But along with the 168th, they were the only ones to make it to the wall.

For four more days, Company B fought house to house through the town of Cassino. When Yuki, Tug, and Kazo joined the rest of the 100th, they would say only that they had been close enough to the enemy to see them in the next room. Company B came down with sixteen men.

Allied command ended the assault. What was left of the 100th Battalion and the rest of the 133rd Regiment watched as, two days later, Allied forces sent 215 planes against the rock walls of the abbey. Plane after plane dropped 2,500 tons of bombs against the ancient stone walls. Burst after burst tore down the mountain sentinel.

The men of the 100th, beaten by the medieval stones like so many of history's armies gone before, stood with their brethren from the other units and watched the onslaught of air power. Artillery hurled round after round into the stone edifice, slowly crumbling its massive walls as plumes of dark smoke rose high in the air. The Abbey of Monte Cassino was reduced to rubble, a smoky pile of rock covering its priceless mosaics and frescoes. Yuki watched in silence. Tug and Kazo were all that was left of his squad.

The 100th pulled back to Alife for rest and regrouping. Without replacements, they would not be an effective fighting force. Without rest, they couldn't push forward to what lay ahead. Days later, the call finally came. The 100th moved around the citadel's hilltop rubble to push into the soul of Italy—Rome.

CHAPTER 55

March 10, 1944
San Giorgio, Italy

It wasn't what he expected. Sammy and the other men plucked from the 442nd as replacements saw burned-out German tanks and blackened American military vehicles as their truck rumbled along the rutted road toward the village where the 100th had been sent for rest and regrouping and to pick up others like him and Freddy. He stared as the convoy pushed to the side of the road. The stale smell of smoke from the charred hulks still hung in the chill March air.

Here and there wisps of green showed in the brown grass edging up to the road. Sammy could see dark evergreens clumped against the hilltops, but near the road all he saw were splintered sticks, a few yellowed leaves still clinging to now-dead branches. Village after village showed the ravages of war as the convoy passed shell-pitted walls.

But it was the people who affected Sammy the most. Old women and young children standing beside the road, asking for help in halting English. He and Freddy tossed out what they had. It was still not enough to feed the masses of people lining the road, mile after mile, eyes sunken, hands out.

All the men in the replacement packet heard or read about what happened at Cassino. They knew that they were coming in to fill the gaps in ranks left by heavy, heavy losses. Some of the men riding in the trucks were wounded in engagements up to and including Cassino. They were riding back to rejoin the unit. As the men jostled for comfort on the hard wooden benches, they listened to the veterans impart their experiences and advice.

The stories they told set Sammy and Freddy's teeth on edge. Even Stubby quieted down when he heard about the Rapido River crossing.

Both Bobby and Stubby lapsed into their pidgin English. As soon as the 100th veterans joined them, they found men who had common acquaintances. The lilting island patois deepened the relationship between the island veterans and the new boys from home. Sammy and Freddy didn't understand most of the conversations but they did understand *katonk*, which they heard repeatedly as the Hawaii boys talked with the veterans.

When they reached the encampment, Sammy and Freddy jumped off the truck and pulled down their barracks bags as they were shuffled into a formation by a chunky two-striper. After Cassino, with so many noncommissioned officers dead or wounded, Tug had been made a corporal and Yuki was now a sergeant.

"My name is Corporal Taniguchi. Now I got a list here of you guys and where you've been assigned. Listen up for your name and company. Then go stand where I tell you."

He called out name after name before coming to Sammy. "Miyaki, Isamu, Company B, Second Platoon. Over there where you see that sergeant," he said, pointing at Yuki.

Sammy looked at Freddy and then moved over to a growing group of men. He looked at Sergeant Watanabe, who shook his hand, and then motioned for him to take a seat on the ground. Sammy watched to see what would happen to Freddy. It wasn't long before Freddy, as well as Bobby and Stubby, made their way over to the same cluster. Freddy sat down next to Sammy, relieved they were still together. Yuki looked down at the two men.

"You guys buddies or something?"

Freddy looked up. "We grew up together, Sergeant."

"Well, that's good. You're going to want a buddy with you." Yuki looked down at Freddy. "You're the BAR man, right?"

"Yes, Sergeant." He held up the eighteen-pound Browning Automatic Rifle that was assigned to each nine-man squad. At more than four feet in length, the twenty-round machine gun was almost as big as he was.

"Good. We lost our last one." Sammy could see something different in Sergeant Watanabe's eyes when he referred to his other BAR man, almost a vacant stare that looked right over him.

Yuki waited until all of the replacements were parceled out to the different companies. "Okay, listen up. We're going to stay here for a little bit longer and maybe get some more replacements in the next week or so. We got mail that came in ahead of you. After that, we'll get you set up with your squad leaders. Then we take you boys through a little training for what it's really like. We'll be moving out soon. The war's not over."

Sammy and Freddy both took their mail back to a wall and sat down, using it to rest their backs. Freddy opened a *Life* magazine that Rose sent, along with a letter, some cookies, and some soap. He passed around the cookies while he read the letter. Rose and her family were being moved to another camp called Rohwer, about twenty miles away from Jerome. The Jerome camp was being turned into a German and Italian P.O.W. camp.

The copy of *Life* included an article about a soldier from the 100th. It bore the title "Blind Nisei" and showed a picture of Turtle Omaya sitting in his pajamas and bathrobe, with each of his eyes covered in cotton patches. The article said he would be blind. Some of the men sitting around Freddy began to look over his shoulder at the picture. Tug walked over when he saw the magazine, and called out to Yuki. Soon everybody was crowding around Freddy. He handed the magazine up to the veterans, who obviously knew the man in the picture.

Sammy sat quietly, reading a letter from Betty. Her parents were grieving over the death of the Machado boy. They were close friends with his parents and they were shaken by the loss. Betty talked about the people leaving the camp and going to the East Coast to work. She felt that Jerome would close soon and maybe Manzanar, but everybody said they wouldn't be allowed to go home. Most people decided they would just stay where they were until they could return to their homes. He folded the letter up and looked up at Sergeant Watanabe.

"Sergeant, where are we going to be sent?"

Yuki responded in a flat, emotionless monotone. "The rumor right now is we're going to spend some time on the beach at a place called Anzio. And don't ask me because I don't know where the hell it is. They won't tell us nothing until we're there. That's the way it's been."

Yuki looked over at the rest of the new men who were listening, his voice softening.

"Couple of things you should learn. Keep an extra pair of clean, dry socks. Make friends with the company clerk and don't piss off the cooks.

After that, everything you'll need to know you'll find out when they start shooting at you. Oh, and by the way, Corporal Taniguchi, the one we call Tug, he's your new squad leader."

~

After rest and regrouping, the 100th, along with the rest of the 34th Division, moved to the beachhead at Anzio. For two days they rode on pitching landing ships until they moved into position on a fifteen-mile stretch of beach. It paralleled a canal that drained a large swamp known as the Pontine Marshes, an area infested with malaria since the days of Nero, who had been born nearby.

Anzio had been devastated by repeated assaults trying to break the German line. Doors and windows stood with no walls behind them. The detritus of war littered the town, burned vehicles and shattered trees lining the rubble-strewn streets. The Americans held the coastline. The Germans held the land behind it.

The 100th sat for two months in a standoff. The Germans reinforced lines separated by an expanse of ground known as "no-man's-land"—a broad stretch of grass and abandoned wheat fields, with barbed wire running down an edge of minefields. Enemy bunkers were placed up and down the line, watching for any night movement. During the day the two sides mostly kept to themselves, knowing that nothing could be done without being seen and prepared for. At night, both sides lobbed artillery shells. These occasional attacks and reconnaissance patrols by both sides kept everyone on edge, but it was an impasse. The Fifth Army couldn't move off the beach area, and the German army had to hold their line to keep the Allies from moving through and on to Rome.

Sammy and Freddy found out quickly that their squad leader, Tug, wasn't much of a disciplinarian. If you took care of the details you were assigned and listened to his stories, you got along. Sammy was surprised by what he had seen of war so far. When he first joined the unit, there were hot rations and a USO show. Now he was dug in on a beach and other than an occasional artillery shell, he and Freddy spent time gathering watercress from the canal and scooping fish when someone dropped a hand grenade into the water. Some of the men picked flowers from abandoned farmhouse gardens and kept them in their dugouts.

On the German side men could be seen with their shirts off, tanning in the Mediterranean sun. Sammy heard stories about the war, and he met the men rejoining the unit after earning hospital stays and Purple Hearts. He and Freddy began to relax during the daytime. Even the few night patrols were uneventful.

The 100th HQ was in one of the few intact farmhouses, while most of the men lived in dugout shelters covered by blankets and dirt. At night they watched the lines and hoped they weren't one of the unlucky ones who caught a shell. It was known by the men as a "vampire" existence.

On April 2, Lieutenant Colonel Gordon Singles, a West Point officer who had been at Shelby with the men, took assignment as the new commander of the 100th. Major Casper Clough became his executive officer. Clough's refusal to send his men across the muddy field at Cassino had not been forgotten.

After discussions with Clough and other officers, Singles called in Lieutenant Kim and made him an S-3, Battalion Operations Officer. Singles had never seen combat and needed experienced men. He looked and he listened, quietly garnering the respect of his new command while his men went through their daily existence of trying to stay alive, avoiding the boredom of the days and the terror of the nights.

Toward the beginning of May, Singles and Kim were called into division headquarters. There were briefing officers from the Fifth Army who first swore them to secrecy and then laid out the problem confronting the stalemate along the battle line. After the briefing, they walked out of Division Headquarters and headed back to the farmhouse.

Singles sat at his makeshift desk, a kerosene lamp providing the only light. His face flickered yellow in the dim glow. He looked at Kim, sitting in the chair near the desk.

"Did you understand it the way I did? They want to make a breakout where we are? They think they can move tanks through here?"

Kim's face was impassive as he leaned his head back and looked at the ceiling. *"They know there's a German tank division somewhere behind this line. They just don't know where it is. If we hit that tank division, they'll cut us to pieces. I've run aerial photographs, used planes to dive in for close up shots. I haven't gotten anything."*

"We need prisoners, Kim."

"We're never going to get a prisoner the way we're going. I don't care if we increase patrols from sixty to one hundred twenty, it isn't going to work. The area is so flat that you have no cover if you try to cross. It's heavily fortified so we can't take it out with shelling and they have snipers just like we do. The only way we're going to get a prisoner is if we cross that barbed wire minefield on the other side of the grass. I've been thinking about it. We cross at midnight and hide out. Then we go across the mine field."

Singles laughed. *"They'll see whoever tries to cross. That's crazy."*

"No, they'll never look down. Once you get on their side of the field they won't be looking for anybody. The trick is to get to the other side of the field and wait. You let me do it and we'll have our prisoners."

Singles sat there silently, looking at his new operations officer. *"No. Nothing moves on Anzio in the daytime. Any man who crosses there is dead. I won't approve it. But I'll send it up."*

Kim nodded. It was the only plan he could think of. Somebody had to do it because they needed prisoners who could answer their questions.

Kim got up and said a terse good night. He walked back to his quarters in part of the farmhouse.

～

Over the next few weeks, more and more men were coming in as replacements from the 442nd back at Shelby. On May 24th, three more officers and 112 enlisted men made it to the 100th. The new men included Akiro Morita and Tommy Doi, Sammy's friends from Manzanar.

Three days later, Akiro and Tommy were sitting in the dugout with Sammy and Freddy. The boys had been up most of the night, telling stories about home and what it had been like so far. They could tell that neither Akiro or Tommy were impressed with their dugout. Tommy kept looking around.

"You guys been living in *this* for two months?"

Sammy looked offended. "Hey, *this* is pretty good. We got moved over here and grabbed this hole. We got a radio." Tommy looked over at the contraption made of razor blades, a dry cell battery, and wire.

"That's your radio?"

Freddy laughed. "You'll see. We got it pretty good. So far, just a few shells coming in, but the Jerries stay pretty much on their side, and we stay on ours unless we get a patrol. We really haven't done much."

The four of them crawled out of the dugout and looked around. The sky was just beginning to turn light with dawn. There was very little movement. Tommy spotted a patrol coming back. One of the men in the patrol was wearing a knit beanie, while the other men wore their steel helmets.

Akiro looked over at Sammy. "Who's the guy with the beanie?"

"That's Lieutenant Kim. Come on, we'll tell you all about him. Let's get Corporal Taniguchi. He tells it best."

Tug squeezed his bulk into the crowded dugout. There was a new audience for his beach boy routine. "You want to hear about Kim? Okay, but you not gonna believe it. That guy's crazy, everybody knows it. We been here living like rats for two months. The Jerries got all kind defenses on the other side, tanks and who knows what kind things. We all trying to take prisoners. Every night patrols go out. Sammy and Freddy here, they been out. No prisoners.

"So Kim goes to the old man and tells him he wants to go across no man's land and bring back prisoners. No way that can be done. Everybody can see you do that and you kill yourself. In daytime the Jerries can see you, and at night they got mines in that field and they're watching. So the old man says no, but he'll tell the division commander, General Ryder, and he says no, but he'll tell the corps commander, and he says tell General Clark, the big kahuna, you know. So I hear that Clark say okay.

"Anyway, other night Kim takes Irving Akahoshi and they crawl across in middle of night to the edge of the Jerry line. So close they can hear the Jerries talking. Anyway, they crawl to the barbed wire and go through mine field for maybe six hundred yards, moving like snakes. They get to a ditch and hide until almost daylight. Irving said they hear some snoring and there's some Jerries asleep in this trench, so they crawl over and Kim shoves his tommy gun in this German's mouth. Irving does the same thing to the other guy in the trench and that wakes 'em up. They take 'em prisoner and crawl back past a Jerry pillbox and then go back to the ditch and keep those two Jerries there all day until night. Then they crawl back with two prisoners.

"We hear that Clark so excited he orders Kim and Irving get the Distinguished Service Cross on the spot. That guy Kim? You want to stay alive, you follow him. Yuki and me were with him when we cross the Volturno and when we at Cassino. He's crazy, but I stick with him." Sammy and Freddy nodded their heads. "He used to be platoon commander of our company, but now he's the operations officer. The clerks say even the colonel asks what he thinks."

Akiro looked over, cocking his head to the side. "You guys are bull-shitting me, aren't you?"

Tug shook his head, his voice serious, the beach boy talk finished. "No, no. He kept us alive at the Volturno. We almost walked into a mine-field but he kept us out of it. He got a silver star there. Lot of guys got silver stars—most of them dead now."

Tug hung his head. "Those guys get medals but the Army sends them home to their families, you know? Don't be thinking about medals when we go out there. You think about staying alive. Stick with Yuki and me. We got this far. Just remember, old Kim is always in front so you see him, then you know everybody else is behind you."

Tommy just sat there looking at the others, his eyes big as saucers. "How long are we going to be here, Corporal?"

"All I know is I'm tired of living like some kind of beach rat. You guys will see action soon enough. When you do, maybe you'll wish you were back in this hole."

~

The prisoners that Kim and Akahoshi brought back revealed the location of a German Panzer unit that would reinforce any attacked position. As a result of this intelligence, the combined Fifth and Eighth armies broke the stalemate and pushed through the German defenses. The 100th waited while others broke the enemy line. Then the 34th Division was ordered up to take enemy positions near the town of Lanuvio, the last stronghold before the road to Rome. Other units moved to the east of Lanuvio and held the hills, but German resistance held the western approaches.

Sammy and Freddy were silent as they rode fifteen miles to the line. There they relieved another battalion from the 135th Regiment that had been facing a German defense of overlapping machine gun positions and had failed to break their line. General Ryder gave orders to the 100th to take the western approach. The 100th moved into position near the hamlet of Pian Marano, just west of Lanuvio.

For Sammy, Freddy, Akiro, and Tommy, this would be their first taste of real combat. For the veterans looking up at the village hanging from the side of the hill, it was like Cassino. As they approached the battle line, the sound of artillery could be heard thundering in the distance. The smell of cordite began to filter into the trucks as artillery blasts grew louder and closer. They came off the truck expecting to face the enemy. It was May 27, 1944. They were held in reserve four days.

~

As night fell on June 1st, Captain Takahashi gathered his platoon leaders and sergeants. "The Jerries have made a bulge into our lines. We'll take Lanuvio, but first B and C companies are going to take out their machine guns and the village of Pian Marano. First, we clear the mines so our boys can come through." Takahashi drew out the positions of the platoons.

Yuki came back to the waiting men in Second Platoon. "Here's what we do. Tug, take the left flank. I'll be the center. The rest of the company will push up behind us. We have to take those machine guns. Third Platoon will be clearing mines. C Company will be with us. The rest of the unit will support. You new guys just watch your squad leaders and the lieutenants. If you get lost, look for me. Just remember to keep going forward and look for mines. I'll see you all in Marano."

Sammy and Freddy looked at one another. By now, the German machine gun fire and shelling was intense. Stubby nudged Sammy.

"Hey, Sammy, *brah*, this some bad shit I think. No more *katonk*, *buta head* out here, okay?"

Sammy looked over, his voice suddenly hoarse. "We watch each other's back, Stubby. Maybe we can all get through this."

Sammy looked around at the other men in the squad. Tommy's eyes were wide and unblinking. His face showed the fear that everyone else was trying to conceal. Freddy's face was drawn and taut. He had two bandoliers slung over his shoulders and he was hunched over from the weight. In the early morning darkness they started walking toward the sound of the guns.

The Germans began to lay fire down on the hill they were about to ascend. Sammy moved forward, following Yuki and Tug. The sound was overwhelming. Screeching artillery mixed with the pinging sound of ricochets off rocky outcroppings. Sammy saw dirt spray upward as bullets hit the ground in front of him. The ripping sound of machine gun slugs tore the air. He saw the muzzle flash of a machine gun ahead of him. He crawled toward it and reached for a grenade attached to his web gear. He felt the sharp gravel of the hill scraping through his fatigues. He pulled the pin in the grenade, counting before he threw. He didn't lob it like he'd been taught, but threw it like a straight throw from shortstop to first base, hitting the dirt berm in front of the machine gun nest. He watched the grenade bounce up and explode, the brief flash covered by smoke and dirt blowing upward. The firing stopped for a moment and he pushed forward.

For some reason, the sharply defined battle sound was gone now. All he heard was a muffled roaring noise. All he could see was the machine gun nest. He stuck his head up to get a better view and felt his head slammed into the ground from behind. He turned his face to the side and saw Yuki moving his lips. It took a moment to separate the sound coming out of Yuki's mouth from the roar of the battle.

"Keep your goddamn head down, Miyaki. Keep moving."

He started pushing with his feet, trying to find traction. The muzzle of the machine gun was starting to swivel. Another grenade sailed over his head, landing behind the gun. All of a sudden he heard Freddy yelling at him.

"MOVE TO THE LEFT! I GOT THE RIGHT!"

Sammy slid to his left and pushed forward, clawing the dirt and rocks to pull himself ahead. He saw Freddy jump up and start running toward the machine gun. Freddy pulled a grenade and threw it underhand, like a toss from shortstop to second, into the machine gun nest.

Sammy got up and ran toward the machine gun. The next thing he knew, he was back on the ground. Flying dirt and small shards of rock hit his helmet and face. He felt the whomp of the blast and then Freddy grabbed him by the arm, pulling him up while he fired his BAR into the machine gun crew. Both of them kept firing into the tangle of men in bloody German uniforms. They kept pushing forward. There was no time to think about what they had just done. There were still more guns up ahead. Around them mortar rounds were falling, the air buffeting them as they tried to gain the rocky ground.

Night turned into humid day and back into night. The 100th pushed forward foot by foot, moving the German line farther back. Sammy felt the heat of the ground as the rest of B Company kept crawling, then running, then crawling next to C Company. After more than twenty-four straight hours, they were almost to the walls of the village.

Sammy's legs burned. His mouth was dry, and he turned over onto his back to get a drink from his canteen. Men jumped up, running forward up the moonlit hill and then dove to the ground, looking for the next opportunity to advance, looking for a hole in the enemy fire. In the light of muzzle flashes he caught glimpses of faces, dirt-streaked and bloody from the chips of bullet-splintered rocks. Freddy was to his right and forward. There was no point in trying to yell. He couldn't even hear the sound of his own voice.

Sammy caught a glimpse of Tommy, moving ahead of him and finding cover behind a rock. A machine gun lay up ahead, its muzzle flash spewing flame and raking the hill to their right. He saw Tommy stand as the muzzle swung back. He was arching his arm to throw a grenade. Everything happened slowly. He could hear himself screaming Tommy's name. He could see the grenade leaving Tommy's hand and the flame of the machine gun barrel sweeping to its right, the muzzle spitting fire like the whipping head of a dragon. It caught Tommy before his grenade silenced the muzzle flame.

The last burst of the machine gun moved Tommy back, his steps uncertain as he reached for the ground to find cover. The gun went silent as the grenade blast took the machine gunners. Sammy moved forward, screaming for Tommy to keep moving. But he didn't. He pulled on Tommy's shoulder, rolling him over. Tommy looked surprised. His eyes were wide open. Sammy kept shaking him, screaming at him to move. He pulled his arm back, a dark stain smearing his sleeve. For one brief moment there was silence all around him as he stared at his sleeve, then he slowly crawled forward.

The hill stretched out the hours. Sammy was surrounded by men, but all he could see was the wall at the top. Artillery rounds started walking down the hill, the shell bursts thudding into the slope, each round stepping farther down the hill than the last. He sensed the forward movement sagging as the shells dropped around them, the blasts pushing men down, digging into the earth to find a safe place to hide.

Yuki watched. The rounds hit above the wall where the Germans were and down the hill where his men were digging in furiously. *Were the Jerries dropping short rounds on their own men?* He heard the whistling sound as the rounds arced down. The sound was coming from behind them. *It's our own artillery!* The concussion of the rounds knocked him to the ground. He looked around frantically to locate his platoon. He heard another sergeant screaming into a radio to stop the artillery, but it didn't stop until rounds had walked right through the center of their line. When it stopped he could see men on the ground behind him, unmoving. He looked ahead. The wall was still there.

~

The early morning sun warmed them as they stood at the top of the wall of the little village. Ahead they heard the sound of sporadic gunfire as other units finished the breakthrough into Lanuvio. The men looked for one another to see who made it through. Freddy reached for Sammy's arm. "We made it." Sammy nodded. He looked over and saw Bobby down the hill, kneeling beside a man. It was Stubby. The medic was working on his chest.

They walked down the rocky ground that seemed so steep only hours before. Sammy could see the tears in Bobby's eyes. When the litter bearers came over, Sammy and Freddy helped Bobby slide their friend onto the canvas stretched between two poles. Stubby never stopped talking. The morphine was beginning to take effect. He started to slur his words. He looked up at Bobby, his eyes questioning.

They watched Bobby walk beside the litter, his hand covering Stubby's hand, holding on to him as far down the hill as he could go before they had to separate. He was crying. "It was ours. He made it through all that and it was our own fire. We got almost to the top. Those rounds started coming in. Stubby grabbed me and pushed me down. That's when he got hit. It was because of me."

Sammy saw the guilt on Bobby's face and the tears couldn't be hidden. The blood from Stubby's wound was still damp on Bobby's chest. Bobby found a rock and said, "Let me sit for a minute."

Sammy walked back across the hill where medics were working on the wounded, and looked for Tommy. Scattered across the slope, upturned rifles marked the men who were lost. Here and there, other men were kneeling by the ones who lay still. He saw Akiro standing where Tommy had been hit, a rifle stuck in the ground with a helmet on it.

Akiro was staring down at Tommy, the dark, cold stains turning his uniform a reddish brown, his round smooth face now pale, his eyes like dry black pebbles, no shine or laughter left in them. Akiro reached down and closed Tommy's eyes.

Both men walked back up the hill. Freddy was sitting on the ground, looking at the sunlight washing across the barren hill. The heavy BAR was lying across his lap. His eyes were sunken, with dark circles under them aging his face. He had streaks of blood on his arms and hands.

"I didn't think it would be like this."

Sammy sat down next to Freddy. They had fought for thirty-six hours without stopping, and now the fatigue was setting in. He never felt so tired. His body ached when he moved. His joints were sore from crawling, from hitting the hard, rocky ground where he had repeatedly thrown himself, and from the adrenaline that saturated his body. He looked down at his hands, blood pushed into the fingernails, ground into the lines of his palm from where he had grabbed Tommy. He stared at the dark brown stains that clung to his hands. He took his helmet off and leaned against his friend. It was the end of his first day.

CHAPTER 56

June 5, 1944

The Hills Outside of Rome, Italy

ROMA—10 Kilometers

The jeep stopped near the road sign. The midafternoon heat and humidity rippled up from Highway 7. Kim and Colonel Singles sat in the jeep, sweat drawing muddy lines in the dust on their faces. The black-framed white road sign stood at a rise in the hill where they halted. Behind their jeep, the men of the 100th lined the side of the highway. Kim looked over at Gordon Singles, his head slowly nodding acknowledgment that they would be the first. He looked back over his shoulder at the men. They saw the sign also. For the first time that day, the men were smiling. The Eternal City was within reach. They were the first Allied troops to stand on an open road to Rome. They had fought for every inch of that road.

The day after the climb to Pian Marano, Colonel Singles took command of a task force which included the 100th and three other battalions. His orders were to clean out the rest of the German 29th Panzer tank unit still blocking the road to Rome. Company A and Company B of the 100th moved up one more hill with Company C on the right and support from the 151st Field Artillery and two companies of tank destroyers. By June 4 they had pushed through to Highway 7. The Germans were in full retreat. They had broken through. Now the objective they had fought toward was in sight.

Singles turned to the column and gave the signal—move forward toward Rome. Progress was slow and came in fits and starts. Harassing machine gun fire would slow the column every quarter of a mile, the staccato bursts riveting the ground, causing the men to dive for cover. The enemy left behind machine gun crews to slow down Allied movement. Kim sent squads up the hills in pursuit, but it was a hit and run attack. By the time they reached the hidden machine gun emplacement the enemy would be gone. The German rear guard succeeded in slowing the advance.

By 4:00 p.m. their jeep came to a halt at the top of a downward slope that led toward Rome. Both men looked through their binoculars. They could see Rome in the distance, the city radiating afternoon heat from the beige and white buildings, the dome of Saint Peter's just barely visible. The road was open. The intelligence reports said that the Germans had abandoned the city and declared it open. There would be no battle at the wall, no house-to-house fighting.

Kim looked over his shoulder when he heard another jeep moving up behind them. Both he and Singles saw Gen. Ernest N. Harmon, division commander of the First Armored Division, riding in the right front seat. Harmon's jeep pulled next to Singles and Kim, while the men of the 100th stood off to the side of the road.

Harmon looked over at Kim and Singles. "Whose forces are these?"

Singles responded. "We're the 100th Battalion, sir. We just opened up the road."

Sammy and Freddy stood on the road, looking at the jeep with three stars on the bumper. Tug moved over to the side and sat on the ground, watching. As the General turned his head, the sunlight glinted from the stars on his helmet. Harmon looked back at the line of dusty, sweat-stained men standing in the middle of the roadway.

"I want you to get your forces off the road. Move over to the side."

Singles sat quietly, but Kim could feel his anger swelling as his face flushed. Singles kept silent, but Kim couldn't restrain himself. *"Sir, we're going to keep going toward Rome."*

Harmon didn't bother to conceal his anger. *"I said to move your troops, Lieutenant."* The general turned around to the driver of an armored vehicle behind him. *"I want you to go through here at forty miles an hour and I don't want you to stop before you hit Rome. Understand?"*

Harmon looked back at Singles and Kim. *"You need to move your men."* The First Armored started to move past the line of the 100th troops standing by the side of the road.

Sammy watched the armored vehicles rolling by and sat down. Freddy was already sprawled on the ground with Bobby. All the men had hoped they would be the first American troops into Rome. Tug looked around at the other men who were expressing their disgust with both words and gestures hurled through the clouds of dust made by the rolling armored vehicles. It wasn't long before word came down the line. The 100th was to stand down and wait for trucks to pick them up. They were going to ride into Rome. But it wasn't going to be until after the First Armored rolled in as liberators of the eternal city.

Captain Takahashi walked over to Yuki. He could tell his men were looking at him, waiting for him to say something. There was nothing he could do. Yuki leaned over.

"Captain, why aren't we marching in?"

Takahashi shook his head. "Sergeant, I talked to the old man. *He said that the First Armored landed before us at Anzio and they should go in first. With their armor they can handle snipers better than we can. And the old man said that we're supposed to wait here so the battalion officers can go to a meeting about us leaving the 34th Division.* Kim says we're supposed to meet up with the 442nd in a few days."

Yuki stood watching the men waving from the armored track vehicles and tanks. "We opened the road, sir. We pushed the Jerries back and got through their line. We were here first. You can see Rome from here."

"Yes, Sergeant, we opened the road. Tell the men to take it easy. They're going to send trucks for us. Somebody has to be first. It just won't be us today." In the background, Yuki could hear men muttering that the only time they were first was when somebody was shooting.

By 9:00 p.m. the trucks were loaded with all of the men from the 100th. At 10:30 p.m. they rolled through the now-quiet streets of Rome. The buildings were dark. A few people could be seen hurrying down side streets as the trucks rumbled by. There was no parade, no cheering crowds. Almost everyone had gone home.

Sammy looked out on the darkened streets. For months this city was all they talked about. All they had anticipated. What they would do when they got to Rome. How they would be treated. He looked over at Freddy, sitting on the other side of the truck. He just stared back. The rest of the men were strangely quiet. The only sound was from the tires on the road and the heavy hum of the truck engine.

Yuki looked at the deserted streets. He couldn't help feeling let down. He didn't know what he expected, but this wasn't it. He kept thinking about all the men who were lost in the battles to get here.

As the trucks neared St. Peter's Square, the silence was finally broken by the cheering of a few small clusters of people who had not finished celebrating. The sound of even a few cheers broke the tension and disappointment.

Tug tapped Yuki on the shoulder. "You know what Yuki? Two years ago today, we left Honolulu."

Two years, 900 wounded and killed—to the day.

~

June 12, 1944
The White House
Washington, D.C.

President Roosevelt reached for another cigarette. His throat was burning from all the cigarettes he had smoked, and the day was still young. Even his ebony cigarette filter didn't help much anymore. No point in complaining, Eleanor would just remind him to quit.

The Japanese internment issue needed to be addressed. At the last cabinet meeting, Attorney General Biddle continued with the same speech he had been making for two years—cancel the exclusion orders and let the Japs go home. Only now the Secretaries of War, Interior, and Justice were all in agreement that this could be done without danger to defense considerations.

General DeWitt had been removed as head of the Western Defense Command and was now head of the Army Staff College. They had to move him out gracefully, without making it look like he was being reprimanded. After DeWitt held his "a Jap is a Jap" press conference, the *Washington Post* published an editorial entitled "A Man is a Man." DeWitt had become too big a political liability.

The problem was the upcoming election. Secretary of State Cordell Hull agreed that it would be a mistake to do anything drastic or sudden in ending the exclusion orders. Out in California, Earl Warren had decimated Culbert Olson for the idea of allowing some of them back into the state to work in agriculture. Now Warren was governor, and it was no secret he wanted to be president. Even Undersecretary of State Ed Stettinius said that *"the question appears to be largely a political one, the reaction in California, on which I am sure you will probably wish to reach your own decision."*

The President rubbed his eyes. Well, Stettinius was right, but it wasn't an easy thing to resolve. He buzzed his secretary. "I have some dictation."

The President paused for a moment and composed his thoughts. "A memo to Secretary of the Interior and to the Secretary of State."

*The more I think of this problem of suddenly ending the orders excluding Japanese Americans from the West Coast the more I think it would be a mistake to do anything drastic or sudden. As I said at Cabinet, I think the whole problem, for the sake of internal quiet, should be handled gradually, i.e., I am thinking of two methods:

a. Seeing, with great discretion, how many Japanese families would be acceptable to public opinion in definite localities on the West Coast.

b. Seeking to extend greatly the distribution of other families in many parts of the United States. I have been talking to a number of people from the Coast and they are all in agreement that the Coast would be willing to receive back a portion of the Japanese who were formerly there—nothing sudden and not in too great quantities at any one time.

Also, in talking to people from the Middle West, the East and the North, I am sure that there would be no bitterness if they were distributed—one or two families to each county as a start. Dissemination and distribution constitute a great method of avoiding public outcry.

Why not proceed seriously along the above line—for a while at least?" *

Roosevelt sat back in his chair. "Read that back to me please."
He listened as his words were read back.

"Yes, that's fine. Type it up for my signature. Thank you."

~

June 21, 1944
Near Grosetto, Italy

The 100th moved some forty miles from Rome to Civitavecchia, where the 34th Division was resting and refitting. The newly arrived 442nd Regimental Combat Team bivouacked next to the 100th, having now arrived from its training at Shelby. The 100th was attached to the 442nd, and both units were assigned to the 34th Division. Even though Sammy, Freddy, and Akiro had trained with the 442nd, they had experienced battle and were now men of the 100th.

When the men of the 100th saw the fresh troops of the 442nd, they couldn't help their swagger. They had nothing to prove. Even though they were not attached, General Ryder and General Clark gave orders that the unit would now be known as the 100th/442nd. The 100th was the only merged unit allowed to keep its numerical designation. General Ryder and General Clark said they had earned it.

The weeks in bivouac were a welcome contrast to the preceding months. Hot meals and hot showers that had been luxuries were now routine as the 100th/442nd Regimental Combat Team merged. The men of the 100th had difficulty adjusting to the inexperienced men of the 442nd. At first, the 100th segregated itself from the new troops. Sammy, Freddy, and Akiro managed to travel freely between the units. They had fought with the 100th and trained with the 442nd. They had friends in both but at night they rejoined the men of the 100th, the fraternity of battle.

~

Troops from different units clustered around a large open field. Today, battle honors would be awarded to men from different units. Sammy and Freddy stood with men from the 100th. They were all waiting for the corps commander, General Mark Clark, to arrive.

Sammy and Freddy stood on the outside of the group, confused and a little embarrassed by the attention. They would receive silver stars for their conduct at Pian Marano. First Lieutenant Kim and Private First Class Irving Akanoshi stood near them. They would receive the nation's second highest medal, the Distinguished Service Cross, for their actions at Anzio. The four men were going to be decorated personally by General Clark. He had told the Secretary of War that the 100th was his best unit. The press called them "the little iron men."

The honor guard held the flags, preparing to enter the field when the General arrived. Music from the band drifted in the wind. The flags rippled in the light breeze. Sammy stared at the red and white stripes curling around the wooden staff, his mind a swirl of images against the blazing color of the flag—the wire fences of Manzanar guarded by men wearing the same uniform as the honor guard—*Obasan*'s rocking chair in the corner of the horse stall at the fairgrounds—the look of surprise on Tommy Doi's face.

The flag began to blur as tears filled his eyes. He knew why he was here. He looked over at Freddy. He knew too.

General Clark and his aides arrived, and the men were assembled into ranks while the orders were read. Kim stepped forward when his name was called while General Clark stood, towering in front of him.

"Attention to orders. The Distinguished Service Cross. Young Oak Kim, First Lieutenant, Infantry, United States Army. For extraordinary heroism in action, near Cisterna, Italy, on 26 May, 1944…"

Sammy stopped listening as the citation recounting Kim's actions was read. His mind was back at the hill below Pian Marano. The snapping flags brought his attention back to the voice of the officer reading the citation. *"First Lieutenant Kim's courageous and daring performance provided vital information and identification of enemy units to a critical sector of the front. Entered military service from Los Angeles, California."*

General Clark removed the medal from its box and pinned it on Kim's chest. He had previously given Kim a silver star for his actions in stopping the German assault on Hill 600. Well over six feet tall, General Clark looked down at the young officer standing rigidly at attention. *"How come you're still a First Lieutenant?"*

Kim stared straight ahead. *"Well, sir, your headquarters denied my promotion five times. Our unit can't promote unless the man who occupied the position first is either killed or out of the unit."*

Clark stared down at Kim for a few moments. *"Well, I'm going to make you a captain right now."* He turned to an colonel. "My junior aide is a captain, get his bars from him." Clark took the bars that had just been removed from the aide's collar. He pinned them on Kim's collar. "You're a captain."

"Yes, sir, thank you."

Clark stared at him. "Well, Captain Kim, you don't look very happy."

"Yes, sir, well, there's another officer in the same situation with me. His name is George Granstaff and he was a first lieutenant before I was and he's still a first lieutenant, and now I'm a captain."

Clark started to smile and then he laughed. "Get me another set of captain's bars." He waited until the colonel found and removed a captain's bars from one of the officers. *"Here, this is for Granstaff. Tell him he got promoted today too. You happy now, Captain Kim?"*

"Yes, sir." Clark stepped back and returned Kim's salute. Then he moved over to Irving Akanoshi.

"Attention to orders . . ."

The assembled men stood quietly while Private Akanoshi's citation was read. He was also awarded the Distinguished Service Cross. Both men looked at each other out of the corners of their eyes. They would be linked forever.

Sammy and Freddy stood quietly until their names were called. As the orders were read, they could almost feel one another's thoughts.

"Isamu Miyaki, Private, Company B, 100th Infantry Battalion. For gallantry in action . . ." He really didn't hear all of it. His mind was on Tommy Doi.

When they read Tommy's name, who was awarded the silver star posthumously, Sammy and Freddy looked at one another. An officer finished reading Tommy's citation, ". . . entered military service from Manzanar Relocation Center, Independence, California." As soon as the ceremony was over, Sammy and Freddy took the medals off and put them away.

CHAPTER 57

June 28, 1944

Manzanar War Relocation Center

Independence, California

The chill of the high desert morning quickly gave way to heat as the women tilled and weeded the small garden they tended for their block. Setsuko wiped the sweat from her forehead, working slowly and carefully with her hoe, turning the thin soil gently, loosening its hold on the roots of the vegetables they all shared, the weeds constantly battling for the meager nourishment the alkaline soil offered. The talk was quiet and subdued.

The papers were full of reports about the intense fighting of the all-Japanese battalion, as well as the heavy losses. Some of the boys from the camp who had volunteered for the 442nd were now with the 100th in Europe.

With the losses, everyone knew that the dreaded telegrams would reach Manzanar eventually. Setsuko said a silent prayer for Isamu and Freddy as she worked the hoe. She looked over at Fumiko. Her lips were moving quietly, a prayer for Tommy. Every day without a telegram was another day they were grateful to have pass.

The letters from Isamu didn't say much about fighting, but Setsuko knew it was because her son didn't want to worry them. They had enough to worry about with Toshi still in Moab, Utah, refusing the draft. He was going to be prosecuted, but he said he didn't care. Shig and Setsuko struggled daily with the conflict in their hearts over their oldest son's rebellion. In Shig's mind he could not accept it, but he could understand it—both his sons on separate paths. Setsuko simply held her sons close to her heart, as she always had.

Setsuko saw Fumiko's head rise up and stare in the direction of their barracks. She turned and looked as the other women stopped working, some raising hands to their faces. The camp administrator was walking down the graveled area between the barracks. The chaplain was walking next to him, as was the block representative. The block captain looked in their direction. None of the women could tell who he was looking at. Setsuko saw him lean over and talk to the administrator, but her eyes were on the envelope the administrator held in his hand.

Setsuko and Fumiko looked at one another, waiting, neither wanting to be the first to walk down the path to the barracks, as if that walk would acknowledge the possibility the envelope was for them. A few of the other women had sons still in Mississippi, but all eyes were on the women who had sons in Italy. Nobody moved. The block captain stopped in front of the door to the rooms that the Shiragas and the Dois shared.

The three men waited quietly, watching the women standing in the garden, not wanting to call out a name. Waiting and hoping that the women would come down the path to them. Finally Setsuko turned to Fumiko. "We will go together."

The women touched hands as others took their hoes. They walked together down the path, long morning shadows carving the light across the gravel, the only sound the crunching of the small, carefully raked stones under their feet.

Setsuko kept her head up as they drew closer. No sound passed between the two women, only the brushing of their shoulders as they tried to gather strength from one another. They walked slowly, staving off as long as possible the answer to the question each kept inside.

By now other women emerged from other doors along the barracks wall, watching. Word traveled quickly in Manzanar. The block captain looked down before raising his head to speak.

CHAPTER 58

October 7, 1944
Septemes, France

Sammy shifted against the wooden slat seat of the truck. Around him, other men in Company B huddled against one another, trying to find some warmth. The cold rain drizzled down his helmet and into the folds of his poncho, slowly finding its way inside. There was no comfortable position, the soaked uniform slowly chilling his body.

The 100th/442nd landed in France at the end of September—three days on a pitching ship, the USS *Samuel Chase*, from the Italian port of Naples to the French port of Marseille. German resistance in France was fierce as the soldiers of the Third Reich felt their backs buckling against the border of the homeland.

Pulled away from the Fifth Army and now referred to as a regimental combat team, the 100th/442nd was detached from the 34th Division and assigned to the 36th Texas Division under the command of Major General John Dahlquist. Most of the men simply ignored orders to replace the Red Bull patch of the 34th with the T of the 36th. They didn't know the 36th and they didn't know Dahlquist. Almost all who had made it this far held fond memories of the 34th's General Ryder. He very publicly said that they were the best he had.

The troops had not been dry for over a week. They hadn't been warm, either. The staging area just outside of Marseille sat in an open field atop a hill. The wind blew constantly, matching the falling rain. The tents were often blown down, drenching the equipment and the men's sleeping bags. Tug tried to find a truck with a canvas top, but most of the men sat on the bench seats and endured the cold rain beating down on them. The ponchos didn't help much. The heavy rubberized material didn't breathe and often the condensation dripping inside the poncho was more uncomfortable than the rain, but they did provide some warmth and cut down the wind.

For two and a half days, Company B sat on the hard, wet benches of the rumbling trucks. The muddy roads wound through green valleys where red-tile-roofed villages nested against the cold and the rain. It was noon on October 11 when they reached the assembly area.

The Vosges Mountains surrounding them were dark green, almost black with heavy forests of evergreen trees that blocked out the sun where the road edged the assembly area. Dense brush and undergrowth rose up under the foliage, making the forest an almost impenetrable wall. The pouring rain mixed intermittently with slushy pellets of snow, drawing a dark curtain over the land.

Even ten miles behind the lines they could hear the thunder of artillery. For the veterans, it was a sound that had become part of their day-to-day environment. For the new men, it had the ominous rumble of the unknown.

~

Captain Kim stood around the map table with Colonel Pence, Lt. Col. Virgil Miller, the 442nd executive officer, Gordon Singles, 1st Lt. Tim Boodry, the new 100th intelligence officer, Lt. Col. Jim Hanley of the 2nd Battalion, and Lt. Col. Al Pursall of the 3rd. General Dahlquist made it clear that the 36th had to take the town of Saint-Die, an industrial center that sat on the intersection of three passes through the Vosges Mountains, a gateway to the entire Rhine region, behind which lay the heartland of Germany.

To take Saint-Die the 36th would have to go through the town of Bruyeres, where there was a rail center. Five thousand people lived in or near the town. The 100th/442nd was ordered to take it.

The 179th Regiment was in a defensive position ahead of them, waiting to be relieved. The commanders were all looking at the objective and then at one another. None of them had a good feeling about this. Dahlquist claimed that the area was lightly defended, but that didn't make sense to anyone standing around the map table. The town of Bruyeres was surrounded by four conical shaped hills they had named "A", "B", "C", and "D". The tallest was only about 1800 feet high, but if there were Germans on it then all approaches to Bruyeres would be visible and subject to fire. The railway line was a vital conduit into the Rhine. It was unlikely the Germans would give it up easily. To take Bruyeres, they would have to take the hills.

Pence looked up from the map. *"Our objective is the road to Bruyeres about four kilometers to the east. The 100th will come in on the left and the 2nd will be on the right. I don't think this is going to be as easy as Division seems to think. Intelligence indicates that Bruyeres is under the control of Waffen-SS troops. They will destroy the railway line if we don't move quickly. We move up today. We advance tomorrow."* Nobody asked questions because they knew Pence didn't have answers.

Kim spoke up. *"Sir, I'm going to take Lieutenant Boodry and reconnoiter the area. Maybe we'll get an idea of what we're getting into up there. The 179th Regiment is supposed to be up ahead somewhere. We'll try to get as much information back before the unit moves up."* Pence nodded his agreement. They needed to know what was ahead. Somebody had to go forward.

The unit moved into position for the morning attack. By early afternoon, the men were ordered to dig in. They made slit trenches and tried to make themselves comfortable in the long shallow holes. The screeching of the Nebelwerfer screaming meemies kept everyone on edge and most of the men dragged branches to their trenches to try and make a roof, some small shelter from the rain that seeped into them.

Sammy and Freddy quickly dug a trench and settled in, covering the top with downed tree limbs. They kept as close together as they could, trying to share body heat and keep their minds off of what lay ahead. Low fog drifted over the forest, shrouding the tops of the trees, wisping down through the branches. Even when the rain stopped, so much water dripped off the trees that it was hard to tell the downpour had ceased. Freddy pulled off his boots and tried to massage his feet, swollen from soaked socks and boots. It didn't do much good, and he decided to save his dry pair of socks until later. Yuki checked on them as the day wore on. There wasn't much to do except sit in the trench and wait, while water seeped into their shelter and slowly turned it into an icy, muddy hole.

~

What light there was in the hours before dawn offered little to help visibility. A heavy mist settled on the area in front of the hills surrounding Bruyeres. The low, dripping branches of the conifers slapped their heads as Kim and Lieutenant Tim Boodry made their way through the brush and splintered wood of the forest. The undergrowth was at least six feet high and very dense. Gnarled roots rose up from heavy bushes that covered the ground like a thick carpet of tangled knots.

Kim and Boodry couldn't see more than five feet ahead. The dead branches below the brush cracked as they stepped carefully through the undergrowth. Kim heard something. Somebody was trying to tell them to be quiet. He couldn't see anything until his eyes made out a slight movement. Through the tangle of brush Kim was startled to see a second lieutenant sitting in a foxhole, along with six or seven other soldiers. The lieutenant had his finger over his mouth and was motioning for them to get down.

Kim looked at the dirt-streaked face of the young officer. He could see the fear in his eyes.

"Lieutenant, who are you?"

"Sir, we're with Company C of the 179th." He was shaking like a leaf. It was difficult for Kim to understand him, because he was stammering from the cold and trying to keep his voice down at the same time.

"I'm the company commander, sir."

Kim's eyes narrowed. *Company commander? This officer is just a second lieutenant and obviously not that long in the field.*

"How long have you been company commander?"

"Three or four days, sir. Look, Captain, we have to be quiet. The Jerries are right over there." He pointed at some bushes about twenty-five feet away.

Kim looked over at the dense brush and then back at the lieutenant. "How many men do you have?"

"Maybe twenty-five or thirty, sir. I get ten new ones every day but we lose at least that many, so we stay even. I'm the only officer we got right now, sir. We haven't moved forward and we can't move back, so we're here with orders to hold."

Kim nodded and looked at Boodry. *This isn't right. Something is seriously wrong with the intelligence we've been given out of Division.*

"Lieutenant, our information is that the Germans have cleared out of this area."

The lieutenant gave him a blank look and then made a guttural laughing sound. *"Sir, whoever told you that hasn't been up here with us. We haven't moved for a week."*

Kim's eyes narrowed into flat lines. *"All right, Lieutenant, we're here to replace you but we're going back to our headquarters. Just hold on. We'll be back."*

As quietly as they could, Kim and Boodry crawled out of the crowded foxhole and made their way back to the battalion HQ. Both men looked grim. Kim spoke immediately to Singles.

"Gordon, we have to talk to Pence. Something isn't right here. We ran into a forward unit. This place is crawling with Jerries. I think the whole area is heavily defended."

Pence's face clouded with anger as he listened carefully while Kim and Boodry reported. He had the radio man get division and waited until General Dahlquist was on the radio. Pence reported his new intelligence, but Dahlquist only said that Pence's men didn't know what they were talking about. They weren't telling the truth. There weren't Germans in force out there. The combat team needed to move forward.

Singles waited until the division commander was finished. He was shaking his head and looking over at Kim and Boodry while he responded. *"Sir, these are experienced officers. They wouldn't make this up."*

They could all hear the response. *"Move your men forward, Colonel."*

"Yes, sir." Pence handed the radio phone back to his aide. "We're in trouble. Dahlquist thinks we can move ten kilometers a day. He doesn't believe there's substantial opposition up ahead."

Kim shook his head. "Easy for him. He isn't up here."

～

The 100th moved out toward Hill A while 2nd Battalion moved toward B. The terrain was very rough, steep, rocky ground covered with splintered wood that had to be climbed over and scratching underbrush that blocked the way. Steady rain mixed with sleet made the frozen ground an icy sheet against which men slipped and grasped at roots and brush to keep their feet. Captain Takahashi led Company B through the half-light created by heavy fog and drizzling rain. Yuki moved ahead of the company with Second Squad following as rapidly as possible, given the difficult ground.

They had been moving over an hour when the air filled with the sound of machine gun and rifle fire. Thudding bullets hit the trees around them. Takahashi radioed back that they were encountering heavy resistance. The radio became crowded with the voices of commanders giving similar reports.

The 100th hunkered down, moving forward in feet instead of yards. Kim called for tank support. He looked over at Singles, shaking his head. There was nothing in front of them except more dense forest, the blackness only broken by flashes of muzzle fire from the enemy, hidden and waiting in the darkness and steep ground.

The 100th and the 2nd Battalion of the 442nd spent the night holding their position. Through the previous day they moved less than five hundred yards with heavy opposition. Company A, held in reserve, had been hit with heavy mortar fire and taken losses. Takahashi kept pushing forward until Company B made it through the first of the forested areas to the outside of a small clearing. Hill A was on the other side. Takahashi could see that it was thickly wooded and rose steeply. Kim called for tanks and they rumbled in five abreast, machine guns firing forward, sweeping the dense brush in front of them. Yuki moved between squads, keeping the men between the tanks until they made it to the foot of Hill A. Company B was on the move.

Sammy and Freddy moved up the hill with the rest of B Company. Sharp explosive bursts of black and orange splintered the crowns of trees. Shards of wood and shrapnel fell down like rain as the German 88s exploded at treetop level. Sammy saw men going down with long splinters of wood piercing their bodies. He looked over at Freddy, whose face was set with grim determination, pushing through the brush as the sky rained wood and metal.

Dusk began to fall, pulling the last of the dim light from the forest. Tug was with Second Squad, taking cover behind some fallen trees. Sammy and Freddy saw Akiro and Bobby crawling through the mud, staying as low as possible. Rifle fire increased. The crashing of brush grew louder.

Tug screamed at his men. "STAY DOWN! THEY'RE COMING STRAIGHT AT US!" Sammy looked desperately to find Freddy. His ears were ringing. Noise filled the swirling fog and fading light. He made out only dark shapes and spitting muzzle flashes. He could hear a sergeant screaming for artillery support, but it was only a disembodied voice in the miasma carrying the smell of gunpowder and charred wood.

As darkness fell, the 552nd Field Artillery, attached to the combat team, and the 83rd Chemical Mortar Battalion poured heavy fire into the enemy positions, grinding the German assault to a halt. The men of Second Squad settled into the mud, moving as close under fallen trees and branches as they could, burrowing into the ground and pulling the shattered tree limbs over them. They would wait until morning. No one could see. Both sides were blinded by the night and the dark shroud of the forest.

~

In the thin gray light of morning the fog still wrapped itself around the shattered forest of Hill A. Sammy raised his head to take a look around. Freddy grabbed his jacket and pulled him down.

"What the hell are you doing?"

"Trying to see what's out there."

"Well, we'll know soon enough."

Before Freddy got the last of his words out, German infantry hit from the left flank. Sammy heard Yuki yell, "FIX BAYONETS!" Tug moved next to them. The rasp of bayonets unsheathing sliced the air around him. Suddenly, Sammy was on his knees firing at silhouettes of men moving through the mist toward them, their ghostly images floating down through the fog.

Freddy jumped up and moved forward, his BAR firing in steady bursts, while the rest of the squad followed. Tug was screaming, "HOLD THE LINE!" *What line?* Sammy thought. He only saw a jumble of rocks, fallen logs, and shattered tree limbs. The Germans fell back. Sammy, Freddy, and the rest of the squad put their bodies down against the trees for cover. And waited.

A few hours later, the Germans reformed their line and hit again, just as Colonel Singles ordered a counterattack. This time, Yuki could see Company B spread in a ragged line across the side of the hill. The line sagged back slowly under the German assault.

Kim was standing with the communications officer, who yelled that somebody wanted him on the radio. "Who is it?" Kim asked. But he knew. Dahlquist's voice barked over the radio and suddenly fell silent. Kim looked at the wires in his hand that he pulled from the radio.

Kim turned back to watch the men trying to push up the slope of the hill. At last, the 100th straightened the line and pushed forward. The hours scratching and pulling up the hill had only purchased scant yards and still the forest rose up ahead, the mountaintops lost in the gray sky that met the rising mist.

All day, the fighting had been close. Both sides saw each other through the fog and drizzling rain, moving over fallen trees and dense brush. Nobody moved easily. As darkness fell Kim could see two houses on the slope of the hill. The enemy put hidden machine guns inside the houses, keeping up a field of fire that halted almost all forward progress.

All of a sudden Lieutenant Otaki from Company C ran toward the houses, leading his men. Kim watched in horror. *Otaki is supposed to be in reserve. What's he doing?*

Boodry was standing near Singles. They heard the order over the radio from General Dahlquist. He had made his way up the hill to speed up the attack and saw the enemy machine guns slowing the line. He ordered Otaki to attack the entrenched German position. They watched helplessly as Otaki moved forward while his legs buckled and his body snapped back. Machine gun fire riddled his chest and then swept through the others from his platoon.

Kim moved back to get tanks and make an advance. He spent most of the afternoon helping their crews rig up a cable so the tanks could be lowered from an embankment that stopped their movement. Two tanks held the cables that cradled another tank as it was lowered. Finally, they managed to get enough tanks down the embankment to help the 100th move forward. The vehicles moved toward the houses while the men of A and B Companies followed them. The Germans fell back, their defenses shredded by the heavy armor that moved into the fight. The 100th was now pushing up the hill.

∼

After six and a half hours of fighting, both Hill A and Hill B were in the control of the 100th/442nd. Company L of the 442nd moved into

Bruyeres and began moving forward, house by house. The town was strangely silent, the muddy and rubble-strewn streets empty as the men walked past knocked-out German half-tracks and down narrow streets walled by two-story homes. As they moved from building to building, they found the homeowners hiding inside with their children. The men didn't have much, just chocolate and a few canned rations, but they handed it out and kept moving.

Not everyone came down into the town. Some men were left on Hill A to hold their hard-won position. Other companies remained on B and D to hold those hills. When Tug led his squad into the village nobody was talking. Hands were shoved into field jackets and heads were down. Sammy spent very little time thinking about what they had been through to take the town. Like most of the others, he was only thinking about a dry place to sleep and the chance to eat something hot.

Elsewhere in Bruyeres, Singles sat down next to Kim to rest for a few minutes before they met with the other officers. He was shaking his head.

"It was Dahlquist who ordered Otaki to attack those machine guns in those houses. Otaki just did what the general ordered him to do."

Kim didn't say anything. *What's there to say? Dahlquist is a general. Otaki was a lieutenant.* He had won a battlefield commission. Now he was dead.

~

Singles and Kim walked into the two-story, red-roofed stone house where Colonel Pence had established his combat team HQ. Pence didn't mince any words.

"The 100th has been ordered to take Hill C."

Neither officer hid his anger. Singles was frustrated at orders that failed to recognize the toll the battle had taken.

"Sir, the men are exhausted."

Pence was just as frustrated. *"General Dahlquist has given the order to take Hill C by noon tomorrow."*

Kim couldn't stay quiet. *"Colonel, there's no time to plan this."*

"It's the order." Both men nodded. It was obvious that Pence didn't like it any more than they did.

Kim walked back to plan the assault for early morning.

~

At the break of dawn, a smokescreen covered the assault on Hill C. By 9:00 a.m., the 100th broke through. By noon, they held the hill. Singles and Kim looked at their men, whose fatigue showed in their drawn faces. Singles had already radioed that while they held the hill, there were still Germans around, and it would take quite a while to make it completely secure.

Kim took the radio when a call came through from Pence.

"Yes, sir?"

"Kim, I want you to move off Hill C. He could hear the strain in Pence's voice.

Kim couldn't believe it. *"Sir, we've just taken it. If we leave the hill the Germans will take it back and we'll have to do it again. We can see the Jerries now. They're about 2,000 yards out and they're going to counterattack. We can hold this hill and keep the high ground."*

There was a short silence on the radio.

"You have your orders."

Kim walked over to Singles and told him about the order. He knew Dahlquist had given Pence no choice. He could hear the General in the background. Singles was furious.

"This is just stupid. Maybe we should just stay here and fight."

"Gordon, we stay here, we get court martialed. We need to go down the hill."

By 6:00 p.m. the 100th moved back into Bruyeres, and the Germans moved back onto Hill C.

~

For another day, they waited until they received further orders. Their faces lit by lamplight, they stood at a map table looking at the terrain around Biffontaine. Thirty men from the French Underground also gathered in the room. The unshaven faces of the French partisans looked around at the Asian faces, gathered with the Caucasian officers of the Regimental Combat Team. They would lead the 100th/442nd to the ridge overlooking the town of Biffontaine. The 100th would take the ridge to secure the high ground. Biffontaine had to be taken in order for the 36th Division to advance.

The 100th/442nd moved out in a long column, with B Company providing rear security. By 3:00 p.m. they held the ridge that looked down on Biffontaine. It stretched out between heavy forest walling the small valley between the ridges on either side, and a small L-shaped farming village in the center of the valley. But they were low on ammunition and supplies. The rain started again.

By dawn, heavy fog settled over the ridge. All the men huddled in their trenches against the freezing cold. The fog made it worse. Soldiers couldn't see the enemy if they came. And everyone knew, sooner or later they would come. The Germans had poured heavy fire against the ridge, shattering the night with tree bursts from German 88s and the banshee shriek of screaming meemies.

Kim moved over to Singles. He had instructions from Pence. "Gordon, we have orders to move down into Biffontaine. Dahlquist wants it taken today."

The first thought that went through Kim's mind when he heard the order was *Why? It's a worthless tactical objective. We need to move along the top of the ridge, take the high ground and hold it.*

Singles listened quietly and then took a deep breath. *"If we go down into Biffontaine we'll be behind the ridge. We won't have any radio communication and we won't have any artillery support. We should hold the ridge. Let the rest of the unit move up into position."*

"I already told him that, Gordon. Maybe you can talk to Pence but I don't think he has a choice."

Singles listened over the radio as Pence repeated the order to move into Biffontaine. He tried one more time.

"Sir, we don't have much left here. If we go down off the ridge we won't be in radio contact. We'll have to have somebody take our place on this ridge so the Germans won't have the high ground."

Singles knew Pence understood. He also knew that Pence was following orders too. Beyond all the logistical issues of exhausted men and low ammunition and food he couldn't help thinking, *What the hell is in Biffontaine that's worth all this?*

Yuki moved from trench to trench, getting the men of Company B up and moving. The men moved slowly off the ridge, pushing aside the thick fog that swirled around them as they walked toward the village. Company C moved to the northern part of the town with Company

A on the left. Company B moved to the edge of the forested area. They planned to set up a pincer movement and close around the village. From what they could see, looking down from the ridge, the village seemed deserted. The church square was quiet, but that didn't mean the town was empty. Or that it wasn't defended.

By late morning the three companies began to close on the village. The houses at the edge stood silent. An area between the edge of the forest and the village outskirts left one hundred yards of open terrain to be crossed without cover.

Yuki led the platoon, following the rest of Company B as it moved to the village's western edge and began to cautiously move house to house. Tug took Second Squad into a home. A family huddled in the cellar. They looked at the heavyset Tug and then at Sammy, Freddy, and the rest, their expressions puzzled, asking if they were *Boche*, Germans. Freddy pulled his BAR up, pointing it at the ceiling.

"We're Americans. Are there any Germans here?"

There had been Germans billeted in the village, stealing all of the animals and most of the food. Sammy and Freddy took what rations they carried and handed them over to the family. It wasn't long before Germans started shelling from the ridge that the 100th had just left. Sporadic gunfire rattled nearby. The Germans were going to make them take the village house by house.

The squad backed out of the house and followed the platoon through the village, watching every door and window. Ahead of them, another company searched farmhouses sitting back from the roadway.

The shrill abrupt, scream of a woman and a burst of automatic weapon fire turned Sammy's head. A gray-haired, middle-aged woman stood in her doorway, holding her chest as blood stained her apron. Her face had a startled expression as she fell to the ground. The men ahead immediately lifted their rifles. Sammy could see the anguished expressions of the men around the soldier who had fired. Tug shook his head and looked back at the squad. None of the men responded.

The squad walked by, casting sideways glances at the rumpled gray-haired form lying in the dirt beside the open farmhouse door, her dress pulled up above her thigh. Sammy could see her hands still covering her chest, clutching at the apron. And her face. The same expression that Tommy had, the surprise—and the eyes, wide and unblinking. He tried to turn away and then walked back, pulling the dress down around her exposed legs. The staccato sound of exchanging gunfire focused everyone's attention. Sammy rose up as the squad moved quickly to the houses ahead.

By noon, the 100th controlled Biffontaine. They took it almost too easily but there had been civilian casualties, and it grieved the men that they had killed a woman who had opened a door too quickly. Their medics were treating a boy who had lost a leg to one of their hand grenades. They hadn't come to fight women and children.

The unit set up headquarters in a house near the edge of town and hoped their food and ammo would be resupplied by division. They were completely behind German lines. It wasn't long before Germans began to encircle the village, moved in tanks, and waited.

In the late afternoon, Kim moved cautiously along the walls of houses, going from company position to company position, taking advantage of the lengthening shadows. He expected an enemy counterattack and tried to ensure that each company was prepared defensively.

Kim moved forward until he slipped into the town church to observe the German positions. Bill Pye was there with men from Company C. They had been holding the position near an open field. There was a German tank sitting in the field, but it hadn't moved. Nobody knew if the tank crew was just waiting for movement or if they were dead, but the situation was too dangerous to risk an approach.

Kim moved a stump of wood over to a window so he could get high enough to peer through. He turned to Pye.

"We need reinforcement. Division says we have to hold out, but we can't do this much longer."

He stepped on the stump and put his hand on the edge of the window to brace himself. The sound of shots rang out the same time he felt searing pain in his hand. He fell back into the house as Pye rushed over. It wasn't hard to see that his hand was badly wounded, hit by three rounds.

The pain was unbearable. Pye started to wrap the hand.

"Kim, we need to give you some morphine."

Kim looked up at Pye. *"We need to get the hell out of here."*

Soon the morphine began to dull the pain, and Pye got on the field radio. He ordered a litter team to take Kim and several other wounded men out. They conscripted several prisoners of war they had been holding in the cellar and moved the wounded back toward the center of the village.

~

The German counterattack came at dusk. The men held the town as darkness fell, but they were under heavy assault. The enemy began to fire on the town with tanks and mortars as the German infantry closed in. Yuki could see Jerries moving around, maintaining cover as they moved toward the two-story house he was in with the second and third squads. The family who owned the house was moved into their cellar, along with the wounded. The Germans pumped shells into the house, and the walls and roof were starting to open up.

Yuki turned to Tug. "Get down to the cellar. We'll guard the windows. When they get close, we'll let you know!"

"I'm staying up here." Tug turned to his squad and directed Sammy and Freddy to take a window on the second floor. Bobby was sent downstairs to help carry the wounded. The woman who owned the house took some bedding and dragged it downstairs for the wounded to use.

Bobby and Akiro carried down two men who had been badly hit. The second time he came down Bobby heard one of them, a replacement maybe eighteen years old, trying to talk to the owner, calling her "Mama." She was trying to spoon water into his mouth while a medic worked on his stomach wound. Bobby could see his entrails exposed while the medic frantically sprinkled sulfa on the open wound and tried to contain the bleeding with torn sheets. As he turned to go back up the cellar stairs, the boy stopped talking.

Bobby went back upstairs and took the other side of the window near Freddy. Ammunition was growing low. Holes began to open up in the walls as enemy rounds slowly reduced the building to rubble. Thick, choking dust shook down from the plaster walls as the Germans shouted in heavily accented English, "SURRENDER! YOU ARE SURROUNDED!" Enemy soldiers moved closer as mortar shelling from German positions struck near the house. Sammy, Freddy, and Bobby moved down to the bottom floor as the roof started to collapse.

Yuki could see German soldiers moving between the darkened buildings. The clanking sound of an enemy tank could be heard in the darkness. The squad fired at any movement it could see. Other units joined in the fire. Grenade bursts blew out windows in buildings where enemy forces concealed themselves.

The roar of gunfire trailed off until the only sound was from American guns. The Germans retreated, firing sporadically. As darkness came, the German guns at last fell silent. They were exhausted, too.

Sammy slumped against the thick walls of the house, gaps opening the room to night air and the sounds of darkness. Most of the two squads were in the cellar while he and Freddy stood watch. He looked over at Freddy. Even in the dim light, his face was gray with fatigue. Both of them shook their heads, too tired to even utter words. The same thought passed between them. *When would it be over?* The night brought only uncertainty.

Sammy drew his jacket around him, looking around what was left of the room. Freddy was leaning near a window, his BAR held loosely in his arms, his eyes staring out into the darkness. The dust floated in the air, coating every breath with grit, the pasty taste drying Sammy's mouth. He waited before drinking from his canteen. The sound of sporadic gunfire broke the silence and men shifted uneasily, waiting for either more fire or more silence.

Sammy let his mind drift back home to Betty. It seemed like he hadn't thought about her in a long time. He hadn't let himself. Now, in the silence, waiting for morning, he let himself be with her, if only for a few moments. He needed his mind to take him home one more time.

～

The dawn was cold as the rain started again. The stretcher bearers from the unit and the German POWs put Kim on a litter along with Captain Sakamoto from Company A, who had a severe back wound. They moved through the darkness, trying to make their way to the back of the village and hopefully meet up with reinforcing units coming into Biffontaine. It wasn't long before they were lost.

The small party stopped to find their bearings. One of the men looked up the slope of the nearby hill. A German patrol moved toward them. The

Germans surrounded the group of medics and wounded while both sides shouted back and forth for the other to surrender.

Sergeant Hagiwara leaned over to Kim, who had lost a significant amount of blood. Kim listened as Hagiwara spoke to him, but he was having difficulty focusing after several shots of morphine.

"Captain, we're surrounded by a German patrol. We need to know what to do. Do we surrender?"

Kim tried to clear his morphine-clouded mind. He was having difficulty assessing the situation. *Surrender?* He looked up at the sergeant.

"No, no surrender. We make a break for it. Help me up."

He rolled off the stretcher. Kim saw the trees. He started moving into the bushes with some of the other men, following as the Germans moved in. Two of the men made it with him into the brush. The rest were putting their hands up. Kim kept stumbling forward trying to clear his head, forcing himself to think about where he was.

~

Captain Takahashi made his way back toward regimental HQ with the other wounded. He had been hit in the arm by machine gun fire and made it as far as an engineering company, which took him away in a jeep. They had also stumbled around in the dark and lost their way. He heard the report coming over the radio. It was Singles, talking to Pence.

"Do you know our situation?"

"Sir, we have A and C on the left and a few men in the buildings in town. B and D are on the north side. We finally managed to have our men fed. We are being attacked on the left. We had a party of litter bearers, also 20 POWs, and Kim was on the litter train when they met a superior force. Kim managed to escape but A Company commander and Lieutenant Sakamoto are probably captured. I came from A and B and they are able to hold."

"Do the best you can on the town. Is Kim hurt?"

"Yes. Captain Kim managed to escape but he's badly wounded."

~

Kim is down? Singles handed the radio receiver back to his radioman and took a deep breath. Dahlquist ordered them to hold out. But they had been promised reinforcements. He knew he couldn't hold much longer. The rumble of heavy armor broke the uneasy silence. He could hear and then see reinforcements starting to move into the village, pushing the enemy back.

Singles felt the weight of the situation bearing down on him. It would be difficult for the men to accept the loss of Kim. They all thought he was invincible. His boys were falling one by one. There would be no replacements. They would have to keep moving forward. Singles could still hear Dahlquist's rasping voice in his head. *"Hold Biffontaine. Push forward."*

He rubbed his eyes. *Who will lead from the front while the generals give orders from the back?* They held Biffontaine, but almost every main company grade officer was down. They lost Kim, their operations and planning officer. They lost twenty-one men killed in action, one hundred twenty-two wounded, and eighteen captured. Even the rumbling American tanks couldn't change that. And they still weren't through the forests of the Vosge.

CHAPTER 59

October 25, 1944
100th/442nd Regimental Command Post
Belmont, France

The village of Belmont, surrounded by small farms and lumbering operations, was not that far from Biffontaine. But it might as well have been the other side of the world, as far as the men of the 100th/442nd were concerned. Canvas tents enclosing hot showers provided welcome relief to the grime and sweat of the last few days. Supply brought in new wool socks.

Tug walked over to see what was available. He could hear some of the men muttering as they rummaged through the replacement issue. It was mostly clothing designed for the Women's Army Corps, as they still didn't have the necessary sizes to fit the small statured men in the combat team. Tug grabbed socks. He wasn't going to take women's underwear. He walked back to change his socks and pin the extra pair to his own underwear. It helped keep the extra pair dry, but only if their uniforms weren't soaked through.

~

Colonel Pence and Gordon Singles were talking in the command post when General Dahlquist walked in with Lt. Gen. Alexander Patch, commanding general of the Seventh Army. It didn't take long before Dahlquist made it clear there was a major problem. He said he would reluctantly have to send the 442nd's Second Battalion and the 100th back into the field. Pence tried to listen without losing his temper.

"Sir, my boys are exhausted. They've been in combat for eight straight days. We barely got out of Biffontaine with our asses intact."

"Colonel, look, I don't want to do this but there isn't a lot of choice here. Part of the 1st Battalion of the 141st is in trouble, boys from Texas. As they were moving to Biffontaine to reinforce your boys, they may have moved too far to the northeast in this damn forest. They're surrounded. It's Company C, Company A, and part of Company B. Near as we can tell there's about 275 men that the Jerries have encircled."

Singles listened quietly. The 141st and the 143rd had relieved them after they had been surrounded in Biffontaine. He knew how those boys got themselves into this. You couldn't see anything in the forest, especially in the dark.

Pence looked at Dahlquist and Patch. Dahlquist's face had a determined expression. *"Colonel, send the 2nd Battalion in tomorrow. They'll join with the 3rd Battalion of the 141st. We need to bring those boys out."*

Pence looked at Singles, who was listening quietly without expression, then he turned to Dahlquist.

"Yes, sir. We'll get them out."

Dahlquist nodded. *"We all do what we have to do, Colonel."*

Pence looked at his regimental officers. He knew what they were thinking. *Some have to do more than others.*

~

Everybody in camp knew that 2nd Battalion had been ordered out, but nobody knew why. Nobody had any illusions. It was only a matter of time until they got sent up. Colonel Singles took meetings with officers all afternoon, and their grim faces told the whole story. As the officers talked to their sergeants, the word began to trickle down to the privates. It didn't seem possible that they were going back in so soon, but so far only the 2nd had gone. The rest of them were glad to get as much time as they could just to rest and eat.

Yuki came back to talk to Company B's squad leaders. The 100th was going in sometime after midnight to support the 2nd Battalion. The men needed to get ready. All he knew was the 141st Regiment had run into some heavy opposition, and the 100th/442nd was being called forward to help. They had been promised several days' rest. They only had one.

Tug walked into the barn where Sammy, Freddy, Bobby, and Akiro sat playing cards.

"Yuki says we go at midnight. You guys need to get some sleep. Check your gear. Carry as much ammo as you can." He looked outside. Light snow was falling, covering the encampment with a veil of white. "It's going to be cold."

He sat down to write a letter to his parents that he had been putting off. Tug looked down at the scrawled words. He wasn't good with letters and besides, it was bad luck to think every letter could be your last. Still, he wanted his Mom to be reassured. He signed the letter and folded it for the envelope. He put it in his shirt pocket. He would mail it later.

~

It was shortly past midnight as Sammy pulled on his gear. His body ached in places he never even thought about. He heard Freddy mumbling about the cold. Tendrils of fog reached into the barn and the straw was sodden. There wasn't a dry place to sit, even inside. Outside, he saw that the snow had slowly deepened with the night.

Both men moved out with Bobby and Akiro to take their place in the line. Movement around him began to take on the shape of men as his eyes adjusted to the blackness. Yuki walked down the line, handing out pieces of torn white toilet paper. "Pin this on the back of the man in front of you." The paper would be something they could see in the dark.

Truck engines rumbled as a line of ambulances and aid stations moved into position while the men formed ranks. The drivers of the trucks with the red cross painted on the side looked over at the men slowly shuffling. The men in line watched as the ambulance drivers turned their faces away when their eyes locked with the drivers. Wherever they were going, it was evident that somebody expected a lot of casualties.

They marched with heavy steps. Fatigue had taken their legs. Each man held onto the pack strap of the man in front of him. It wasn't long before they were moving up a road, slipping in the slick mud and tripping over holes hidden by the dark. When one man went down he took several with him, dominos slowly toppling.

Swirling mist transformed the men into vague shapes, slowly disappearing into the fog. Towering trees reduced the few slivers of moonlight able to penetrate through the forest. Sammy shivered as the damp seeped through his jacket and into his uniform. His underwear began to chafe and he felt the burning sensation of raw patches on his legs. Nobody talked. It took too much energy and they were too busy looking around, waiting for the enemy to attack.

Freddy lifted his feet out of the muck, step by step. He felt the mud building on his boots and the damp soaking through to his socks and feet, which were already starting to swell. It had only been a few hours.

Yuki looked back at Second Platoon. The roadway narrowed so severely that the 100th moved off the road and down to the right. The 3rd Battalion took the center and the 2nd Battalion the left. Rain drizzled through the mist and trees as he led the platoon through the heavy forest. By the time they stopped and dug in, they were too tired to eat. Some were even too tired to sleep.

~

The men had been marching since well before dawn. Finally, they were allowed a two-hour rest. Yuki asked Second Platoon for a final ammunition check. The trucks following them bogged down in the mud, sinking to the axles. The morning light was so dim that visibility provided very little security.

They started to pass men lying motionless in foxholes, their war over. The 141st had fought hard. The men looked at the dead soldiers, the morning mist beading on their cold faces, lips blue and hair slick with icy spikes. Sammy stared silently as they saw frozen soldiers lying against the dirt walls. He knew, every man knew, they were the replacements. They were close to the enemy. The grave detail followed behind them.

Yuki couldn't see far enough ahead to feel like he had any sense of what was going to happen. He heard it first, the thumping sound of German 88s opening up. Tree tops shattered into deadly splinters as the 88s cut their crowns. Then the sound of machine guns reverberated, but they couldn't see where it was coming from. Men were beginning to go down, but they couldn't see where to fire. The mist held them inside its shroud, sound and sight directionless, fire all around them and nowhere to be seen. All the men tried to find cover while the rattle of German machine guns kept them from moving forward, slowly slicing men away, sliver by sliver.

∼

The 100th, the 2nd and the 3rd moved very slowly. Resistance was heavy and losses were mounting. German machine guns kept the men pinned down most of the time on their bellies, crawling through the mud and brush. By nightfall, the 100th gained 900 feet. Sammy and the rest of Second Squad dug trenches in the rocky ground. It was slow going. Eventually they got enough earth shoved aside to make a slit trench, which they covered with branches as thick as they could find or cut.

Forward scouts crawled back to the position. At the sound of their movement they were hit by machine gun fire from their own boys. Shouts of "*shi-shi-ni*" ("442") and "*bakatare*" ("asshole") came back as the forward scouts squirmed into their lines. Ahead lay nothing but Jerries. The only security was the dark where nobody could move.

∼

At dawn, Lieutenant Colonel Singles moved the 100th forward. He could see that the 3rd and the 100th were in between two hills, with an open area in the saddle between them. Both battalions moved down and across the saddle. They were without cover.

Yuki motioned the men in Second Platoon to move forward. He was now in command of the platoon. The platoon had lost half their officers, but at least he now knew why they were up here. A lost battalion of men from the 141st were encircled somewhere up ahead. He talked to his squad leaders to let them know they had to get those boys out.

Yuki led the platoon across while the other platoons moved abreast. The Germans waited until they were almost across before opening up. Shells fell all around them and men were going down. The 100th pulled back to the opposite side of the saddle. It was right where the Germans expected them to run. The shelling lasted an hour. The men scraped and clawed their way into any cover they could find. Anything that would give them some protection.

Second Squad scrambled back to the cover of trees on the opposite hill. Sammy and Freddy ran ahead, followed by Bobby and Akiro. Akiro felt a white-hot pain shoot through his back and then, nothing. He could tell he was flying through the air, but it was like his body was in water. There was no pain. When he hit the ground, he could see the sky. He couldn't move and lay on the muddy ground while mortar rounds fell around him. He stared up at the dark gray sky as big drops of rain hit his face. But there was no pain, just the roar of the artillery, the sound of men screaming. He couldn't help thinking how peaceful he felt. He wondered what his parents were doing now. Manzanar seemed a lifetime ago. How miserable he had been in that wooden room, with the wind whistling through the walls. And all that dust. He closed his eyes. He could see his mother now.

The 100th moved across the open ground, leaving their dead and wounded to the medics. Freddy saw that Akiro was not moving before Tug pulled him forward.

Yuki moved out in front of Second Platoon, toward Colonel Singles on the ridge ahead. They were now down to two second lieutenants and two sergeants.

"Sergeant Watanabe, you're taking command of Company B. Lieutenant Boodry is dead and Lieutenant Pye is wounded. Listen, we're going to be okay. We're going to move forward—"

Singles was interrupted by his radioman. "It's a message from division, sir."

Singles looked at the field telephone and pulled the wire loose. He didn't have time to listen to Dahlquist now and was so angry he could hardly talk.

"We have to keep moving. Just keep the boys going forward." Singles looked at the men who now had command of his companies. "Do the best you can. I'll be here with you. I'm sending a patrol back for more ammo and supplies. We'll carry the wounded back down."

~

By late afternoon the three battalions pushed forward another thousand feet. They could see a line of fire spread across the hill. The enemy was dug in directly in front of them and there was no way around the entrenched line. They could only go through it. Yuki led Company B straight ahead. Companies A and C were right beside them. Sammy saw Tug walking, firing from the hip while he moved forward. The Germans had a roadblock along the line of the ridge. It would be only moments before they engaged.

Sammy felt Freddy next to him as they plunged into the underbrush. Germans defenders were shooting at them. They were so close Sammy could see the stubble on the faces of the enemy, shooting and falling back, shooting and falling back. Freddy swept his BAR back and forth through the brush, tearing apart leaves, branches, and anything behind them. Men in gray uniforms tumbled and fell as both of them fired as fast as they could.

Sammy kept pushing forward, firing from the hip while he moved, ignoring writhing men on the ground, guttural cries in German mixing with the screaming men of Second Platoon, ripping at anything in front of him that moved.

Finally, the enemy fell back. Both Sammy and Freddy looked at one another. There was only Tug, Bobby, and them left in the squad. Behind them lay what had once been Second Platoon. Across the open ground, pieces of Company B were all that was left for Yuki to command.

~

At dusk, Dahlquist made Lt. Col. Virgil Miller regimental commander of the 100th/442nd. Colonel Pence was down. The steady rain turned the ground into a quagmire. Rations and ammunition were moved by hand. The dead and wounded could no longer be carried back in trucks. They had to be carried down the hill by litter bearers. Only two lieutenants were left to lead the 100th, along with its battalion commander.

Miller listened over the radio to Dahlquist's latest order. *"Rescue the First Battalion and drive the Jerries south of the ridge. Your objective is that ridge and push out to the south."* Miller handed the phone back to his radioman. Fatigue was in every part of his body. He felt his neck tighten listening to Dahlquist. They were his boys now, and he was losing them with every foot of the hill.

429

⁓

The ridge above the Biffontaine-La Houssiere Valley was cloaked in dark gray. Stinging sleet and cold rain drenched the open area at the top of the ridge. From far below, the fierce sound of battling men echoed, muted at first, blunted by the dense forest, but growing louder slowly. Whatever was happening down below was growing closer.

Tall, lanky, and sharp-featured, 1st Lt. Marty Higgins looked out from the entrenched position where the Alamo Regiment of the Texas Division was trapped and surrounded. The perimeter of the entrenched position of the 264 men he now commanded was a morass of shattered tree limbs and shell-pocked, muddy ground.

The Germans had been probing them all day, with scattered shots and intense focused attacks that were sapping the strength of the men. The wounded were increasing. Higgins had men badly disabled by trench foot due to the constant damp. They could hardly walk but were still willing to fight.

Higgins tried to stare through the fog to see any movement down the hill, any emerging shadows and any outlines of soldiers. All he could see were the immobile shadows of trees that drifted back into a surrounding gray wall. There wasn't a choice. His men had to fight and he had to lead them.

There was no one over the rank of lieutenant left, but the other officers agreed to put Higgins in charge. He thought about his last message to command: *"Out of food and water, critically low on ammunition. Medical supplies next to nothing, wounded need attention. No way to evacuate."*

Radio batteries were low and Higgins had to conserve them. He had just given Lieutenant Blonder the order to send one more message: *"Contact with enemy forces at three different points. Twenty-eight wounded. Request artillery on enemy positions on Bois de Biffontaine, southeast of Devant le Feys."*

It was a calculated risk. The artillery rounds were dropping close to them. If they didn't already know, the enemy would soon find how thin Alamo Regiment's perimeter was. When they did, Higgins's command would be overrun. He continued to stare out at the fog. *Maybe volunteers to try and break through?*

The Corporal sat in a hole near the middle of the perimeter that he and some of the other men had dug. It was a long way from Texas and even further from the small town where he grew up. The ground was hard and rocky. He used his bayonet and folding shovel to dig a hole as deep in the frozen ground as he could.

Some of the men cut tree limbs with their bayonets and penknives, pulling the limbs over the top of their trenches to protect against the constant tree bursts from incoming German artillery and mortars. He couldn't get used to the sound of the splintering wood and the torrent of searing shrapnel that rained down on them, ripping everything in its path. The idea of trees falling from above like spears was something he couldn't get out of his mind—the explosion and burst of red flame and black smoke, then the sound of metal and wood splinters shredding leaves, then wood, then men. He watched the medics pull shards of wood out of men, saw the jagged gaping holes, heard the cries of pain that even morphine couldn't silence. Now the forest was as much an enemy as the Germans.

The Corporal listened to the rumbling in his stomach, feeling the twisting pain in his bowels from diarrhea that had been eating away at his insides for the last two days. He was very hungry, but the thought of eating made him nauseated. They hadn't eaten fresh rations for three days. What water they had was tinged with algae. During the night, he and a few of the others crawled down the hill to a depression where water had settled. They filled as many canteens as they could while others kept their rifles ready. The enemy was filling their canteens from the same slime-rimmed hole. It wasn't a neutral place. Either side would kill the other if caught. It didn't matter how the water tasted or looked, it was wet.

It seemed so long ago that he had been soaking up the sun, working in the fields and complaining about the heat. *What I wouldn't give now for some of that heat.* He had never been so cold for so long. The skin on his feet was gray and pasty. Already he was loosening the laces of his boots because of the swelling. He looked toward the perimeter and the young lieutenant standing at the edge. There wasn't much difference in their ages. The Corporal felt a twinge of pity for him.

The Corporal folded the letter to his parents and put it in the breast pocket of his shirt. Maybe it would be found, maybe not. At this point it was obvious to him and the others that sooner or later they were going to have to fight. If he made it out, he would keep the letter. If he didn't, then he hoped somebody would make sure his folks got it. He listened to the whispered conversations between a few of the men nearby. There were supposed to be units coming to get them, but nobody knew if they would arrive in time.

All day long they heard the gunfire raging below them. They even smelled the burned gunpowder drifting up the ridge. He let his mind drift away from the conversation. He kept thinking about when he was a boy, how he wished he had spent more time with his dad. He resented his father's expectation that he should always work when he wanted to play ball. All his father ever talked about was the farm. He just wasn't interested in it. *I might not be able to make that time up to him now.*

He crawled into a trench and huddled under his blankets, trying to stay warm. He was too tired to care about the tree bursts anymore and too tense to sleep. In a couple of hours it would be his turn to take the watch. Down below, the rattle of gunfire finally tapered off with the night. Men were fighting down there. Men were coming for them. They had to hold on.

CHAPTER 60

October 29, 1944
100th/442nd
The Ridge Above Biffontaine-La Houssiere Valley, France

The early dawn of Sunday morning did little to enhance visibility under the trees. The nighttime blackness grudgingly gave way to dim gray apparitions of trees and muted battle sounds floating through the forest. The fog settled over the men while freezing rain fell, a gray shadow-world hiding the enemy behind dripping clouds.

The 2nd, the 3rd, and the 100th were on a narrow ridge. The sides dropped off steeply, almost like cliffs. The men moved carefully, scrambling and grabbing at gnarled tree and branch roots jutting from steep rocky ground, leaning into the sharply rising earth, digging in their boots to keep balance step by labored step.

Company B was down to seventy-six men, Company A seventy-seven, and Company C eighty. More than fifty percent dead and wounded losses since Biffontaine. Yet still they moved forward. Tug was exhausted. It was hard to move at all. It was even harder when he looked around and saw that most of the squad was gone.

The night had brought only exhausted restlessness, minds drifting on the edges of sleep because every sound brought the potential of attack. The screaming meemies shrieked overhead, exploding wherever the enemy thought they might be. Mortar rounds came whistling in sporadically.

They were so close to the German lines that often they weren't sure which side of the line they were on.

In the middle of the night one of the men had just about fallen asleep in his foxhole when he felt another soldier climb in and huddle next to him. He was too tired to care. It was a body for sharing heat. When they woke up in the morning, he realized the other man was a German soldier. They took him prisoner.

German machine guns covered the area above the ridge. Yuki looked at the men struggling to take that ground. He knew they were all in bad shape. Some of the men had diarrhea from the cold, greasy rations. Others were struggling with trench foot. Slowed by heavy resistance, casualties were mounting in the already thinned ranks.

Singles couldn't make out much through the heavy forest, but he knew the enemy was out there. The 100th had not made much progress. The 3rd also made no headway, already passing through an open area where mines left substantial casualties. They had to be close, less than a thousand yards from the trapped battalion, but it was obvious they were going to pay for every foot.

In the thin light of early afternoon, Singles spotted a German machine gun position through the underbrush. He felt a presence behind him and turned to see General Dahlquist standing there with his aide, Lt. Wells Lewis. It startled him to see the two stars on the general's helmet. Division commanders didn't normally lead from this close, but he wasn't sure that it was going to be an improvement over Dahlquist's constant badgering over the radio.

"Singles, have you got a map?" Singles shook his head. Boodry had the terrain map and he was dead.

"I need a map."

"Yes, sir." Singles walked back to his radioman to have a map brought forward.

Lieutenant Lewis moved in front of Dahlquist. *"I have one, sir."* He reached inside his jacket and then pitched forward as a machine gun burst sprayed the area. Dahlquist caught Lewis as he fell to the ground. Singles looked back and then turned and kept walking. *Men die, even aides to generals.*

He moved over to survey the situation through his binoculars. He glanced over when Dahlquist approached. The General's uniform was sprayed with blood from Lewis's wound. Singles could see the ashen look on Dahlquist's face as he stood near him.

"Wells is dead."

Singles nodded. "Yes, sir."

"He was Sinclair Lewis's son, the author." Singles nodded, thinking, *Everybody out here is somebody's son.* He kept silent. Finally Dahlquist turned and walked back toward the rear. Singles kept his attention forward until he heard Dahlquist's voice, again asking if he had a map. Singles remembered that he did have Boodry's map. He pulled it out and handed it to the General.

Dahlquist walked back to the radioman and began calling in coordinates. Singles shook his head. They hadn't been using radios for most tactical maneuvers because the enemy could intercept the transmissions. They used runners or field telephones if they could keep the wire from being cut.

Singles overheard the conversation. *There's something wrong. It's the coordinates. Dahlquist is calling in artillery fire directly on the location of the trapped battalion!* He waited until Dahlquist walked back down the hill and got on the radio. He could hear Lt. Col. Henderson of the 552nd Artillery questioning the coordinates with the forward observer.

Singles interjected. "That plots right in the middle of the lost battalion!"

The forward observer interrupted. "The general wants us to fire on that point."

Singles snapped an order. "We're not going to fire on those coordinates." He didn't have time to be relieved that he caught the mistake. Obviously Dahlquist was shaken by the death of his aide, but he had come dangerously close to shelling the men they were trying to save.

He didn't have time to worry about it. One of his sergeants reported that Germans had circled behind the 100th, firing at the backs of the men as they moved forward. The field telephone lines were cut. He sent runners for what was left of his three companies. The only course of action was to move forward—to attack—to push as close to the lost battalion as possible. They would deal with the Germans behind them as they pushed forward.

Lieutenant Colonel Pursall looked up the hill ahead of the 3rd. The enemy was in an entrenched line across the hill, machine gun nests and mortars sweeping fire across the 3rd's position. He called for artillery. The trees caught the incoming rounds. The road was too narrow for the tanks to move any closer. Only a frontal assault was possible. He knew what that meant to his already decimated ranks. The 100th moved along the flank of the ridge below him, but they were running into stiff resistance. Pursall stared up the steep ridge. He called forward the cooks and clerks. Whoever could carry a rifle, must.

By midafternoon, the 3rd and the 100th had moved almost a thousand yards since dawn. Dahlquist ordered the 3rd to push through and finally, exasperated at the slow progress, he came up himself to prod Pursall. At this point, the commander of the 3rd had his fill of Dahlquist.

"Yes, sir?"

The short, stocky Dahlquist leaned into the chest of the six-foot, five-inch Pursall, looking up at the younger regimental commander. His voice came out in a rasping bark.

"We're close. You need to get these men moving forward."

Pursall motioned for the General to come with him to the edge of the tree line.

"Sir, we are pinned down. Company K has taken heavy losses and the Jerries are entrenched up above us." Both men stayed low because of the constant rattle of machine gun fire from the German positions.

Dahlquist looked up the hill, his face reddening, the veins on his thick neck visibly throbbing. *"You need to send your men up that hill, Colonel."*

Pursall looked down at the face of the division commander. *"Sir, I'm not sending my boys up that hill by themselves. I'll lead them. I'll give the orders to them."*

He got on the radio and called for tank fire on the German position. He waited until tanks had poured in heavy fire, then gave orders to the lieutenant in charge of K Company, Lt. Ed Davis. Davis rose up, clutching his stomach from the pain of diarrhea. The men could hear him yelling, *"FOLLOW ME!"*

The roar of enemy machine guns splintered the air as the men began to crawl forward. Pursall walked down, following Company K while the men advanced, shooting from the hip, slowly pushing up the hill. He jumped into the lead, his pearl-handled .45 automatic in one hand and a dark blue .45 in the other. He wasn't wearing a helmet. He turned to his men.

"LET'S GO, BOYS!"

The 3rd rose as one and began charging up the hill. Cries of "bastards" and "sons of bitches" could be heard across the line, mixed in with shouts of "*Make!*" ("death," in Hawaiian) and "*You baka, you bakayaro!*" ("You lose, you assholes!"). The men surged forward all the way to the tree line, pushing the Germans back.

Japanese bodies fell over German bodies. Men writhed together in agony, their cries a mélange of German, Japanese, and English. The 3rd pushed relentlessly, firing, firing, men stumbling over the man ahead who was down. Shrapnel from mortar rounds caught men from behind. Machine gun fire swept the ragged line as the 3rd surged forward, throwing grenades, men firing their submachine guns, drawing the barrel across the enemy positions, shredding anything in the path of the Tommy guns.

The Germans began to fall back in the face of the maddened charge and, at last, Company I and Company K made it to the top. It was 3:45 p.m., and the 3rd held the high ground. The Germans fell back, but Pursall looked around at what was left. The hill below was strewn with the dead and dying of his command. He called for the field telephone. There was still the ridge ahead.

"We have no officers left in K Company. We are up the hill but may get kicked off. There's a road block and we took a lot of casualties. We have to get that roadblock knocked out." He could hear Dahlquist on the line.

"The 141st is moving up. They say they are getting tank fire. Is it yours?"

"It could be but we have to shoot our way up. An enemy tank is coming in from the south." Pursall needed reinforcements and he needed them now.

Dahlquist came back on. *"We are sending an engineer company toward you. It's all we have. How is Singles doing?"*

He wasn't doing any better than they were. *"He is up against the same thing. The Germans are well dug in. We have many casualties. How about some infantry help? I have men down all over the ridge."*

"I can only give you engineers." Pursall handed the field telephone back to his communications man. He needed infantrymen.

Pursall looked at his men, holding a thin line in the black light of the forest. Except for him, almost all officers were dead or wounded. Sergeants were in command of companies. Seventeen men were left in K Company, and forty-five were dead or wounded in I Company. He needed boots on the ground now—riflemen, not engineers or cooks or clerks.

~

At 9:00 p.m., Yuki sat with Tug, Sammy, Freddy, and Bobby. They ate quietly from cold rations. It was so dark that they could barely make out whoever sat next to them. The rain started again, the cold water dripping off their helmets and sliding in rivulets down their ponchos. Colonel Singles was down. All the men in the 100th knew it. His jeep had taken a mortar round and he was wounded. One of the men with him was killed. There were only two lieutenants between the three companies. Yuki was the ranking sergeant. They had a little more than 200 men left.

Sammy scraped out a trench in the rocky soil and crawled in, pulling branches over the top. Freddy was on watch. The tree bursts shattered the silence of the night. The battle had become one long roar of deadly sound that changed only by the fall of darkness. The sound never ceased, the fear never left. He shivered in the biting cold and pulled his feet inside his poncho, pulled his blankets around him, and breathed down into his jacket to help keep himself warm. In the distance he heard a guttural sound that was hard to make out. It was a wounded German crying for help. He heard a hoarse "*wasser, wasser,*" over and over again. He closed his eyes until the only sound was the tree bursts.

~

The German artillery shattered the morning, breaking the brief respite of stillness that arrived with the dawn. At dawn, Yuki moved among the men of Company B, a thin skim of snow dusting the ground. The cold rain had finally turned. He heard the frozen mud crunching under his boots as he moved from foxhole to foxhole, reaching in and rustling the shoulder of whoever was closest to the opening. Always the same three words, "We're moving up." It was hard to tell the difference between night and day, except by his watch. The forest was so heavy that its canopy let very little light come through. What light there was only strengthened the feeling of being closed in.

Freddy slept in the trench with Sammy. He leaned back and pulled his legs inside his poncho and blankets, reaching for his canteen to wash some of the film from his mouth. The water was frozen solid. Even the water that had seeped overnight into the trench was frozen solid.

"Sammy, you got any water? Mine's frozen."

"Yeah, I put my canteen inside my poncho."

Freddy crawled out of the hole and crouched. He dug through the few rations he had left and took out a chocolate bar. He looked down at Sammy.

"You going to marry my sister?"

The shadows didn't hide the startled look on Sammy's face. "Why you asking that now?"

"I don't know. You and me . . ." Sammy stared at Freddy's face, thinner now, almost gaunt. Freddy reached a hand down to pull Sammy up out of the trench. "You and me . . . we're like brothers. I need you to know that."

Sammy wrapped his hand around Freddy's wrist. "I've always known that."

Freddy's eyes fixed on Sammy's puzzled expression. "Guess I've been thinking a lot about home, the folks. I decided I'm going to marry Rose."

Sammy nodded. Freddy never talked about things like this. Home— that was something he didn't want to think about right now. Freddy turned his head away.

"You think we'll get to those guys today?" Only the day before had they learned that the unit they were trying to reach was completely surrounded.

"I don't know. We're pretty close, but if the Jerries have much up ahead we don't have many men."

Freddy was silent for a moment. "We got enough."

Tug motioned to the two of them. "Let's go."

German artillery was getting heavier. The 100th pushed abreast of the 3rd. Yuki moved out ahead while the 552nd Artillery dropped rounds in front of them. Second Platoon moved up the hill but it wasn't much, only fifteen men left. There were only seventy-six in the whole of B Company. It was the fifth day on the hill. They were close, less than a thousand yards from the lost battalion.

Snow was falling as the men moved their aching bodies into the dark gloom again. Sammy's fingers were so cold they tingled. He had to be careful touching the metal of the rifle for fear his fingertips would stick to the gun and freeze. More than one man the last few days had left the skin of his fingers on the barrel of his weapon.

They were within five hundred yards of the crest of the ridge where the Texas boys were trapped. The Germans laid down heavy smoke. Company B pushed forward through the acrid fumes, each man blinking his eyes against the burning smoke. Each man knew German tactics—the smoke would precede an assault.

Tug moved ahead, motioning for his squad to follow on him through the small open area to the trees ahead. Sammy saw movement through the trees, across the open area. He raised his rifle and started firing, advancing steadily. He spotted a German up ahead, moving across his line of fire. He aimed and followed him with his rifle, leading the Jerry, waiting before he squeezed the trigger.

Sammy felt the impact on his body from behind, sucking the wind out of him, knocking him to the ground. *It isn't like I expected it to be.* He felt like he had been hit by a two by four. He reached out to break his fall, one hand searching for the wound. Freddy stepped over him. He could see Freddy's mouth moving, but his ears felt like they were closed.

"I told you to keep your ass down, you stupid son of a bitch!" Freddy was standing in front of him, sweeping the area with his BAR. He had hit Sammy from behind with the butt of the Browning to knock him down.

Sammy saw Tug off to the right, crouched down as machine gun fire stitched the ground around them. He kept feeling for a wound but couldn't find it. Dirt and sharp splinters of rock stung his face, and he instinctively covered his eyes. Tug motioned forward. The thud of bullets hitting the trunks of trees and ripping the evergreens filled the air. Green needles from the trees rained down, the cries of a man down and then another pierced the roar of German machine gun fire. They were so close.

The next moment seemed to imprint itself on his mind. Freddy crouched in front of him, firing and yelling. Then Freddy slowly slid backwards, sitting down. It was like he had just decided to rest. A stunned look crossed his face. He turned and looked back at Sammy, shaking his head. His mouth was moving but nothing came out, only a thin trickle of blood seeping from the corner. He laid back against Sammy, who pulled him over. Their faces were very close. Sammy put his hand on Freddy's chest. He could feel the warm stickiness soaking his sleeve and hand.

Freddy's mouth parted in a half-smile. "I told you to keep your ass down." It was difficult to understand him, pinkish froth was coming out of his mouth. "You never listen."

His breath was coming in short gasps. His chest made a sucking sound.

"You have to go."

"No, I'm not leaving you here."

Bobby crouched down next to them and pulled on Sammy's sleeve. He was screaming. "WE HAVE TO MOVE FORWARD!"

He, too, could see the wound in Freddy's chest. "Sammy, there's no cover here."

Sammy looked up at him with a vacant expression, like he didn't know where he was. The sound of bullets ricocheting off the stony ground and hissing through the air near his head kept him low.

Bobby reached down and grabbed Freddy's sleeve. "Come on." Both he and Sammy pulled Freddy toward the cover of trees, out of the open, his blood staining the frozen ground. Bobby helped lay Freddy down as carefully as possible. He looked at Sammy and spoke as gently as he could.

"We have to move forward."

Freddy looked up and nodded. "They'll come get me. You got to go forward." He was choking as he tried to talk. "Tell Rose . . ."

Sammy leaned as close as he could to Freddy's mouth, but it was Tug's voice he heard.

"Goddamn it, Sammy, come on. Freddy's gone." Tug stopped for a brief moment, realizing what he had just said. It didn't matter—there was no time for compassion.

"You gonna get killed here. We got to move forward."

Sammy looked down at his best friend, the man he had known all his life. He drew his bloodstained hands across Freddy's chest, trying to push the life back in. There was no more light in his eyes. He put his mouth close to Freddy and whispered, "I'll bring you home, Freddy. I promise."

Sammy reached into Freddy's pocket and took out the letter that he knew was there—the last letter home that they all carried. He pressed his cheek against Freddy's forehead, feeling the warmth slowly fading, drawing a last moment with his best friend. All he could feel was overwhelming emptiness. For the first time in his life he felt alone. There was no sound of battle, no screaming men. Only emptiness.

~

The Texas Battalion, Alamo Regiment, Above Biffontaine

Lieutenant Higgins looked around his perimeter. Dahlquist radioed that he should try to send a patrol down to break through to the men coming up the hill. Before he could give the order, the besieged men were attacked on three sides. He looked over at his machine gunners. They were pouring fire into the forest, sweeping anything that moved. The enemy was pressing in hard. They hadn't hit them this hard before. He didn't know how much longer they could hold.

The Corporal wasn't used to the machine guns. He laid out the ammo belts as fast as he could, trying to keep the feed steady while the gunner moved the machine gun from side to side. His mind was clear and his hands were steady. The men on either side of him kept intently on their task—to keep the machine gun a living, deadly weapon. Whether they lived or died was going to be decided very shortly and they all knew it. The Corporal thought for a moment about his parents, about his sister and her new baby. He hoped somebody would find his letter.

Finally, the firing tapered off. The smoke from the German positions had not led to an attack. The men watched the trees, waiting for another probe.

Through the fog and dim light it was difficult to make anything out. One of the men pointed at men moving from tree to tree. They had been told if men came in from a specific point that they should hold their fire and take them prisoner, in case they were Americans. Their boys had to be close. The only thing that was clear was the helmets of the men moving carefully up the last yards of the hill to the perimeter of the embattled Alamo Regiment—their helmets were too big for them. The men were small, very small, almost like boys wearing their father's clothes.

Somebody said, *"Holy crap, are we fightin' Japs?"* The other men told him to shut up. They knew who these boys were. They were the 100th/442nd. They were Americans.

Yuki peered through the dim light trying to make out the position of the Texas boys. At this point, his biggest concern was to keep them from shooting his men. He moved carefully from bush to bush, trying to keep his profile low. They were close, maybe fifty yards. He looked back and could make out Tug's bulk as he led what was left of his squad up the hill.

Yuki moved as carefully as he could through the trees, watching the position ahead of him. He knew the lost battalion was there. He saw men from the 3rd moving cautiously inside the perimeter. He felt the eyes of men watching him from behind brush and logs that lay over the shattered open area. After a while, he straightened up and moved quickly toward the dim shapes watching him from dug-in positions.

The faces of the men in the first foxhole were drawn and streaked with dirt. He saw from the way they looked at him that they had not fully realized that American troops had broken through. All of a sudden he felt arms encircling him, hugging him. He heard one of his men ask. "You boys want a cigarette?"

Quickly, other men began moving through the heavy mist and walking among the Alamo Regiment. They stared at the men still in foxholes looking back at them and grinning, faces black from dirt and gunpowder.

Sammy watched the few men from the 3rd making their way into the area where the Texas Division, the Alamo Regiment, were crawling out of trenches. The thought went through his mind that they had made it. He had made it. But hanging on the edge of that thought was the realization of who had not. He thought he would have a different feeling when they made it here, but he felt drained of emotion, used up.

Sammy and the rest of the squad walked across the trenches to the outside perimeter. German snipers and the sound of the 2nd battalion, staving off a German counterattack, could be heard from the other side of the ridge.

As he walked inside the line of the Alamo Regiment he saw the faces of men worn down by the stress of combat—tired, weary faces. There weren't that many men here. They were dug in over an area no more than 300 yards wide. Most were so filthy that the whites of their eyes and their teeth were a stark contrast to their mud-encrusted uniforms and dirt-blackened faces.

Men climbed out of foxholes slowly and met with the first advance of the 100th/442nd. The larger men of the Alamo grasped at the small brown men working their way through the encircled position, hugging them, some crying.

Sammy looked at the face of one grinning soldier who reached up with a grime-covered hand, waiting until Sammy would take it. As he reached out toward the man, his eyes focused on the blood crusted on his own fingernails. He touched the outstretched hand and pulled back, barely acknowledging the gesture. The realization that it was Freddy's blood on his hands, blood from the last moments of his friend, began to scroll through his mind in scattered flashes of memory. Freddy died for these men—these strangers. His childhood friend, his best friend, and none of these men would know it. How could they know what had been given by so many for so few?

It was all rushing back to him—Manzanar, the barbed wire, the faces of his parents, and, most of all, the face of his friend lying on the frozen ground a few hundred yards below. He kept looking at his bloodstained hands. It wasn't the fault of these men, and he knew it, but he just couldn't find the spot in his heart that would make room for their gratitude. *Maybe later but not now.* He turned and saw Tug sharing his canteen with a man in a foxhole. Bobby pulled out cigarettes while men took them with shaking hands.

The Corporal stared as Sammy walked to the edge of the outpost. Sammy saw the Corporal watching him, the muddy course of tears down his face, drawing lines in the heavy black stubble of his beard. The Corporal was by himself, alone in his foxhole, hands on his rifle. He didn't make any effort to come out of his dirt sanctuary. He just stared, the whites of his eyes glowing through the dirt and grime. For some reason Sammy couldn't ignore him, as he had the others. There was something in his eyes that made him different. He heard the voice, the lilt of an accent he hadn't heard for so long.

"You boys with the Japanese battalion?"

Sammy looked down. He couldn't keep the tinge of bitterness out of his voice.

"Yeah, what's left of us."

The black eyes staring back didn't blink. "Thank you for gettin' to us. I don't think we had much time left." It was the voice, the slight Spanish accent. Sammy heard it before, somewhere. He looked more carefully at the dirty-faced man who held out his hand.

"José Duran from San Antonio, Texas."

Sammy took off his helmet, the liner leaving a clean stripe above the rest of his grime covered face. He stared at the face, looking for a familiar feature. He couldn't wrap his memory of José around the haggard man standing in front of him. "José? Is that you? It's me—Sammy Miyaki." It sounded so strange to use his name like that, almost normal, like they were back at school, meeting at the ball field instead of this muddy killing ground.

José looked at the dirt-covered face of the man standing above him. "Sammy?" José climbed out and pulled off his helmet. His black hair was matted and sweat slicked. Now roughened by whiskers that he didn't have back in school, José's face was lean and harsh.

Sammy stood for a moment, looking at his friend. Then he reached out. He felt his body begin to drain as both men sank down on the frozen ground. He could feel José's body shaking against his as the two men knelt in the frozen mud, their heads together, no more words passing between them. They were both shedding tears as men now, tears that as boys neither would have allowed the other to see.

José didn't know what to say. He thought of the men fighting their way up the hill to his unit, but there was no face to any of them. Even the men in his own unit had no faces anymore. He didn't see them when they talked and, he imagined, they didn't see him. They had just become screaming voices. Now it was all back. These were men who had come up for them, and one of them his friend. Thank you wasn't enough. No words were enough.

They stood together until the order came for the men of the Alamo Regiment to go back down the hill. José reached out and embraced Sammy one more time. Sammy told him about Freddy. For a moment they were silent as they both thought about what they had lost. It was too soon to feel the grief that would come. It was too soon to feel anything.

Two hundred and eleven men of the Alamo Regiment slowly walked down the hill. Some were wounded. Many were crying. The rest were either litter cases or dead. They held out for six days, waiting for American boys to make it to them. Some 800 men from the 100th/442nd were killed or wounded climbing up the ridge to save them. But they made it. The men of the 100th/442nd stood silently watching from the top of a ridge they had purchased with their blood.

CHAPTER 61

November 10, 1944
The White House
Washington, D.C.

The November election was over. He had won an unprecedented fourth term. An aged and increasingly infirm President Roosevelt looked around the long, polished table at his cabinet officers. The discussion had gone on long enough. Everyone was agreed. The Secretary of the Interior, Harold Ickes, made it clear that since there was no longer any military necessity for exclusion that there was no basis in law or in equity for the perpetuation of the ban.

Attorney General Biddle, Secretary of War Stimson, the Secretary of State, even Admiral Ernest King, Chief of Naval Operations, and Chief of Staff General Marshall agreed. The military situation no longer justified the mass exclusion of Japanese Americans from the West Coast. Word of the rescue of the Texas Battalion had been all over the news. It was likely the Supreme Court was going to rule against the government on the constitutionality of the exclusions.

Biddle had advised that he thought the Supreme Court, in the Japanese test cases, would turn down the government. It would be wise to lift the exclusion before being forced to do so. It was time to put this whole matter to an end.

The President spoke. *"So it is agreed then? The exclusion orders will be lifted?"* He saw the nods around the table. *"Fine—all right, the Attorney General will develop a plan for implementation."*

The President looked at the Attorney General, who had finally heard agreement to the position he had taken from the beginning. *"How soon, Francis?"*

Biddle did not take any satisfaction in this resolution. *It should never have happened.* *"By mid-December, I think, Mr. President."*

Roosevelt nodded thoughtfully. *"We must be careful about the release of any information. We will approach it cautiously. Perhaps some questions at a news conference—prepare the American people."*

CHAPTER 62

November 12, 1944
Biffontaine, France

General Dahlquist ordered the men to gather so that they could be honored for their actions rescuing the lost battalion on the mountains above Biffontaine. The officers listened quietly. They were devoid of emotion, as were their men. After taking the ridge above Biffontaine-La Houssiere, the men were ordered by Dahlquist to hold the ridge and fight on. For nine more days they struggled through the bitter cold and constant German assaults. The 100th had been further decimated by friendly fire from the 143rd.

Singles was now back on the line with the 100th. Hanley had the 2nd and Pursall had the 3rd. But they commanded battalions that were shadows of what had been. The 100th had 260 men left in four companies. They began at Biffontaine with almost a thousand. The Second Battalion had 333 men remaining. The Third Battalion was a shattered shell, down to four men in one of its companies and the rest with sergeants in command.

When the 100th/442nd started at Bruyeres, they marched 4,000 men and officers strong. Now they had less than 1,200. The rest were wounded or lined up on the snowy ground at Epinal with the dead of the 36th Division. Men were also down with trench foot and exhaustion.

But more than anything, the commanders who listened to Colonel Miller tell them that their boys would have to stand for honors knew that it would be a long time before their men could recover their ability to fight effectively. They hadn't lost their pride or their spirit. They lost friends and brothers.

The men of the 100th/442nd moved onto the assembly area slowly. The open field near Biffontaine was lightly dusted with snow. The frigid air burned faces already roughened by wind and cold. Some of the men could barely walk because of feet swollen with trench foot. Yuki led the men of Company B to their place along the line with some confusion. They were used to standing in ranks, next to men who were no longer there. Now they had to look up to see where to stand.

Yuki could not help thinking about the men he boarded ship with that day in Honolulu harbor, all the leis that had been cast in the water with the scented promise of safe return. Now, so many of those young men were gone, never to walk the island sands again. He looked down the line of the formation of the 100th, where once almost fifteen hundred men stood proud.

Sammy stood next to Bobby. Winter clothing had finally come. They were dressed in overcoats and woolen scarves, but in the chill air they could feel the cold seeping through as they stood waiting for the ceremony to begin. Ahead of them Lieutenant Colonel Virgil Miller, acting regimental commander, stood next to a file of riflemen, the American flag slowly moving on a pole stuck in the ground.

The trees rustled in the background, their branches creaking instead of shattering from tree bursts. Bobby watched the riflemen standing straight, waiting for the moment to raise their guns in salute instead of anger. He was grateful to be standing here, and he was grateful that Stubby was able to stay home. At least one of them made it back. *And if I'm lucky*, Bobby thought—*if I'm lucky.*

The air carried the strains of the "Star-Spangled Banner." Normally the men stiffened with pride at the sound, but their eyes filled with only exhaustion and weariness. Tug barely heard the music. His mind was not on the field before him. His mind was on the field of battle that he had marched through and the men he had marched with.

Chaplain Hiro Higuchi walked to the front of the ranks and began to read the names of the fallen as a single bugle player blew "Taps." There were so many. Not a man moved. Tears filled the eyes of the living as they remembered the dead. Sammy looked down the ranks, Tug to his right and Bobby to his left. They were all that was left of his squad.

As the chaplain read Akiro's name, Sammy's mind went back to that first day at Manzanar when the confident young man led his family to their barracks. With Tommy, they had played ball and talked of what they would do with their lives. The great things they would accomplish, the future that lay ahead. Now Akiro and Tommy lay in the cold ground of Italy and France, far from home, forever young.

It was when Higuchi read "Frederick C. Shiraga" that Sammy felt the tears chill against his cheeks. So many warm summers they had shared together. So many dreams. So many days that they threw the ball back and forth with Mickey. Freddy was more than his friend. Freddy was his brother. He had been there at the endless ball games of their youth. He had been there when they both found the young women that held so much promise for the future. And he had been there when one gave his life for the other.

A light snow began to fall on the silent formation. The quiet moment when the sound of "Taps" faded was broken by the sharp retort of the honor guard firing a salute to brothers fallen. Each man stood erect as the order came to present arms. Hands snapped to the brim of steel helmets. One last salute.

General Dahlquist watched the ceremony and surveyed the spare ranks of men from the combat team. He turned to Lieutenant Colonel Miller.

"Colonel, I ordered all of the men to be assembled for honors."

Miller felt his throat tighten. A hundred thoughts went through his mind as he felt the words come to his lips.

"Yes, sir. These are all the men."

EPILOGUE

April, 1998
Manzanar, California

Isamu leaned forward, feeling the winds of Manzanar pushing against him as they had so many years ago. Air that once slid over him in his youth now chilled his aging body, shivering him. He could feel the thin warmth of the sun falling on shoulders that stooped with years that somehow too passed quickly. The sudden cold pierced the thin skin of his face, bringing images rushing forward in his mind, reaching back to that day so long ago, a soldier's face pressed against the glass window of the train. It did not seem so long ago. Nothing seemed so long ago, and yet it was, a young soldier then, returning home.

He kept his face pressed against the window and stared out as the train rolled through the great Central Valley. There was a comfortable familiarity to it— the dark fields of winter fallow dirt, the vines stripped bare by frost. Soon it would all be green again—and he would be a part of it. In a few hours he would be home. It seemed like he had been gone a lifetime. There was no way that he would ever be the same. All the killing, all the death, all the days spent wondering if there would be a tomorrow—it was over.

He watched the flat countryside of the Valley pass by. He could feel the warmth of the winter sun on the window, even though his breath condensed on the glass. He remembered the last time he had been home, leaving the assembly center with his family, bound for Manzanar, shades drawn. And shades drawn when he left for Shelby. Now sunlight streamed into the car and bathed his face.

He looked down at his hands, roughened by months of combat. The fighting had not ended on that ridge in the Vosges Mountains. The 100th/442nd fought on—through the rest of France and then back into Italy where they helped break the Gothic Line, opening the way into Germany. And then it had all been over.

On May 9, 1945, Germany surrendered. The 100th/442nd became part of the occupying forces. They stayed in Italy but slowly men with the highest Adjusted Service Rating Scores began to return home. Yuki received a battlefield commission after the Vosges Mountains. Tug become a sergeant and then a staff sergeant. Bobby and he became sergeants. They were the old veterans. He had ended up in the 522nd Artillery–and at the gates of Dachau. They were the old veterans.

Now it was all over. They said their goodbyes and began to scatter. Tug insisted he was going to be a lawyer. Bobby planned to go to medical school and Yuki decided he was going back to Wisconsin. He had met a girl there during training and they had been writing each other.

He looked at the image reflected in the window, obscured by the misting of his breath on the cold glass, lines creasing the corners of his mouth, cheeks now sharply drawn against a face that looked back with the eyes of a man he had not seen before. He moved his hand across the fogged window and looked out again.

He had fought for his country, for his family, but most of all, he had fought for the men who stood with him in those terror-filled moments of noise and thunder. Yes, that was it—the men who stood with him. Without them, he could never have stood alone. Lives had been given to prove loyalty. But one life had been given for him—that he understood clearly. That he would not, could not, forget.

The soldier sitting next to him looked at his shoulder patch, an arm thrust up holding a torch. "Sergeant, you were with the 442nd?"

He turned and looked at the young private. "Yes, I was with the 100th/442nd."

"We read about you boys in the papers. You fellows saw a lot of action, I guess. I just got in and finished training and now it's all over. I sure wanted to see what it was like." The young man's eyes lingered over the ribbons, the silver star, and the campaign medals on his chest.

He looked at the private, who was staring back at him with evident admiration. He could tell that his answer surprised the young man.

"It was cold and it was muddy. There were days when you didn't know if you would live through the next few minutes. There were men that came into the unit as replacements and died before you even learned their name. There were men whose names I will never forget as long as I live. I'm going to spend the rest of my life trying to forget what it was like."

He felt the train slowing to a stop and looked out the window. He was home.

Isamu smiled at the memory of his mother and father, how they looked standing there waiting for him. They had been home from the camps for months. *He could see Mr. and Mrs. Bagdasarian, Sack and Carmen holding a wiggling little boy, and Betty with Mas and Satomi and Luis and Maria. They all came to the station.* He had not shared that memory with himself for many years and now it was before him again.

His parents standing quietly, clouded by steam from the train. They looked smaller somehow. He stopped in front of them and sat his duffle bag down. His father's face was even more weathered than when he had last seen him through the wire fence at Manzanar. His father reached out and touched his face.

"Your mother . . ." His father began to cry. He had never seen his father cry before. He put his arms around his mother and touched the wisps of hair graying along her temples.

"I'm home."

He never really heard what everybody else said while his mother held him, moving her cheek next to his.

Isamu lifted his hand to his face. He could almost once again feel the warmth of his mother's cheek. *Tears streamed down her face as she looked at him, a man now. He reached out and wiped the tears. "There's no need to cry now, I'm home."*

He could see her clearly now, the warmth of her hands reaching out through the years since she had passed on. *His mother reached up and covered his hand on her cheek. The whispered words. "Not tears of sadness. You have brought our honor home."*

Isamu heard his grandson calling to him, pulling him back from his memories, remembrances of his life fluttering away like ribbons in the breeze. Yuki had made his way back to Wisconsin and married the girl he met in Sparta. He became a dairy farmer and then a politician. Just this last year he had passed away. Tug went home and became a lawyer and was now a retired judge. Stubby became a teacher, surprising all of them. Bobby was a surgeon in Honolulu. Mickey had stayed in the military and then worked in a job so secret nobody ever knew what he did.

Isamu smiled at the memory of the face of the man who never wore a helmet. Captain Young Oak Kim became a legend. When he finally recovered from his wounds, the war was over. He returned to the Army in Korea where he led forces behind the lines, winning the Korean equivalent of the Medal of Honor, honored as a hero by France with their highest military honor, and by the United States as one of its most decorated soldiers, retiring as a colonel.

José became a high school principal at the school they attended as children. Sack sold him the Cadillac he rode in and Sack and Carmen's son carried the rings at his wedding to Betty. The memory brought an ironic smile to his face. He became a farmer, just like his father before him. He and Toshi bought the ranch his father worked on but could never own. Toshi lived out his days in the farmhouse where they both had been raised.

He looked at the silent ground of the old baseball field and reached down for a stone. His mind paused for a moment on the one he kept in a special place. *Perhaps Freddy's spirit was playing an eternal game of baseball with Akiro and Tommy. They were there, out on that field.* He could feel it. He could see their faces smiling at him, sunburned faces, unlined by age. Soon, he too would know their secrets and join their endless game.

He returned the stone to the ground. So many years had passed and yet, in memory, just a moment ago. He saw the drops creating muddy dimples in the dust before he felt the tears on his cheeks. So many years since he had shed tears. Not since he had brought Freddy home from France and laid him to rest in the veteran's cemetery in Fresno. *The sad refrain from the bugle and the sharp retort of the honor guard's rifles—and Rose standing there silently.* She had never married. Even when his precious Betty died, no tears.

He felt a hand on his shoulder. He heard the muffled sound of his son's voice, but it was lost to the whispered sounds of battle carried by the wind from the hills of Italy and the forests of France. He could not shut his eyes and keep them back. He didn't want to. The tears fell freely into the dust of Manzanar.

SOURCE MATERIALS

Many people spoke to me about the atmosphere of the times and how they felt on December 7, 1941. The manners of life and bits and pieces of personal experiences were pulled out and utilized as part of the lives of the fictitious characters in this book. I visited many places to gain historical context, sometimes personally and sometimes through the Internet.

I spent six months interviewing Col. Young Oak Kim, going over and confirming the actions he participated in as an officer in the 100/442, as well as his memory of the events the unit participated in. All I have depicted regarding him and his combat actions has been confirmed, either through eyewitness accounts, battlefield reports, or historical documentation. My accounts of the rescue of the lost Texas Battalion are based not only on the historical records of that event, but also on personal interviews with Capt. Marty Higgins, the battalion's ranking officer and a First Lieutenant at the time. Al Tortolano, a battalion PFC, also contributed valuable reminiscences. For his actions, Higgins received the Silver Star. As with many others, it was not enough.

Both Kim and Higgins are gone now, but it was an honor to know them. They were real American heroes.

I was privileged to go to our National Archives in Suitland, Maryland, and have access to the voluminous records related to the 100/442nd. If you ever have the opportunity to visit the Archives, please go. It will make you proud and humbled to be an American. The records of the 100th/442nd Regimental Combat Team are in over 50 banker's file boxes, and I was allowed to go through them page by page. I would read daily combat records, compare them to historical descriptions, and then call men whose names were in those records to confirm their accuracy.

As I said, I set out to answer the question of why young Japanese men would go to Europe and fight for a country that held their parents in concentration camps. I got my answer. It was a matter of honor.

Documentary Resources

Bendetsen, Carl. Papers, Hoover Institution, Stanford University.

442nd Regimental Combat Team. Private personal interviews.

Go for Broke National Education Center (www.goforbroke.org). This resource contains hundreds of personal interviews related to individual battles, as well as the detentions.

Higgins, Capt. Martin. Personal interviews.

Kim, Col. Young Oak. Personal interviews.

National Archives and Records Administration, Suitland, MD. 442nd Regimental Combat Team records.

Olsen, Culbert L. Papers, The Bancroft Library, University of California, Berkeley.

Relocation camp internees. Private personal interviews.

Torolano, Al. Personal interviews.

Warren, Earl. Papers, Library of Congress.

Books

Adler, Bill, and Tracy Quinn McLennan. *World War II Letters: A Glimpse Into the Heart of the Second World War Through the Words of Those Who Were Fighting It*. New York: St. Martin's Griffin, 2003.

Allen, Gwenfread. *Hawaii's War Years: 1941-1945*. Honolulu: University of Hawaii Press, 1950.

American Historical Association; Community College Humanities Association; Organization of American Historians; United States, National Archives and Records Administration. *Internment of Japanese Americans: Documents from the National Archives*. Dubuque, Iowa: Kendall-Hunt, n.d.

Burton, Jeffrey F., Mary M. Farrell, Florence B. Lord, Richard W. Lord, Tetsuden Kashim, Eleanor Roosevelt, Ronald J. Beckwith, and Irene J. Cohen. *Confinement and Ethnicity: An Overview of World War II Japanese American Relocation Sites*. Seattle: University of Washington Press, 2011.

Clarke, Thurston. *Pearl Harbor Ghosts: The Legacy of December 7, 1941*. New York: Ballantine Books, 2001.

Cooper, Michael L. *Fighting for Honor: Japanese Americans and World War II*. New York: Clarion Books, 2000.

Cooper, Michael L. *Remembering Manzanar: Life in a Japanese Relocation Camp*. New York: Clarion Books, 2002.

Crost, Lyn. *Honor by Fire: Japanese Americans at War in Europe and the Pacific*. Novato, Calif.: Presidio Press, 1996.

Daniels, Roger. *American Concentration Camps: A Documentary History of the Relocation and Incarceration of Japanese Americans, 1942-1945*. 9 vols. New York: Garland, 1989.

Daniels, Roger. *The Decision to Relocate the Japanese Americans*. Malabar, Florida: Krieger, 1990.

De Nevers, Klancy Clark. *The Colonel and the Pacifist: Karl Bendetsen, Perry Saito, and the Incarceration of Japanese Americans during World War II*. Salt Lake City: University of Utah Press, 2004.

Dempster, Brian Komei. *From Our Side of the Fence: Growing Up in America's Concentration Camps.* San Francisco: Kearny Street Workshop, 2001.

Duus, Masayo. *Unlikely Liberators: The Men of the 100th and 442nd.* Honolulu: University of Hawaii Press, 2006.

Falk, Stanley L. *MIS in the War Against Japan: Personal Experiences Related at the 1993 MIS Capital Reunion, "The Nisei Veteran: An American Patriot."* Washington, DC: Japanese American Veterans Association of Washington, DC, 1995.

Grapes, Bryan J. *Japanese American Internment Camps.* San Diego, Calif.: Greenhaven Press, 2001.

Hanley, James M. *A Matter of Honor: A Mémoire.* New York: Vantage Press, 1995.

Harrington, Joseph Daniel. *Yankee Samurai: The Secret Role of Nisei in America's Pacific Victory.* Detroit: Pettigrew Enterprises, 1979.

Higa, Thomas Tarō. *Memoirs of a Certain Nisei, 1916-1985.* Kaneohe, Hawaii: Higa Pubs.,1988.

Hohri, William Minoru and Mits Koshiyama. *Resistance: Challenging America's Wartime Internment of Japanese-Americans.* Lomita, Calif.: The Epistolarian, 2001.

Hosokawa, Bill. *Nisei: The Quiet Americans.* New York: Morrow, 1976.

Ige, Tom. *Boy from Kahaluu: An Autobiography.* Honolulu: Kin Cho Jin Kai, 1989.

Japanese Eyes, American Heart: Personal Reflections of Hawaii's World War II Nisei Soldiers. Honolulu: Tendai Educational Foundation, 2000.

Jasper, Joy Waldron, James P. Delgado, and Jim Adams. *The USS Arizona: The Ship, the Men, the Pearl Harbor Attack, and the Symbol That Aroused America*. New York: St. Martin's Paperbacks, 2003.

Lord, Walter. *Day of Infamy*. New York: Owl Books, 2001.

Masaoka, Mike and Bill Hosokawa. *They Call Me Moses Masaoka: An American Saga*. New York: William Morrow, 1987.

Masumoto, David Mas. *Distant Voices: A Sansei's Journey to Gila River Relocation Center, 1982*. Del Rey, Calif.: Inaka/Countryside Publications, 1982.

Matsuo, Dorothy. *Boyhood to War: History and Anecdotes of the 442nd Regimental Combat Team*. Honolulu: Mutual Book Company, 1992.

Murphy, Thomas D. *Ambassadors in Arms: The Story of Hawaii's 100th Battalion*. Honolulu: University of Hawaii Press, 1955.

Nakagawa, Kerry Yo. *Through a Diamond: 100 Years of Japanese American Baseball*. San Francisco: Rudi Publishing, 2001.

Nakasone, Edwin M. *The Nisei Soldier: Historical Essays on World War II and the Korean War*. White Bear Lake, Minn.: J-Press, 1999.

Odo, Franklin. *No Sword to Bury: Japanese Americans in Hawai'i During World War II*. Philadelphia: Temple University Press, 2004.

Shirey, Orville C. *Americans: The Story of the 442nd Combat Team*. Nashville, Tenn.: Battery Press, 1998.

Steidl, Franz. *Lost Battalions: Going for Broke in the Vosges, Autumn 1944*. Novato, Calif.: Presidio Press, 2000.

Tanaka, Chester. *Go for Broke: A Pictorial History of the 100/442d Regimental Combat Team*. Novato, Calif.: Presidio Press, 1997.

United States. Commission on Wartime Relocation and Internment of Civilians. *Personal Justice Denied*. Seattle: University of Washington Press, 1997.

Weglyn, Michi. *Years of Infamy: The Untold Story of America's Concentration Camps*. New York: Morrow Quill Paperbacks, 1976.

ACKNOWLEDGMENTS

No book like this is written without the cooperation, advice, and the benefit of resources written by scholars and participants. As is apparent, I am not Japanese. Some will find the language of the participants to be archaic, and perhaps a little trite, from a modern perspective. It was carefully crafted to reflect the times and the reality of ethnic differences, which were more pronounced in our language at the time of *Tears of Honor*. I want to acknowledge the tremendous input and advice of my good friend, Judge Dale Ikeda, who not only introduced me to people I could consult but also acted as a resource to ensure that my use of accents and behavior was accurate. If any offense is taken by readers, none was intended.

I also want to thank Dan Smetanka, who edited this book. I am embarrassed to admit that the original manuscript exceeded one thousand pages. I thought that every page was important. Dan agreed that every page was important, but he convinced me that some pages were more important than others. It is, after all, a book of historical fiction, but the events all really happened. I just tried to make them come alive for today's readers.

ABOUT THE AUTHOR

James A. Ardaiz is a former prosecutor, judge, and Presiding Justice of the California Fifth District Court of Appeal. From 1974 to 1980, Ardaiz was a prosecutor for the Fresno County District Attorney's office. In 1980 Ardaiz was elected to the Fresno Municipal Court, where he served as assistant presiding judge and presiding judge. Ardaiz was appointed to the California Fifth District Court of Appeal in 1988 and was named the court's Presiding Justice in 1994. Ardaiz retired from the bench in 2011 and remains active in the legal profession.

Ardaiz has received many civic honors, including the Distinguished American Award presented to him in 2008 by the Japanese American Citizens League for his service to the Japanese American community.

Ardaiz's previous books include *Hands Through Stone*, a first-hand nonfiction account of his work on the investigation and prosecution of murderer Clarence Ray Allen, the last man executed by the State of California, and *Fractured Justice* and *Shades of Truth*, the first two novels in Ardaiz's Matt Jamison mystery series.

Ardaiz wrote *Tears of Honor* after five years of extensive historical research, including interviews with one of the central real-life characters in the novel, retired U.S. Army Colonel Young Oak Kim.

Ardaiz's website is **jamesardaiz.com**.